THURMOND'S SAGA

CHRONICLES OF THE MEDIEVAL UNDERWORLD, BOOK 1

ROBERT JOHN MACKENZIE

Distributed by Bublish, Inc

ISBN: 978-1-64704-125-0 (paperback)
ISBN: 978-1-64704-126-7 (eBook)
LCCN: 2104916117

TO CRISSY, OF COURSE

THURMOND'S
SAGA

CONTENTS

PART 4   UNDERGROUND

PART 5   THE HARD JOURNEY HOME

PART 6   THE TURNING OF FORTUNE'S WHEEL

GLOSSARY OF CHARACTERS

Aborax: imp with a foul disposition

Artos: sergeant-at-arms in the employ of Bartholomew Staynes

Bartholomew Staynes: son of Lord Percy Staynes

Bodo: soldier in the employ of Bartholomew Staynes

Red Charles of the Border: religious fanatic and eater of liver

Derkyn: evil half-wit

Lord Drakar de la Pole: terrifying warrior and brother of Lady Renata de la Pole

Drax: mercenary in the employ of Lady Renata de la Pole

Einarr Badhand: maimed Adventurer and proprietor of a fencing academy

Giles: butler to Lord Percy Staynes

Gregorio: diviner in the employ of Bartholomew Staynes

Gyre: bastard child of Bartholomew Staynes

Father James: handsome and charismatic cleric

Jarvis: purveyor of used and unusual items

Jasper: mercenary with an odd appendage in the employ of Lady Renata de la Pole

Lars: soldier in the employ of Bartholomew Staynes

Nod: riverman and the son of Scrymgeour

Oscar: household servant of Lord Percy Staynes

Lord Percy Staynes: invalid father of Bartholomew Staynes and others

Friar Plutonius: Black Friar in the employ of Lady Renata de la Pole

Earl Sir Ralf Mortimer: Earl of Avincraik

Lady Renata de la Pole: powerful sorceress and sister of Lord Drakar de la Pole

Roscoe Appleman: Thurmond's friend and Adventurer in good standing

Rupert de Pugh: scoundrel and current plaything of Lady Renata de la Pole

Sarah: plucky young sorceress who is not Thurmond's ladylove

Scrymgeour: boat owner and father of Nod and Sod

Sims: henchman of Lord Rupert de Pugh

Sod: riverman and son of Scrymgeour

Thurmond: would-be Adventurer and our hero

Torgul Bonelip XXIII: doughty dwarf and Adventurer in good standing

Trollkeeper: strange man with an even stranger vocation

Una: wife of Trollkeeper

Whisper: tree-dwelling spirit

PART 1

THE INNOCENT LAD

CHAPTER ONE

THURMOND FINDS
HIS PATH

Thurmond dashed through the crowd as fast as the narrow, twisting streets would permit. He dodged a donkey cart laden with firewood and squeezed by two men with a basket of river eels. His legs were beginning to weaken, and his breath came in hot, jagged gasps as if his chest were filled with small, sharp stones, yet he dared not pause or even slow his pace. He knew they were still back there and coming up quickly.

He knew as well that he could expect no help from any of the crowd that thronged the busy street. The dwellers of Old Shambles understood the wisdom of minding their own business. If a trio of corner boys wanted to rob him or beat him, perhaps even kill him, they would simply look away. In Old Shambles, it was always best to take no notice of other people's affairs.

This was the poorest quarter of the city. Its denizens were left to feed freely on one another, and they did so with abandon. Strong-arm robbery, rape, and assault were daily, sometimes hourly, occurrences. More often than not, the break of day revealed the grotesque remains of the night's victims—strangled, bludgeoned, and stabbed.

Corner boys were young street thugs who preyed upon whomever they thought they could victimize for sport or profit. They were notorious for their cruel and reckless deeds as they strove to gain recognition in the city's criminal underworld. Those surviving to adulthood, if sufficiently blooded, could apply for membership in the Brethren, Gorgonholm's crime cult.

Thurmond risked a quick glance over his shoulder but then nearly collided with a washerwoman carrying a heavy load of wet laundry. She was taller than he and as stout as a stone pillar. Her immense forearms looked like a blacksmith's, and he thought she might in anger seize and hold him. But instead, she said something unintelligible, laughed, and proceeded on her way.

That brief delay was costly. His pursuers were gaining. He heard the slap of their shoes on the hard-packed earth of the street and their shouts of triumph as their quarry came into view. Without thinking, he slipped into a small opening between two houses. This was risky. The corner boys were residents of Old Shambles and knew its turnings and bystreets far better than he did. He could easily find himself trapped in some blind passage.

The alley opened into a weed-choked court, bounded on all sides by buildings. Other alleyways diverged from it, leading off in different directions. This was good. If he could slide into one unseen, he just might manage to give them the slip. Exhausted now, he skirted an open cesspit and selected a passage partially hidden by a ramshackle chicken coop.

He had just made it to this opening when a great savage dog rose silently from the weeds and plunged at him. Caught unawares, Thurmond stumbled and fell. He stared helplessly as the monstrous creature launched itself at his face. But at the last instant, the force of its lunge threw it backward as it reached the end of the chain bound around its neck. Its yellow eyes bulging with rage, the brute immediately rose and resumed its attack, but the boy managed to scuttle beyond the reach of its fangs. It again threw itself against the chain, causing a stream of drool to fly from its jaws.

It was at this moment that shouts announced the approach of the corner boys. The dog at once turned and flattened itself on its belly in the weeds. It offered no warning bark or growl. Thurmond stole a quick peek around the edge of the coop just as the trio surged into the court. They paused, taking stock, but the chicken coop screened him from view. He pulled back, regained his feet, and made his way quietly down the passage toward the street beyond.

The corner boys remained unaware of the dog until it was too late. They came straight across the yard, three abreast—all were well within the radius of its chain. Thurmond could hear the squeals of surprise and agony as the dog at last found victims within its reach.

He chuckled. He was in Lady Fortune's good graces today. He had outrun three ruthless criminals and dodged an even more malevolent dog. This was all good practice, for he needed to keep his skills finely honed. When he was at last permitted to join the Adventurers, he would need all the endurance and agility he could muster.

Above all things, Thurmond longed to join the Brotherhood of Underworld Adventurers, an exclusive fraternity of seasoned warriors who ventured into the depths of the subterranean caverns to wrest wealth from the fell creatures that dwelled within. Such a man must have astounding luck, skill, and courage. He had to be willing to risk all, to face unimaginable hardship and agonizing death. But limitless riches and a life of infinite luxury could be his rewards. The eager youth deemed the risk well worth taking.

To Thurmond, any danger was preferable to the tedious village existence to which he had been born. He had never fit in. His thick brown hair was considered dubious in a community composed mostly of mousy blonds. Moreover, he was naturally intelligent, articulate, and ambitious. With such terrible disadvantages working against him, he could never expect the simpleminded laborers who tilled Lord Beaufort's farm fields to wholly accept him.

But worst of all, he had what his mother called the *bing*—an engaging, vivacious gleam in his eyes that was altogether lacking in your typical peasant. The village wives knew such attractive eyes could only be trouble. They might sour the ale, curdle a cow's milk, or bring carbuncles to one's buttocks. Thus his neighbors often turned away when they saw him coming and crooked their fingers behind their backs to ward off evil.

So he had fled his village, secure in the belief that he possessed all the requisites to become a top-tier Adventurer. Though of medium height and build, Thurmond was strong for his size, and his exceptional nimbleness had always served him well in village games. He had arrived in Gorgonholm supremely certain that the Adventurers would at once recognize him as a kindred spirit and admit him to their company.

Unfortunately, none of this had worked out as planned. He had, so far, been soundly rebuffed in his efforts to ingratiate himself into their ranks. The Adventurers were entirely unimpressed with his unbridled optimism, and his enthusiastic overtures had met naught but insult, mockery, and indifference. Even his *bing* had failed to move them.

Alas, Thurmond possessed no weapons, no armor, nor any money with which to purchase these essential tools. He was untrained in the use of the sword or spear or bow. He could not find his path by the stars, follow a track, scale a castle wall, pick a lock, or handle a galloping horse. He had no influential friends or family on which to draw.

The Adventurers were practical men who demanded more than bubbling energy from those seeking admission to their order. They wanted experienced fighters and stalwart outdoorsmen. Men of proven mettle. Men of ability and means. Callow boys were decidedly unwelcome, and they made sure poor Thurmond was well aware of this fact.

Nonetheless, his passion remained undimmed, for he was a tenacious lad who refused to be discouraged. He was certain that his worth would sooner or later be recognized. Thus he often lingered about a notorious drinking den that flourished under the name of the Old Traitor's Head, more typically called the Severed Head or sometimes simply the Head. Its signboard depicted a freshly decapitated head held aloft by fingers entwined in its hair. Gouts of blood oozed from its stump of a neck.

This was where the Adventurers gathered to swill, relive past exploits, and discuss upcoming projects. Thurmond would often hang about, making himself useful in whatever way came along, usually running errands or delivering messages. But mostly he listened to the wild stories the Adventurers told, sometimes horrid accounts of death and deception but also fabulous tales of valor and treasure.

He had been en route to the Head when the corner boys jumped him, but with them disposed of, he was able to resume his journey. The sun had set beneath the city's western wall when he at last took his accustomed place on a bench just outside the main entrance. This was a good spot. By now, the Adventurers all recognized his face, and some of them knew his name. So he was often asked to tend to the horses of new arrivals or to carry messages to such and such that such and such was back in the city.

Thurmond had been sitting on that bench for nearly two years now, but he would not give up. His determination must eventually pique the interest of some Adventurer who would then give him the chance to prove his skill and courage. Seldom, though, did he actually venture inside the tavern, where he would be expected to spend his scant coin on their notoriously overpriced ale.

But tonight Lady Fortune was indeed smiling on the lad, for he found himself—after only a moment and to his great surprise—summoned inside. A surly man-at-arms emerged from the tavern's door, poked him on the shoulder, and without a word beckoned him to come along. Thurmond's attempt to question the man was met with only a grunt and an impolite gesture, so he followed him through the main room and into one of the side chambers reserved for the more affluent clients.

There he met a well-groomed man with all the trappings of a gentleman—elegant clothes, long curled hair, fine jewelry, and expensive weapons. The man-at-arms took a position behind him, glaring, arms folded in a stance of physical menace.

Though trembling with excitement, Thurmond tried to keep all emotion from his voice.

"You sent for me, sir?"

The gentleman's voice was controlled, silky, and soft.

"You are Thurmond." This was a statement, not a question.

"Aye."

"I have seen you about and asked after you. I have been told that you are a man who understands things, who knows how things happen."

Thurmond had no idea who might have said such things about him, but he was pleased to hear them.

"Aye, sir. I always keep my eyes skinned and my ear to the wall."

"More to the point, are you a man who knows how not to ask questions?"

"I am."

"And how not to reveal what he has heard if questioned by others?"

"Aye! I certainly am such a man."

"Then, as such a man, I am certain that you are already aware that good things often come in a series of threes. Perhaps a marriage, a child, and unforeseen wealth."

Thurmond was confused. Why would the man mention such things to him? What could he want?

"Aye, sir. I have heard tell of such."

"And ill things also come in threes. Loss of fortune, defamation, death."

"I have heard that, too."

Thurmond was growing impatient with these seemingly meaningless questions, but the well-groomed man seemed not to notice.

"Well, perhaps you haven't heard that tests of character—of courage, intelligence, and skill—also come in threes. Those who pass such tests find themselves on the path to their heart's desires. What is your heart's desire, my friend?"

This, at least, was easy to answer.

"To become an Adventurer. To gain wealth and renown by the doing of great deeds. To ride a warhorse and wear armor of iron plate. To be remembered for my fortitude and honor."

"Then you may be the perfect man for a job I have to offer, for it could start you on the path you wish to follow.

"And what job would that be?"

The gentleman now had Thurmond's full attention.

"I cannot tell you now. This place is too public, and the personage I represent demands the utmost discretion. Come tomorrow, one hour after the setting of the sun, to the small hill halfway between the South Gate and the mill of the Gray Friars. Do you know the place?"

"I do."

"Good. Then come tomorrow at the appointed hour. I will wait on the summit for one-quarter hour, no more. Consider this appointment the first test of three. If you appear at the agreed place and time, you will be given a task, which will be the second of your trials. Succeed in that, and you will be charged with a third and much more difficult undertaking.

"Bring that off successfully, and you will be granted a position that will lead to the fulfillment of your heart's desire. You will become a soldier for a great lord, be given weapons and armor, and be trained in their use. You will be well fed and earn a generous stipend. After a given term, you will be allowed to leave service should you so choose. What say you?"

This was the answer to all of Thurmond's most fervent prayers, but he still kept his voice controlled.

"I say aye! Of course I will meet you tomorrow one hour before sunset on the hill halfway between South Gate and the mill of the Gray Friars. I am your man already. Command me, and I will do your bidding at this moment."

"Your zeal is commendable but premature. Appear at the appointed place and hour, and you will be informed of what is expected. You are dismissed."

"By what name should I call you?"

But the well-groomed one just shook his head.

"We have no need to become acquainted."

†

The next day dragged with excruciating lassitude as Thurmond awaited the appointed hour. The sun hovered stubbornly in the sky as if refusing to give way to evening. He had been waiting for this moment since his arrival in Gorgonholm. At seventeen years, he was a man—no longer a mere child at the mercy of others but a fully-grown man who must take what he needed to create his own place in the world. And he would meet this challenge today. By God's teeth, he would! He felt the hand of Lady Fortune propelling him toward his destiny.

He spent the intervening hours in Market Square. This was in the Hilltop Quarter, where he had often gone in the hope of finding a day job, perhaps unloading a wagon or carting refuse. And almost as often, he had found nothing. The families of quality who lived in the district already possessed servants and minions, so they were seldom in need of a casual laborer. And unless business was brisk in the square, the vendors and craftsmen would not require his help.

He chose this spot because he preferred the Hilltop to any of the other sections of the city. This was where the rich and powerful made their residence, where the enormous stone houses were guarded by high walls and sported roofs of tile or the more expensive slate.

He liked to sit on the cathedral steps and watch the elegant ladies in their lavish gowns as they perused the merchandise in the square. Even more, he liked the proud gentlemen on their tall horses, with swords of fine steel girded about their hips. Now the time was at last approaching when such a sword, such a horse, and perhaps such a lady might be his.

Next to Market Square, the spire of the cathedral pushed assertively into the sky. He had heard this massive structure referred to as a prayer in stone, but it seemed to him much more like a tribute to money and power. No citizen dared to defy the Blue Friars, who enjoyed supreme spiritual authority in the city and controlled scores of farmsteads and villages throughout the land.

Beyond the cathedral, the foreboding edifice of City Keep loomed on the crown of the high hill around which the city had grown. It was the domain of Sheriff Brandon and his constables, the site of public hangings and whippings, and a good place to avoid whenever possible.

Market Square was always exciting. Tinkers, potters, and cordwainers hawked the excellence of their wares. Foreign merchants held forth spices, jewelry, and lengths of fine cloth brought by caravan from the East or South, while effete nobles picked their way disinterestedly among the stalls.

The official market days were much livelier, with country people bringing cartloads of beets and turnips, live ducks and geese in wicker cages, baskets of eels and fish. Holy feast days were even bigger events, with jugglers and jongleurs, strolling players, and sometimes bear wrestlers. Cutpurses, amateur and professional, plied their happy trade.

The many self-proclaimed sorcerers, with their love charms and jinx spells, always annoyed Thurmond. He knew them for no more than cheap hucksters. Magicians possessing genuine occult powers had real shops and did not peddle their wares for mere copper farthings. He did not much care for magicians in any case.

At least there had been no dwarves underfoot today. And none of the snotty elves with all their superior airs. They were often about, blathering in their strange language, which made him distinctly uncomfortable.

When the sun finally touched the top tower of the River Gate, Thurmond knew it was time to leave for his meeting on the hill. He headed down Castle Wynd, intent on reaching his destination yet all the while pondering the meaning of the well-groomed gentleman's puzzling offer. He found himself consumed by nervous anticipation.

What could this mysterious undertaking be? And how dangerous? Would he be expected to kill someone? He hoped not. He had not been in a fistfight since childhood, and he did not know whether he was as yet prepared to take the life of another. It had never before occurred to him that his quest for fame and treasure might entail murder.

Farther down, Castle Wynd took him through one of the narrower, less prosperous neighborhoods as it proceeded toward the South Gate. The houses were mostly half-timbered affairs with thatched roofs. This street, like all the streets of the city, was of dirt, straw, and animal dung packed down by a continual traffic of foot, hoof, and wheel. It was hard and dusty in the dry summer months, turning to foul sucking mud whenever it rained.

Here were the shops of bakers and brewers, chandlers and tanners. The air was infused with a perplexing blend of wood smoke, badly rendered tallow, half-cured hides, and human waste. Street vendors argued with surly apprentices. Swaggering bravos shouldered through a steady stream of housewives, haberdashers, and chicken pluckers.

Still farther down the Wynd, he came to Old Shambles. Here individual houses gave way to sprawling tenements in an appalling state of squalor and decay. Neither Sheriff Brandon nor his constabulary ventured willingly into this quarter, leaving its denizens to live or die by their own hands.

These streets abounded in cutthroats, beggars, rogues, and smugglers. Poxy gutter sluts beckoned from doorways. The thin wailing of a child wafted down from an upper window and then stopped, replaced by the hoarse voice of an angry man. The vicinity reeked of rot. It was here the day before, in a foolish bid to prove his own courage, that he had encountered the corner boys.

Then the South Gate stood before him—a massive stone structure pierced by a long tunnel more than ten feet in length and guarded at either end with huge oaken doors. Outside, a drawbridge spanned the city's moat, which, when lifted, reinforced the outer doors. Within the tunnel, a pair of stout portcullises could be dropped to impede the progress of an invader who penetrated the drawbridge and first set of doors. Openings in the ceiling allowed defenders to drop unpleasant things on those seeking to fight their way through the tunnel.

Two city constables lounged on a bench in the shade. Their official job was to prevent undesirables from entering the city, but mostly they collected a toll from anyone coming through the gates. They gave little thought to those leaving and did not look up as Thurmond passed them by on his way out.

He knew the gates would be shut at sundown and not opened again until daybreak. He thus hoped his meeting could be concluded quickly so that he would not have to spend the night sheltering in the woods beyond the city. That would be a dangerous and most unwelcome eventuality.

CHAPTER TWO

A STRANGE TASK

Thurmond arrived at the designated hill a bit before the assigned time. He waited in the bushes beneath its crest until the cathedral bells sounded the hour, then climbed the rest of the way only to find, to his grave disappointment, that his contact had not yet appeared.

He was nervous and sought to reassure himself by touching the weapon he carried beneath his shirt on a cord passed around his neck—a dagger with a long, narrow blade. He did not know how to fight with it, but it was his prize possession. His first and only weapon. His first step to becoming a warrior. He was afraid to wear the dagger openly, worried that it might tempt a would-be thief or that someone might assume anyone wearing such a piece must have something of value to protect.

He waited with growing anxiety until nearly sundown when he heard the hoofbeats of an approaching horse. Judging from the frequent pauses and slow pace, the rider was being very cautious as he made his way to the hilltop. When he finally appeared, he was wrapped in a bulky cape that effectively concealed his body. The hood was pulled down low over his brows, but Thurmond recognized the intense eyes and neatly trimmed beard of the well-groomed gentleman who had promised to make his fortune.

The man did not dismount but got right down to business.

"Are you ready to learn of your mission?"

Thurmond had never been so ready in all his life, but he did not want to appear overeager. He kept his voice flat.

"Aye."

The man said nothing, he just stared at the young man as if sizing him up. His expression suggested he did not much care for what he was seeing.

Thurmond had come to be given a task that would set him on the road to wealth. He wanted only to conclude this business and get about whatever was to be required of him. He had long since despaired of making it back to the city before the gates were closed at sunset.

Finally the rider spoke, his tone aloof and slightly condescending.

"The personage I represent has need of a very unusual item. I have been informed that you might be the very person who could acquire it for him. Succeed in this, and you will be rewarded handsomely. Moreover, you will be given a third task that will bring even greater reward and the promise of a position in a very prominent household. Does this still interest you?"

The gentleman's eloquence impressed Thurmond. He tried his best to match the tone.

"More than ever. May I inquire as to the nature of the item that I am to provide?"

The well-groomed one leaned down and spoke quietly in Thurmond's ear. What he heard left him aghast.

"Eeyeew! Why would anyone want that?"

He could not imagine why anyone could require such a loathsome thing. But then he remembered—he had heard of a man from whom this very thing could possibly be obtained. The business would be disgusting and highly illegal, as it bordered on blasphemy and abomination, perhaps even heresy, but Thurmond accepted it without hesitation.

The rider handed over two small leather pouches.

"One of these contains ten silver pennies. That is your pay for this undertaking. The other contains five gold sovereigns to allay any expenses that may occur. Whatever is left over, you may retain. When you have the item, return to the Old Traitor's Head, where you will be informed as to where and how the final delivery is to be accomplished."

That said, the well-groomed rider turned his horse and rode off down the hill.

Thurmond was astounded by the quantity of money that he gripped in his hand. A silver penny was the customary daily wage of a laborer, and he had been given ten of them. This was the equivalent of a gold sovereign! And five more sovereigns were in the second pouch! Never before had he held so much coin. He was momentarily tempted to simply abscond with the money—perhaps join a departing caravan or buy passage on a barge traveling down the Mad River, which ran its course just beyond Gorgonholm's western wall. However, he quickly abandoned such thoughts, realizing that the reach of his unknown benefactor might be of great length. He might well employ magical resources to track down and chastise a deceitful servant. Furthermore, he sensed that this gold was but a pittance compared to what would come his way if he promptly and correctly fulfilled his task.

†

Knowing the city gates had been barred for the night, Thurmond made his way toward the Gray Friars' grist mill. This was an elaborate stone structure situated in the bottom lands of the river south of the city. A narrow channel brought river water to turn the mill's huge wooden wheel. The neighboring farmers were required by law and custom to bring their grain for the Grays to grind into meal. For this service, they retained a given percentage of what they ground, which was originally intended to provide them with bread. In actuality, the friars received far more meal than they could consume, so they sold their gleanings in the markets of Gorgonholm. The avaricious Blue Friars had made several attempts to seize this lucrative enterprise for themselves, but the Grays held the mill by right of an ancient royal warrant that had, so far, held their rivals at bay.

Arriving at the Grays' walled compound, Thurmond rang the brass bell suspended above a small door built into the main gate. The red-faced porter appeared at a peephole set at eye level. He seemed jocular enough.

"Well, young fellow, what brings you to honor the Gray Friars with your illustrious presence? What is your pleasure? How might we bring fame and credit to ourselves by being of service to you? How is it possible that this unworthy abode could come to your exalted attention?"

Thurmond unlocked his tongue. He understood the importance of responding properly to the porter's formal diction. He might be no more than an impoverished village boy, but he need not sound like one. Over the past two years, he had learned that lofty language was a golden key that would often open doors. He had thus listened carefully while others spoke and amassed a substantial word hoard of his own.

"Well, sire, I am honored by the praise you lavish on my lowly self. It is not often that the innate quality of my character is so readily recognized. I must assume that I am in the presence of one possessed of extraordinary perception and discernment. I am flattered, sire. I, your humble servant, bow to you."

"Why, in sooth. You are a fine young laddie. A well-spoken laddie. A likely laddie, as I live and breathe."

"I can only pray, good friar, that I can prove worthy of such generous approbation. I find myself stranded for the night beyond the locked gates of the city. I have come to throw myself upon the mercy of your venerable order, well known for the charity and compassion extended to wayfarers such as myself."

"You may rejoice in the knowledge that you have not been misinformed. The Gray Friars will spare no effort in providing a warm and homey refuge in which a gentleman such as yourself may make merry and take his ease. We can depend, of course, on your largesse and munificence?"

"The very thought of such opulence sends me into a transport of delight. What exactly mean you by my largesse and munificence?"

The friar's voice now assumed a quiet, regretful tone.

"Alas, we are but an impoverished order with scant resources even to feed ourselves. We would ask that your lordship would be so kind as to donate a very modest amount—say, a silver penny—to help allay the expense of the banquet we will lay before you."

Thurmond nearly choked when he heard these words. He had sufficient monies, of course, to pay the asking price and gain admittance. However, he was quite aware that the fee was well beyond the value of the austere accommodations he could expect within.

"By the holy feet of God, good friar, I am assured that the comfort and good cheer you offer are worth far more than the meager price you ask. But as you can see from my apparel, I have taken a sacred vow of simplicity and austerity. I need no grand chamber nor lordly meal. Perhaps just a corner of a storeroom or barn and a small bowl of gruel. Nothing more would be required."

The friar's face lost a degree of its former amiability.

"Just how much would you be willing to pay then?"

Time for some *bing*. Thurmond looked pleadingly into the porter's eyes.

"Holy friar, I was hoping that the satisfaction of giving succor to an unfortunate might be an adequate recompense."

All trace of cordiality was at once removed from the red face that thrust itself into the peephole. Saliva flew from angry lips that had formerly been so sugared.

"Depart at once. Git ye gone! Go! I'll not have some thieving, ragged-arse vagabond lurking about my gate. What? Still here? Git ye hence, or I'll release my dogs, and you won't like 'em—not one bit."

Clearly the *bing* was not working as well as Thurmond had hoped. The peephole abruptly slammed shut, but he could hear the porter's voice coming from the other side of the gate.

"Here, Gnasher! Ripper! Come on, boys!"

Thurmond was profoundly inspired to withdraw from the compound of the Grays and be content with whatever shelter the woods could provide. How bad could it be?

†

The sky squatted and pissed on the city of Gorgonholm—that is, at least, how it seemed to Thurmond as he huddled miserably beside the bole of an ancient oak. The rain poured down from the cold night sky, soaking his clothes and leaving him agonizingly chilled. His body trembled uncontrollably. His efforts to find a hollow tree proved futile in the rapidly falling dark. In the end he could only wait the weather out, sitting hunched forward with his arms held rigidly against his sides and his face pressed against his soggy knees.

While he sat and shivered, he looked back on the unlikely series of happenings that had brought him to this sorry state. But cold and miserable though he was, he had to admit that he was still far better off than had he stayed in the small, dreary village of his birth. He assumed it must have an official name, but he did not know it. The people who lived there just called it *the village* because it was the only place that mattered in their narrow lives.

At age fourteen he had been apprenticed to the local carpenter, a situation he at first had found vastly preferable to spending his life behind an ox-driven plow. The carpenter, his mother had insisted, had taken him because Lord Beaufort, the minor noble who owned the village, had fathered him. This claim could be true, of course, but Thurmond doubted it. He knew his mother kept close acquaintance with many men—the carpenter could just as easily be his father. Besides, he knew that almost every nameless whelp like himself tried to trace his or her lineage to the local lordling.

He entered into his apprenticeship with a degree of buoyancy and enthusiasm, as it promised to at least free him from hauling and spreading the endless piles of dung needed to fertilize the village fields. And the carpenter, an older man, had a pretty young wife named Alison, with whom Thurmond believed himself to be in love.

Unfortunately, Thurmond's optimistic mood was not long lived. The carpenter proved petty and bilious, thrashing his young apprentice for every trivial mistake or imagined shortcoming. Alison, too, disappointed him, having already awarded her affection to the strapping son of the village beer brewer. And to get right down to the bottom of things, Thurmond found carpentry every bit as uninteresting as shoveling mule shit.

After an especially severe beating—he had chosen the wrong piece of wood to replace a broken spoke in a cartwheel—Thurmond resolved to make an escape. But such a step was quite dangerous. The force of law and custom bound him to serve his master until the completion of his apprenticeship. For him to run away was no different from a thief seeking to escape justice.

Runaway apprentices were zealously pursued and, if captured, publicly whipped and then branded with a special sign that marked them forever as disobedient, ungrateful, and dishonest. And wherever he fled, he could expect no aid or comfort from those he encountered. Villagers were inherently hostile toward strangers, and runaway apprentices were considered no better than criminals. Anyone might raise the hue and cry and set an entire village against him.

Thurmond's one real chance—and every downtrodden serf and disaffected apprentice had heard of this—was an old law stating that anyone living in a chartered city for a year and a day would be released from all previous obligation and bondage. If he could but make his way to such a city and survive for a year, he would be free to make his own way without interference. He had heard of a great city—he had not known its name—lying somewhere to the west of the village. This then was to be his destination.

So Thurmond began to scheme. He was strictly forbidden to enter the carpenter's house unless summoned. His place was in the shop, a long, rather low shed attached to the side of the house. This was where he took his meals and slept on a pallet on the floor. However, he was quite familiar with the habits of the carpenter and his wife. His master routinely drank himself into oblivion after his evening meal. The wife would take this opportunity to join her lover in a lean-to behind the alehouse. He had only to wait until he heard the carpenter's drunken snore and the soft *thunk* of the door as Alison departed to the lean-to.

He then entered the house and gathered all the food he could carry in the ragged blanket that had covered his pallet. He tied the corners together, forming an awkward sling that could be carried over a shoulder. Returning to the shop, he took the most expensive iron tools: a saw, several augers, light and heavy hammers, a drawknife. This deed significantly compounded his offense. If apprehended, he would be hanged.

He bade a silent good-bye to the village as be passed along its single street for the last time. He did not stop to speak to his mother. Dodging behind the alehouse, he saw the bare feet and naked ankles of the brewer's son protruding out through the opening of the lean-to.

CHAPTER THREE

THE TROLLKEEPER

The next morning, the trees were still dripping from the night's storm as Thurmond made his way along a dark, leaf-strewn path toward an obscure glen hidden deep in the woods. There, he had heard, lived a man who could provide the unlikely item he had been tasked to acquire. The air was musty with decaying undergrowth and the rotted wood of fallen trees. Vines and brambles pushed in close on both sides of the path. Unseen creatures, disturbed by his approach, scuttled beneath the branches, causing them to rattle and shake.

The woods were dangerous. Even experienced woodsmen and hunters sometimes failed to return from their shadowy depths. In addition to such workaday dangers as banditti, poisonous snakes, and flesh-consuming beasts, forests tempted the fell creatures to venture up from their underground lairs. Goblins especially, but sometimes kobolds, and even trolls and ogres, had been known to lie in ambush along woodland paths. Shape-shifters and vampyres, though less common, at times took up residence in the ancient ruins of castles and monasteries the woods had overgrown and reclaimed.

Of course, Thurmond had never actually laid eyes on any of these creatures, but he had heard all about them from the Adventurers at the Old Traitor's Head. He knew it always paid to be wary when braving such primal environs.

Thurmond strove to keep his wits about him as he endeavored to recall

18

the route to the location he sought. He had heard it told in one of the many random conversations on which he routinely eavesdropped while sitting in his spot outside the Head.

He headed south on the Royal Highway until he came to the decayed and rutted track known as the Old Forest Road. From there, he went east until he crossed a stream with the broken remains of a tower on the far side. He knew better than to approach this ruin too closely. He then veered left at the next fork and left again at the one after. Here the road was little more than a deer trail and often hard to recognize as it wound uphill through the dense and tangled foliage. Finally he arrived at the critical landmark, two large boulders in the shape of a plump woman's tits. Between these boulders, a narrow crevasse led to a secret glen, in which there lived a most unusual man.

After about a mile of scrambling over shattered rocks, Thurmond knew he was getting close. He smelled the place long before it came into view. It exuded a heavy fetid stench far worse than anything produced by man or livestock. Then came a low, guttural snarl that grew to a thunderous roar, as if a dozen bears were being roasted alive over a slow fire. Thurmond was certain that he had come to the portal of hell.

But when he came around the final bend and his destination was revealed, it was far less imposing than he had expected. A simple thatched cottage and a small shed stood next to a sheer cliff-face of solid rock. Running from the back of the cottage, a pen held a herd of goats. An iron door in the cliff-face stood open, revealing the mouth of a cave. It was from this that the frightful scream and the horrid smell emanated.

Such was the abode of the infamous Trollkeeper. He was, so the story was told, a man who had abandoned morality and common sense. Isolating himself from all normal human society, he had taken residence in this hidden glen, where he engaged in a most foul and hideous practice. He maintained a number of live trolls. Body parts could be harvested from these loathsome creatures to provide ingredients necessary in certain rites of necromancy and black magic. Such practices were, of course, strictly forbidden by law and custom, as well as reason and decency. But where there is a need, someone will always be willing to supply it.

Gathering his courage, Thurmond approached the cottage.

"Hallo! Hallo in the cottage! Is anyone there?"

The cottage door swung wide. A woman stood in the opening, aiming a crossbow at Thurmond's chest. She was fat, ugly, and looked as mean as a troll.

To his relief, a man now emerged from the door in the cliff and called to the woman.

"Wait! Una! Don't shoot him! Let's see what he wants first. Then you can shoot him."

She peeled back her lips in an evil snarl.

"Whadda you want, mister? Speak up now! Be quick about it! I can't be foolin' around here. I gotta shoot you quick and get back to work. I got trolls to feed."

Thurmond called out urgently.

"Nay! Nay! Please don't shoot me. Really, I'm harmless…here on business for a great lord. *Please*…don't shoot me."

The man stepped closer. He was huge and shaped like a turnip. His head was bald and scabby. A wispy, white beard grew to a point halfway down his chest.

"Put down the bow, Una. This guy ain't gonna give me no trouble."

"Kiss my ass! That's what you said last time, and you know what happened."

"This guy ain't like that. It'll be okay. Just put down the bow."

"Go screw yourself then."

And with that, Una stepped back into the cottage and slammed the door with a kick.

The Trollkeeper, for that is who he was, now turned to Thurmond.

"Well, mister, what can I do you for?"

"I've been dispatched to purchase an item from you…for a great lord of the city of Gorgonholm. I can't, of course, reveal his name, for my mission is one of great delicacy, but rest assured that he is a very great lord and…"

"Stop yammerin'. Shut up, slow down, and tell me what you want. And I don't give a dead rat's ass about yer great lord. Now what exactly do you want?"

"The left hand of a live troll. Fresh cut and not too large. The smaller the better."

"Why?"

"I don't know...I wasn't told...didn't ask. Do you have one available?"

"I got one. No problem there. How much money you got?"

Thurmond always grew cagey when it came to money.

"Isn't it customary for the seller to set the asking price?"

"Looky here, you little lump of dung, when you come to my place, botherin' my wife and askin' me a bunch of damned questions, I get to make the rules. Now how much money do you got?"

"Five gold sovereigns."

"Well shit, that ain't near enough. What I got here is known as a specialty item. You can't just buy a troll's hand in the Market Square in Gorgonholm, and if you did, the priests would have you arrested and hung. So if you really want such a thing, you gotta be willin' to pay."

Thurmond had not expected this and did not know how to respond.

"Couldn't we work something out? I mean, I'll give you all the gold I have here. You could give me the hand and tell me how much more it costs. I'll bring back the rest as soon as I can get it from my lord."

"Do you think I'm stupid? That I believe that you'd really come back? Nay, that ain't no good. Here's what we'll do. You can work for me to make up the rest."

"Work for you? Here? Doing what?"

"Cleanin' troll cages. Whadda you think, shithead?"

And so the hand of fate once again turned Thurmond's footsteps in an unforeseen direction. He handed over the gold and followed the Trollkeeper into the cave.

CHAPTER FOUR

THE LABORS OF AURELIUS

An old legend tells of the god-king Aurelius who appeased the wrath of the Elder Gods through an act of humility and contrition. Taking human form, he appeared in the realm of men, where he accomplished a series of difficult and unpleasant chores. Among other things, he slew the water hags of the Sea of Nith, who for so long had lured sailors to their demise. He found the golden key that unlocked the purity girdle of Queen Iantheena, releasing her from a confinement of 157 years. But most challenging of all was the cleaning of the menagerie of King Zafridi, in which the dung of a thousand animals had accumulated for five generations. For his efforts, Aurelius was given a magic sword that could defeat any foe.

Thurmond tried hard to believe his labors, like those of Aurelius, would bring him great reward. That task was difficult, however, because nothing could be fouler than troll dung. He stood in a tunnel-like cave, illuminated by smoky torches stuck in sockets along the wall. He was sweating despite the subterranean chill. His sleeves were rolled above his elbows, and a rag was tied across his nose and mouth.

The cave's sides were lined with a series of cells, fronted with extremely heavy iron bars mortared into the living rock. Two contained trolls, one very large and the other a bit smaller. The vestigial nubs of breasts suggested the second was a female. Both shook the bars and screamed in rage when Thurmond approached.

Trolls were weird. They seemed neither fully mammalian nor reptilian but an obscene mixture of both. The skin was scaled and hairless, yet they propagated in the normal way. They were unspeakably hostile and foul, yet they showed a rough affinity for their offspring. And they could regenerate. Cut off a part, and it would grow back, which made them ideal for someone in the Trollkeeper's line of business. At least that is what the Trollkeeper explained to Thurmond as he drove the female to a second cage to allow the cleaning of the first.

The Trollkeeper gave a squeaky little laugh and continued his story.

"The only reason I kin control 'em at all is that I got this here spear." The item referred to looked like an ordinary spear except that its point blazed with a blue fire.

"It's got elf magic in it, and they know it kin really hurt 'em, so they's afeared of it. But if I was to turn my back on 'em, they'd swallow me whole in about a heartbeat. You watch yerself when yer about 'em. Got it?"

"I…got it."

With the female secured, the Trollkeeper disappeared into the recesses of the tunnel. Thurmond proceeded to scrape at the appalling residue trampled into the floor of the cell. He bent forward, concentrating on a particularly stubborn spot, unaware that something hitherto unseen had risen from the shadows of the adjacent cage and was reaching through the bars. As he straightened, he took only a slight step backward, but it was enough.

The young man was suddenly grabbed by the neck and pulled off his feet so his back slammed into the bars of the neighboring cell. Talons dug into the flesh of his throat and stifled his air. He was in the grip of a young troll that had hidden itself beneath the pile of rags it used for a bed. He had been entirely unaware of its presence until it struck.

Thurmond was just starting to black out when the terrible grip was released. The Trollkeeper stood beside him with a heavy cleaver. He had chopped off the troll's left hand, which now flopped on the floor at their feet. The injured troll howled and retreated to its rag pile, while the elder trolls shrieked in sympathetic rage.

The Trollkeeper retrieved the severed member. It squirmed like an injured reptile, the fingers flexing and unflexing. He dropped it into a cloth bag he carried in his belt.

"Here's yer hand, sonny. Jest soon as you finish cleanin' up in here, I'll give it to you. No extra charge for the bag."

Thurmond was furious.

"You knew that thing was hiding in there, and you didn't tell me. You knew it would try to get me, didn't you?"

"'Course I did, you damned fool. I wanted him to reach out nice, just like he did, so I could lop his hand off easy. You weren't in no real danger. I was always standin' ready with my chopper here. Now git back to work."

The scouring of the troll cages was slow, vile, back-straining labor. Thurmond was dejected. He had still not escaped the shoveling and hauling of dung. His work at last complete, he leaned morosely on the shaft of his wooden-bladed shovel. Una entered the cave, dragging the carcass of what looked to be a freshly slaughtered goat. Her former hostility seemed to have evaporated.

"You'll be wantin' somethin' to eat afore you go. Keeper says you can't come in the house, but I can fetch you up somethin' after I feed my trolls."

Thurmond was indeed famished but also skeptical about the nature of the provender she might have to offer. The reappearance of the Keeper exacerbated his apprehension.

"He ain't goin' nowheres tonight, Una. Too dark out. And we don't need nothin' to eat neither. Just fetch the jug. We'll be up late."

Thurmond cringed. He had had quite enough already of the Trollkeeper, Una, and their trolls. He was exhausted and stank of troll. The thought of a late-night drinking bout with this maniac both frightened and disgusted him.

Una moved farther into the cave and began butchering the goat with the keeper's cleaver. She threw the head and legs between the bars to the youngster. He bellowed in appreciation, his dismemberment apparently forgiven and forgotten. The elders, anticipating their portions, set up a tremendous din that reverberated deafeningly along the walls of the cave. The female received the stomach and guts, which she sucked down with gusto. The large male got the rest, the largest portion. He squatted menacingly over his repast, snarling and snapping as if to ward off any attempt to take it from him.

Her charges fed, Una left the cave but returned a few moments later, bearing a large crockery jug. The keeper caught it up by the handle and had

THURMOND'S SAGA | 25

a long, slow swig. Smacking his lips and wiping his thin beard, he handed the jug to Thurmond.

"Take yourself a pull, boy. You earned it."

Thurmond did so but immediately had to suppress a gag. It was mead, a very popular drink he normally enjoyed, but this was the worse mead he had ever tasted. Something about it was just wrong. Was there an aftertaste of decayed meat?

The Trollkeeper grinned.

"Good, ain't it? Make it myself. Best mead in the world. Old family recipe, you might say. Come on, drink up now. We got a long night ahead of us, and there's a lot of mead in that jug. Hey, what say we give some of this here to the trolls? They love it. Then I can put the female into the male's cage. You won't believe how they kin go at it. Hee-hee-hee-hee-hee!"

Thurmond's belly roiled at the thought. The path to becoming an Adventurer was taking some strange twists and turns.

†

Hours later the jug was empty, and the Trollkeeper was incoherent. Normally Thurmond enjoyed the strange tales of exotic people, but he found the Trollkeeper's mental wanderings impossible to follow. He had swallowed far too much of the detestable mead in an effort to ease the grinding tedium. When the Trollkeeper at last announced it was time for bed, a new fear struck him. Would he be expected to sleep in the cave with the trolls? God forefend!

To his relief he was shown to the small shed next to the cottage. The Trollkeeper pushed open the door and swept away an accumulation of spider webs.

"You can stretch out in here."

The interior was clammy and had an unhealthy smell, but it was vastly superior to sleeping with trolls.

Thurmond paused. The thought came to him that perhaps the keeper meant to lock him in the shed, to hold him prisoner for some obscene purpose. Troll food? His own dining pleasure? His host seemed to read his thoughts.

"Aw...go on in. Ain't nobody gonna do anything to you. Ain't even a latch on the door. Looky here, see for yourself. But just one thing—once you git yourself settled down, don't be goin' outside agin. Not for nothin'. Even if you hears some strange goin's on, don't go out agin."

Thurmond took the keeper's advice to heart, having no conceivable reason for venturing beyond the walls of the shed. He curled up on the dirt floor and fell fast asleep. But his repose was of brief duration. He awoke abruptly, his bladder bursting. Too much nasty mead! He was in agony, afraid to go out to relieve himself but much too uncomfortable to go back to sleep.

He had about decided to take a chance, to open the door a little and pee through the crack, when he heard a quiet snuffling sound coming from just outside. He held his breath and listened intently. It came again, louder, and then again and again. Was it a troll? Una? Did the Trollkeeper shift shape and wander about his yard at night? Was there such a thing as a weretroll? In desperation Thurmond peed across the bottom of the door, hoping whatever was out there would respect this ancient method of marking one's lair. Perhaps it worked, for the snuffling gradually receded, and he spent the rest of the night undisturbed.

In the morning Thurmond froze in midstride as he emerged from the shed. Large, strangely splayed footprints were embedded in the mud just in front of the door. They had not come from trolls, of that he was sure. They lacked the horrific talons that projected from each of a troll's three toes. But the length and depth of the prints indicated a creature of impressive stature. Several of them had apparently approached the shed from different directions, stood congregated before his door, and then departed from whence they had come. A single set of prints, a bit smaller than the rest, led off toward the Trollkeeper's cottage. Thurmond recalled the snuffling he had heard and gave an inward shudder.

He proceeded to the small creek running behind the cottage and tried to wash off the stench of the trolls. He hated bathing. He knew it to be a most unhealthy practice that brought disease, but he was desperate. Removing his clothes, he scoured them as best he could against a rock. Then he rubbed himself down with eel grass pulled from the creek bank. When he looked up, Una was standing there with her toes in the water.

"Want I should scrub down your backside? I can give a powerful scrubbin'."

"Nay…I thank you, though, for your kind offer. I…was just finishing up."

Thurmond donned his wet clothes as quickly as he could and stepped up onto the bank. He thought he heard an odd gurgling sound coming from the cottage.

"Is your husband up and about yet?"

"Aye, but he's gone already. Had to go see a man about some business. Hey, I brang you a sack of victuals for your trip back."

She held out a battered grain sack.

"That is, unless you'd rather stay awhile maybe."

"Nay! I mean…uh…I really have to get…to get…back to my mission for my master. Where is my hand?"

"In the sack with your food."

"Oh…well…that's wonderful. Thank you ever so much for your hospitality."

She smiled broadly and seemed entirely unaware of his insincerity.

"You sure you don't wanna stay a bit?"

Thurmond looked down at the bag in her hand. The sides heaved and convulsed as if a small animal were confined inside.

"What's really in there?"

"Just the hand and your food. Troll parts ain't ever proper dead. That thing'll crawl around for days before it starts to settle down."

"The Trollkeeper said that cutoff troll parts grow back. That right?"

"Sure do. Them are real tough buggers."

"This hand isn't going to grow into a whole new troll, is it?"

Thurmond began to have grave misgivings about touching the squirming sack.

"Nay, one little hand can't grow a whole new troll. Go on and take it. You'll be all right."

"How should I protect it from the sun? I don't want it to turn to stone."

"Ever'body thinks that's what happens, but trolls don't really do that—leastways none of ours never did. Stop frettin' 'bout ever' little thing."

With that he accepted the proffered sack but then stepped deftly away as Una sought to clasp him in her arms.

"You got nice eyes, boy."

Sometimes the damned *bing* was more trouble than it was worth.

"Nay…sorry…I must away. Perhaps next time!"

He was now pretty much certain that the gurgling sounds coming from the cottage were the Trollkeeper's snores. And was there not also an odd snuffling?

Peeved, Una took a step back, too.

"Well, I guess ol' Keep really put one over on you, didn't he, city boy?"

"I fail to understand."

"I mean he took you off one. Got you with that line about not havin' money enough."

"What?"

"You had plenty money, you idjit. He was just scammin' you."

"Why?"

Thurmond was thoroughly confused and flustered.

"'Cause he's lonely. He likes somebody to listen to his stupid stories, and he knows I ain't no good at it. Anyways, he don't like shovelin' troll shit any more than you do."

And with that Thurmond made his departure.

†

Thurmond kept up a good pace on his way back to town, pausing only long enough to throw Una's provisions into the bottom of a deep ravine. Besides the hand, the bag contained a number of strips of dried meat. He found the coarse texture and greenish-brown tint unsettling. It was probably goat, he realized, but he was not about to take a chance.

He had tried to carry his bundle slung over his shoulder, but the hand soon poked a claw through the cloth of the sack and prodded him between the shoulders.

Angry, he cried out.

"God's blood! Stop that, you stupid troll hand! That really hurt!"

He swung the sack with both hands and bashed it against the side of a rock. Then, feeling ridiculous, he resumed his journey back to town.

CHAPTER FIVE

THE HERO'S RETURN

Thurmond was triumphant! He had successfully accomplished the second of his three great trials. The city walls of Gorgonholm were growing closer and higher with each confident step. He would soon meet with the well-groomed gentleman and deliver the item he had been sent to procure. Then he would be given his third and final task, which, he had not the slightest doubt, he would fulfill with equal dispatch and aplomb. A position as a man-at-arms in a great household would soon be his.

He would be given armor and be trained in the use of arms. Defending his lord's interests, he would have the opportunity to demonstrate his courage, loyalty, and prowess. When his term of service was complete, he could again approach the Adventurers, but this time as an equal. They would be, must be, glad to welcome such a one into their Brotherhood.

During his journey back to the city, Thurmond continued to experience great annoyance from the ungodly troll hand. Although it had made no further assaults on the skin of his back, it continued to flop and writhe as if attempting to escape from the sack. Its antics grew so irritating that he was at last forced to stop and seek a remedy.

He gathered a quantity of long-bladed grasses from the roadside and braided them into a robust twine. He then bound the hand's fingers into a compact mass. He hated having to touch the thing, but that was better than having it crawl around.

As he withdrew it from the sack, a terrible thought struck him—what if the damned thing turned to stone? He was relieved when it remained twitching, crawling flesh and blood. So maybe not everything they said about trolls was true.

The hand was a good deal larger than that of a man. It proved extremely strong and resisted with all its might. Thurmond, however, persevered and eventually prevailed. He then doubled the fingers into the palm and tied the whole affair into a package resembling a fist. It continued to twitch but was effectively denied the ability to enact further mischief.

His one moment of real danger came when he unexpectedly encountered a squad of the Royal Road Guards. This was a troop of mounted men-at-arms who patrolled the king's highways that stretched east and south from the city. They were officially tasked with discouraging the numerous banditti who worked the roads. In reality, they were ruthless bullyboys who often abused the very travelers they were sworn to protect. They were also authorized to demand a road toll from all wayfarers. Though law and custom set the amount, they often extorted far more than was their rightful due.

Thurmond kept a wary eye open for the telltale dust plume that would signal the approach of the Road Guards even before their thunderous hoofbeats came to his ears. Usually he had plenty of time to dive into the cover of bushes or behind a fallen log. On this occasion, however, they were dismounted, taking their ease in the shade of a large linden tree. They saw him before he saw them.

"Hey you, boy!"

Thurmond froze. There was no chance to escape from these well-mounted men. If they found the hand, there would be serious trouble. There could be no respectable purpose for such a thing. It was useful only to magicians casting a spell of regeneration or for the reanimation of the dead. Everybody knew such rites were absolutely forbidden by all by the church, who reserved for itself the exclusive privilege to such practices.

If arrested, Thurmond knew he would be tried in an ecclesiastical court, where he would be tortured to reveal the name of his accomplices. Since he had nothing to reveal and nowhere near enough money to bribe the judges, he would undoubtedly be hanged.

"Stand fast where you are, boy, till we can get a look at you."

There were six guards beneath the tree. Three rose and approached Thurmond. The other three continued to pass a skin of wine from hand to hand. They were rough-looking men in rusted mail and tattered leather armor.

One of the men stepped in close. His face was deeply scarred, and he had only one eye. The empty socket of the other was left uncovered.

"So, whatcha got in that... Ohhhh! Damn, boy, you stink! Whadda you been doin'—rollin' in somethin' dead?"

It was, of course, the residue of troll stench lingering in his clothes and hair. One-Eye and his two companions recoiled two or three steps.

"Nay, sir. I was just helping a neighbor, and there was this cesspit...and..."

"Shut up, boy! I don't care what happened to you. But I don't want ya stinkin' up the place around here. So git! Go on about yer business."

And with that, they went back to their tree and their wine. Thurmond was left to continue on his journey.

During the encounter he had been afraid that the guards would notice the incessant jerking of the hand in the sack. They would no doubt have inquired about its contents if not distracted by the repellent smell. But strangely the hand had remained quite motionless while in their presence. Now that the danger was past, it was again twitching like mad. What did this mean? Could a troll hand be sentient? Could it actually sense danger and modify its actions accordingly? Thurmond doubted even a fully intact troll was capable of this kind of reasoning.

Thurmond knew very little about fell creatures. He was certain he was destined to slay a great many as soon as he became a famous Adventurer, but his knowledge of their specific characteristics was slight. The Trollkeeper's trolls had been his first look at anything in that category. He knew there were also ogres, goblins, and kobolds. Thurmond was fairly sure there were many other kinds of strange beings, but he was not familiar with those as of yet.

All such creatures shared a single, common trait—they were instinctively loathed by human beings. There was just something innately wrong with them, some indefinable quality that evoked both great hatred and great fear. When faced with such creatures, people were immediately filled with a compelling need to attack or flee. With the exception of a few extreme eccentrics—the Trollkeeper and Una came to mind—humans simply could not abide their presence.

This antipathy was reciprocal. The fell creatures universally despised humans and took every opportunity to do them ill. Many centuries of conflict had resulted in their banishment to vast underground grottoes and cavern complexes. Here they gathered strength and planned dark deeds. And woe to any unlucky human who came too close.

From time to time, bands of marauding goblins would emerge from their holes, perhaps with an allied contingent of ogres or trolls, and fall upon a town or farmstead. Most of the population would be slaughtered. An unlucky few would be driven back to the goblin caves to spend the rest of their miserable lives as slaves, never to see the light of day again.

Kobolds sometimes joined the goblins in their above-ground forays, but in general they were more reclusive and less destructive. For one thing, they were small. While a tall goblin might reach the height of an average man's breastbone, a kobold seldom exceeded two feet. What kobolds lacked in stature, however, they made up for in numbers. There were always too many of them. They would abruptly boil from hidden openings in a hillside and swarm over their victims before any real defense could be offered.

Trolls and ogres, Thurmond had heard, were big, dumb, and ugly. He had now had a good, close look at trolls and could add vicious, deafening, and foul to the list. Ogres were…well…still just big, dumb, and ugly.

To counter this evil, a unique society of brave men had come into existence, the Brotherhood of Underworld Adventurers. Bands of these doughty heroes risked their lives in desperate incursions into the fell creatures' underground lairs, where they slew them without mercy and reaped the rewards of their valor.

For the fell creatures were rich with treasure. They amassed great hoards of gold coins, gems, and magical items taken as booty in their raids. Such creatures instinctively loved such things and collected their treasure in great subterranean storerooms that they guarded with their lives. The happy Adventurer who won a goblin hoard could find himself well set for life.

In addition, there were other nonhuman races that maintained more cordial relations with human society. Parties of dwarves, elves, and less frequently gnomes passed through Gorgonholm with some regularity, buying and selling sundry goods, joining caravans, and forming adventuring expeditions.

Thurmond, like everyone else in his home village, had been raised to dislike the nonhumans. The gnomes were the least offensive. At least they knew they were short—about hip high but very stocky—and acted accordingly. Not so their cousins the dwarves, whom Thurmond found insufferably boastful. They were always harping about their illustrious ancestry—as if anybody cared—and bragging about their great skill with weapons, the length of their beards, and the number of goblins they had killed.

At least that was what people said about them. Thurmond had never personally spoken to a dwarf, but from what he had heard, he did not we want to. He had seen a few at the Old Traitor's Head, where they drank too much and took great offense to anything that might possibly be interpreted as an insult. Nobody liked them.

Elves were even worse. Effeminate and condescending, they exuded an air of superiority. Yet for all their vaunted sophistication, they were not above kissing arse to get their way. Thurmond had never seen elves before coming to the city, but back in his home village, his mother had always warned him not to trust an elf.

The encounter with the Road Guards made Thurmond aware that he had another problem to solve before he could return to Gorgonholm. He would never be allowed through the city gates reeking of troll as he did now. Coming to a stream, he immersed himself in the water for a considerable length of time. He scrubbed his entire body with mud, pine needles, sweet grasses, and rough tree bark. His clothing was more of a problem—the ferocious stench clung to it tenaciously.

But at that moment, Lady Fortune smiled upon him. As he sat soaking in the water, a washerwoman, apparently from a nearby village, lugged a large basket of clothes down to the edge of the stream. Unaware of his presence, she dipped the garments into the water and began beating them against a rock. Finished, she gathered her washing and returned the way she had come.

Here was the solution to his problem. The thought of stealing from this poor washerwoman caused Thurmond a sharp twinge of guilt. Her customers would be angry and might demand payment for their pilfered garments. But, as he often did, he cast the occasion in mythic terms. Just as a reptile sheds its skin and is born anew, he would cast off his old apparel and assume the identity of a professional Adventurer. Someday he would repay the washerwoman by slaying the monsters that lurked in the woods around her village.

Rising from the stream, Thurmond found the path that led to the woman's village, but he waited until after dark to make his approach. Every dog immediately started to howl, offended by the lingering troll stench on his clothing. Doors opened, and lights appeared. Irate voices demanded quiet, and some of the canines obeyed. Others continued to raise a clamor. Frightened, Thurmond threw himself beneath an oxcart and waited.

The washerwoman's cottage was easy to recognize—she had hung the wet clothing on some bushes to dry. Thurmond moved fast, snatching hose and doublet, and as a final thought, he tossed a silver penny onto her doorstep. Inside, what sounded like a herd of goats began a frantic bleating. He withdrew into the shadows and escaped into the night. Village dogs continued to bark long after his departure.

The clothes proved badly chosen. He had selected them because in the uncertain light they had appeared to be the most elegant. Unfortunately, the hose were far too large so that they hung on his slender legs like sacks. Even worse, they were badly worn, and the knees were permanently stained with dung. The doublet was too small, obviously that of a boy, with the sleeves too tight and reaching but halfway down his forearms.

He would not be entering Gorgonholm in the grand style he had imagined. He looked like a peasant wearing his master's castoffs. Adventuring, he reflected sadly, seemed like nothing more than a long series of unpleasant encounters and unavoidable setbacks. He slept the rest of the night shivering in his new clothes, which had not had time to dry. At least he no longer reeked of troll.

Thurmond arrived at the city gates well before noon the next day. His situation had change dramatically since he first entered those gates two years ago. Then he had lacked the copper farthing needed for entrance. He had watched until the gate guard's attention was turned to a wagon stacked high with teetering cages full of live chickens. As the guard haggled with the driver and poked at the squawking poultry, Thurmond crept along the vehicle's far side and out into the city street beyond.

With no other option, he then took the desperate chance of trying to sell the stolen tools. He half expected to be seized and delivered to the constables, or at the very least quizzed about his possession of the tools, but no questions were asked. The merchant, an older man with hairy ears and a continually dripping nose, had immediately agreed and produced a pouch of coins.

The steep prices demanded by even the seediest of accommodations resoundingly thwarted his efforts to secure lodging. Even a vermin-infested attic room in the most sordid tenement was beyond his meager budget. Happily, a chance encounter with a friendly stableman led to an arrangement in which he was allowed to sleep in the tack room. In exchange, he would help with the horses, clean the customers' saddles and bridles, and when necessary, alas, shovel the manure from the stalls.

Every day Thurmond ventured out to the streets to earn whatever he could with whatever came his way. He might help a mason unload a cart of heavy stones or a builder whose regular helper was injured and could not work. Such work was piecemeal but provided coin enough to keep him fed. The constant strenuous work toughened the muscles of his body.

Nonetheless, he remained dissatisfied. Thurmond was determined to become an Adventurer of great acclaim, to accomplish legendary deeds, and to win fabulous treasure. For two years he languished, frustrated with his inability to escape the workaday drudgery and live the life of a hero.

But that was all in the past. Today the young man was smiling as he passed through the city gates and handed over the gate price to the guards. He had enjoyed his adventure immensely. More importantly, he had accomplished a difficult task that would earn him the gratitude of some powerful and mysterious nobleman.

CHAPTER SIX

AT THE DROWNED RAT

As instructed, Thurmond returned that very night to his customary spot outside the Severed Head. Gone were the mismatched doublet and hose. His remaining silver had bought him the nicest garb he had ever owned. He was especially proud of the jaunty cap embellished with a large white feather.

His wait was short. The same burly man-at-arms who had first brought him to the well-groomed gentleman appeared before him.

"You got the item?"

"Aye, of course."

"Where?"

"Somewhere safe. I couldn't just walk around town with something like that, could I?" Actually, it was stashed behind a loose board in the wall of his tack room lair. It had become increasingly docile. Was it gradually losing its vigor or merely growing complacent? Thurmond had no idea.

"Be at the Drowned Rat just when the moon sets behind the cathedral tonight. Don't be late. And bring the item." The burly man disappeared into the darkness.

Now, the Severed Head had a reputation as a dangerous place. Its clientele were in general a rough-and-tumble bunch, not at all averse to the spilling of blood. Adventurers, of course, committed acts of extreme violence on a regular basis as a requirement of their chosen line of work. But this gave them a much more professional and detached attitude toward mayhem when they were off duty. For them, killing was simply their job, so they were not particularly eager to jump into a fight for which they were not being paid.

Besides, there was little percentage in starting a drunken death duel when your opponent was most likely as well armed and well trained as yourself. In a barroom filled with professional killers, only the most foolhardy forgot his manners. Thus the Adventurers who frequented the Head remained relatively cordial and polite.

The Drowned Rat was another story. It was a waterman's bar, crammed into a corner of the city wall by where the River Gate opened on the wharves that lined the east bank of the Mad River. The Rat's customers were largely bargemen and riverboat runners. These tended to be loudmouthed and aggressive, completely lacking the professional restraint of the Adventurers in the Head.

There was also a sizable criminal element among the drinkers in the Rat. Smugglers waited there for consignments of illegal goods. Stolen merchandise was fenced. Notorious outlaws and river pirates were reputed to lay low in the upstairs rooms. Anyone taking too much notice or asking the wrong question was promptly knifed, dragged out, and heaved into the river.

It was with great trepidation, therefore, that Thurmond approached the establishment at the stated hour. He had never ventured inside and had no wish to do so now. To his relief, he spotted the rude man-at-arms standing outside the door, his hand on the hilt of his sword. He offered no word of greeting as Thurmond stepped up.

"Go around the right side. There's a well in the courtyard—stand by it." He gestured with his thumb in the desired direction.

Thurmond did as he was told. The troll hand, tucked inside his new doublet, began to quiver and twitch. He at first saw no one, but then the well-groomed gentleman materialized out of the darkness. He was once again swathed in a huge cape with its hood pulled down to conceal the face.

"Have it?"

"Aye, right here."

Thurmond reached into his doublet and produced the bag.

"Take it out."

Thurmond did as he was bidden. The hand convulsed violently, still entwined by the strands of braided grass. He was a bit puzzled by its antics. It had been so docile of late.

"Let me see."

Thurmond held it up to catch the dim light filtering from the upper windows of the Drowned Rat.

"Hand it over."

Thurmond again complied, offering both the bag and the hand to the gentleman, who flinched and refused them.

"Not to me! To him."

A figure emerged from the shadows—the man-at-arms. Thurmond had had no idea the man was lurking behind him. He opened a large leather wallet and thrust it in Thurmond's direction. The quivering hand was dropped inside, and the man again disappeared into the dark.

The well-groomed gentleman began to speak.

"Now for your third and final test. It is by far the most important and the most difficult. But if you succeed, your dreams will come true."

"I stand ready."

"Well said, very well, indeed."

His voice grew silky and inviting.

"Know you that my master is a man of great learning, a highly cultured man, a man who sees far beyond the limitations by which lesser men bind themselves. He loves beauty above all else and surrounds himself with many beautiful things."

Thurmond, who had always had an impatient temperament, longed for him to hurry up and get to the point.

"He is also very rich, which is fortunate, for it allows him to add new acquisitions to his collection of beautiful things. He can purchase almost any worthy item he might chance upon. But at times there are misguided souls who reject his generous offers, who through selfishness or greed decline to sell an item my master…"

So that was it! They needed a burglar, someone to steal an item for which gold had been refused. Thurmond's mind raced ahead, and he stopped listening to the words of the speaker. What could it be? What risks would the job entail? More importantly, why him? Why not a professional burglar? Surely, they must have ways of finding such a person.

"…And so you can understand that we cannot go through the…uh… regular channels with this job. We need an outsider, an unknown. You're perfect. Will you undertake it?"

"Aye, certes! What is the nature of the item I am tasked to retrieve?"

"A very small thing, really. A small silver mirror no bigger than a dinner plate. Nothing elaborate but of great antiquity and bordered with exquisite etching. Etrusian work and a marvelous tribute to the glory of their empire. Master's heart is set on it."

"Where is this item to be found?"

"In the house of a certain low-ranking noble here in Gorgonholm. He is very old and apparently lost to all reason, for the sums Master offered for the piece were beyond imagination."

"What else can you tell me?"

"According to my source, you'll find it in the library, in an elegant wooden chest with a pentagram carved on the lid."

"A what?"

"A pentagram. It looks like a star surrounded by magical symbols."

"Are there guards?"

"There are the household retainers, but most of them are almost as old as their master and will be of little account. One or two may be younger and more robust, but they will be servants, not trained fighters. And we anticipate no magical defenses."

"You *anticipate* no such defenses?"

The gentleman gave a small shrug.

"One can never be absolutely certain, can one? However, I can provide you with a pair of special items that will give you a considerable advantage during the undertaking."

Now the gentleman drew a leather wallet from beneath his cape. It was identical to the one the man-at-arms carried.

"There are two items inside that will prove very useful. The first is a golden street door key. A charm has already been placed on the lock of the door by which you must effect entry. Merely touch it with this key, and it will open without a sound. It will work only once and only on the designated lock."

He held up the key for Thurmond's perusal.

"The second looks like this."

He now held a plain wooden box with a hinged lid, no bigger than the palm of his hand.

"I am aware that it looks harmless, but be very careful with it. When opened, the box will emit a blinding blast of light that will dazzle the eyes of anyone caught in its rays. Take care to be directly behind the lid when you open it, not in front or even to the side. That way, you will remain unaffected."

Thurmond nodded his understanding.

"A final word of caution. When you have the mirror, do not look into it directly. It may possess certain arcane properties that you will find disturbing. This is most likely no more than a silly old legend, but best not to take chances. Just drop it in the wallet."

Thurmond did not like the sound of that. He knew nothing about magic and did not want to learn. He had had enough trouble with the damnable troll hand. He certainly had no desire to involve himself with a magic mirror, especially one with disturbing properties.

The gentleman continued.

"In three night's time, my representative will once again meet you at the Old Traitor's Head. I will expect either the mirror or a valid explanation of why you have not fulfilled our agreement. Take this as a down payment."

He tossed a small leather pouch. Thurmond caught it and was surprised by its weight. He was even more surprised to find it contained ten gold sovereigns. The idea of a magic mirror suddenly became far less troubling.

"Succeed in your task, and you will receive five times that amount upon delivery. In addition, steady employment will be yours for the asking."

Thurmond merely nodded, disoriented by the fortune in his hand and by the nagging doubt that he had been drawn into something far beyond what he was being led to believe. The well-groomed gentleman was far sharper of wit than he. It occurred to him that there was another important aspect of this enterprise that needed to be clarified.

"Has this job been cleared with…I think they're called the Brethren?"

Gorgonholm, like all cities, was rife with crime. Citizens and visitors were routinely plundered and not infrequently murdered. Most of this activity was conducted under the auspices of a brutal crime cult known as the Brethren and their even more hidden shadowy, the Patron. No one could say who the Patron was, but of his existence there could be no doubt. It just did not pay to defy the Brethren.

"Do you mean, have we secured the permission of the Patron? Of course. We are well versed in the steps that must be taken in such matters. You may put your mind at rest."

Thurmond certainly hoped he could believe this promise. He had heard too many tales of the Brethren's fearsome methods to heedlessly risk falling afoul of them. Every illegal activity required the approval of the Patron and that a percentage of the take be given over. Those failing to comply were given no warning. Their butchered bodies were simply left on display in a public square to encourage obedience.

The conversation lapsed, and the gentleman began to turn as if to leave.

"Hold on! You have yet to tell me which house I am to burgle. Might I at least be told how to find it?"

The well-groomed gentleman turned back for a moment, leaned in close, and whispered into Thurmond's ear. Then he turned yet again and glided back into the gloom of the moonless night.

†

Thurmond never did get to sleep that night. He flopped and fidgeted just like, he thought grimly, that frightful troll hand. His mood swung wildly from jubilation to despair. At one moment, he was confident his natural abilities would lead him to the successful completion of his mission. In the next, he was on the edge of tears because he knew nothing about being a burglar, and the chances that he would be killed or captured were very great.

But he was not about to abandon his dream by backing out now. He owed himself better than that. Plus, he had given his word to the well-groomed gentleman. An Adventurer could always be relied on to keep his word.

He did not trust that silky gentleman to do likewise. As repulsive as he found the Trollkeeper's trolls, at least their evil natures were quite evident. That they would kill you and eat you was beyond dispute. Dealings with humans were not so simple. Something was amiss with his bargain, but he knew not what it could be. But at this point, there was no other option but to go forward. So a burglar he would become.

CHAPTER SEVEN

A Nocturnal Intrusion

In spite of his resolution the night before, ethical concerns still plagued Thurmond the next morning. He had stolen before, but his previous thefts had been different. They had been amateur efforts conducted only to satisfy the vital needs of the moment—survival needs. Simple things like food and clothing. This new job was poles apart. He had been engaged as a professional burglar and was expected to enter a private home and make off with an antique item with magical properties. The monetary value of such a thing would be astronomical.

It was stealing for the sake of profit and personal advancement, not to fill an empty belly or replace clothes fouled with troll stench. It defied everything he'd ever been taught about right and wrong.

But what exactly was right and wrong, after all? Did the rich not routinely steal from the poor, calling it feudal obligation or hereditary privilege or some other meaningless crap? Did the church not steal from everybody, promising hellfire to anyone who failed to hand over? And did it not all just add up to the same thing? Those who were able to take from others did so. You could be a taker, or you could be taken from. It was just that simple.

So why should he, a person of intelligence, a person of merit, not refuse to play the victim? Why not become the predator instead of the prey? He did not particularly like this idea, the reduction of life's values to such a simple equation, but he did not get to make the rules. They were set indelibly by law and custom. He could only abide by them, taking the world as he found it. If his goals could be reached only through stealing, then steal he must.

Yet how could he do this and still aspire to become an Adventurer, one of a Brotherhood of heroes renowned for their deep commitment to honor? Would he not forever bear a stain far more odious than the reek of troll? If he did this thing now, would he ever be able to redeem himself through heroic and selfless deeds?

Aye! This had to be the answer! He would steal at present only because stealing would allow him to serve the cause of good in a larger way later on. He would recover the valuable items stolen by fell creatures and return them to their rightful owners. In this way, he could easily atone for such a minor transgression as he had agreed to commit.

With his ethical dilemma resolved, Thurmond set out to become the best burglar he could be. If he was to be a thief, he had to learn to think like one. To this end, he took to the street—not to seek work, but to learn to see the world through the eyes of a predator. Find the weak spot, the angle of approach. Find the trust that could be betrayed. Lie when there was no need to lie. See other people only as a means to an end, as a resource to be exploited. No compassion, no hesitation, no regrets.

He spent the rest of that day and most of that night perfecting this new identity. He was delighted with himself when he successfully filched a long strip of cloth from a street vendor's stall. It was a dark charcoal gray and would make an excellent mask or head scarf. In addition, he tried to follow random passersby without being discovered. He slunk in shadows, peeked around corners, and tried to catch overhead tree branches with a running jump. He had a great time pretending to be a thief.

On the second day, he grew more serious. Assuming the guise of a lowly day laborer in search of employment, he climbed to the exclusive Hilltop Quarter and searched out the abode of Lord Staynes, the name the well-groomed gentleman had whispered in his ear. It was a town house, ancient and ornate. Unlike many of the adjoining houses, it was not set within the confines of a walled compound but removed from the street only by a short setback. The windows were secured by elaborate but thoroughly functional wrought iron bars. The street door was massive and reinforced with more bars. A large keyhole was centered in a heavy lock.

Not wanting to be conspicuous, Thurmond gave the place a quick look-see as he proceeded up the street. He lingered awhile and then gave it another as he came down. There were no concealing bushes or shrubberies in the narrow yard that bordered the street. He would have to make his approach directly and quickly.

✝

The moon finally settled in behind the cathedral, causing a shroud of darkness to descend over the Hilltop Quarter. Thurmond was ready. His new scarf was tied across his face, bandit style. He wore his new hat, which he deemed his lucky token. His dagger was in its accustomed place under his arm. The leather wallet containing the wooden box was over his shoulder. The golden key was in his hand.

Rising, he scuttled across the street from his hiding place in the topiary of a neighbor's garden. He had spent the last several hours lurking beneath a shrubbery cut to resemble what might be a horse. Having had the opportunity to evaluate it at some length, Thurmond thought it looked more like a sheep with the head of a bird. Or perhaps a dancing human with an exceptionally long nose.

He had been clutching the key for some time, worried that he might fumble and drop it if he waited until he was at the door to draw it from his pouch. Of course, he was also concerned that he might, by holding it in his hand, drop it and lose it in the dark. Fortunately he did neither. Coming up to the door, he touched the key to the lock as instructed. Without a sound, the door swung slightly ajar. He was in!

Thurmond stood in a large entrance hall, dimly lit by the glow of two or three hanging oil lamps that cast flickering shadows. Chairs and large urns lined the side walls. At the opposite end, an open door beckoned. Above it, an open balcony ran the length of the far wall. As quietly as possible, he moved to the left-hand wall and began to proceed toward the open door.

There was a loud, mechanical *clunk* and then an even louder *thwak* as something struck the wall next to his head. It was undeniably the sound of a crossbow being fired. Someone was shooting at him from the balcony. The bolt had come very close. He had felt its wind as it passed by his cheek. He heard the clicking sounds of the weapon being recocked.

Thurmond stood frozen for an instant, scarcely believing this could indeed be real. But his instincts for survival were good, and he jumped for cover behind an enormous stone urn. Again he heard the distinctive *clunk,* but this time neither heard nor felt the arrival of the bolt, only the sensation of his hat being lifted from his head. He ran straight to the far door, striving to get beneath the balcony before the crossbow could be cocked and fired again.

He found himself looking down a long hallway, along which a series of doors opened on either side. Without hesitation, he plunged into the corridor, and, choosing a door at random, hurled himself inside. Behind him a horn began to blow, presumably an effort by the crossbowman to rouse the rest of the household.

The room was very dark, but he could make out a large table covered with a long cloth. Lacking a better idea, he dove beneath it. He could now hear a cacophony of frantic shouts and approaching footsteps. He peeked out but could see no other means of egress. Looking about, he discovered he was in an armory. A dozen helmets were piled on the floor beside the table. He saw mail hauberks, shields, swords, and spears heaped on tables or hanging in racks.

Then the door opened, and two men entered. Both carried very long, very lethal-looking daggers. The second one held a lamp.

"Take care, Oscar! If he came in here, he mighta picked up a weapon."

"Aye, I will. Bring the light over here."

As if by instinct, the pair came directly to the table, beneath which Thurmond cowered. In utter terror, he drew his dagger from its sheath and prepared to defend himself. Then he remembered the wallet and reached a trembling hand inside. Just as the edge of the tablecloth began to lift, Thurmond opened the wooden box.

An intense beam of light shot from it, directly into the eyes of the two men. It lasted only a second, but that was sufficient. Both were immediately struck blind. Thurmond sprang out and kicked at the first man's stomach, but as he was scrambling backward, it hit him squarely in the nuts. He went down with a loud, sucking sound.

Thurmond tried to shoulder past the second man but tripped on the first, who was writhing on the floor. Falling forward, he reached out and inadvertently thrust his weapon into the bicep of the second man. Wounded and blind, the man screamed and fled to the far side of the room, hoping to escape. His way now clear, Thurmond regained his feet and ran down the hallway to another door on the opposite side. He was afraid to go back the way he had come in, dreading that the crossbowman would shoot him in the back as he crossed the entrance hall.

This room seemed to be a library, the very place he was looking for. Various books and scrolls were arranged on shelves along one wall. Others were strewn upon a massive desk, where on one corner a single lamp offered a feeble light. And there, on that desk, among the sundry books and papers, an elaborately carved box sat open. Next to it was a silver mirror, about the size of a dinner plate. Thurmond did not stop to think about it. He just shoved the thing into his wallet.

He considered starting a fire with the parchments strewn on the desk. Such a diversion might give him the opening he needed. But caution prevailed. It was more likely that he would find himself trapped in a burning house. Nonetheless, he swept a number of them into the wallet, thinking that, under the right circumstances, fire could still be an option. He again heard the sounds of approaching pursuit, of a household roused and angry.

And then a face, seemingly from nowhere, was thrust into his.

"Want to get out of here?"

"What? Aye, I most certainly do."

"I can get you out, but I want something in return."

"Okay, anything. Get me out of here, and I'll do whatever you ask. Just hurry, please."

"Come on then."

The mysterious figure was shorter than Thurmond and apparently deformed—one shoulder rose substantially higher than the other. He moved to the far side of the room.

"I said, come on."

Thurmond obeyed.

"This house is filled with secrets. Secret deeds, secret deals, and secret passages. I know them all."

The small man fumbled with the ornate corner of a bookcase, and a concealed door suddenly popped open before him.

"Come on. They'll be in here any moment."

Thurmond followed the figure into the hidden passage, and the door snapped shut behind him. The way was narrow and dark, and he was forced to grasp the back of the small figure's tunic to keep from being left behind. The little guy was fast. They went straight, left, down a steep flight of stairs, and straight again for a long time. They at last emerged through a small door that also clicked closed behind them.

Thurmond tried to catch his breath as his companion lit a small lamp.

"Where are we?"

"In a warehouse behind the house and way down the hill. We're safe enough here, at least for the moment. Over there is a door to the street."

"Who are you?"

"Who am I? Who are *you*? You're the housebreaker! Just what were you trying to pull off in there?"

"I was on a mission of…acquisition."

"You mean, you came to steal something, don't you? You're a thief, right? So just admit it."

"Okay, okay—I'm a thief. All right? Happy now?"

Thurmond got his first good look at his new companion. He was small and quite thin. The drooping left shoulder lent him a lopsided stance. The facial features were miserably hard favored.

"Well, I don't happen to care what you were doing in there, Mister Thief. I only care about your promise."

"My promise?"

"Aye, your promise. You promised that if I led you out of there, you'd do whatever I asked."

"Oh, come on! I might have said something like that. But they were after me. A fellow will say anything at a moment like that."

"So, you're not only a thief but also a liar. A breaker of promises. A swearer of false oaths. Is that what you are, Mister Thief? That can bring mighty bad luck, you know."

"Nay!"

"Aye! Mighty bad luck. Years of ill fortune and betrayal. You get as you give, you know."

Thurmond knew this was neither the time nor place to stand and argue with this scrawny cripple.

"All right, you win. What do you want?"

"For you to help me find a way."

"A way? What does that mean? What way?"

"I mean a way. A way to live. I can't go back there now, and I have no other way of living. I've never been allowed out of that house, not once in all my life. So now you have to help me find a way. A life for a life. My life for yours. That's fair, don't you think? If you have any sort of decency at all, Mister Thief, you'll help me. You'll keep your word."

Thurmond groaned inwardly. This misshapen little toad had found his weak point, his innate sense of honor. He could no more break this promise than break the one he had made to the well-groomed gentleman.

He had to admit, though, that things were going very well. He had the mirror, he had escaped with his life, and he would soon be coming into a deal of money. A whole new life awaited. What did it matter if he was saddled with this twerp for a couple of days?

"Very well. I agree. A promise is...a promise."

CHAPTER EIGHT

AN ODD COMPANION

His sack of golden sovereigns certainly gave Thurmond the chance to raise his standard of living. Better living quarters were easily now within his means. But he thought it prudent not to reveal his newfound wealth in a conspicuous flurry of extravagant spending. So he stayed in his room in the stable and kept up the pretense of being no more than an out-at-elbows laborer. He felt it was a most clever disguise.

When he and his companion arrived at the tack room, Thurmond threw himself down on his pallet of saddle blankets. The night's escapade had left him utterly exhausted.

"You'll find a big pile of blankets over in the corner. Take as many as you want. You can sleep over there, too."

He indicated an empty spot on the far side of the room. But tired as he was, sleep would not come. He eyed his new companion who was arranging his blankets in a far corner.

"What do they call you?"

"You may call me Spoon."

"Spoon? What kind of a name is Spoon?"

"It isn't my real name, if you must know. I won't tell you that because it isn't any of your business. My mother was in charge of polishing Master's silver, and I guess when I was little, I liked to play with the silver spoons. I don't remember any of it. That's just what I've been told. She started calling me Spoon, and the name stuck."

Thurmond knew all about concealing one's real name. His was actually Wido. It was a common name in the village—so common, in fact, that things got confusing unless the various Widos assumed some additional designation. Wido Long was the tallest man in the village, and Black Wido pounded horseshoes at the forge. He had been known as Marge's Wido after his mother.

But Wido had always sounded like the name of a man destined to haul dung, so he had changed it upon his arrival at Gorgonholm. After considerable reflection, he had chosen Thurmond, the name of a legendary hero from the olden days. Everyone knew the legends of Thurmond's great deeds. He was exactly the kind of man young Wido intended to become.

"You say that they never let you out of the house? Not even once?"

"Aye, that is fact. Not even once. Master was too ashamed of my crooked body to let me be seen in the street. I think he was so touchy because he's my father."

Thurmond rolled his eyes at this. He had heard that said so many times before.

"But Master has grown old. He'll die soon. And Young Master hates me, hates my ugliness and twisted body. Hates me because I'm his half brother. As soon as our father dies, he'll put me in a sack and throw me in the river. And nobody will care. So, you can see, I couldn't stay there. I didn't know what to do, but then you came along, and I saw my chance. I was reading in the library when…"

"You can read?"

"Aye, certes."

"Teach me then. I've always wanted to read."

"Well, okay, but maybe not right now. Anyway, when I heard you coming in, I ducked behind a hanging…"

"Why not now?"

"Look, I can teach you. Maybe. But it's going to take a long time. I can't do it in one night. It's something you have to work at."

"So who was shooting at me from the balcony? A professional bowman?"

"By the fingers of God, nay. That was only Gyre, the son of one of the maids. Can't be more than about ten. He likes to pretend that he's a great Adventurer, so he takes a crossbow from the armory and stands guard up there. He says he's protecting us from invading trolls. You were never in any danger. The bow is almost as big as he is. He couldn't really hit anything."

Thurmond was not so sure about that.

Spoon continued.

"I guess he's allowed to do it because Young Master is his papa."

Same old story.

Sleep was finally coming over both of them, and they let the conversation lag. Within moments, they drifted off.

†

The conversation resumed in the morning while they were breaking their fast on a loaf of stale bread dipped in beer. Spoon thought a fish would be nicer, he was used to a fish in the morning. In Master's household, he was accustomed to eating well. But he knew he had to be satisfied with whatever Thurmond could provide, and judging from his appearance and his quarters, things were going to be lean.

Spoon felt fairly sure he had handled things well the night before. Thurmond was a trusting boy. That was good. Gullible, too. Even better. He just had to be careful not to slip and give himself away. The best thing, he decided, would be to keep him talking about himself.

"So, judging from the accommodations, I'd have to say you're not much of a thief."

Thurmond bridled a bit.

"I'm not really a thief at all—at least I wasn't until last night."

"So you're really just a stable boy."

Did this little runt intend to insult him, or was he unwittingly being impolite? Thurmond was unsure. But either way, he was not going to swallow such rudeness. His voice grew stern.

"Nay, not a stable boy. This is just temporary until I join the Brotherhood of Underworld Adventurers. I'm sure you've heard of them."

Spoon heard the change in the young man's tone and knew he had made a mistake. He had not yet had enough experience with strangers to know how to speak to them. Time to try a different approach.

"I beg your pardon. I didn't mean to give offense. Prithee, tell me your story. Have you lived in the city all your life?"

Thurmond was flattered. No one had ever expressed interest in his life before. He jumped in at once.

"By God's liver, nay. I was in a dull farming village and apprenticed to a carpenter, but I ran away two years ago when I was fifteen years. I had heard there was a great city somewhere to the west, so that's where I went, and here I am."

"You're a runaway apprentice? That's against the law."

"Not for me, not anymore. I've been here for more than a year and a day, so I'm legally free now. That's the law."

"But you weren't when you ran away—weren't you scared?"

"Aye, plenty scared. I had to stay away from people and villages. It's bad enough being a runaway—they might whip you or brand you for that—but I stole my master's tools too. If I'd been caught, they'd have probably hanged me. I stole food along the way as well."

Spoon's eyes gleamed in amusement.

"So you are an experienced thief after all."

"So would you be if you were as hungry as I was. It wasn't easy. I tried to sneak into hen roosts and gardens and orchards, but I never got much to eat. Mostly I got chased by farmers and bitten by dogs. Once a woman with a slingshot shot me in the back with a rock."

"Why? What did you steal from her?"

"A flitch of bacon from her smokehouse. It was pretty good once I cut off the mold on the outside."

The young man was now relaxed and talkative. It was time, Spoon thought, to move to more important questions.

"So, Thurmond, what were you hoping to steal last night? When I first saw you, you were digging around on the parchments on Young Master's desk. You obviously weren't looking for coins or jewels in that mess."

Thurmond did not know what to do, what to say. He was loath to confide in Spoon—he had no reason to trust him. But he surely needed to talk to somebody. He was mired in complicated issues he was not prepared to cope with, and he needed help. Spoon was obviously highly intelligent, and even if he had been kept locked in the house, he seemed somehow worldly wise.

And he had read books! Wise men wrote books, men who had solved life's mysteries. Spoon must have found the answers in books Thurmond so desperately needed. And Spoon had no reason to betray him. Had he not said that he had nowhere else to go, no one else to turn to? He needed Thurmond and would only injure himself by turning against him.

"Look, Spoon, if I tell you something, do you promise to keep quiet about it? Can I trust you?"

"Of course. We are sworn to aid one another."

"I need information. I think that you may have it. You may have found the answers I seek in the books you have read."

"Ask then."

"Okay. Is it possible for a man to retain his honor if he breaks an oath when it was a bad oath taken without proper forethought to the painful consequences it may hold for innocent folk who have done the oath-taker no ill, though the oath-taker stands to gain from the breaking of the oath whe—"

"What?"

"I mean, can a man still be called virtuous if he has done something that violates all concepts of decency and honor yet has done so only for the best of reasons, perhaps to lessen the suffering of innocent souls or—"

"Peace! Enough! I neither know nor care about such drivel. Let's speak of something of real consequence. What did you take from Master's house?"

Thurmond gave in.

"This."

He drew the silver mirror from the wallet and held it up. Spoon gave it only a cursory glance.

"Ah, Young Master's mirror of scrying. I'm surprised he left it lying around like that. But he has always been of a careless nature."

"I am told it is very old and very valuable."

"Old, perhaps. Valuable, aye. Scrying mirrors don't come cheap."

"What's scrying?"

"Divination. The ability to see things far away or mayhap back in the past. Some claim to see the future as well, but I doubt that is really achievable."

"I was hired by a certain person, who wants it for his collection. A certain very rich person."

"If this *person* is so rich, why didn't he hire a real thief? Why come to you?"

These words stung Thurmond. Was his inexperience really so obvious?

"I was told they needed someone unknown."

"Well, I think he certainly got what he was looking for then."

Thurmond did not take kindly to Spoon's sarcasm.

"Hey! I would appreciate it if you watched what you say to me. I got the damned mirror, didn't I? And without me, maybe you would be floating in the river in a couple of days. In a sack!"

Spoon knew there had to be more to the story than this simpleton was aware of, that whoever had hired him had to have some angle. Spoon also knew he had to be more circumspect with Thurmond. He had always had a caustic tongue, and if he did not watch out, it might spoil everything.

"Okay, sorry. No offense meant."

The boy seemed genuinely placated by his apology. Spoon decided to shift their conversation in a new direction.

"Too bad you didn't bring along any of those parchments from Young Master's desk. Some of them might have been of real value, too."

"But I did! Here, I'll show you."

Thurmond began pulling them out of the wallet.

"Take it easy! Some of those are old and crumbly. You don't want to ruin them before I can read them."

"Maybe you can teach me to read while you look at them."

"Listen, I need some time to try to read these…and quiet…and solitude. Isn't there somewhere you could go while I do this work? Maybe for two or three hours?"

"Aye, I suppose so."

"Very well then, why don't you run along? Come back in the afternoon."

†

Thurmond did not fully trust Spoon—he could tell there was something the small man was not saying. Leaving the stable, he settled in behind a fence across the street. The stable's big barn doors were wide open, and Thurmond, peeking through a knothole, could keep close watch on the tack room door. If Spoon made a break, he would see him. Hours passed. He was hungry and desperately needed to go to the privy. Happily, his new companion made no attempt to make off.

When he reentered the tack room, Spoon was lying unconscious on the floor.

"Spoon! Spoon! What's the matter with you? What happened?"

Thurmond splashed the leftover beer on his face. Spoon's eyes popped open and seemed alert, but his face was deathly pale.

"Spoon! Damn it! What's wrong with you?"

"It was the mirror. I looked into the mirror."

This frightened Thurmond more than trolls or crossbows ever had. He was shaking as he grasped Spoon under the arms and half carried, half dragged him to his own sleeping pallet.

"Why'd you do that? You shouldn't be messing around with magic. It's too dangerous unless you know what you're doing."

"Look, Thurmond, you have to listen to me now. I haven't told you everything. Remember when I said I knew all the secrets of Master's household? Well, the most important ones are in the books in his library. He collects old and rare volumes, especially those on magic. But I read them all. I have the power to work some spells, but you are the only one I have revealed this to."

"What happened with the mirror?"

"I performed a ritual of gazing, something I'd read about but never tried before. I focused on the mirror's most recent target, presumably something Young Master was interested in. He has no arcane knowledge, so he's hired a magician to do this for him."

"What did you see?"

"A man and a woman, deep in conversation. Both affluent, judging from their dress. The woman was tall, dark of hair, and attractive, I suppose, if you like them mature. The man was also tall, with long curly hair and a beard. I'd call him well groomed."

"And? Go on!"

"Now we come to the disturbing part. They seemed to be speaking of you. At least, I heard your name mentioned before… Oh, God's holy blood, I feel ill."

Spoon bent over, clutching his stomach and emitting a series of dry heaves.

"Before what? Tell me!"

"Before the woman became aware of me. She sent something after me. Some kind of a demon. It was coming through the mirror, but I managed to break off. I shoved the mirror back into the wallet and must have passed out. I feel terrible. Do I look bad?"

"Aye, very bad. Even worse than usual. Just lie still. I'll go fetch some more beer. Or would you rather have wine?"

"Wine, please. And hurry. I don't like being left alone just now."

Both eyed the leather wallet lying in the middle of the floor.

CHAPTER NINE

THE UNLOOKED-
FOR ALLIANCE

Spoon sat propped up against an immense pile of horse blankets, a wooden cup of wine in his hand. More wine waited in a small stone pitcher on the floor beside him. He was still weak and pale, and his head still ached, but the infirmity seemed to be leaving him.

"What was it, Spoon? What did it look like?" Thurmond was desperate to know the details.

"Couldn't really tell. Just kind of a blur or a blob. But very definitely alive. It was something she turned loose and sent after me. I know that for sure."

Thurmond let out a long, soft groan. "Ooohhh, God's blood, what are we going to do?"

"Maybe it's not so bad. See here, the woman knew I was watching her, but I don't know if she actually saw me. In any case, she has no way of connecting me with you. So maybe you're still okay. Not in danger. Go deliver the mirror and get paid. We can just disappear after that."

"But you said they were talking about me!"

"Maybe—I heard the name Thurmond. It could be somebody else with the same name."

"I don't think so! Plus, you mentioned a well-groomed gentleman? I know him. He's the fellow I'm supposed to give the mirror to."

"There's no real problem, then. That explains things. They were discussing the delivery and were angered because I intruded. Can't blame them, really."

"What if there's a demon hiding in the wallet?"

"Just give it back to them, then it's for them to see to. It's their demon after all, isn't it?"

Once again Thurmond found himself acquiescing to Spoon's suggestions. He could think of no good reason to do otherwise. Nevertheless, he was mortally afraid of the demon-infested wallet and felt a pronounced distrust toward his employers.

†

He made his way to the Severed Head, wallet slung on shoulder, and took his old spot on the bench by the door. Immediately, the well-groomed gentleman appeared. He had obviously been awaiting Thurmond's arrival. There was no sign of the ruffian, but Thurmond assumed he was close by.

"You have it?"

"Aye, I do. In the wallet."

Thurmond set the accursed wallet on the bench and then pulled back slightly as the gentleman opened the flap and looked inside, but no demon flew forth in his face. The gentleman, satisfied, gave a smug smile.

"Excellent. I have your promised remuneration. There is a ten-sovereign bonus for a job well done. Would you like to count it?"

He handed over a bulging leather pouch. Opening it, Thurmond saw it was jammed full of gold coins. He bounced it in his hands as if checking it for weight.

"It looks about right."

"I must away anon. But come again to this place tomorrow night when the conditions of service in Master's household will be made clear. Then, knowing the particulars, you will be admitted if you desire it still. But the choice must be made with full awareness on your part."

"I eagerly await this great chance and am grateful to your generous master."

Thurmond boldly lied to the well-groomed gentleman. Never in his life had he felt so justified violating the sanctity of truth.

Returning to the stable, he found Spoon fully recovered and in a high state of agitation.

"Thurmond! Glad you're back! How did it go? Get the money? Was there anything in the wallet? I mean, anything besides the mirror?"

An endless stream of questions came boiling out of him. When Thurmond tried to answer, he didn't listen but jumped into another topic.

"While you were out, I read those parchments you took from Young Master's desk. Some secret plan is afoot. He's buying weapons, and there's a map and even a spell scroll. I'm surprised. I never thought him ambitious enough or smart enough to conspire in some scheme, but I think it must be so."

"What is he up to?"

"I know not, but I think it must be desperate. Listen to this ledger entry for armor and weapons, all of recent purchase.

Six habergeon of maille, well riveted; six corslet of lether, boyled in wax; six swerd, long and brood of blayde; six swerd, stiff and shorte of blayde; ten speer on staves of ashe; two ax, hevy and brood; twelve helm of open face; six crossbowe…

It goes on and on, Thurmond. He's outfitting a troop of soldiers. Is he planning to start a war?"

"Tell me about the map."

"From the looks of it, I'd say it's a treasure map. Some kind of a cavern complex. It shows a great cave mouth by a bend in the river and what looks to be a smaller opening leading in from the rear."

"I know what he's doing! Your Young Master is equipping an expedition to go treasure hunting. He's arming a troop for an underground adventure. He must be expecting stiff opposition to require such a well-appointed troop."

"That explains the spell scroll."

"Spell scroll?"

"Young Master has taken a magician into his service, otherwise the scroll would be useless. They're very dangerous to the uninitiated."

Thurmond wrinkled his brow.

"What are these scrolls for?"

"When a magician casts a spell, he depletes his psychic energy. When that energy runs out, his powers desert him until he rests, sometimes for a goodly while. But the really powerful magicians, the masters, know how to store a spell by writing it on parchment. When it is read, the spell is cast without depleting the reader's psychic energy."

The young man's brow unwrinkled.

"So you could the use the scroll we've got?"

"Mayhap, but there's a problem with scrolls, you can't read what's on them before you use them, because as soon as you read them, the spell is cast. So you have to be willing to take your chances. You might blast your enemies with a ball of fire or pelt them with a barrage of dead rats. You have to be satisfied with what you get. And after you read it, it's used up. The spell disappears from the parchment."

Thurmond stood for a moment, gathering his thoughts. For the first time he perceived his true destiny stretching inexorably before him, the disparate pieces coming together in an intricate web of beauty and perfection. He could see with new eyes. His past mistakes were not mistakes at all, but stepping stones to the fulfillment of a purpose ordained by a gracious providence.

"Spoon, I've just had the greatest inspiration."

"I know, you want us to become partners, to beat Young Master to the treasure. Okay…sure…maybe. But nay, such a thing cannot be. The two of us alone can't do something like this. Do you know anything of treasure hunting? Because I sure don't."

Thurmond abruptly produced the pouch he had received from the well-groomed gentleman.

"That will not be a problem. We can hire men to help us, just like your Young Master. I have plenty here."

He emptied the sack on the floor between them so that the candlelight gleamed on the golden coins. Thurmond began to run them through his fingers.

"Have you ever seen so much gold? When I was a lad, I couldn't have imagined… Oh, even now, I just can't believe that this gold is really real."

And with that, the gold coins abruptly transformed to flat gray stones, the kind found in abundance along the banks of any river. Both screamed in unison.

"What? No!"

Spoon pointed an accusing finger at Thurmond's face.

"Why did you do that? What possessed you to do that?"

"I did nothing!"

"You did, you great idiot! You did! You disbelieved. These stones had a glamour spell put on them, so they looked like gold—nay, they *were* gold—until you disbelieved. And that's just what you did. We could have spent them. The spell wouldn't have worn off for a long time. But you had to go and disbelieve. Don't ever do that!"

The vehemence of Spoon's anger took Thurmond aback. He liked Spoon and did not want to disappoint him, but this outburst piqued his ire.

"Hey, Spoon, why are you so burned up? This was *my* gold, not *our* gold. Anyway, how was I supposed to know it wasn't real?"

Thurmond rose to his feet.

"I hope you still want to be partners, because I do. But take it a little easier. I'm going to go down to the Head and have a few beers while you cool down."

Spoon sat in a silent snit as Thurmond left and shut the door behind him.

On his way to the Head, a terrible thought struck Thurmond. Had the rest of his money turned back into rocks as well? Frantically he checked the gold, silver, and copper coins in his purse. He was very much relieved to find them unchanged. At the Head, he took a seat inside and ordered a mug of their costly ale. What the hell, he could afford it.

He needed to figure things out. The well-groomed gentleman had betrayed him, so there would be no position as a man-at-arms in the household of some great lord. Though disappointing, this realization was not a crushing blow. He now had the map, and it opened the door to a far more promising possibility.

He regretted the loss of the gold, to be sure, but it was just money. The map would bring him more, probably much more. Then he could pay for the training and gear he needed to become an Adventurer. It was a much better way, far more to his liking than breaking into houses at the behest of some curly-haired fop.

Thurmond's spirits rose. His destiny had finally been revealed. That was much more valuable than mere gold.

He drank three mugs of bad ale, and each one tasted a little better than the one before it. It was potent ale, which accounted for its popularity in spite of its price. By the bottom of the third mug, he was sleepy and starting to drift. His eyes closed, and he settled back against the wall. But in the next instant, a conversation being held at a nearby table brought him to full attentiveness.

Two men, rough-looking sorts, were discussing the break-in at Staynes Hall the previous night.

"You're tellin' me the thief got inside but didn't carry nothin' away? Ain't much of a thief then."

Thurmond smirked to himself, that fellow should get his facts straight.

The words of the fellow's companion were more to his liking.

"But he didn't get caught neither, and that says somethin', 'cause young Staynes roused the household to find him, but they didn't. Got himself away without a trace—there's a bloke what's good at thievin'."

This made Thurmond's chest swell a bit. His skill was being recognized, had become the topic of conversation. He had finally done a deed worthy of acclaim. But the next words completely shattered his moment of self-congratulation and filled his veins with cold terror.

"I'm tellin' you this to see if you wanna be partners. The Brethren's put a bounty on the bloke's head. Seems he's workin' freelance. Five gold pieces. You in?"

"God's tongue, aye! For that kinda coin I'd strangle my own mother."

The well-groomed gentleman had lied! The job had not been sanctioned. Thurmond had been set up to take the blame for their crime. That was why they had chosen him. Because he was naive enough to believe their far-fetched tale and because he was absolutely expendable. No one would care if he were killed.

Thurmond sat and contemplated a very grim fact. A pitiless cult of professional murderers had now marked him for death. His issues with Spoon forgotten, he ran back to the tack room in a panic. Spoon took the news more calmly than Thurmond had expected.

"Let's don't make rash decisions until we submit our plight to close scrutiny, Thurmond. There are only three at present who can connect you to the deed. Myself, the *well-groomed gentleman*, as you label him, and his retainer. Perhaps the dark-haired woman, the witchy one, makes four. I have no reason to betray you, nor do they. They were the ones who received the mirror, after all, so they share your guilt. Is there any other way a connection could be made?"

"Well, I lost my hat in the entrance hall. The kid shot it off my head with his crossbow."

To Thurmond's surprise, Spoon dropped his head into his hands. "No! No! By God's holy toes, no. We are undone then. Young Master's hired sorcerer can use it to track you down. He knows such spells, or he wouldn't have been able to use the mirror. This is the worst possible eventuality. Goodbye, Thurmond. I can't stay here. I don't want to be killed when they come for you."

"You'd leave me now? I thought we were partners. You'd run out on me when I'm in this kind of trouble? I don't believe you—"

And then occurred a thing supremely strange. Stranger even than the turning of golden sovereigns into river rocks. Spoon simply disappeared, and now a young girl stood before Thurmond. She was brown of hair, sharp of eye, and nearly as tall as himself. Certainly she was pretty, with clear, even features. Her cheeks blushed with a rosy hue. Her garb was different as well. A long woman's kirtle had replaced Spoon's tunic and breeks.

Thurmond was completely dumfounded.

CHAPTER TEN

A SECRET REVEALED

"Idiot!"

The girl slapped Thurmond's face with her right hand.

"Imbecile!"

This time with the left.

"You're a girl!"

"Aye, I'm a girl. Is there something wrong with that?"

Then she burst into tears.

Thurmond was thoroughly perplexed. He couldn't quite grasp how his friend Spoon had been transformed into a female. More importantly, he had no idea how to respond to a female who was crying, and she was doing so with zest.

"You've ruined everything. You broke the glamour. I told you not to disbelieve, but you had to go and do it anyway. I hate you! You've ruined my entire life. What's going to happen to me now?"

"Look, I'm sorry I…"

"Shut up! Go to hell!"

Thurmond sat on a stool and stared down at his feet. He wanted to reach out, maybe hold her until she was cried out. Maybe stroke her head as his mother had done for him when he was a child and had fallen and skinned a knee. He could think of nothing else.

"Spoon, I…"

"My name's Sarah. I haven't gone by Spoon since I was little."

"Okay, Sarah. What is going on? Don't I have a right to know? Haven't I been your true friend?"

"I don't know. Have you? All I know is that my life has only gotten worse since I met you."

"Maybe so, but only because you didn't tell me the truth. At least I did that for you."

She began to get herself under control. She stopped crying, but her voice was still heavy with emotion.

"I don't know, Thurmond. I'm so confused right now. I don't know what to do. I have nowhere else to go. I can't go home. And if I stay here, they'll kill me. You lost the money, which was the only thing that would let us get away, and—"

Thurmond, quite unexpectedly, started to laugh. Sarah stopped talking and stared at him in astonishment.

"Spoon, I mean Sarah, maybe it's not as bad as you think. I'm pretty scared of being murdered, sure enough. But the map gives me the chance to have a grand adventure, and that's the very thing I've been burning for all my life. This is what I ran away from home for, what I've been trying to find since I came here two years ago. Here's my chance to become what I've always wanted to be, a real Adventurer. Nothing else matters. I've got to try.

"And this is your best chance as well. You said you can't go back to your old life, and you have nowhere else to go. You have little to lose then, and maybe Lady Fortune sent you this chance to find what you've always longed for. So come with me.

"I've been in this city long enough to know some people who can help us. And I still have some gold, so we're not broke. If we're going to beat your Young Master to the treasure, we need to make some plans. I don't know how to prepare for an adventure, but we can figure it out."

Sarah began to get her overwrought emotions under control. She wiped her eyes and blew her nose on her sleeve. Something about Thurmond made her want to trust him—something in his eyes.

"Maybe I could begin my initiation. The process is long and costly, but if

I could become a real magician, I could read spell scrolls. Plus I could throw much better spells than anything I can do now. I'm barely a beginner."

"How does one get started in something like that?"

"Like in anything else, I guess. I'd have to apprentice to a master magician. You have to pay them to take you on. It requires years to complete and is supposed to be very difficult."

"Listen, I've been an apprentice, and it's just shit. The master works you to death and beats you for everything that goes wrong. Or even when things don't go wrong. It's a bad choice. And we don't have the time. Isn't there some other way?"

"I'm not sure. I taught myself some basic spells using Master's books. Mayhap something like that is possible, but it's contrary to custom."

"Certainly I give custom all due regard, but I think necessity must take precedence. But before we lay further plans, tell me your story. Why did you disguise yourself as a lopsided man?"

"My story…the real story? Very well, I'll tell you. A great deal of what I told you is true, but not all of it. I really am the child of a housemaid who cleaned Master's silver, and I was, once upon a time, called Spoon. I really am Master's natural child. I can tell by the way I've been treated. Though he is often indifferent to others, he has always been kind to me, especially after Mama died. That I was never permitted out of the house is not true. But my father is so very protective that I was always strictly chaperoned when allowed out except for the times when I snuck out. I have had scant experience in the world beyond Father's walls.

"Even so, it wasn't a bad life. I had good food, nice clothing, and a warm bed. The servants were generally civil. But all that is bound to change as soon as Father passes. Young Master, my brother Bartholomew, won't put me in the river in a sack. That was a lie. But he promised me a fate that I contemplate with equal trepidation. Father, of course, has never allowed him to touch me, and Bart is quite afraid of him. But when he is gone, there will be nothing to stop him from having his way."

Thurmond was horrified.

"But if your master is your father, then his son is your brother! But he still wants to…"

"Makes no difference. The ways of nobles are not the ways of lesser people. So I've been experimenting with simple spells, casting a glamour that would make me unattractive and undesirable or that would disguise me so that I might escape from the house. That's what I was doing when you barged in. That moment was quite fortuitous. I knew I was unlikely to have another like it, so I revealed myself to you."

Thurmond was awestruck —how rapidly his life had changed. A few days ago he had been a simple stable boy and a common day laborer, whose grandiose dreams seemed to be dissolving in the harsh reality of the world. But then, by the turning of Fortune's Wheel, a conniving witch-woman and her well-groomed minion had selected him to be the sacrificial victim in their deceitful scheme. He had swilled mead with a madman and had been assaulted by both a troll and the madman's wife—well, sort of.

He had survived an encounter with brutish Road Guards and had smuggled a twitching troll hand into the city. Then he had nearly been killed by a ten-year-old with a crossbow as big as himself. He had dazzled two men with a magic box of light and stabbed one of them in the arm. He still felt bad about that.

He had stolen a valuable item with magical properties that a demon used as a portal. And he had made a new friend—a lopsided, runty man—only to have him transform into a damsel in distress—or near enough. A cult of killers was hunting him, but he also had more gold than a humble stable boy could ever look for. He had a treasure map and would soon be embarking on his first bona fide adventure.

All this was thrilling, strange, and wonderful. He was at last living the life of which had always dreamed.

†

Although the hour was late, they resolved to quit the stable at once. Thurmond was well known in the neighborhood and would not be hard to find. At least they were not encumbered by baggage. Sarah had no possessions of her own, and the few things Thurmond had amassed were easily carried in one simple bundle.

They spent a rather miserable and uncertain night huddling in dark corners, and in the morning, they sought shelter in a more obscure corner of the city. To Thurmond's frustration, Sarah insisted on a lodging with two separate rooms. This seemed like a frivolous and extravagant luxury. Whole families typically housed in a single room, where they ate, slept, shat, and coupled in sight of each other. Privacy was so uncommon that the lack of it went unnoticed, was not something to be especially desired. The lad saw no point in her demand for such superfluity, but she would not be dissuaded, and in the end he acquiesced.

Eventually they found new accommodations in what had once been a storeroom, one end of which was screened by a partition of rough-cut lumber. Nonetheless, it was the cleanest and most spacious abode in which Thurmond had ever resided.

He had grown up in a typical peasant's hut with a dirt floor and a roof of decaying thatch. The carpenter's workshop had been cold, leaky, and filled with a suffocating blanket of sawdust. The stable reeked of horse urine. He had shared all previous residences with robust colonies of lice, mites, bedbugs, ticks, and fleas. So in spite of the cost, the young man found the new lodging quite pleasing.

Sarah entertained a very different opinion.

"Thurmond, I understand that this dreadful shack is the best that you can afford at the moment and that it must do until you can provide something better. But even in these downcast circumstances, a degree of decorum must be observed. I therefore claim the rear room as my private chamber. Please do not enter it without first receiving my explicit invitation."

He was taken aback.

"What? What are you saying?"

Her tone became aloof and haughty.

"I believe you heard me well enough. I am a young lady of gentle birth, at least on my father's side, and I fully intend to act like one in spite of our current condition. So you will be pleased to respect my privacy. Agreed?"

Sarah did not wait for an answer, but picked up one of the ragged horse blankets they had brought from the stable. She then entered *her* room and shut the door, leaving him standing alone and feeling, for reasons he did not entirely understand, vaguely foolish.

Growing up, he had always heard that women should remain meek, humble, and submissive to men. Everybody said so. Sarah was anything but that. The strong line of her jaw suggested the determination of a warrior, not some nobleman's pampered daughter. Her shoulders, broad for a young girl, betokened strength.

Still, her unwavering insistence for a room of her own suggested that she truly was a child of privilege. Perhaps she really was the fruit of the master's loins. Maybe. But did that give her the right to get high handed with him?

Their new accommodations were austere. The furnishings consisted of a single small table and two stools, one of which had a short leg and rocked precariously when sat upon. Thurmond sighed. He had no illusions about which stool would be peremptorily consigned to him.

There was also a cracked chamber pot in one corner. He foresaw it quickly coming to reside in milady's chamber, where he would be denied the use of it. Would he be expected to attend to its emptying? She may have managed to snag the best room, but he would be damned before he would clean her personal crapper. He had just escaped a lifetime of hauling dung, and he meant to keep it that way.

Yet he found himself liking her—nay—admiring her. She was good looking and seemed to possess real pluck. Her eyes bespoke intelligence, and she could carry on a worthwhile conversation. She was altogether different from anyone, man or woman, he had ever before encountered.

He heard a low moaning sound coming from Sarah's room. Crying again? Nay, some kind of chanting. Most likely some kind of mystical rigmarole or other. Whatever was going on, he was probably better off not knowing. Magic had always scared him.

Thurmond began to plan out the steps he now must take. He must be audacious and aggressive if he expected to lead an adventuring party in search of treasure. He must set the example by thinking, acting, and speaking like the Adventurer he was striving to become. He must acquire mastery of the requisite adventuring skills.

And he knew just the man to talk to.

CHAPTER ELEVEN

ROSCOE APPLEMAN

Thurmond had first met Roscoe at Einarr Badhand's Academie of Fence, a simple two-story structure of half-timbered construction with a thatched roof. Behind it, a stout palisade of trimmed tree trunks enclosed a sizable yard. But despite its humble appearance, the Academie offered its scholars a most rigorous curriculum, for within its confines, young men honed their abilities to slay one another with sword, spear, axe, mace, war hammer, or dagger.

Einarr had been an Adventurer of renown until an unlucky blow had removed two fingers and part of the palm of his right hand. He had attempted to learn to fight left-handed but had been forced to concede that he was exceptionally clumsy in that mode and would manage only to get himself and his companions killed if he persisted.

Thurmond had learned of the Academie soon after his arrival in Gorgonholm and had made the proprietor a proposal. He would clean the place, help the clientele, make necessary repairs, and run Einarr's errands in exchange for lessons in armored combat. He would even shovel the dung of the customers' horses, if required. His services would cost the proprietor nothing. He remembered what followed very clearly.

Though well advanced into middle age, Einarr was an imposing man—tall, heavily muscled, and still trim of waist. Long blond braids and a drooping blond mustache betrayed his Vanarian blood. He was jesting and drinking ale with another older man when Thurmond presented himself. Setting aside his ale cup, he squinted down at the lad with obvious distaste. Then he held up the mangled remains of his right hand.

"Take a right good look at this. That's what you can expect if you take up my trade."

He shoved the stub of his hand right up to Thurmond's nose and pressed it hard against his lips.

"Take a taste too, if you've a mind."

Thurmond knew he was being tested, but he could only guess what a proper reply would be. Keeping his face absolutely blank, he ran his tongue along the ridge of grimy scar tissue. He searched the Vanarian's face for some indication of approval, but the irascible scowl remained unchanged.

"Well now, if it's that good, maybe I should join you."

Einarr ran his tongue along the same spot.

This, Thurmond concluded, must be a positive sign.

"You'll have me then? I could start now if you like."

"Sorry, sonny, I ain't in need of a boy just now, so on your way."

But then, quite unexpectedly, the other man came to his aid. He was as tall and broad as Einarr but had grown a great, round belly while the Vanarian remained lean. His dark chestnut hair was flecked with gray.

"Be nice, Einarr—can't you see the laddie has his heart set on learnin' to fight. Are you grown so old that you've forgot what it was like to feel them things? What can it hurt? And like the boyo says, it ain't gonna cost you nothin'."

Einarr shot Thurmond another scowl. It seemed to be his favorite expression.

"Roscoe here thinks I should give you a try. Don't be gettin' underfoot or causin' no trouble. If you does, I'll throw you right out on your arse. Some of my students be so dumb, they can't even get their own armor on and off by theirselves. So maybe you can make yourself useful. Just don't piss me off."

And then to Thurmond's great delight, the other man, the one called Roscoe, said the words he most wanted to hear in all the world.

"There's no one here at the moment, Einarr, so why don't you loan the laddie that old coat-of-plates and a pothelm. I'll go fetch a couple of shields and give him his first fightin' lesson."

He then turned to Thurmond.

"My name's Roscoe Appleman. What do they call you?"

"Thurmond."

"Well now, that's a fine name you have, so it is."

The young man soon found himself strapped into a most cumbersome assortment of iron plates, leather straps, and random scraps of mail. His head was enclosed in an iron pot that made it hard to see and harder to breath. Mostly it was just as uncomfortable and heavy as hell. Einarr had laughed at his discomfort.

"Wearin' a shell might come natural to a turtle or a snail, but never to a man. So you'll be right uncomfortable at first. But when you're used to it, it ain't bad at all. You could wear it all day. Sleep in it if you had to."

Roscoe next produced two very strange-looking weapons, like swords but with thick, heavy blades made of something that looked like bone.

"We call these *wasters*. They're practice swords made from the bones of a whale- fish. They're as tough as troll-hide and last for a long time. Very good for what we're doing."

"What's a whale-fish?"

"Some sort of sea monster, so I've been told. Big as Sheriff Brandon's keep. I'd have my doubts such creatures was real, but we've got their bones here, so I guess they must be."

As uncomfortable as he was, Thurmond was ecstatic. He had burned for this moment for as long as he could remember. However, that first session had not gone anything like he had expected.

Roscoe was old and fat, and he walked with a heavy limp, so Thurmond had assumed he would at least be able to hold his own against him. Wrong! Try as he might, he could not land a single blow, while his opponent could strike him at will.

The lesson continued until Thurmond was so battered and exhausted that he could hardly stand. In spite of his best efforts, the fat old man had defeated him soundly. God's holy elbows! He had never before had such a grand time!

Afterward, over pot of ales, Roscoe told Thurmond about his life. He had, like Einarr, been an Adventurer of some renown until a debilitating blow to his hip ended that career. Now he sold fruits and vegetables—apples a specialty—from a stall on Market Square.

Of course, he missed the wild adventures of his younger years. Selling apples could in no way compare to the sting of battle or hair-raising escapes. He earned a sufficient living, but it was miniscule compared to the gold he had won and squandered as an Adventurer.

†

And so it was from Roscoe that Thurmond now sought counsel. He found the man in a stall in Market Square, clad in an oversized smock bespattered with fruit juice. Spying the young man, he smiled broadly.

"Well, it's my old friend Thurmond, so it is."

"Greetings, Roscoe, you look well. Can you leave your stall long enough for a mug of ale at my expense?"

"Your expense, you say? My, my, you must have come into a bit of coin. Maybe you'd like to buy a bit of fruit as well? Nay, I'm but jestin' with you. Certes, I get can away for a bit. Things is slow right now anyway."

He called for a man in a neighboring stall to mind the fruit, wiped his hands on his smock, and pointed to a small alehouse across the square.

"There's a fine place that rejoices in the name of the Golden Eunuch. Good ale and less pricey than at the Head. Sadly lacking the boisterous crowd, but it'll do."

Once seated in an isolated corner, mug of beer in hand, Thurmond sketched out the basics of his plan. He told of the map but was careful not to reveal from whence it had come. His voice rose in pitch as his excitement waxed huge. His eyes watered as he strove to exude a maximum of *bing*.

"Easy, boyo. Keep your voice low. No sense tellin' the world what you're about. Now, you say that you don't know exactly what the treasure might be."

"That is correct."

"Nor if this treasure, for a fact, exists."

"Well, nay."

"Nor the nature of the present ownership—who exactly that might be."

This conversation was not at all going as Thurmond had expected.

"I do not."

"Lad, have you ever faced, I mean really faced, your own death? Like when some howling lunatic is running straight for you with a sword and means to slice open your guts?"

"Aye, that I have. Well, to a point. Do crossbows count? Guys with daggers?"

"Have you ever had to fight with a sword? Or an axe? Or a spear?"

"Nay."

Roscoe turned and looked toward the ceiling as if he were talking to a third person.

"I can only conclude that my friend here has been deprived of his reason. That he is in the grip of madness and should be confined for his own good. He has concocted a scheme that is nothing less than a thinly veiled act of suicide. And that's a deadly sin, so it is. None but a mooncalf or a love-struck friar would for a moment consider such an ill-considered undertakin'. No loyal friend would ever encourage such an insidious quest for self-destruction. His idea is utterly daft, nothing less."

Thurmond was heartbroken. He had been certain Roscoe would embrace his plan, but his friend was rejecting it in no uncertain terms. When he said nothing, Roscoe continued.

"Why, you'd have to be desperately tired of your own life. You'd have to be willin' to lose everything."

Roscoe paused and gave Thurmond a long look. His face was a strange mixture of irritation and good humor.

"Be willin' to lose everything…to likely die for a chance to never again touch or smell another apple."

Thurmond perked up.

"So, are you telling me…?"

"I'm tellin' you that I'm sick to death of being a has-been. That I need one last chance to feel like I used to feel, and to have a better life than sellin' apples at that soddin' fruit stand.

"When I think back on all the gold I've won and how little I've got now, I feel a mite foolish, like nothin' I've done was worthwhile. I'm gettin' old and need someplace where I can settle down and be comfortable when the years really set in. So, I'm agreed. At least, if the arrangements is right."

Thurmond was ecstatic. Good old *bing*! He was well aware that the adventure would be impossible without Roscoe. But he wanted to be careful not to give too much away. Roscoe had the skills and experience. But Thurmond was possessed of unbounded enthusiasm and the supreme confidence of youth. He also had a willing, if somewhat reluctant, magic user as an ally. And best of all, he had the map.

"What arrangements would you find agreeable?"

"Adventure Captains customarily get three-eighths of the take."

"You fancy yourself the captain then?"

"Do you flatter yourself that you possess the ability? How many times have you been underground, laddie? Do you really want the job?"

Thurmond had to concede that his aspirations of being the group leader were absurd. He had just assumed that he would fulfill that role. So he would have to agree to serve as a lieutenant for at least an adventure or two before stepping up to a captaincy.

"Agreed—three-eighths, but after expenses."

"After expenses, agreed."

"All costs before the adventure to be charged against it before we divvy up."

"Agreed, but all costs are to be approved by the captain."

Thurmond paused here. Aware of Sarah's extravagant tendencies, he anticipated problems. Roscoe, sensing his hesitation, jumped in before Thurmond could reply.

"But all reasonable expenses will be approved, just as long as they directly serve the needs of the adventure party. So if you've had your eye on a stately carriage drawn by a matched team of four and attended by liveried footmen, you'll have to wait until after the adventure."

Roscoe burst out laughing at his own joke.

"Come on, boyo, it'll all work out. We've always been friends, so don't let a few gold sovereigns come between us. Not when there are so many of them to be gathered in. Not when such a marvelous adventure beckons."

Thurmond conceded to his friend's good reasoning.

"Agreed. But Roscoe, we're going to need some more people. Can you take care of that?"

"For a fact, I believe I can."

"And I need more fighting lessons. Can you teach me?"

"Aye, laddie, but you should know by now that it takes years of hard study to become skilled with weapons. Only in foolish legends do young sprouts such as yourself master the techniques and surpass their teachers in a brief span of time."

Roscoe chuckled again, amused by the intensity of his beginner's enthusiasm.

"How many times have you been in armor, Thurmond?"

"Five times. Twice with you, twice with Einarr, and once with some little boy whose father brought him in for lessons."

This made Roscoe laugh aloud.

"So you got to fight a wee laddie—who won?"

"Neither of us. I wasn't allowed to hit him, but I wasn't about to let him hit me."

Roscoe shook his head in amused disbelief.

"Looky here now, boyo, we ain't got time to make you into a real fightin' man. So just remember this—you gotta forget all them things you heard in stories and songs. That's just a bunch of blather made up by some bard who don't know nothin'. If you try fightin' like that, it'll get you killed. You know what I mean—like when the hero throws his sword at the last minute and kills the bad guy. That's just horse dung. You can't throw a sword. It don't work. And if you did, you'd be throwin' away your weapon. That's just stupid. If you want to throw something, throw a javelin.

"And forget all the fancy moves you've heard about—spinnin' around, holdin' the sword backward, things like that. You keep the enemy in front of you, hold the sword by its hilt, and hit 'em with the blade. Pretty basic common sense, but I guess it ain't dramatic enough for the poets."

Then Roscoe's smile faded, and his voice assumed a lower, more serious tone.

"There's one other thing we've got to get straight. This is important. You cannot go around calling yourself an Adventurer. That's going to get you in big trouble mighty fast. The Adventurers' Brotherhood is sacred. You've got to earn the right to join us. We'll be the ones to judge if you're fit to be a Brother."

"All right. How do I do that?"

"First off, you got to have a mentor. A full member has to agree to learn you everything you need to know."

"Someone like yourself? Could *you* be my mentor?"

"I could be. But we'll have to wait and see how the adventure goes. In the meantime, you have no official status. You're what we call a *hang-around*. You can come along on the venture, but you have to take orders and keep quiet. I want to see how you conduct yourself, how you fight, how you react to problems."

Thurmond was again disappointed. He saw his dreams of a lieutenancy fading before his eyes. Roscoe continued.

"And then if I like what I see, maybe after a while you get promoted to Prospect—a prospective member. Kind of an apprentice Adventurer. Kind of like being a squire if you want to become a knight. This is where you really got to prove yourself. Prove you ain't afraid to fight. Prove you don't run away and leave your brothers in a big pile of shite. Prospectin' is hard because everyone wants to test you to cull out the weak ones. Sometimes it takes years. Lotsa guys don't make it."

"And if I prove myself?"

"Then you get one of these."

Roscoe pulled up his sleeve to reveal a large tattoo on his right forearm. It resembled a grotesque dragon-like creature with a battle axe gripped in its oversized talons.

"It's what's called a wyvern, laddie. When you get your tattoo, you're an Adventurer forever. You can only quit when you die. Even when you're old and crippled like Einarr and me, you're still expected to act as a Brother."

Thurmond absolutely loved hearing such talk. All his life he had needed someone to recognize his true worth. The Adventurers were the fiercest and most courageous men in all the land. If he could prove himself to them, be recognized as worthy of their Brotherhood, his lifelong need would be fulfilled. He continued to belabor Roscoe with questions.

"What's to stop some guy from just getting the tattoo and passing himself off as an Adventurer from far away? How can you tell if they're really one of you?"

"Woe to anyone who tries that. That's a path to certain misery, so it is. We have secret signs and countersigns. When you meet an unknown brother, you flashes them a sign, just subtle like. If they know how to respond proper, then they're a Brother. 'Course if you get suspicious, there's other ways of tellin'. But I ain't tellin' you about that stuff yet."

"And what happens if they're not a for-real Brother?"

"That ain't pretty. There's fire and there's the knife, but one way or other, that tattoo is comin' off. And they'll get beat like they've never been beat. Sometimes worse."

Then the old Adventurer's face brightened again.

"So, laddie, what time tomorrow would you like some fighter practice?"

"Let's at least wait until cockcrow. I'm not too lively before the sun is up."

Roscoe laughed again.

"Let's say midday at Einarr's. I have to see a man and make some arrangements first. And with any luck, I may be able to rid myself of the damned fruit stand."

CHAPTER TWELVE

SARAH MAKES UP HER MIND

S arah knew she had probably hurt Thurmond's feelings by walking off so abruptly, but she needed time to think. The events of the last couple of days had left her afraid and confused. She did not know what else to do. She just needed time to think.

She had made good her escape from Bartholomew's clutches. That was good—but she had now become ensnarled in an escapade highly dangerous and somehow even ludicrous. She had at first felt nothing but a sort of amused disdain for this naive boy, Thurmond, but now, she had to admit, she had started to feel a need to stick by him.

He had, after all, come to her aid when he saw her as nothing more than an ugly little man, and he had asked nothing in return. He had shared with her generously and included her in his treasure-hunting scheme. After such unconditional acceptance, she could not just abandon him. And he was, in his own boyish manner, rather attractive. He had such nice eyes.

He really needed her, needed her magic. He might well die if she withheld her support. And was this not, after all, the most expedient way to acquire the funds necessary for her advancement, both in the occult arts and in her rightful place in society? Perhaps it be the first step toward her formal recognition as the daughter of Lord Percy Staynes, perhaps someday as Lady Staynes. The foolish boy might be right—his idiotic adventure could be her best bet. If she could win enough treasure, she could purchase an apprenticeship with a magus and equip her own magical workshop. This would allow her to live her own life, one free from a controlling father, a lecherous brother, or a domineering husband.

She must have money. Only money would allow her the independence she so desperately sought. Money would bring power and position. With money she could claim the birthright to which she was entitled as the daughter of Lord Percy Staynes. Why should Brother Bart, through nothing more than an accident of birth, inherit all—title, lands, money—and she receive nothing? It was not fair.

In the meantime, she had to develop her magic. She did not know whether it was even possible to do so on her own, but she knew she had to try. Their survival would most likely depend on her occult abilities, and that meant bringing them to a far higher level than she currently possessed.

Remembering a simple ceremonial for the clearing of the mind, she positioned herself on the bare floor and began to chant. Her mind began to gather on the task before her. The manipulation of magic was contingent on a number of factors. Largely, it depended on the ability to focus one's will to a needle-sharp point. This represented a tremendous concentration of psychic energy.

True masters had the power to alter the material world, to call down lightning or shift large stones. Lesser magicians could only alter the perceptions of the human mind. They could, for instance, bring on a sudden sleep or cast a disguising glamour.

To acquire even the most fundamental skills, a demanding course of study and training was necessary. Initiates were expected to commit to memory thousands of bits of arcane lore—spells against an infestation of worms, herbal recipes to cure a farmer's bunions, the secret names of demons, and the order of the progression of the spheres. They had to read a myriad of forgotten languages and know the best phase of the moon to cast spells against festering sores.

At the end of his or her course of study, the new magician would be formally inducted into the Most Sacred Fellowship of Spellcasters, Alchemists,

Diviners, Sorcerers, Philter Mixers, and Thaumaturgists of Gorgonholm. This august body served as the local magicians' guild and was supposed to ensure that its membership maintained the highest of professional standards. In reality, the guild did very little except collect dues from its members. Necromancers were naturally banned from joining, theirs being a forbidden art.

Sarah also knew that female initiates were quite rare and that those who were accepted possessed either great wealth or familial connections. Only recognition as Lord Percy's daughter could open that door.

She knew all this and much more because, among her father's piles of occult tomes, she had discovered and read a copy of the guild's meeting minutes from twenty years before. It had been a tedious read, but she had persevered because she aspired to membership and was eager for whatever advantage such inside knowledge of the organization might provide.

Sarah had learned much in her father's library. She knew, for instance, that a new magician must have a wand or staff that served as the repository of their psychic energy. The magician fed energy into the wand in times of rest or study. This could then be drawn upon when extra energy was required for the casting of a spell.

Without a wand, a magician soon expended their energy and could cast no more spells until well rested. If a wand was lost or broken, their power was drastically reduced until a new one could be made.

Wands were often made of hazel wood, but she didn't know why. Some of the old books had included inscriptions and designs to be carved along its length. One source recommended an iron tip if the wand was to be used as a weapon of war. This sounded like the kind of wand Sarah was going to need.

She did not doubt her ability to physically construct a wand. She had nimble fingers and had always enjoyed making things. But she did not know how to infuse it with psychic power, only that the procedure involved focusing one's will. The ability to focus the will was the key to all magic. To alter physical matter was the most difficult. It might require the same effort to levitate a pebble an inch off the ground as to cloud the minds of a crowd of fifty.

Strength of will also gave the magician the power to summon, and hopefully control, the host of disincarnate entities with whom the world was shared. And it was the will that lifted the veil, allowing the magician to see and manipulate the vibrations of which all things were composed.

At least that was what her father's books had told her.

To achieve the necessary focus of will, the magician fasted, meditated, chanted, consumed substances of unspeakable foulness, and stood in strange and unnatural postures for hours on end. Sarah was well versed in such practices and was quite willing to undertake them to achieve her goals. But would they work without the guiding hand of a master magus?

There was also the problem of money. When Thurmond had brought home the pouch full of gold, she had suddenly possessed the means to purchase the numerous arcane items the magician required. Now that was gone.

She did not know how much money remained in Thurmond's purse, but she suspected it was far short of the amount they needed to fund the adventure he was set on starting. She knew no spells strong enough to make river pebbles appear as gold coins. What could she do to make money? Surprisingly, it took but a moment before she thought of a way.

†

When Thurmond returned to the lodging, he found Sarah in a state of high excitement. She guided him into her private chamber, where he was amazed to find an assortment of candles, incense burners, various parchments, an ink pot and pen, a dagger, and other implements of the magician's art.

"Where did this come from?"

"I bought them."

"Bought it? With what? I've got all the money we have left."

"I found a way to earn my own money."

"How so?"

"Strong-arm robbery."

"You robbed someone? Nay, you but jest!"

"At knifepoint. I told him that if he didn't hand over his purse, I'd slice open his belly so his guts'd slither out to the ground."

"Nay!"

"Aye."

"You really did that? You said that?"

"Aye! In sooth I did."

"Weren't you scared? I mean, what if he had fought back? You're...well... you're just a girl."

"I used a glamour spell. I'm not yet able make river rocks shine like gold sovereigns, but I can cloud a person's mind. So when I saw this rich-looking merchant fellow, a fat old geezer who just had to be carrying a fatter purse, I jumped him. I made him think I was the most dreadful, scar-faced brigand he had ever seen. It was easy, actually. And what's wrong with being a girl?"

"Nothing's wrong with being a girl. I just meant.... Where did you get the knife?"

"I used a stick. He just thought it was a knife. I didn't get the knife until later, when I bought it and the other stuff. And don't touch that knife. It's for ritual purposes only. You'll render it useless if you use it to cut cheese or something."

"Are you planning to make a career of strong-arm robbery?"

"Nay, this was strictly a onetime event. To be honest, I was scared to death. If I had said the wrong thing and he had grown suspicious, the spell would have been broken. Or even if I had just gotten too nervous and lost my concentration."

Her face clouded with guilt.

"I know what I did was wrong. I was just so desperate. I need things if I am going to develop my magic skills. It's the only way we'll have a chance of surviving your adventure."

Once again, her voice grew resolute.

"And I've already begun. I put a charm on our rooms that should ward off that demon thing if it comes poking around. I also cast a cloaking spell in case that witch tries to use the mirror on us."

Thurmond could only shake his head and grin in amazement.

"Wondrous well! With Roscoe coming along and you at my side, we can't fail."

PART **2**

THE HANG-AROUND

CHAPTER THIRTEEN

THE CONCERNS OF SORCERERS

Meanwhile, in a small crenellated tower a bit southwest of the city, a powerful witch, Lady Renata de la Pole, was expressing her own apprehensions. She was tall, stately, dark of hair, and attractive, if you like them mature. She spoke to a well-groomed man who was considerably younger than she.

"Is it done? The river again?"

"Naturally—why wouldn't it be?"

"Sometimes there might be regrets."

"None at all."

"By your own hand?"

"Nay, I instructed Sims."

"Were you fond of her?"

"Impossible! An absurd question! Why would you ask such a question?"

"I want to know, Rupert. I want to make sure."

"Fine, ask what you will."

"What was her name?"

"She was called Henrietta, a servant's name."

"Not an inappropriate appellation. Did you *woo* this servant girl, Rupert? Woo her properly? Woo her thoroughly? Uhhmmm?"

"Aye, you know I did."

"And did you find it pleasurable?"

"You know I did not. She was a spindly, little bitch with a disagreeable face and no meat on her bones. Her conversation was insipid, and her lovemaking was…well…she had not much time to perfect her technique. I believe I was her first and only."

Renata's response was icy.

"It must have been dreadful. You may take comfort in the certainty that your great sacrifice on our behalf will pay a great dividend. You did, after all, achieve your goal. You found out what we needed to know."

"Aye, that I did, but I still want to spit her abominable taste from my tongue. By the feet of God, I feel defiled."

"Poor Rupert, your gentility sullied by a common housemaid. Yet for her, we would never have known about young Master Staynes's map and mirror. So, bravo, my jolly profligate. You have indeed put us on the path to a life of comfort. I do so enjoy my comforts."

"Aye, milady. Of that I am quite aware."

"Dear Rupert, I pray that you will find *me* more inspiring than that poor lass. I hope too that our arrangement will be more long lived and result in our mutual satisfaction."

"Of course it will, milady. How not?"

"How not, indeed—but no matter. 'Tis pity that your little trollop couldn't tell you where the map is hidden. Are you sure she wasn't holding back?"

"Aye, very sure. Sims is quite thorough in that regard."

"What word on that imbecilic thief you hired?"

"None. He has disappeared. He has apparently joined with a short, ugly man with crooked shoulders. But none know whither they have gone."

"Perhaps slain by the Brethren as we planned?"

"Likely not, or their butchered remains would have graced a city thoroughfare."

"I like it not. I want to make sure. I like still less that someone tried to spy upon us through that mirror. Any idea who?"

"I would guess Staynes or someone in his employ. I believe we were observed just prior to the mirror being stolen."

"Aye, I concur. I was caught off guard for a moment. I suspect Staynes has retained a magician of considerable power. Most likely the little crooked man.

"I'm thinking that we should take no needless chances. I mistrust your young thief, this Thurmond. I tried scrying for him and for Staynes, but the mirror remained dark. The hour is wrong at present. I will send the faithful Aborax. I am certain he will succeed where the Brethren and the mirror have failed."

"You would release an imp into the streets of Gorgonholm?"

"Only a little one."

"But is that wise, milady? It seems overbold, even for yourself."

"Nonsense! Aborax is completely under my command. No one will be able to see him or even know he's there. And there will be no untoward outbursts this time. He has given me his word of honor."

"The word of honor of a spawn of hell?"

"Peace! Enough! He is perfectly well behaved when he wants to be, and I have promised him certain rewards for his good behavior. I will need that leather wallet that your thief handled so Aborax can get a good sniff.

"Come, Aborax! Come! Time to do Mama a service. Come on, now! Here kitty, kitty, kitty, kitty, kitty."

†

It was a day like any other. Shopkeepers and craftsmen, prostitutes and vagabonds bustled though the streets of Gorgonholm. The summer sun was warm, and the air was filled with the jangle of harness chain, the cries of street hawkers, and the bleat of goats. The people were joyful or gloomy, satiated or ravenous, industrious or slothful as dictated by their own individual circumstances.

Yet in a single moment, the citizens who thronged a certain street were brought to a pause. Those on the verges were less affected. Some felt a chill wind that seemed, in an instant, to bite to the core of their souls. Others paused in midstride, assailed by a putrid stench as foul as the depths of hell.

Those in the street's middle fared far worse. Many were struck insensible with blinding head pain. Roiling waves of nausea smote a few, and fits of dry heaves seized others.

And then, as suddenly as they had come on, the afflictions passed. Those who had been so instantaneously discomfited could now straighten and continue on their way.

†

The stable man sprawled motionlessly on the stable floor, a shoeing hammer still clutched in his hand. The horses had been driven to frenzy, breaking their tethers and kicking themselves free from their stalls in a panic-stricken bid to flee. Such was their fury that these thoroughly domesticated creatures, normally quite docile and obedient, took great bites of flesh from the flanks of their fellows as they stampeded out the stable door and down the street.

All the while, an unseen presence moved throughout the stable, lingering here, sniffing there, especially in a side room where the tack was stored.

CHAPTER FOURTEEN

UNLOOKED-FOR GUESTS

The sun was reaching its zenith. Thurmond was about to depart for his midday fighting lesson when Roscoe appeared unexpectedly at the door of his lodging. This was disturbing. With the Brethren on his tail, Thurmond wanted to keep his new residence a closely guarded secret. He had told no one, not even Roscoe, where he and Sarah were hiding out. He knew that if Roscoe could find him so readily, the Brethren's professional assassins would have no difficulty at all.

"How did you find me?"

"Not hard at all, boyo. Most folks are happy to help out long as you grace them with a big, pleasin' smile. *'Scuse me, madame, but would you happen to be acquainted with a laddie goes by the name of Thurmond? Suppose to live somewhere hereabout. Can you help me?* So I just asked around a bit, and here I am. And there you are."

Thurmond was too unsettled to respond, so he just stood and gawked. The person on his doorstep only slightly resembled the Roscoe he had always known. Gone was the fruit-stained smock. The rugged attire of an Adventurer had replaced it: jerkin, breeks, and high boots of sturdy leather. His huge black hat with an immense brim—the traditional headgear of the Underworld Adventurers—added dramatically to his already-imposing stature.

"I thought we were to meet at Einarr's at midday."

"I couldn't wait to see you. I bear grand news. We have had the great good fortune of enlistin' an experienced Adventurer as my lieutenant, my second in charge. A stout fighter and dependable companion."

Thurmond was a trifle disappointed, still having had some vague hope of functioning in that capacity himself.

"When can I meet our new lieutenant?"

"Thought you'd never ask."

Roscoe gave a loud whistle, and a figure emerged from the shadow of a nearby overhang. He at first seemed strangely misshapen, but as he drew closer, Thurmond realized he was just short. Very short. By God's twelve toes! He was a dwarf.

This one stood a bit taller than the young man's breastbone, with a beard nearly half as long as he was tall. He was, like Roscoe, dressed in adventuring garb, but his hat was of absurd proportions, with a brim reaching well beyond his shoulders. It was topped by an immense feather, dyed a burning scarlet, which curled down his back. He bore a gigantic rucksack that had added to his misshapen appearance. Strangely, he had no axe. Thurmond thought all dwarves carried axes.

The young man was vaguely amused. This dwarf, he surmised, must be sensitive in regard to his lack of stature and thereby driven to make his accoutrements of such a size to compensate. But if the dwarf felt such personal hesitancy, it was not revealed in his first words, which were delivered in a tone of high hauteur.

"It is your pleasure, young man, to be in the company of Torgul Bonelip, twenty-third of that name and direct lineal descendant of Torgul the First, known as Torgul the Great. My distaff side is hardly less illustrious. My mother, bless her, carried the blood of Borik the Bold, of whom the legends tell. I am a lord of the Spear Mountain Dwarves, fierce and terrifying in battle. I have slain goblins beyond count and men, too, when they warranted it."

Thurmond struggled against an impulse to slam the door in the braggart's face. It was always the same with dwarves. They were always boasting about their lineage and ferocity. He supposed this one would soon start praising the length of his own beard.

Roscoe recognized Thurmond's aversion to Torgul's boasting. People who were not used to dwarves always reacted this way, misunderstanding that it was simply their way of introducing themselves.

In fact, Torgul was going to some length to put his best foot forward, to win Thurmond's confidence by establishing his credentials as a worthy warrior. He was actually paying the young man a great courtesy, considering that he was a full-fledged member of the Adventurers' Brotherhood and Thurmond was a mere hang-around.

Standing behind the dwarf, looking over his head, Roscoe gave Thurmond a smile and a wink. Thurmond caught the wink, softened, and opened the door all the way.

"Gentlemen, please, won't you come in?"

Torgul threw his rucksack against the wall and settled back against it, apparently making himself at home. Roscoe produced a crockery jug of beer, which he uncorked and passed around. When Sarah entered from the back room, Thurmond introduced her to the others. Torgul went through all his customary rigmarole but this time doffed his hat and made a sweeping bow.

"You're the spellcaster then?"

"In my own small way, I suppose such a description would not be entirely inaccurate."

"Then you've seen the thing across the street."

"The thing?"

"Aye, a small one but vicious of appearance. Does it belong to you?"

Sarah was confused.

"Please, enlighten me. One what?"

"One imp, of course—perched on a limb of that elm tree across from your door. It thinks nobody can see it, but I possess a bit of the second sight, inherited from my great-grandmother, who was a renowned seeress among the Spear Mountain Dwarves. I assumed that you, being a sorceress, would at least be aware of it."

"Oh, God's holy bones!"

Sarah ran to the door and looked out. She could see nothing. She had not yet developed the power to see beyond the veil. She turned again to the dwarf.

"I see him not. He must be under a glamour to cloak him from my sight. Watch him for me. I think I know what to do."

With that she ran into her chamber and slammed the door. Torgul looked at the others, clearly a bit bewildered.

"She ain't what I imagined when I was told we'd have a magic user along. How old is she?"

Thurmond immediately rose to her defense.

"Never sell her short. She encountered that demon thing once before and knows what to do. She is smart and resourceful, and she is possessed of great daring. Sarah will come through when we need her."

His own words surprised him. He had entertained his own doubts, but Sarah always seemed to justify his faith in her. Anyway, her ideas usually seemed better than his own.

A pounding commenced in the backroom, as if Sarah were striking something with a hammer. After a while, there came a long series of lighter taps. Then scratching. The backroom door flew open, and she burst back to where the others sat talking.

"Quick! Finish that beer! I need the jug."

Roscoe was happy to oblige. He drained the last remnant in a single swallow and handed it over. Sarah once more disappeared into her chamber. When Torgul moved to the door to check on the imp, Roscoe focused his attention on Thurmond.

"She's a saucy one, this paramour of yours."

"She is by no means my paramour. She is simply someone who I...who fate threw in my path. Nothing more."

The old Adventurer gave Thurmond a sly look.

"Whatever you say, lad. However you want to play it."

Then he grew more serious.

"But listen, boyo, we have a wee problem. You see, it is a difficult thing for a dwarf, even an esteemed one like Lord Torgul there, to secure accommodations in this town. And you havin' so much extra room... I thought maybe..."

Thurmond did not like the way this was going. He did not like dwarves, especially this swaggering, boastful runt. But he found it difficult to say no to Roscoe, even when he really needed to. Instead, he tried to equivocate.

"I'm not sure how Sarah would feel about that. Magicians need a lot of solitude for study and such. With another person in here..."

Roscoe drew Thurmond to one side.

"Look, laddie, you got to see that Torgul's in real need here, so he is. His own people won't have him back 'cause he's spent too much time with humans—he carries a taint, you might say. Plus there's nothin' for him in the dwarf lands anyways. And most human people won't abide him neither. Most of the inns won't have dwarves. They say they're bad for business, that they offend the other customers.

"The Head's one of the few place's what'll take 'em, but they're full up. Booked solid for some reunion or other. Bunch of old timers gettin' together to show their scars and tell lies about how things used to be.

"So how about it? Are you willin' to help a brother out? It's the adventurin' way, after all. And it seems like having Torgul on the premises would be distinctly advantageous—him bein' the only one who can see your visitor in the tree outside."

Thurmond began to weaken, but before he could reply, Roscoe laid a meaty hand on his shoulder and continued.

"And there's another small issue, very small in the bigger picture of things. Tiny actually. You see, Torgul's financially embarrassed at the moment. Flat busted. And since you recently come into a tidy sum, perhaps you could see clear to float him a small loan. A trifle. A couple of sovereigns just until we get the treasure. Then he'll repay you in full. It's the kind of thing we adventurin' brothers do.

"And of course you might slip a few sovereigns into my purse as well. Just for necessary expenses, don't you know? All to be credited to the adventure and repaid off the top. That's the way we always do it."

Thurmond was perplexed. He desperately wanted to emulate the behaviors of the *adventurin' brothers* he hoped to join. But the poverty of his youth had made him ever cautious when it came to money. He was just working up the gumption to refuse, or at least to give an excuse, when Torgul's shouting from the doorway abruptly interrupted their conversation.

"Here it comes! Here it comes!"

With that the dwarf slammed the door, ran across the room, and tried to cover his body beneath his rucksack. Roscoe gave Thurmond one quick look and curled up in a ball in the corner, face to the wall. Completely taken aback, Thurmond stood frozen and did nothing.

From the backroom, there came a terrible rending sound, then several loud crashes as if a heavy object were being flung against the wall, followed by a long, agonizing screech. Then silence. Thurmond realized he had been holding his breath. He had no idea what to do. The two Adventurers seemed equally unsure. They rose and, like Thurmond, stared at the door to the backroom.

It opened. To Thurmond's surprise, Sarah stood there, smiling and apparently unscathed. She held forth Roscoe's beer jug in one triumphant hand.

"Got him!"

"Got what? Are you all right? What happened in there?"

"I got him. He's trapped in the jug. Look here."

The mouth of the jug was stoppered with a crude cap hammered out of copper and inscribed with what looked like some magical symbol. Sarah smiled again and gave the jug a hard shake. This stimulated a loud buzzing, as if a host of enraged hornets were trapped within and seeking to break out. She laughed aloud, mighty pleased with herself.

"Just listen to that. I got him."

Roscoe approached, obviously with a high degree of apprehension.

"That thing sounds mad as hell. How'd you get 'im?"

"I've read all about imps, and I know they're stupid. So I outsmarted him. Imps don't have bodies in the normal, physical sense, but they still can't just come through a solid wall. They need a regular opening like a door or window. There's a little hole in the back wall of my chamber that somebody had covered with a scrap of copper.

"I took it down and made this cap for the jug, inscribed it with my anthame. Then I removed the warding spell I had placed on these rooms. I knew that this dummy..."

With that she gave the jug another vigorous shake that induced an even louder buzzing.

"...this dummy would sense it and come flying straight through the hole. I just held the mouth of the jug up against it and clapped on the lid when he did so. Pretty smart, huh?"

Her audacity dumbfounded Roscoe and Torgul. Thurmond was still too naive to appreciate the scope of her deed. It was Torgul's turn to speak next.

"Missy, I hope you realize what you have in there. It's a hell-fiend that could tear us all to fragments with its claws. And that cap doesn't look particularly well fitted."

"Not to worry. It's the mystical properties of the inscription that's keeping him in, not the tightness of the fit. Aye, a hell-fiend but just a little one. What can we do with him?"

†

Such was the mood of jubilation attending their survival that Thurmond could not find it in his heart to refuse the requests Roscoe had made just prior to the arrival of the imp. Indeed, they now seemed most reasonable. He had a quick, private word with Sarah, who was still exalting in her own cleverness and was therefore unstinting. Thurmond's resources were already getting depleted, but Sarah dipped into her stash of ill-gotten gold. She passed it to Thurmond, who passed it to Roscoe, who passed it, a bit of it anyway, off to Torgul.

Being seasoned Adventurers, Roscoe and Torgul were well experienced with close calls and unanticipated assaults. Once the excitement of the moment had passed, they returned to their ordinary demeanors almost at once. It was time to look at the map. Thurmond unrolled it on the floor, its corners held down with a dagger, two cups, and the demon jug.

It revealed what could only be a section of the Mad River, bending in a great horseshoe loop. This was followed by two much smaller oxbow bends set close together. Between the small bends, a cave entrance was depicted as a grotesque face replete with a gaping mouth, fangs, and glaring eyes.

Beyond the mouth, a labyrinth of intersecting lines appeared to signify subterranean rooms and passages. One chamber was marked with a rune commonly used to represent gold or other valuables. Inland from the cave mouth, surrounded by markings that seemed to represent forest, a second runic symbol suggested another location of import. Sarah, however, was unacquainted with the meaning of this rune.

"I don't know this one. Dwarves are supposed to be good with runes. Do you recognize it, Torgul?"

"Nay, missy. 'Tisn't dwarvish nor gnomic."

"Roscoe?"

"Sorry to say, I've never seen its like. Neither Vanarian nor Keltin. Probably some occult *futhork*. And my best guess is that it shows a back door."

But that was all the map could offer. There was nothing to indicate where on that great expanse of river this particular location was to be found.

Roscoe looked up at last.

"I'm baffled. I've got no idea where this might be, none at all. It's a distinctive bit of river, so it is, and someone will know of it. But we can't go showin' this map around, not to just anyone. We don't need any competitors now, do we?

"I think I'll talk to an old waterman I know. Goes by the name of Scrymgeour. He's been up and down the Mad all his life. He was probably born on a riverboat. And I can trust him, at least if I make it worth his while."

With that Roscoe departed. Torgul curled up on the floor with his rucksack for a pillow and within moments was snoring vigorously. Thurmond and Sarah just stood and stared at each other in silent amazement.

CHAPTER FIFTEEN

THE ABOMINATION

Father Plutonius was not an impressive physical specimen. He was skinny and old, and his voice tended to crack when excited. He was excited at the moment, and his shrill screech was greatly annoying to Rupert.

Plutonius was dressed in the long, dark habit and cowl of the Black Friars, the clerical order to which he belonged. Though the Blacks were a powerful and respected denomination, they were not known for their deep piety or spiritual devotion. They controlled the city's loan-sharking and spent far more of their time tallying numbers than mumbling prayers.

Nonetheless, if Plutonius's superiors had any inkling of the blasphemous undertaking in which he was involved, he would have faced immediate excommunication, followed most likely by torture and death. The Charonite church was very jealous of its authority. Rejuvenation and resurrection spells were reserved for bishops and above. They commanded the highest imaginable fees, euphemistically called "love offerings," and were only rarely performed. Moreover, the mingling of the human with the nonhuman was deemed a dire abomination. The current activities of Father Plutonius were, therefore, a very serious offense.

He stood in a simple peasant's cottage, in which a man with a bandaged arm sat on a bed. There were no windows, but just enough light came in through the open door for Plutonius to see what he was doing. Rupert and

Sims stood on the other side of the patient, watching intensely as Plutonius unwound the wrappings around the man's left wrist.

The friar grew even shriller as the last of the wrapping came free.

"I told you so. Didn't I tell you so? I told you I could do it. See that? Clean as can be."

The man might belong to a holy order, but there was something decidedly unholy and unwholesome about him. He turned and addressed his patient.

"Now you, bend your fingers. Show the gentleman how you can bend your fingers."

The patient complied.

"Now make a fist. Now open it and spread your fingers wide. See that? Good as new. Didn't I tell you? Better than new. Much better than new."

The patient was a rangy, muscular, and dangerous-looking man with the air of a soldier. He was decidedly not a peasant, and this was not his cottage. He had, however, been forced to spend several days confined therein while Plutonius conducted an endless ceremonial. He sat passively, almost oblivious to the ministrations of the friar, but he immediately became attentive when Rupert spoke to him.

"How does it feel, Jasper? Does it possess normal feeling, like a regular hand?"

"Not really, lord. Just kinda itchy and dead feeling. Moves all right, though. Guess it's better than not havin' a hand."

Plutonius, growing impatient with their quibbling, snapped at them.

"Of course it feels bit strange, but he'll get used to it in time. That's to be expected. Now I want my money. You swore an oath to pay the remainder just as soon as the operation was complete. Well, it's done."

Rupert put on his best silky-smooth demeanor.

"Certainly, Holy Father. I have the full balance right here. It would be supremely foolhardy to break a sacred oath to one possessing such skills as you have demonstrated."

He handed over a heavy purse. Plutonius opened it and dumped a cascade of gold sovereigns onto a nearby table. He began a careful tally, examining each coin individually. Rupert was relieved that Renata had not insisted on substituting river rocks this time. The friar was too canny.

Rupert then bent to have a closer look at the hand. It was much larger than a normal human hand. The skin had a greenish tint and seemed composed of fine scales. The fingers terminated in large, hooked claws that twitched a bit.

Concerned, he looked at the friar.

"It seems to be experiencing some form of palsy or spasm. Will he have trouble controlling it?"

Peeved at being interrupted, Plutonius did not look up from his counting.

"Certainly not. I told you, it turned out perfectly. That's just a normal nervous reaction. It will all settle down if you give it a little time."

But instead, the fingers began to jerk violently, to flex and unflex as if trying to perform a grotesque dance. Rupert grew doubtful.

"Perhaps, good friar, you should come and have a look."

With an expression of disdain, Plutonius ceased his counting and returned to his patient. He was just opening his mouth to make a further complaint when the hand suddenly shot forward and grasped him by the throat. He face darkened, and his tongue protruded. The eyes began to glaze.

Rupert wanted to allow the hand to finish him. He could then pocket the gold and free himself from the company of this dreadful little man. But a rogue friar had his uses, and in the upcoming venture, he might prove quite useful indeed.

"Let him go, Jasper."

"I can't, lord. I'm really tryin', but it's strong as a mule, and I can't make it let go."

"Well, you must, Jasper. Either you release him, or I'll cut it off your arm with my sword."

Rupert's threat was idle. The operation had cost far too much to squander it over the life of a friar.

"I'm tryin', lord, but I just can't…aughhh…"

Sims stepped in and delivered the hand a hard blow with a length of firewood. It released the friar, who collapsed to the floor. His breathing resumed in a series of ragged, jerking gasps. Rupert led the others out of the stinking peasant hovel he found so distasteful. Plutonius was left behind in a swoon.

Once again in the clean, fresh outdoors, some of Rupert's good humor was restored.

"I trust, Jasper, that the next time you get in a barroom tussle, you'll have the common decency to get yourself killed rather than dismembered. I'll not be paying to replace another hand. Perhaps you should have your head instead of your hand removed next time. I think you'd look much better with a troll's head on your shoulders. You'd probably be smarter, too."

He laughed at his own joke. Sims and Jasper trudged silently along behind him. It had been Rupert's idea to graft a troll hand on Jasper. He had heard that such a thing was sometimes done, the regenerative powers of the troll making the grafting easier. Jasper had been easy to convince. Better a troll hand than no hand at all.

It had been difficult sweet-talking Renata into paying for it. She was always tightfisted with him, even though her brother provided her with lavish funds. It had taken an extended period of flattery and arse kissing before she would at last relent.

But she had then insisted on defrauding the simpleminded thief, substituting enchanted river rocks for gold sovereigns. She obviously resented being asked to spend her money, even in her own best interest. Perhaps victimizing the thief had somehow assuaged some of that anger.

Rupert put these thoughts from his mind. He really did not care. Not, anyway, as long as he was getting what he wanted. He had been occupied for some time now, and he knew Renata would be missing him. Time to keep her happy.

†

Father Plutonius lay on the dirt floor of the peasant hovel, trying to restore himself with a healing spell. It was a good, functional spell, but it never seemed to work correctly when he tried to cast it on himself. His throat felt terribly swollen, and it was still hard to breathe. He could see his partially counted gold on the table across the room. He was in a rage about being left like this, but at least that arrogant blackguard Rupert had not robbed him.

He had been given to the Black Friars as a boy by a father who had had no use for so many sons. His father had also presented the friars with a substantial love offering for his unwanted progeny's room and board. If, over the years, Plutonius had learned anything from the Black Friars, it was to appreciate the value of money.

They made no pretense of being a charitable order. The poor did not gather at their back door for a dollop of gruel. The Blacks understood that the existence of their holy order depended on money and that their bellies could not be filled by prayer. They were highly skilled at keeping their bellies and their coffers filled.

Years ago the Black Friars had been proclaimed, by royal decree, the official moneylenders of the kingdom of Poitiers. They were the only ones permitted to issue loans at interest, so they became astronomically wealthy. Part of their success was due to their reputation for ruthlessness in the collection of bad debts. Each church maintained a squad of well-trained goons to break the legs of shirkers and deadbeats.

Such affluence naturally created an intense rivalry with the larger and more powerful Blue Friars. The Blues had long been the predominate sect. The Holy Pontiff, supreme head of the Charonite church, was always drawn from the Blues. Determined to retain their preeminent position, the Blues felt a natural enmity toward the upstart Blacks.

This hostility had, on occasion, flared into open warfare, with secular nobles choosing to champion one sect or the other. But in general, both orders agreed that bloodshed was bad for business and eschewed armed conflict whenever possible. In Gorgonholm, the Blacks and the Blues mostly ignored one another. The Blacks were obliged to remit a percentage of their annual income to the local bishop, who was of course a Blue. They grumbled about this but complied.

There were other sects in the city as well. The White Friars exerted considerable influence among the lowest classes but were not nearly as wealthy as the Blacks or Blues. Their ceremonies were given in the vernacular and consisted of the most simplistic of precepts, consisting of little more than demanding utter obedience to church elders and encouraging a distrust of foreigners coupled with a hatred of all nonhumans. Such spiritual principles were generally well received by the parishioners.

The Gray Friars operated the grist mill just south of the city. They produced most of their own sustenance on the grounds of the associated monastery and purchased whatever else they needed with revenue gleaned from the mill. They were, for the most part, an introverted sect who preferred to be left to their own affairs.

The Brown Friars were much the same, but their orientation was even more rural and self-contained. They maintained a large monastery still farther to the south and were famous for the excellent quality of their mead. Huge hogsheads of this beverage were transported into the city on ox-drawn drays.

There was also a wide array of schismatic and fanatical sects that passed in and out of the city gates. Troupes of flagellants, death dancers, dirt eaters, and snake handlers would appear, admonish the citizenry to give alms, and then move on before the established denominations could take stern measures against them.

The creed of the Purple Friars was perhaps the most bizarre of any. They believed that the fell creatures of the underworld—ogres, trolls, goblins, and that ilk—could attain grace. They would, firm in their faith, venture unarmed into those subterranean lairs in search of converts. For this reason, there were very few Purple Friars.

CHAPTER SIXTEEN

LADY RENATA'S IRE

In the top floor of her tower, Lady Renata was in a transport of wrath. She hurled an expensive cloisonné vase against the stones of the fireplace. With a sweep of her arm, she sent an array of silver goblets crashing to the floor and then kicked over the table on which they had stood. The room was littered with broken furniture, smashed crockery, and tapestries torn from the walls. She shrieked in rage as loud as she was able, though her voice was by now growing weak from all her prior shrieking.

Rupert finally made an entrance. He had been listening to the din from the ground floor for some time but was unwilling to climb the stairs until the bulk of her fury had been spent.

"Milady, whatever is the matter? What is troubling you? I am just now in from some business and heard you in distress. What can I do to end your pain? Prithee, tell me how I may help."

She paused, about to fling a silver platter through a stained-glass window.

"Where have you been, Rupert? I've been calling for you for hours. *For hours*! I don't like it when things go against me. And things are going against me now. We have big problems."

"Prithee, milady, describe the nature of your woe so that I may seek a remedy."

"Something has happened to Aborax. He hasn't come home, and that's not like him. Not even for his usual feeding, and you know how he gets when he's hungry. Something is wrong. Something has happened to him."

"God forfend that ill should befall your imp! Can you not employ the mirror to ascertain his whereabouts?"

"Fool! Think you that such a thought didn't occur to me? Of course I tried the mirror, but something there, too, is amiss. The proper hour has come and gone, but the mirror failed. I turned it first on Staynes. Since we don't have his map, I hoped to read it over his shoulder if he should unroll it. But the mirror was dark. I could learn nothing. He is obviously under the protection of a counterspell."

The corners of Rupert's mouth drew down almost imperceptibly, but only for an instant. When he spoke, it was with the same reassuring calmness that he always affected when dealing with Renata.

"But if you cannot see the map, how can we locate the treasure?"

"Dolt! Must you always state the obvious? That is why I am so upset. That and poor Aborax, of course."

"Any luck finding the young thief?"

"Nay, there, too, the mirror remained dark. I fear that he and Staynes may be now allied and under the protection of a master wizard who sets my best efforts to naught. Most likely that short ugly person who tried to spy on us with the mirror. In fact, I am certain of it."

"Perhaps in my own small way, I can ease your mind a bit, at least in this regard. Sims and I were just out checking on things with the friar. All went well. And it occurred to me that Sims might be the answer to our missing thief. I suggested that he send two or three of his associates into the city to find the boy and tidy things up. He promised to do so straightaway."

"Might your Sims help us with Staynes as well? Perhaps stage a raid on his house and seize the map?"

"I doubt that such a course would prove productive. Staynes is young and foolish, but he could hardly be so stupid as to fail to take precautions now that he has been alerted. He has, as we know, a large body of well-trained mercenaries and, as you say, a master magician in his employ. The map must now certainly repose in the most secure of hiding places."

Renata felt her anger rising once again. Her voice grew strident as she vented her frustration.

"So am I supposed to do nothing? To let that young oaf have the treasure? I won't just stand here and let that happen. You must find a way!"

Rupert suddenly brightened, his broad smile revealing straight white teeth.

"Well, perhaps there is another way. Not as elegant as simply reading his map with the mirror and beating him to the treasure, but it could work. I will instruct Sims to assign men to watch Staynes Hall. When the young fool departs on his treasure hunt, we will follow him. We will let him lead us to the treasure and allow him the honor of battling who or what may be guarding it. Whichever side wins will be weakened. That will be when we step in and seize it for ourselves."

Renata's foul mood was at once forgotten.

"It is at moments like this, dear Rupert, that I am fully aware of why I find you so attractive. You may kiss me."

CHAPTER SEVENTEEN

NOCTURNAL VISITORS

Thurmond sat on the floor of his lodging, trying to sharpen his poniard as Torgul had shown him to do, but he was not having much luck. Sarah was in the back, presumably studying her magic. The dwarf sat on the far side of the room. He was using the pommel of his knife, a short, choppy weapon known as a scramasax, to tap the cap of the demon jug into a tighter fit. Dwarves are famous for their craftsmanship, and this one was sparing no effort to seal in the inhabitant of the jug. He paused and looked at Thurmond.

"Have I told you that the blood of Borik the Bold runs in my veins?"

"Uh…you may have mentioned it."

"You are, of course, familiar with his great deeds, with the exploits so well recounted in the six hundred and thirty-six stanzas of the *Borikinga Saga*?"

"Not entirely."

"Shall I sing it to you? Refresh your memory?"

"Not at all necessary. I'm sure the briefest of anecdotes would suffice."

"Good, I will start at the beginning."

> *"Hwæt! I sing of Borik, son of Axe Mountain, yclept The Bold, bravest and most ferocious, bane of night-wraith and ogre. May his beard flourish! Borik, who departed from the caverns of his forefathers, then but a cub, to seek fame and fortune in the realm of man. Many were his trials and troubles, but great*

he was in courage and terrible in his wrath. That was a good dwarf!

"We have all heard of the mighty deeds wrought by this lord of the axe, this intrepid war-onion. Many foemen did he slay and much gold amass, but the greatest treasure was the cauldron Hrunfling, from which flowed an endless stream of nutritious and well-seeming provender, wholesome and sustaining, though sickly vile to the taste. Yet this remained the favored fare of Borik, slayer of trolls, for despite the noxious flavor, it kept his fighting spirit keen.

"Fortune favored the axe lord, and so he gathered unto him a war band of young dwarfling fighters most eager for fame. Nor did the stew-giver renege, but to these worthies he doled out the bounty of Hrunfling...."

Thurmond was just on the verge of nodding off when his front door burst open and a man with a shortsword rushed inside. Another followed close behind.

Thurmond was completely stupefied. The first man came straight at him, his weapon raised. Only at the last moment did the attacker become aware of the presence of Torgul. Thus his attention was turned slightly in that direction. Thurmond did not consciously think about what to do. He just reacted.

The knife he had been sharpening was still in his hand. He lunged forward. The point took the intruder just under the breastbone and penetrated upward. He gave a hideous shriek and collapsed to the floor, bleeding and kicking.

The second man fared no better. Torgul was on his feet in an instant. He bounded across the room, leaped high in the air, and struck the intruder at shoulder level. The force of the impact propelled him over backward, and by the time he hit the floor, Torgul had cut his throat with his scramasax.

A third man appeared in the doorway. He held a short, heavy-bladed sword and was standing directly over Torgul, who was still floundering on the floor in an attempt to free himself from the corpse of the second man.

Thurmond, on the other side of the room, could only watch in horror as the third man prepared to smash the skull of the helpless dwarf.

Then something smashed into the wall beside the intruder's head, splashing him with a thick, black liquid. He jumped back, trying to wipe his eyes, and that was his undoing. Torgul rebounded from the floor, stabbed his scramasax into the man's stomach and ripped across. The third man also shrieked, but only briefly, for Torgul's next blow slashed across his throat.

And then it was over.

A fit of trembling overtook Thurmond as full realization of what had just happened began to dawn on him. Men he did not know had broken down his door and tried to kill him. He now noticed Sarah standing behind him. She seemed equally dazed. Only Torgul was unaffected.

"Say, missy, whatever that was you threw, that was well done. Would have been better, of course, had you took him right in the face, but it did the job. Well done!"

"It was my ink pot."

"I'm just grateful for whatever it was. That one had me, sure enough, but you drew his attention, and that was sufficient. I thought for a minute it was the demon jug. That would have been bad all 'round."

Thurmond thought he saw the dwarf almost crack a smile. Sarah returned to her room and shut the door, obviously very distraught. He then turned his attention to the man he had knifed. He still lived and was breathing in great gurgling gasps. Torgul stepped over and joined him.

"Best finish him."

As a farm boy, Thurmond had killed his share of chickens and rabbits. He had helped his neighbors slaughter hogs, sheep, and cows, yet he had never before seen a man killed. He had had his share of boyhood fistfights and had inadvertently stabbed an unfortunate servant in the arm when he stole the map and mirror. But he had never taken a human life.

"Go on, boy, finish him. You're not doing him any good by waiting around. He's dying and suffering while he's doing it. So end it."

Thurmond continued to hesitate, but while he did so, the man on the floor gave one last frightful gasp and made an even more terrible burping sound as his final breath escaped his lungs. Then he was dead. Thurmond had taken a human life. He wanted to sit down and rest, maybe weep, but Torgul grabbed his arm.

"Listen to me, boy. We've gotta dump these bodies somewheres. It's dark out now—that's good. Look him over. Keep his weapons and anything else that might be useful. Then we'll drag 'em out. Is there a hog pen anywhere nearby? Pigs we could feed 'em to? And get little missy to come out and clean up when we leave."

Thurmond felt like he was in a dream as he began to rummage through the clothing of the dead man at his feet.

†

Two hours later, the door opened, and three more men entered the room. Torgul, Thurmond, and Sarah were much better prepared this time and rose as one, weapons in hand, to defend themselves. They knew they were taking a risk by staying in the lodging, but they had nowhere else to go, and it seemed more defensible than being caught in a city street.

Fortunately, it was Roscoe with two young men of about Thurmond's age. He also carried in another jug of ale, which they all agreed was exactly what was needed. After they had recounted the events of the evening, interrupting each other and arguing over details, Roscoe took a long swig of ale and smacked his lips.

"To be sure, someone's got it out for us. Do you see now, laddie, how fortunate you are to have a formidable warrior like Torgul here in residence? 'Twas providence, so it was. And how lucky that Sarah is no quiverin' girlie girl who is too timid to fight back. I doff my hat to you, young lady, so I do.

"And with you, friend Thurmond, I am also impressed. Though taken entirely by surprise, you rose from a sittin' position and skewered your foe in exactly the right place before he could strike you. That was superbly done. You might make a warrior yet."

Roscoe's praise made the young man uncomfortable.

"To be honest, I only got him because his attention was turned toward Torgul. Otherwise, I would have been the one dead on the floor."

"That don't signify. Not in the least. Torgul might have gotten chopped had Sarah not thrown the ink pot. You might have died had Torgul not risen when he did. All is merest chance, and our lives always hang by a thread. So when Lady Fortune smiles, don't resist it. Accept it as your due. You'll have plenty of bad times to even things out. When the good ones come along, just enjoy them."

Roscoe glanced down at the ominous stains on the lodging's wooden floor.

"What became of the bodies, by the way?"

"We put them in the river."

"Aye, that's good. The river's good."

"Torgul wanted to feed them to pigs."

"Pigs is good too, so they are."

He then gestured to the young strangers, who stood silently behind him.

"Now let me introduce you to our new companions. You couldn't pronounce their real names, so let's agree to call 'em Nod and Sod. Them's good names that are easy to say and remember. They are the sons of Scrymgeour, an old friend and an expert waterman. These lads, despite their youth, are also master watermen. They have agreed to take us to the location indicated on our map."

The focus of the conversation abruptly shifted from the intruders to the treasure. Thurmond looked dubiously at the newcomers.

"They know where it is? For certain? We can believe 'em?"

"Aye, for a fact. Turns out, the large cave by the river is scarcely a secret. It's well known to all the watermen. What's important here is not the main cave entrance but that we know where to find the back door.

"The cave is, in fact, the lair of a host of goblin river pirates who have grown most troublesome in recent times. They don't much bother larger vessels with a well-armed crew, but smaller ones, like Scrymgeour's boat, are always imperiled on that stretch of river. Scrymgeour has agreed, for a modest consideration, to loan us his boat and his two good sons to assault and eliminate that nest of vermin."

Torgul was on his feet in an instant.

"*Assault and eliminate*? Has your mind withered in its skull? I joined this group to find treasure, not clear the river for boatmen. Them goblins are *their* problem. They ain't no concern of mine."

"Now, Torgul, my old friend, you have to understand the nature of my negotiations with Scrymgeour. 'Tis true enough, certain promises were made concernin' the elimination of said vermin. But if we don't manage to exterminate them entirely…well…I imagine it will be enough to weaken them by depletin' their essential resources."

"Do you mean by takin' their gold?"

"Aye, indeed I do. You take my meanin' entirely."

At this point Torgul seemed placated, but Thurmond was growing increasingly wary.

"You mentioned offering Scrymgeour a *modest consideration*. What might that be?"

"A mere trifle. Hardly worth mentionin'."

"How much?"

"One-eighth."

"One-eighth of what exactly?"

"One-eighth of the total after expenses."

"And how much is a lieutenant's customary share?"

"Two-eighths. A mere pittance."

"If the captain gets three-eighths and Torgul gets two and the boatmen get one, what do the other members of the party receive?"

"They divvy up the other two-eighths. That is, they do if they are full partners and not just hirelings servin' for a fixed fee."

"Which means that Sarah and I…"

"Receive one-eighth apiece. Right fair wages for a brace of hang-arounds."

Thurmond was not at all pleased with Roscoe's arithmetic.

"This hardly seems fair! I stole the map!"

"Aye, laddie, so you did. But findin' the map and winnin' the treasure—if there really be a treasure—are clean different things. Anyway, these things is all worked out accordin' to Brotherhood rules. I'm the captain, and the captain always receives three-eighths. 'Tis the custom, plain and simple. Torgul's my lieutenant, so he gets two. We can't find the cave without the help of a waterman, and Scrymgeour is our best chance.

"You must appreciate that hang-arounds ain't normally entitled to a percentage—just a flat wage. Maybe a hundred sovereigns. So we're already cuttin' you in for a lot more than your rightful share. Plus, you'll be receivin' fightin' lessons from a master swordsman at no cost. But also, I'm thinkin' that you aspire to be joinin' the Brotherhood, and this is the way we do things. We all had to start at the bottom, laddie. Any other questions?"

Thurmond had one more.

"Are you planning to add any more members to our group? Each new member costs Sarah and I dearly."

"Nay, boyo. I believe our little family is complete."

The group spent the remainder of the evening drinking ale and listening to Roscoe's tales of the escapades he and Scrymgeour had shared in years gone by. They had been partners in a smuggling operation that ferried illegal weapons to the far side of the river and brought back the powerful and illegal beverage known as *uisge*.

Scrymgeour was half Keltin by birth and maintained a passable working relationship with the wild tribesmen on the western shore. He spoke their language and had, at one point, purchased a Keltin girl for his wife. She became the mother of Nod and Sod.

These days the family earned a modest living by hauling small loads of freight up and down the river in a nearly flat-bottomed keelboat. Roscoe was pretty sure they were still involved in some illicit dealings in weapons and *uisge*, but larger, more powerful criminal gangs had long ago seized the main smuggling operations.

Nod and Sod drank lustily when the ale was passed to them, but otherwise they sat silently and expressionlessly. It was Sarah who finally spoke to them directly.

"Do you understand us? Do you speak our language? Can you follow our conversation?"

Both immediately responded but spoke in a fashion that was only remotely comprehensible. Roscoe intervened.

"These laddies understand you right enough. And they just replied to your inquiry in the common tongue, though I doubt your recognized it. They speak with a heavy waterman's flavor, and then that's overlaid with their mother's Keltin tongue. So it makes them difficult for most folk to comprehend. They can understand you, but you followin' them, that's another story, so it is."

CHAPTER EIGHTEEN

THE TRIBULATIONS OF NOBILITY

The dead of night was long since deceased and forgotten. The witching hour had already retired to her clammy bed. The ghoulies were again snug in their crumbling tombs, and the ghosties were tucked away in weird corners of abandoned attics. Even the long-legged beasties had completed their nightly bumping. Yet Bartholomew Staynes, the young lord, remained in his father's library, staring blankly at the empty desk. Had he had a candle, it would have been burning at both ends.

He was a stocky, red-faced, healthy-looking man in his early twenties. His blond, close-cropped hair and shaven face lent him something of a boyish look that could have been mistaken for lightheartedness. But he was, at that moment, anything but light of heart.

Things were not going his way, and he was never pleasant at such times. His magic mirror, for which he had paid an exorbitant price, had been stolen, along with his map, one of his spell scrolls, and a number of other important documents.

Someone was obviously aware of his plans and had sent an expert thief, one well versed in magic as well as burglary, to thwart him. Such a professional did not come cheap, so his adversary must be a person of means.

He had shared these deductions with the Brethren. His father paid them an annual tithe, and his family was supposed to be protected against this kind of outrage. They called it the *boot tax,* a kind of insurance policy they offered throughout the city. Merchants and householders foolish enough to decline found themselves with their bones broken, goods pillaged, and premises burned. Brethren representatives had promised to investigate the break-in, but they had seemed anything but sincere.

Bart Staynes had what some would call a low threshold of frustration. Perhaps this was due to the privileged existence that had always been his, or perhaps it was an innate weakness of character. Either way, he grew sullen when crossed and remained so until he found a suitable victim upon whom to vent his spleen. It mattered not whether he was impeded by the weather, an incompetent servant, or his father. Somebody would inevitably be made to suffer for it.

His father was the illustrious and venerable Lord Percy Staynes. Holder of an ancient, if relatively insignificant, patent of nobility. Possessor of several outlying estates that provided a perfectly sufficient income. He had been a notorious rakehell in his day—wenching, brawling, taking what he wanted from the world. But now he was reduced to an enfeebled graybeard who collected old books and stubbornly refused to die.

This fact, above all things, was the stumbling block that grieved his son. He had grown up under the old man's iron thumb and had been forced to submit to years of humiliation and abuse. The intimidation continued to this very hour, when the father lay on the verge of death and the son was in all his manly vigor. Yet somehow he still could not break free from the boyhood terror that had been inscribed so indelibly on his soul.

Many were the frustrations of the moment, but behind all of them was the forbidding awareness that he could never be his own man while his father lived. He had, of course, considered measures to remedy this problem. A mere dewdrop of poison, easily acquired, would, if placed in the old man's wine cup, have brought his dilemma to a happy conclusion. But something deep within Bartholomew Staynes recoiled at the prospect of patricide.

So even in his extreme dotage, the father controlled the son, issuing detailed injunctions about what he might and might not do. He was expressly forbidden to indulge himself with the serving wenches. Certainly his father had never held himself back in that regard. Several of the household servants were reputed to be the products of his passions.

Yet when Bart, at the lusty age of thirteen, had impregnated a kitchen girl, his father had flown into a towering rage and had strictly prohibited any further carnal involvement with the domestic staff. The point was made very clear. The servants belonged to the old man.

He could now hear the consequence of that misadventure running up and down the hallway outside his door. He was shouting and laughing, obviously locked in battle with some imaginary foe. He had been told that the boy wanted to play at being an Adventurer and had taken to stalking the house at all hours with a crossbow. The old man, of course, had allowed it. Bart hoped the brat would somehow shoot himself.

Lately, the wretched urchin had begun wearing an ugly hat with a ridiculous white feather. Bart wondered where he had gotten it. When the old man finally gave in and died, things were certainly going to be very different.

A knock on the library door brought an end to Bart's musings. It was Giles, the butler, a self-important prig whose loyalties lay entirely with his father.

"I thought you'd want to know, milord. Sarah is still not found."

Giles seemed to delight in bothering him with such trivial details when he had much more important matters to occupy his thoughts. This would matter only if his father got wind of it. So he was not especially concerned. That headstrong, little wench had disappeared before. She had most likely snuck out for some illicit purpose and would, he was sure, reappear in her own good time.

Soon enough she would get her comeuppance. She might be his father's pampered favorite now—some said she was his bastard daughter—but things would change when the old man went over. Things would very much change.

Giles continued to annoy him with petty details.

"And there is still no news of Henrietta."

"Who?"

"Henrietta, the housemaid gone missing two days past. I assumed you would want to be apprised."

Giles's words carried a subtle warning. His father would, of course, expect him to search for the missing members of his household. He might even rise from his couch and descend from his sick room, demanding to know the status of said search. Bart had better have a ready answer.

In fact, he scarcely remembered Henrietta, only that she was bony, hatchet-faced, and vapid. Entirely unworthy of his notice. Not at all the kind of girl who would elope with a lover—she was much too plain and dull for that. Nor was she the type to be carried off by procurers or even drunken ravagers—she was just too dreary. So she had probably been murdered for no good reason at all.

"Continue in your efforts to find them, Giles. Keep me informed."

"Very well, sir."

To be fair, Bartholomew Staynes was not an always a bad fellow. He could, when so moved, be quite affable. He, like most people, enjoyed good cheer and fine fellowship. He was generous and considerate with his friends. Allowed his own way, he felt no compulsion to be cruel.

Bart's interests were all in the realm of what is called the *manly arts*. He adored his stable of thoroughbred horses and was never happier than when astride one in pursuit of a noble stag. He kept a pack of trained hunting hounds on which he lavished his fond affection. Bart also enjoyed a circle of other young lordlings who joined him in the hunt, drinking bouts, and fencing matches.

Bart's boyhood dream had been to become a belted knight. He had seen many such men while growing up and loved their air of natural authority. Such a goal could have certainly become his reality. He was of the correct social class. His father had the means to provide the expensive armor, weapons, and warhorses that were a knight's tools of trade. He could easily have been placed with a noble family, first as a page then as a squire, to develop such skills as a knight must have.

But his father, of course, had excoriated that dream by adamantly forbidding Bart to pursue a martial career. He preferred to keep him home and under his own control. And now, even if his father finally died, it was too late. Bart was too old to become a knight.

He was naturally bitter about being deprived his dream, but he had lately hit upon a scheme by which he could win, if not knighthood, at least a measure of glory and renown. It had begun when he kicked over a pile of his father's books. He hated those books. Hated how they were always in his way. Hated their musty smell. He hated them because he did not know what was inside.

Bart, like most of the nobility, had never learned to read, and he distrusted anyone who could. Did they think reading books made them somehow superior to him? He did not know whether his father could read, but suspected that he could not. Why then had he become so smitten by these damned books?

Yet it was a book that had given him his grand design. When he kicked the pile, its pages had flapped open like the wings of a dying bird, and a map had fallen out. Bart was illiterate but far from stupid. He had scrutinized the map, and the more closely he looked at it, the more it looked like a treasure map.

He decided then and there to lead an expedition to recover the treasure. It was the perfect means to win the recognition that had always been denied him. He had not revealed his plans to any of his young noble cronies. If he had told even one, the rest would have known in a heartbeat. And then they would inevitably insist on horning in on his adventure. One way or the other, they would end up with the greatest portion of the treasure. More importantly, they would contrive to steal the renown this undertaking was sure to bring. Above all, Bart needed to assert his skill and daring to the world, and he did not want to share it.

He knew his father would never recognize his worth. But maybe others would. It would be pleasant to hear one's praises sung. And he himself, at least, would know that he had finally accomplished something worthy. This was what he needed to challenge his deep-set feeling of failure.

But now his map had been stolen, and unless he could get it back, his great design would come to naught. Thus, he now sat late in his father's library, frustrated and angry, the day's events churning in his mind.

The morning had started badly—during the previous night an eviscerated corpse had been laid in the street in front of his house. Word quickly spread that this was the remains of the thief who had robbed him, courtesy of the Brethren. Bart had his doubts. The dead man was middle aged, rotund, and had a stunted left leg. Not at all what one would expect an expert burglar to be like. Of course, no one but Gyre had gotten a real look at the thief, and he swore the intruder had been seven feet tall, covered with scales, and possessed a set of huge yellow fangs.

Bart refused to buy it. He knew the Brethren had dumped any old corpse just so they could call the case closed and their debt to him square. Bastards! He strongly suspected that the Brethren might have sanctioned the break-in and then offered up some fat, old fool as a dodge. In spite of his father's payments, they had played him false. Bastards!

And then an urgent message had arrived, calling him to Gregorio's stinking den, insisting that he must come at once to attend to a vital matter. *Summoned! Him!* Summoned as if he were a lackey to be ordered about. He resented the interruption and decided that if the wizard asked for more gold, he would simply kill him and be done.

Bart had hired Gregorio, a specialist in divination, to use the magic mirror to determine the location of the treasure as indicated on his map. But now that both items had been stolen, he had given him a new task. The magician was to cast his spells to discover who had taken Bart's property and where it was to be found.

Bart loathed Gregorio, as he did all magicians, and had hired the man only because he could see no other way to proceed. Almost all magic users were frauds. Nothing but weak men and social misfits who tried to grab some shred of respect and recognition by claiming to command supernatural powers. For all of their supposed wisdom and vaunted book learning, not one of them seemed especially bright. Gregorio personified all his misgivings.

For one thing, magicians were always so awkward and unappealing. Gregorio was very tall, absurdly tall. Long of leg, of arm, even long of face—this unbecoming trait accentuated by his habit of leaving his mouth to gape open. He dressed in a voluminous orange gown Bart assumed was supposed to conceal his gangling frame. If so, it did not work. The gown's sleeves were embroidered with an elaborate array of occult symbols obviously intended to convey the wearer's advanced esoteric knowledge. His efforts left Bart unimpressed.

Bart's mood did not improve when, at about midday, he entered Gregorio's workshop. It was just what he expected—dim and squalid, cluttered with greasy jars and yellowed parchments. A work table was piled high with decaying books and arcane instruments. He even had a stuffed lizard hanging from his ceiling. Why did all magic users think they had to have a stupid stuffed lizard?

And the place just reeked of something unhealthy and unnamable. He realized Gregorio carried some of that same stench, which explained some of Bart's strong dislike for him.

At least Gregorio knew how to address his betters when he chose to.

"I beg your forgiveness for the impertinent summons, my gracious lord. I did so only because I am in the midst of a most delicate magical operation and dare not leave it. And I knew that you would want to be made aware of a recent development. My efforts on your behalf have proven fruitful."

Bart immediately perked up. This was good news.

"What have you learned?"

"It occurred to me, milord, that I, like yourself, had touched the map that was stolen from your library. You see, a diviner's ability to see across the veil depends on his ability to recognize psychic vibrations. No vibrations are more recognizable than one's own, and I left traces of mine on the map. I have now located it for you."

"Where is it? Who has it?"

"In the city. In an old storeroom converted to a lodging. I cannot see who has it. There is some kind of magical cloak in place."

"Come! I will gather my fighters, and we will retrieve my property at once."

"I would advise restraint, milord. There is a powerful demonic presence in the lodging, obviously in the service of a powerful sorcerer. We in the trade call them *familiars*. Without equally powerful magic, it would tear your men to pieces. Unfortunately, I cannot contend with this creature. My skills are elsewhere. I do not treat with infernal entities."

The pieces of the puzzle suddenly came together in Bart's mind. He was indeed the victim of an elaborate plot. Someone of great power was conspiring to steal his treasure. It might well be the Patron, overlord of the Brethren. He would have the full resources of the crime cult to draw on and could easily engage both a master burglar and a master magician.

"Just what then do you advise I do?"

"I would suggest patience, milord. He who has the map obviously seeks to win the treasure. Allow him to do so. Send someone to keep his lodging under surveillance. Then simply follow along behind when he begins his quest. Wait until he takes it or dies in the attempt. Then step forward and claim what is yours by right. A simple plan, actually, but effective."

Bart experienced a great surge of optimism.

"I begin to see why you came so highly recommended, Gregorio. I think I may have to permit you to live after all."

This announcement made Gregorio appear somewhat relieved. He continued.

"I am also honored to inform you, milord, that I have located the mirror."

"Very, very well done. You are indeed the best of wizards. Where is it?"

"In a small tower out where the river swings to the west. There is a small collection of peasant huts, not what I'd call a real village. I have seen a dark woman and her foppish companion."

That was all Bart needed to know. The tower, the location, the woman's description led to an easy deduction.

"Lady Renata! I should have seen this long ago. She and the Brethren are undoubtedly in league against me."

Now it all made sense.

"Gregorio, do you know who she is? She's the sister of Drakar. That ought to be enough for you to see what we're up against. Everybody knows she's a witch. She keeps her own household and lives in an old watchtower exactly as you described. She's tall and dark of hair, just as you said. It's got to be her."

"She's Drakar's sister?"

"Aye, Drakar. So you understand how serious this is. Nobody dares to challenge Drakar. He's far too powerful and completely without restraint."

"Pray, tell me more of the sister, this Lady Renata."

"I've met her a few times. Once during a royal progress. Other times at functions held by Earl Ralf. She fits your description exactly. It has to be her."

"And her relations with her brother? How stand they?"

Bart was completely nonplussed by this question.

"In sooth, I have no idea. I know she lives apart from him. Neither is married. He resides in the family estate, while she makes her abode in an ancient tower in a nondescript hamlet. Beyond that, I am unapprised."

"That the brother enjoys opulence while the sister resides in obscurity says much. Does it not seem probable that she resents her downcast condition and seeks to better it?"

"Aye, possibly."

"That would explain her desire for your treasure map, not so?"

"I would assume so."

"Is it not likely that her plot against you is conducted then without the sanction—perhaps even without the knowledge—of her sibling? That he is entirely uninvolved?"

"Perchance."

"In such case, milord, let us take heart. Powerful forces may indeed be arrayed against us, but we need not assume that they include Lord Drakar, whose name I cannot mention without trepidation. He and his sister seem to live disconnected lives."

"I completely concur with your dread of Drakar. As for Renata, I know not the extent of her powers or her relationship with her bother. What is your estimation?"

"She has clearly harnessed an infernal entity that now wards the thief who stole your mirror. We must assume the thief was in her employ, since she now holds the mirror. But he has retained the map. So he is either leading an expedition on her behalf or has withheld it from her and is striking out on his own. I would assume the former."

"And the Brethren has sanctioned all this? She must have paid them off."

"As it would appear, milord."

"Can you counter her magic?"

"She is obviously well versed in the summoning and governing of things demonic. I am a diviner and so not prepared to give battle to the pit spawn she may send our way. On the other hand, I possess the ability to observe their movements and anticipate their intentions so that you may always be one step ahead. Our best course would, therefore, be to remain unsuspected until the moment we strike a decisive blow."

"I like that, Gregorio. I like that very much. Let them walk into our deadfall entirely unaware. But wait! What about the mirror? Can't they turn it against us?"

"Not to any great effect. I have cast a spell that will keep it dark whenever it is turned on us. But she will be able to turn it in other directions. With any luck, she will use it to find the treasure and lead us to it. And I sent her a little something special to keep her entertained, a bit of an itch."

Bart's confidence soared as if launched from a catapult. This fumbling magician had, against all expectations, saved his adventure! The man had found Bart's map and mirror, identified his perfidious rivals, and suggested a clever plan for their destruction. In his jubilation Bart actually began to feel a degree of affection for the previously despised wizard.

CHAPTER NINETEEN

THE YOUNG LORD'S FRUSTRATIONS

Bart's enthusiasm was unfortunately short lived. After departing Gregorio's workshop, he stopped by Einarr's to watch Artos drill his new war band. What he saw soon soured his good mood.

He had had such high expectations. He had engaged Artos to acquire and train the men he would need for his treasure quest. The latter was a veteran sergeant-at-arms, grizzled and hard, who had served as a sergeant in the mercenary company of the legendary Hawkwood. He had given Bart every assurance that he could turn a motley assortment of plowboys and shopkeeper assistants into a loyal cadre of highly lethal soldiers. All Bart had to do was provide sufficient resources and then stand back and let it happen.

Artos would train them to fight as a unit—shields up front, spears behind and thrusting overtop. Archers drifting wide to the left—the unshielded side. He would turn a pack of simple laborers into a cohesive team that could attack with the concentrated force of an armored fist or, when necessary, close ranks and hold ground. They might flow backward in mock retreat but then suddenly wheel and hit an exposed flank.

The mercenary's stirring descriptions of battlefield maneuvers had completely captivated Bart, and he had readily agreed to the exorbitant costs. Would the treasure not more than compensate?

He had also allowed Artos purchase all the requisite arms and equipment. A sizable quantity of good, serviceable weapons and armor had already been delivered to his house. Bart had naturally gotten something special for himself. He was, after all, a noble by birth and therefore a natural leader. His wealth and station demanded that he equip himself in a fashion that proclaimed his quality.

Only the most up-to-date and stylish harness would therefore meet his needs, custom fitted with every detail answering to his whim. Arms and legs lapped fully in steel, with knees and elbows guarded by articulating plates. His body protected by a short habergeon of riveted links, covered by a bright jupon bearing his family's arms. His head guarded by a close-fitting basinet, the visor drawn out to a dramatic point in a style known as a hound's skull.

Bart was confident that once he looked like a lord, he would feel like one. And feeling like a lord, he would act like a lord. And in such case, his men would treat him accordingly, obeying his commands without question and willingly giving their lives in his defense.

Such items were, of course, extremely expensive, and Bart was beginning to worry that his father would sufficiently recover to review their finances and realize how much of the family fortune he was burning through. The Staynes were by no means short of funds, but his was due to the diligent husbandry of his father and his forebears. If Bart were to continue spending in his current manner, the ancestral capital would be substantially depleted.

It would all be worthwhile, however, if the adventure brought Bart the acclaim that was rightfully his due. He would be a great warrior-captain, leading a party of desperate men in a life-and-death situation. His father had denied him this glory. Now, at last, by God's holy molars, he would have the chance to demonstrate what he was truly made of.

But the uninspired performance of his men on Einarr's practice field had shaken his confidence. They had acted much more like common rabble than trained soldiers, apparently incapable of maintaining a coherent battle line or responding correctly to Artos's commands to advance, fall back, or wheel. Their attempts to charge were more a halfhearted lurch than a vigorous attack. Worse still, they seemed utterly inept in the handling of their weapons.

In short, the men looked like peasants, smelled like peasants, and talked like peasants. He had no reason to believe they would fight like anything but the lowborn bastards they were.

Artos's excuses had not reassured Bart. He had previously had every confidence in the abilities of that experienced sergeant-at-arms. The fellow had seemed so knowledgeable and professional. But now he was not so certain. Artos's training had not produced the highly skilled warriors he had been led to expect. The sergeant had promised to work his men harder, to bring about a dramatic improvement in their martial performance. Bart remained unconvinced.

Time was very short. The other party might make its move at any point, forcing Bart and his men to begin an immediate pursuit. Their next practice session could well come in actual battle.

Upon returning home, Bart dispatched his servant—what was his name? Oscar? The one the thief had stabbed—to keep watch on the lodging where the map was located and send word if anything important occurred. Though the wound was but slight, the slacker carried on as if it were mortal. Well, he could at least keep watch, though Bart doubted his ability to fulfill even this simple mission with any proficiency.

These reasons and more had put him in a foul temper as he sat alone in the dim light of the library. Everyone, it seemed, was working against him—his father, his servants, his soldiers, his friends. All of them were stupid, greedy, self-serving, and incompetent. Even Gregorio's glad tidings were probably false. He could feel his one chance for real success steadily slipping away.

†

As a new dawn was breaking in the sky, the young lord's bleak musings were interrupted. The library door flew open. Oscar ran in, sweating and out of breath, his injured arm swathed in a huge bandage and carried in a sling.

"Milord…milord…uhhh…"

He was gasping and seemingly unable to formulate a coherent thought. Bart felt himself growing impatient but tried to remain calm rather than exacerbate his servant's confusion.

"Take a deep breath. Now let it out slowly and try to collect your thoughts. There! Well done! Now, sirrah, what is so important?"

"Me 'n' Gyre was watchin' at that old storeroom like you told us. Well, me anyway, but I took Gyre along in case I needed some help. But anyways, these guys come out, a real big guy and two smaller ones who looked like maybe they was from the other side of the river…"

"Do you mean they looked like Keltin tribesmen?"

"Nay…aye…I dunno…maybe… Maybe like that. But what's important is that I told Gyre to follow them, and he did."

"And?"

"They went down to the docks and got into a boat."

"A boat? What kind of a boat?"

"I dunno what kind it's called, milord. I didn't see it, and Gyre, he didn't know. He said it's one of them flat-bottomed ones what carries things up and down the river. The kind that brings in the good stuff from over the river."

Bart allowed himself a knowing smile. So they were finally making their move, and it was to be by water. His sense of purpose restored, he at once turned on the hapless servant.

"Back to your post, sirrah. Get back and keep watch. Go do your job."

The young lord once again felt his dismal mood evaporate in a flood of energy and optimism. He must hire a boat.

CHAPTER TWENTY

THE ITCH

Dawn rose gently over the ancient tower in the tiny village of Grimsgard. Smoke crept from the kitchen as scullery maids rekindled the fire to prepare milady's morning repast. The sky was clear, and the day promised to be pleasant. All comings and goings were conducted in a hush until a piercing scream shattered the peace of that early hour.

Milady was awake and unhappy. Maids scurried up the spiral stairs toward their mistress's chamber, all too aware of the penalties that attended tardiness. Male servants followed at a discreet distance in case milady was not yet fully attired or wanted a moment of privacy before their services were required.

They had all been through this many times before and were well versed in how to avoid Lady Renata's wrath. When milady was distressed, it was necessary to be as prompt and attentive as possible.

She had maintained her own household for over ten years now, without the interference of her brother, Lord Drakar. The relationship between the siblings had never been congenial, so when she had suggested making her residence at Grimsgard, her brother had readily agreed. He supplied her with resources sufficient to indulge her whims, yet they were never enough. Lady Renata had an insatiable appetite for wealth and the comforts it brought her.

The ancient watchtower at Grimsgard, originally an austere military installation, had been reborn as an opulent estate. Grinning gargoyles now leered down from the battlements. Stained-glass windows bore the de la Pole family arms, while others carried disquieting occult symbols. Elaborate gardens covered the surrounding grounds. Milady liked to take the air there.

A staff of servants who resided in the decrepit cottages in the nearby village maintained the estate. Though the tower was sumptuous, Grimsgard's village was squalid and dilapidated. There were a few craftsmen to provide the goods and services needed in any village, and only a handful of ragged serfs tilled, sowed, and harvested milady's fields. The mistress cared little for agriculture.

All this was under the absolute control of Lady Renata, who enjoyed the power of life and death over her many lackeys and minions. To be sure, it was extraordinary for a woman to hold such authority in her own hands. But the de la Pole family was no ordinary family. Lord Drakar de la Pole was one of the most ruthless nobles in all the realm and one of the most feared. His reputation for cruelty and callous disregard for human life was unsurpassed.

While his sister embellished her dwelling with grotesque faces carved in stone, he routinely lined the walls of his castle with the heads of those who displeased him. Many were those of Keltin tribesmen, taken during his frequent raids into their tribal areas. Others came from lazy serfs or inattentive servants. It was not prudent to annoy Lord Drakar.

Though the bond between Renata and Drakar was far from warm, neither was it hostile. Indeed, it was rumored that she often employed her occult skills to further his military exploits. 'Twas said that he possessed a direful weapon in the form of a noxious black gas that brought death to all who inhaled it. Such a horror could have been born only in the workshop of an experienced magician.

†

That morning, Renata awakened to the sensation that her skin was crawling with insects. As she instinctively moved to brush them away, she saw that her body was covered with tiny red bumps. The mere touch of her hand was enough to initiate a maddening itch, such an itch as she could not help but scratch. It was scratch or surrender sanity, but the scratching brought no relief.

Rather, it caused the bumps to burst, and this turned the itch into a burn as agonizing as the sulfur pits of hell.

So Renata screamed for her servants, and when they entered, she called for soothing balms, for cool water, for anything on hand that might relieve her misery. She knew nothing so mundane could offer much remedy, for her suffering was of magical derivation, but the itch was intolerable. Worse still, she knew someone had sent it to her.

Renata was naturally livid. She had, of course, in her own time, sent scores of such visitations to those unfortunate enough to have aroused her ire. But this was the first time some brazen caitiff had dared to afflict her. She rose, burning, itching, and angry beyond words. Clothes were a torment, so she cast off her nightdress and stormed out of her room and up the stairs to her workshop on the topmost floor. She worked better naked anyway.

Seeing her coming, the servants fled back down the stairs to the lower level, all thoughts of cooling unguents and comforting salves forgotten. They understood it was time to get out of her way.

The itch was really a very minor spell, one Renata had learned while still a girl and had used frequently to chastise any who denied her adolescent desires. She could dispel it easily enough. What was more, she had long since mastered the technique of returning the spell to its sender.

It had to be that ugly, crook-shouldered man who had tried to spy on her with the magic mirror. The one, she suspected, who had confounded her familiar, Aborax. Let him then fall into his own itchy trap. She would increase its intensity tenfold just to keep him entertained. She laughed in spite of her discomfort, called his abhorrent visage to her mind, and began the spell of turning.

By midafternoon Renata was much improved. The angry red bumps had been reduced to blotchy patches, and the itching and burning were almost entirely gone. She hoped that Rupert would not appear until the blotches too had dissipated altogether. She was vain of her looks, which she took great care to maintain. Further, she knew Rupert set great store by a woman's beauty, and she was still at a point where his feelings were of some account.

She was under no illusions concerning Rupert. He was but the latest in a long series of very pretty men with whom she had dallied. She was well aware he was using her just as she was using him, that neither felt any genuine commitment to the other's well-being. He would, therefore, be indulged as long as it pleased her to do so. After that, it depended.

The theft of the mirror had all been Rupert's idea. He knew she was always keen for more gold, so he had pleaded and cajoled until she had acquiesced to fund the adventure. Watching him beg like that had pleased her.

Success would be a certainty, he had said. He had an informer inside the Staynes mansion who would make it inevitable. Renata did not find out until later that this was a hatchet-faced little trull with whom she had to share Rupert's favors. That bitch was now disposed of, and she would, of course, settle the score with Rupert at some point later on.

Rupert had sworn that he would recover a treasure beyond imagination. He would, he promised, bring her a ruby necklace with stones the size of swallows' eggs, and the rarest magical items, powerful beyond human reckoning. She doubted all this. How could he possibly have such information? But it pleased her to play along, at least for the time being. And if he actually succeeded, she could always use the wealth.

Rupert, she knew, was a nobody. The youngest son of the youngest son of some impoverished family from the most minor stratum of the nobility. The pitiable child of some uncouth backwoods knight with no money or land holdings. Indeed, he was little better than a peasant. But he was entirely without honor or character, which she found useful. And he possessed the charm of the most polished courtier combined with the beauty of a cherub. She adored his long, curled hair. So for the time being at least, she would indulge him.

And she had indulged him. She had even provided the means for that business with that hideous troll hand, as if she could really concern herself with something so vile. These were her thoughts when Rupert arrived, out of breath from charging up the steps at full speed.

"Milady, I bear the most urgent news."

"Well, Rupert?"

"Staynes and his men are on the move."

This was important news. She had maintained a regular surveillance with the mirror, but the images had always remained cloudy. Staynes, she knew, was under the cover of a cloaking spell. Rupert, however, had most thoughtfully posted men to keep watch on Staynes Hall.

"Sims's men saw him come out early this morning. They followed him down to the docks where he hired a riverboat, one large enough for a score of men. He's going by water."

"Then it stands to reason, dearest Rupert, that you should do likewise. Hie thee hence to the river and acquire a boat."

"Large river-going vessels come dear, milady."

"Silly Rupert! Simply use my name. 'Twill suffice, I'm sure. Go now. Away with you!"

In fact, Renata's only real interest in the matter was to see him off until her blotches cleared up.

†

When Renata turned the itch spell, she sent it scurrying back to Gorgonholm. As quick as thought, it ascended to the aether and retraced its steps to the city in search of the short, ugly, lopsided man to which it had been dispatched. But that person was only an illusion, created by the clever Sarah, so the spell had nowhere to land.

Ever dutiful, the orphan spell circled and circled in the clouds above the city, desperately seeking to deliver its message of itch and burn. A multitude of other spells crossed its path as it hunted. Engorged purple lust spells were by far and away the slowest, while the red spells of vengeance were much quicker. There were also envy spells, green of course, nudged by the golden spells of greed. A death curse, black as midnight, was shown due deference and given right-of-way. The itch spell was itself a dark yellow, the color of disease.

Finally, the itch slowed, descended, and hovered above a remarkably ordinary shop in a nondescript neighborhood. Smoke rose slowly from an oven chimney, along with the smell of baking bread. Hesitating no longer, the spell swooped in to make its awful delivery.

Inside, an elderly baker was mixing still another batch of dough. Though he was heavily spattered with flour, the spell could nonetheless discern the unpleasing features of his toothless, pockmarked face. He stirred the huge crockery mixing bowl with some difficulty. He had, as a child, been pushed down a flight of steps in a tumult with an older brother. His right shoulder, broken in the fall, had not been properly set, causing it to droop substantially lower than the left.

The spell was delighted to be able to accomplish its mission and flew at once straight up the baker's nose.

†

Back at Grimsgard, Renata was rewarded with that warm, tingly feeling she always got whenever one of her spells hit its mark. That feeling alone was sufficient motivation to keep her casting spells. It was far more gratifying than anything she had experienced during her carnal endeavors with Rupert—with any of her Ruperts, for that matter.

CHAPTER TWENTY-ONE

FINAL PREPARATIONS

Sarah was beginning to panic. If she was going to be of use to these impetuous men on their harebrained adventure, she would need to advance her magical abilities far beyond her present level. But she had no more time. She would have to try to study on the boat.

She had constructed a wand but was still unable to charge it with her psychic energy. She had scarcely begun her spell book, the study of which was important to the rejuvenation of her power. She knew only a half-dozen spells.

On the other hand, the spells she had recently cast had worked wonderfully. Her glamour spells had easily deceived Thurmond and the man she had robbed. Her warding spell had frustrated the destructive intentions of the imp, and her charm was keeping it imprisoned in the jug. So she was not displeased with the results of her efforts to date.

Sarah worked desperately to prepare for the journey—meditating, chanting, and studying—but how could she be expected to focus her will when she was always so damn tired? She remembered reading that while most magicians garnered their psychic energy through abstinence and self-denial, a few relied on indulgence and physical dissipation. She sincerely hoped this might work for her.

She tried to recall the myriad of spells she had encountered in the ancient tomes of her father's library. Which would be the most useful? More importantly, which ones could she master in the short time she had left?

She seemed to have the best luck with spells of illusion, spells intended to disguise, delude, or misdirect. The effectiveness of such spells depended not only on the power of the magician but also on the willingness of the target to be deceived. Thus, they drew less psychic energy than other forms of spells.

The more Sarah thought about it, the more it became obvious that illusion was her best option. She tried to recall the ones she had encountered. A sleep spell would be useful. If you can convince an enemy that he is exhausted, he might prefer having a nap to trying to kill you. A cloud of darkness would be good. And perhaps something more dramatic, like the sudden appearance of an illusory monster.

Could she acquire such spells in time? She just did not know. But she did know that it was extremely perilous for a magician to cast a spell that was not perfectly mastered. Anything could happen. At best, the spell would simply fail. At worse, it could turn against the caster rather than strike the target. Or an outcome altogether unintended or unexpected could result. Perhaps a deluge of sewage instead of a cloak of invisibility.

She was worried that her cloaking spell had failed. The imp and the three would-be assassins had discovered their hideout. Somebody had penetrated their magical camouflage. She could almost feel unseen eyes upon her.

And she needed a new ink pot, damn it.

Sarah forgot her worries when Thurmond, Roscoe, and Torgul came clumping into the lodging, laughing, swearing, and bearing tremendous burdens that they threw to the floor such force that the structure shook. When she peeked out through the door, Roscoe, who was red faced and had obviously been drinking, greeted her.

"Holla, Sarah! We come bearing the manly tools of war! Come and see! Come and see! We have somethin' special for you. Weapons and armor from the holy smithy of God, so they are."

The pile of rusty mail, worn leather, battered shields, and shabby weapons strewn on the floor seemed to her to be of anything but divine origin.

Their boyish antics annoyed her, but her mood brightened when Torgul presented her with a new ink pot, a replacement for the one she had smashed while saving his life. If was much nicer than the old one, with her name inscribed in gold leaf. He handed it to her without a word. Dwarves tended toward the laconic.

She looked doubtfully at the pile of weaponry

"Where did you get all this stuff?"

"On loan, you might say, from friend Einarr. A gesture of love from one brother to another."

Thurmond interjected,

"We had to promise him part of the treasure."

Sarah was leery.

"How large a part?"

Thurmond named a figure.

"What? That's not coming out of my share, Roscoe! Nay, this is not to be borne."

Roscoe assumed his most soothing and placating tone.

"Nay, lassie. You misunderstand. Thurmond and I already worked it out. This expense comes off the top before we divvy up, so we all share in it. Each of us will have to contribute but a little. A tiny trifle in the long run. And 'tis an entirely necessary expenditure.

"We can't go facin' the fell creatures of the underground without proper harness, now can we? And looky here—we have the nicest little mailshirt that's just your size. Must have been made for an elf maiden, so it was. And a lovely wee helmet to keep your pretty head from harm. Just a small one, light as a feather, so as not to tire your sweet neck."

As much as she resented the added expense, Sarah was irresistibly drawn to the pile of armaments. They had an undeniable allure. She had seen such items often enough. Armored men were a common sight in the streets of Gorgonholm. But this was her first opportunity to really heft a sword and experience its weight and balance. She was surprised by how light and wieldy it actually was. The blade just seemed to want to work, to jump out and stick someone in the belly.

The armor had much the same appeal. Her mailshirt was supple and comfortable, if a bit heavy. Roscoe showed her how to cinch a belt tight around her middle to take some of the weight off her shoulders. She might not win any races while wearing her mail, but she knew she could run and even jump if she had to.

Roscoe addressed her with a playful twinkle in his eye.

"How would you be takin' it off now?"

Sarah crossed her arms and tried to lift it off over her head, the same as she would a chemise, but the mail bunched at her elbows and stuck there. The more she struggled, the more entangled she became. She let it go, hoping it would drop back into place, but it stuck fast around her arms.

Roscoe and Torgul, obviously familiar with what would happen, broke into loud guffaws. She tried again and thought she was making progress, but then the cursed mail grabbed a handful of her hair and seemed determined to pull it out by the roots. It snagged her ears, then her nose, and threatened to tear them loose.

Her arms were growing tired from the weight of all those iron rings. She yanked and tugged, but the shirt only bunched up beneath her chin and grasped her throat as if to strangle her. Her nose received another savage tweak.

Finally Roscoe came forward.

"Here, lassie, we meant no offense. 'Tis an old joke that we always play on beginners. Gettin' free of a mailshirt is easy when you got your head lower down than your…uh…hindquarters. Just point the top of your head at the floor, like. A little lower now. There!"

The shirt slithered over her effortlessly, taking no more than a small clump of hair with it. Her shoulders gave a sigh of relief.

"You should wear it as much as you can to get accustomed to the weight. We also brought you an adorable little bow. Have you shot a bow before, lassie? Nay? Well, you should try to practice while we're on the boat. Thurmond, too. I'll show you the basics."

Sitting in a circle on the floor, they parceled out the war gear. Roscoe and Torgul each had a long hauberk of riveted mail and an open-faced helmet with a stout nasal bar. Both had heavy shields, Torgul's round and Roscoe's triangular. The helmets of Sarah and Thurmond were lighter and close fitting, little more than metal skullcaps. Thurmond was presented with a coat of plates, which fit him much better than the one he had worn on the practice field.

Thurmond had his old poniard and the shortsword of the man he had slain. He was also given a short bow. Roscoe explained that he and Sarah would annoy any approaching foe with their arrows, but when the fighting was hand to hand, it would be up to him and Torgul. The archers would stand immediately behind the Adventurers, who would protect them with their shields. If they saw an opening, they should take it, but mostly they should keep back out of the way.

Roscoe promised to give Thurmond as much fighter practice as he could while they journeyed down the river. Then he solemnly announced they would embark at tomorrow's dawn.

There were so many things to get ready before that early hour. Torgul immediately began repairing their tattered armor and battle-worn weapons. The floor of the lodging was soon strewn with leather lacing, iron rivets, and small shards of metal that stuck in Sarah's feet whenever she walked through barefoot.

Thurmond was set to work honing the edges of each sword and dagger. Sarah gathered her magical items and then began tying their food, bedding, and extra clothes into bundles. Roscoe left for a final conference with Scrymgeour.

The next morning Sarah emerged from her room, not in the flowing kirtle of a woman, but in the tight breeks, high boots, and short tunic of a man. Thurmond was uncertain as to how he felt about this. He had been raised to believe there was a proper way to go about things—that women should dress and act like women, and men like men. But he had of late been forced to reconsider many of his basic assumptions. And he had to admit that the form-fitting outfit was becoming.

Sarah seemed to read his mind. She scoffed.

"You didn't expect me to go adventuring in a long dress, did you? Not bloody likely! Take a good look and get used to it."

PART 3

THE RIVER VOYAGE

CHAPTER TWENTY-TWO

THE RIVERBOAT

Scrymgeour's riverboat, according to Roscoe, was a spacious vessel that would permit them to wend their wide and merry way down the river in ease and pleasure. It was, he claimed, an expansive forty cubits in length and twelve in width, ensuring ample space for personal comfort. Thurmond had no idea what a cubit was, but he had learned to be cautious of Roscoe's hyperbolic praise. Mostly he was uneasy about the water. Like most people, he had never learned to swim—even sailors saw no point in it. He had never been on a boat before and had no particular desire to do so now.

When he finally saw the vessel, it was hardly the stately pleasure craft he had been led to expect. Rather, it was a simple working riverboat much like the many shallow-draft boats that hauled goods up and down the Mad River. Almost flat bottomed, such boats drew so little water that their captains boasted they could make way in a heavy dew.

Though devoid of ornament, Scrymgeour's craft bespoke efficiency and practicality. On downriver excursions, it relied on the current for propulsion, though a flat, square sail could be hoisted if the wind was right. Or the crew, usually comprised of six to ten, could man long sweeps to augment a sluggish current or hesitant breeze. At places where rapids or drops prohibited nautical traffic, teams of oxen could haul such lightweight craft from the river and drag it overland on log rollers to a location agreeable for safe passage. In shallow, currentless sections, the crew could push the boat along with long poles, or it could be drawn by oxen trudging along a towpath running parallel with the river.

A long, low cabin occupied most of the available space. Here the crew slept during inclement weather, and the more sensitive items of cargo were protected against the elements. Its flat roof was walled by a bulwark of strong timbers, behind which the crew could defend themselves with slings, spears, and arrows. A light ballista was mounted on a tripod in the roof's center. Though small, the weapon looked powerful enough to dissuade all but the most bellicose of attackers.

As a stipulation of his arrangement with Roscoe, Scrymgeour had agreed to provide his boat, his sons, and four able boatmen to serve as crew. In exchange for his designated cut of the proceeds, Nod and Sod would accompany the party on the entire adventure, sharing whatever tribulations befell them. The four remaining boatmen would stay with the vessel, guard it against any marauders, and provide whatever nautical services were required. Scrymgeour himself would not be joining them on this venture.

The quayside was all bustle and clamor. Boats and barges of all sizes and configurations were pulling in or pulling out. Gangs of dockers sang slow, doleful work songs as they loaded or unloaded the endless piles of freight. The air stank of hot tar and rotting fish.

Scrymgeour greeted Roscoe with a bear hug and then instructed the rest of the party to stow their gear in the cabin. Even though the boat was not laden with proper cargo on this journey, it was cluttered with bundles, buckets, barrels, sheaves of ballista bolts, and baskets of dried fish.

With the final details attended to, Scrymgeour produced a stone bottle. Holding it on high, he offered a loud but wholly incomprehensible proclamation. Roscoe chuckled and translated.

"He's wishing us a successful venture. It's an old waterman custom."

Scrymgeour took a long pull from the bottle and passed it to Nod and Sod, who drank as eagerly as their father. Roscoe and then Torgul drank deeply. When the bottle came to Sarah, she sniffed it suspiciously before lifting it to her lips for a first tentative taste. But then satisfied, she too took a careful swig.

Thurmond was determined to drink like a true Adventurer. He upended the bottle and poured a stream of the unknown liquid down his throat. Horror! His mouth seemed to be filled with fire. Eyes and nose began to run in a steady stream. He choked as his throat tried to close itself. It was uisge, the drink so beloved on both sides of the river, and it left Thurmond unable to see, speak, or even breathe.

The ritual done, Scrymgeour stepped off the boat and onto the quay. The adventure was officially underway.

As it turned out, Thurmond loved the boat. The allure of the open river proved irresistible, and he claimed a spot in the very point of the prow where he could feel every plunge as the craft made its way downstream. Never before had he known the exultation of movement or such an intense awareness of freedom.

The countryside stretched out on both sides of the river, like a great scroll being unrolled. The western shore, the wild side, was densely forested and revealed little evidence of human habitation. The eastern shore, the civilized side, was replete with farms and villages. Church steeples and the crenellated tops of towers rose above clusters of thatched roofs.

Thurmond wanted to see it all. He realized for the first time how confined his former life had been, even after his arrival in the city. The boat ride opened the door to a whole new existence.

The river had, over the centuries, caused Gorgonholm to grow into a wealthy trade city. The fertile soil of the region yielded great harvests of rye, oats, and millet. Heavily loaded wanes carried these crops to the merchants' warehouses along the inner sides of the city wall. Peasant farmers brought in apples, nuts, onions, and eggs to sell in the Market Square. Great herds of cattle, pigs, goats, and sheep were driven daily to the slaughterhouses, the New Shambles, that lined the eastern bank of the river. The shops and stalls of vendors and artisans were crammed into every available space.

People came from every direction with something to barter. Frequent caravans from the south and east offered luxury items and manufactured goods. The descendants of the Vanarians, far less aggressive than their fiery ancestors, brought exotic furs, raw amber, and fine whale oil down from the frozen north. Tattooed Keltin tribesmen crossed the river with honey, beeswax, and unrefined lumps of copper, tin, and gold.

However, the real business of these tribesmen was the smuggling of uisge, their volatile distilled liquor. It was exceedingly popular in the city, being far more potent than anything to be found in the more civilized lands where the process of distilling was unknown. The tribesmen guarded this secret religiously for they held the drink to be sacred. Only small quantities were brought across the river, keeping the price high—very high. They would not accept gold, or silver, or even gems for this treasured liquid, the name of which was translated as *water of life*. The warrior-traders would accept nothing less than weapons forged of the finest steel.

Providing weapons of any sort to barbarians was a capital offense in Gorgonholm. There had been far too many cross-river raids—along with the occasional invasion—to permit the arming of such hot-tempered and capricious neighbors. But not even the death penalty could deter the Gorgonholmers from slaking their thirst with uisge. On dark nights, small boats would put out from either side of the river, and weapons would be swapped for beverage. Where there is a need, someone will always be willing to supply it. In actuality, little was done to stifle such trade. Uisge was too popular, and it was said that Sheriff Brandon enjoyed it as much as anyone.

Large barges and smaller, nearly flat-bottomed riverboats brought the products of civilization to the far-flung north and the raw materials of the northern wilderness to the south. It brought traders, along with their families, guards, and servants, from a wide array of distant lands. Thus Gorgonholm, though tucked away in the kingdom's northwest corner, enjoyed a cultural diversity unknown in many larger cities.

Sarah sat beside Thurmond for a time but gradually lost interest in the countryside and retired to the cabin to study her magic. Roscoe yakked with Nod and Sod in their incomprehensible riverman dialect. Torgul, obviously an experienced traveler, immediately launched into one of his stories.

"*Hwæt! Much have ye heard of the dwarves of yore. Of the fullness of their beards and the keenness of their swords. Of how they brought terror to their foes and amassed treasure beyond reckoning. Aye—and of their vengeance and valor. But none was more eager for fame than Torgul, first of that name, and yclept the Great.*"

By the twelve toes of God! Nay! Thurmond was not, at that moment, eager for another recounting of the glorious deeds of Torgul's ancestors.

"And so the dwarves of Spear Mountain, sore beset by the boundless goblin hordes, by savage trolls and brute ogres without number, by unnamable creatures called forth from hell's darkest corners, were with certain starvation faced if the siege was not relieved."

Actually, Thurmond had come to like the dwarf far more than he had thought possible. In spite of his boasting, he had an earthy quality Thurmond found endearing. And he had given Sarah the new ink pot. That said a lot.

"Only the most valiant Torgul—with whose blood my veins run full—did possess the courage to break through the iron ring of treacherous foes and fetch a train of vital provender to bring the siege to end."

But right now he was not sure what was worse—dying at the hands of a rampaging goblin or enduring the tedium of Torgul's interminable story.

"And yet in this very moment of his greatest glory was his heart ripped from his breast by the claws of a craven creature, yet still did he fight on, slaying the foul beast and goblins by the thousand until at last he was stuck down from behind in a most perfidious fashion."

Thurmond always loved good adventure stories, but this was too much. Dwarves always exaggerated to the point of absurdity. The beards of their ancestors were always at least twenty feet long.

"And so for his potent deeds and utmost sacrifice was raised a stone wondrous high with his name in runes thereon carved."

Thurmond was certainly eager for fame and fortune, but he hoped his deeds would be recalled in some other fashion than as a dreary old story told by dwarves.

†

The river was broad, and the current was gentle, its endless loops like the slow bends of a great lazy serpent. Nod and Sod took turns manning the tiller, keeping the boat well to the middle of the flow where they would be the greatest possible distance from an attack mounted from either bank. The passengers were assigned lookout duty.

River pirates and Keltin raiders sometimes preyed on such cargo craft. Archers, charging suddenly from hidden positions, would line the riverbank and attempt to reduce the boat crew with flights of arrows. At the same time, swarms of warriors packed in small, fast boats would set out to overtake and board their hapless victim.

To discourage this, Scrymgeour's men were well armed and thoroughly trained in the use of weapons. In addition to the ballista, which was stout enough to punch a hole in the hull of a pirate rowboat, there was a profusion of individual arms: bows, boarding pikes, long pointy daggers, and short choppy swords.

There were other dangers, of course. Unseen rocks or floating logs could stave their boat. A storm could capsize them, or a whirlpool could engulf them. Rapids waited downriver, and the boatmen swore that behemoth-sized water monsters occasionally rose from the Mad River's murky bottom to seize an ill-starred vessel and pull it to its watery doom.

However, when bad fortune did arrive, it came from an altogether unlooked-for direction. Overhead an eagle was soaring back to its nest in anticipation of a fine repast, but the snake clutched in its talons had other ideas. Twisting about, it sank its fangs into its captor's feathered breast. The bird, outraged at this affront, immediately released its prey.

The plummeting reptile landed with a hard thump squarely on the shoulders of Nod, who was at that moment manning the tiller. Seeking its bearings, the creature made one quick circuit around Nod's neck before slithering down his leg, across the deck, and over the riverboat's side.

Nod was in no way injured, but the sudden appearance of such cold, scaly horror sent him into a panic. He threw up his arms and shrieked. In so doing he released the tiller, which allowed the boat to drive hard to the starboard side. Another boatman rushed to right their course, but too late. The boat caromed from a granite boulder, not hard enough to shatter the planking of the hull but sufficient to open its seams and admit a steady stream of water.

Sod suddenly developed a capacity for clear speech in the common tongue.

"All hands to bailing! Lively now! Bail like yer lives depend on it—'cause they does!"

This was true. No one on board could swim.

Sod took over the tiller while the rest of the crew grabbed buckets and began to frantically hurl water over the boat's low gunwale. The passengers joined in, catching up water in whatever receptacle came to hand. But no matter how feverishly they labored, it soon became obvious that more water was coming in than going out.

Happily, the western shore was at that moment a gentle shingle on which the boat could be safely run aground. Sod turned the lumbering craft in this direction, while the others bailed as hard and fast as they could. Skill and perseverance prevailed, and it was at last brought up onto the beach. The brothers inspected the damage. Again Sod was the spokesperson.

"Needs a power of caulkin', which we can do, havin' the necessary pitch and twine. But 'twill take a while, and I ain't likin' this place. Wrong side of the river, you know. And I don't want to be meetin' with the guy who lives 'round these parts. Nod feels just as I does. This ain't no good."

Thurmond was exhausted from all the bailing, but Sod's words made him forget all about that.

"What guy? Who lives here?"

Sod, it seemed, had expended his capacity for speech, so Roscoe took up the conversation.

"There's a strange character lives hereabouts. Never met him, but heard all the tales, and if half of 'em are true, let's just say that he has some exceptional accomplishments to his credit. Goes by the name of Red Charles."

Thurmond had heard of him.! He had been the subject of some of the stories told by Adventurers at the Severed Head. He especially recalled that Red Charles was reputed to enjoy singular dining preferences. Torgul interrupted his reverie.

"Look to your weapons! We got guests comin'."

Sure enough, a line of warriors had crested the low rise behind the shingle and was approaching the boat.

CHAPTER TWENTY-THREE

THE BORDER LORD AND THE BEASTIE

There was no time to pull on their armor, but in a frantic scramble, they grabbed up helmets, shields, and weapons. Two boatmen ascended to the cabin's roof and manned the ballista. Roscoe signaled Thurmond and Sarah to take their bows and climb up, too. He then joined the others in a line of battle along the boat's gunwale.

Thurmond counted fifteen footmen with spears and shields. Behind them rode a single horseman. It seemed likely that they could hold their own against such numbers, unless of course there were greater forces yet unseen. As they grew nigh, he saw that the rider was an old man with long white hair and beard. The latter was of such prodigious length that Torgul already held this stranger in high esteem.

The spearmen halted just beyond bowshot, but the rider came forward, alone and seemingly undaunted. He was a tall man and lean, dressed in rusty mail. His mount was a pony so short of hock that the rider's feet nearly touched the ground. He called out in a voice far more cultivated than one might expect from so outlandish a personage.

"What men are you, bearing weapons in hand, who come unbidden to these lands? I am Charles Borderer, called The Red. These are my lands and my people. Come you in peace or in war? I would be informed! Speak now!"

With a grand ceremonial flourish, Roscoe laid down his sword and shield. Affecting his most winning smile, he stepped over the gunwale into water up to his knees. Then he unleashed his golden tongue.

"I am Roscoe Appleman, member in good standin' of the Brotherhood of Underworld Adventurers, Gorgonholm chapter, and the son of an honest merchant. My boon companion is Torgul Bonelip the Twenty-Third, Lord of the Spear Mountain Dwarves, and likewise an Adventurer Brother in good standin'. These others are our henchmen and minions.

"We mean you no ill, but find ourselves thrust on your shore by no intention of our own. We were on our way to exterminate a nest of goblin river pirates when our boat made an unfortunate acquaintance with a rock. So we find ourselves stranded here until we can make repairs. We will cause you no inconvenience."

Charles urged his pony down to the edge of the shallow water in which Roscoe stood. They were now no more than ten feet apart. Both parties were edgy, alert for any sign of perfidy.

"So you mean to fix your boat and then be on your way. You'll be wanting nothing from me."

This was not said as a question.

"Perhaps only one small favor, generous lord. It seems that when our boat was awash with river water, much of our provender was spoiled. If you could spare but a morsel of meat or bread, just enough to fill our bellies while we make our way…"

"You have a dwarf, you say. He'll be that short fella on the end with the round shield."

"Aye, that's Torgul, so it is."

"Well know this, mister fancy gab, your big smiles won't get you anything here. Life in these parts is hard, and everybody must earn their keep. So you can have the riverbank for the fixing of your boat. But if it's food you want, then you'll have to work for it. Just so happens that I have need of a dwarf at the moment. We've a special problem that's just come up."

"We would be delighted for the chance to aid our gracious host in whatever reasonable task he might set us. May I inquire as to the precise nature of your present difficulty?"

"Some beastie crawled out of a cave and killed three of my beeves. My men tracked it back to its lair and have it trapped, but they're not used to the underground and don't know how to kill it. So a dwarf is just what I need."

"And the exact nature of this creature?"

"I'm no authority on cave-dwelling varmints, but it looks to be like the garden slugs that eat the leaves from my turnips. Only much, much bigger."

So it was settled. The boatmen would stay and make repairs while the others went off with their host to slay a giant slug. Ignoring his guests, Charles kicked the pony into a trot and headed inland. His file of spearmen followed him, and Roscoe and the others followed them. A narrow path wound its way up the slope of a rocky hillside. Thurmond, bubbling over with eagerness, sidled up next to Sarah.

"Sarah, I know who he is! I've heard stories about him. He's legendary!"

"Who? The old guy on the pony? He looks more like a scarecrow than a legend to me."

"That's Liver-Eatin' Charlie, that's who. He's nobody you want to cross."

"Why? What will he do? What did you call him?"

"Liver-Eatin' Charlie. Story goes that years ago a bunch of drunk Keltins wiped out his village, including his family. This was back when he was young, and it made him go kind of barmy. Started raiding their villages, sneaking in at night, and cutting their throats. And you want to know what he did then?"

"I guess so—what?"

"He'd cut out their livers and eat them raw. That's how he got his name, Liver-Eatin' Charlie. All the Adventurers hold him in high regard."

"Ugghh, sorry I asked."

They now arrived at the crest of the hill and looked down on a huge point of rock that thrust out from its side like the prow of a ship. A ditch-and-bank fortification topped by a palisade of logs stretched across the base of the point, isolating it from the rest of the hillside. Beyond that, a semicircular wall of unmortared stone offered a second layer of defense.

Within this, a squat, drystone round tower of a type known as a *broch* rose above a clutch of very low and dreary huts. The air was smudged with smoke and reeked of dung. One hut, just slightly larger than the rest, bore a crude rendition of the solar symbol that marked all Charonite churches. The huts in the outer enclosure were even more dreary, being little more than great piles of gorse with tiny openings that seemed to serve as doors.

Red Charles reined in at the ramshackle bridge that spanned the ditch and waited until the others caught up.

"We'll be taking the path on around the hill to a cave where the beastie is at bay. But the wench stays here. This be no business for a female. She'll be safe until we return. But tell her to stay in the first ward, not to pass through the stone gate or venture back out. She can look through the gate and admire our fine kirk if she's of a mind."

These words were addressed directly to Roscoe, though Sarah stood just by his side. To Thurmond's surprise, she obeyed this injunction without demur and began at once to cross the bridge to the first enclosure. Such meek acquiescence was not at all typical of Sarah. He felt certain she was up to something.

The column began to move again, this time along the side of the hill. Thurmond got his first good look at his host. The old man was clad in rusty mail that quite literally hung in rags. Years of wear and neglect had left large holes in its weave. Links dangled loose in long, tattered strands. An ancient helmet, badly rusted and battered almost beyond recognition, was suspended from his saddle. Liver-Eatin' Charlie was unquestionably the most ill-equipped warrior he had ever seen.

They came at last to a mass of boulders, in the midst of which Thurmond spied the mouth of a cave. Another half dozen of Red Charles's spearmen were lounging on the grass around it but immediately jumped to their feet at the arrival of the column. The entrance was about half as high as a man is tall, so even Torgul would be forced to stoop a bit. Charles again spoke to Roscoe.

"It came out of here sometime last night and killed my beeves. My men followed its slime back to this spot. This morning I sent Hamish down the hole. He says it's in there, curled up in a blind alley and can't get away. He shot some arrows at it, but they had no effect, just kind of sunk in without doing damage. Then it spat some kind of venom on Hamish that burned his face bad. He won't be so pretty after today, I think."

"Did you try fire?"

"Of course, we tried fire. We're not stupid! It just spat more venom and put it out. And be wary as you descend. This cavern abounds in lethal serpents."

There was nothing for it but to go down for a look. Torgul led the way, followed by Roscoe. Thurmond, as ordered, brought up the rear. His job was to hold a torch because only Torgul could see in the lightless confines of the underground. The passageway was low, narrow, confining, and, Thurmond was quite certain, stunk of snake. He and Roscoe were forced to scoot along as best they could on their knees. The latter's stiff leg made this operation most difficult.

Sure enough, the creature was holed up in a small chamber that branched off the main passageway at a downward angle. Removing his helmet, Torgul peeked carefully around the corner. The thing was perhaps twenty feet long if fully stretched, but this was hard to determine with any certainty. At the moment it was little more than an amorphous blob, roughly in the dimensions of the chamber it occupied.

It steadfastly declined to acknowledge the presence of the intruders until the torch was brought forward to give Roscoe a look. Then two long eyestalks extended from what appeared to be its head. Roscoe stepped back at once, having seen what he needed to see. He had no wish to be splattered with the thing's caustic slime. His brief glance had revealed the shafts of several arrows embedded in its translucent, gelatinous bulk. Half-burnt torches and a scorched bundle of tow were scattered on the floor before it, evidence of the prior attacks.

"Ever seen the like, Torgul?"

"Nay, nor heard no stories neither. But our host is correct—it bears strikin' resemblance to a common garden slug. Only much, much bigger."

"Well, I see no profit in an attack with sword and shield when arrows did it so little injury. Could we perhaps impale it on a great sharpened log?"

"And how would you have us bring such a thing through the twists and turns of this passage?"

"How about salt then? I remember cruel games played on slugs by children armed with common salt."

They returned to the surface and related their findings to their host. At the mention of salt, Red Charles began to bluster.

"And who is to pay for this salt? Salt is very, very dear in these parts. We need every bit to preserve the fish that come from the river. I hired you to kill this cursed creature, not squander my precious resources."

Roscoe and Torgul stood silently and clearly at a loss. It was then Thurmond's turn to proffer a suggestion.

"How about uisge? That stuff of Scrymgeour's almost melted my throat. Maybe it would do for the beastie."

Roscoe and Torgul liked the idea, but Charles again made a vehement objection.

"I don't approve of ardent spirits. We are all Reformed Charonites here, and it is not permitted that we sully our god-given brains with such heathen drink. 'Tis base sin. You'll find no uisge on my premises."

Roscoe gave Thurmond a knowing look and a secret wink before turning to their host.

"Lord Charles, we've had a look at the beast and taken his measure. Leave it to us. The vile creature is as good as dead, so it is. Torgul here is a genius when it comes to rooting fell beasts from their underground lairs. You might as well go home and relax a bit. We'll take care of this for you."

"I shall do as you suggest. I like it not to hand over my problems to others, but you are to receive fair compensation for your efforts on my part. And I have, at the moment, much work to do in preparation for the harvest. How many of my men will you require?"

"No more than two or three."

†

As soon as Charles set off for home, Roscoe had conversation with the three spearmen left behind. Coins were passed, and these three quickly departed. Roscoe and Torgul stretched out on the hillside as if preparing to sleep. When Thurmond asked them to explain, they reminded him that he was a mere hang-around. He was to keep a close eye on the cave mouth and wake them if the creature started to emerge. With that, they began to doze.

Before an hour had lapsed, the three spearmen returned, each bearing a cask. The two Adventurers stood up, stretched, and laughed. Torgul procured a hatchet from one of the men and handed it to Thurmond. A cask was likewise thrust into his hands. Torgul and Roscoe hoisted the other two casks, and the three of them went back down the tunnel.

Kneeling just around the corner from the creature's lair, Roscoe beckoned for Thurmond to give him the hatchet.

"No matter what that holy joe of a lordship might say, laddie, there's no way on God's green earth to keep a man from the honest pleasure of uisge. Red Charlie might not want to believe it, but a bit of money will always buy a wee drink. Or even perhaps a couple of casks."

With that, he swung the hatchet and smote open the end of the cask he had been carrying. The pungent aroma of the liquor filled the tunnel.

"This seems like a terrible waste, so it does, but it serves the greater good."

He rolled the shattered cask down the slope into the chamber of the slug thing. Torgul's cask followed close behind.

As soon as the uisge made contact with the slug's body, it surged upward as if attempting to launch itself into the air. The eyestalks shot forth again, but this time they were three times longer than on the previous occasion. The outer membrane began to hiss, bubble, and boil. The creature rolled from side to side as its flesh began to dissolve into thick, yellow ooze. The eyestalks fell limp, landed in the pool of liquor, and shriveled to nothing.

Roscoe broke the end from the third cask. It contained salt stolen from Red Charles's larder.

"All righty, laddie, time to prove yourself. The thing's done for, but we want to make sure. Go down and dump this salt on that puddle of seething ooze. Show us you've got the stuff Adventurers is made of."

CHAPTER TWENTY-FOUR

THE THREE BOATS

They returned to Red Charles's stronghold in good spirits. The spearmen had the good sense to fetch a flask of uisge as well as the casks, which they all shared on the way back. Even Thurmond managed a few careful swallows. Sarah saw them coming and met them at the bridge. She too was beaming and was about to relate a story when Charles rode up on his pony. Roscoe, as party leader, again stepped forward.

"You may delight in the knowledge that the foul beast will trouble you no more. We sent it back to the hell from which it crawled. Utterly and completely destroyed."

"You're telling me it's dead."

"Dead, dead, dead. Deader than hell, so it is. Your men will confirm if you like."

Charles's men, of course, had not ventured back into the cavern and had, therefore, neither witnessed the destruction of the slug nor inspected its liquefied remains. But Roscoe had bribed them generously to confirm his assertions.

Charles waved his hand dismissively.

"I take you at your word. I have an ass ready to be loaded with food. It will be delivered to your boat within the hour."

"And what, if I may inquire, is the nature of the victuals that you so generously provide?"

"Oats."

"Aye, oats are fine. And aught else?"

"Oats. Oats. Only oats."

"No salt pork? Nor fish? Nor even a bit of cheese? Naught but oats?"

"If it's such elegant sustenance you're craving, then you should have stayed in the city where they delight in such things. But God loves simple fare that don't distract from our duty to him. Oats will keep you going. Food need not do more than that."

So oats it was.

†

Thurmond was so eager to tell Sarah of his adventure that the words came bursting from him in an incomprehensible stream. She apparently felt the same way, for she jumped into an equally unintelligible tale. Neither was even remotely listening to the other. Finally Thurmond relented.

"Okay, okay, ladies first. Go ahead."

"Well, when we were first standing by the old man's bridge, I saw that one of those brush huts had magical charms hanging all over it—bones, feathers, strips of cloth tied in special knots. So I knew a witch or wizard lived there, and I thought maybe they could tell me something useful. That's why I was so cooperative when the old guy was being such a pig's arse and wouldn't even talk to me. I wanted to go in there.

"But things turned out better than I hoped. Used to be a druid lived there, but he died. And that Charlie guy has got the whole village so drowning in Charonism that the people are still afraid to go inside. They think it's some demon's den. But, of course, I went in as soon as nobody was looking.

"Druids aren't allowed to write anything down. They have to keep all their spells in their heads. But this one had a big book on ceremonial magic. Not druid magic, but the kind I do. I don't know why he had it. Anyway, I took it, and it's going to help us a lot."

"You stole his book?"

"Aye, he doesn't need it anymore. And I got some scrolls, too."

"What do they say?"

"I don't know. They're in a language I can't read, but maybe I'll figure them out in time. This book might help us get the treasure—might help us stay alive."

Thurmond was a little let down. He had been extremely eager to tell her of the slaying of the slug thing, especially how the veteran Adventurers had chosen him to venture alone into its very lair to deliver the final killing blow, though he knew that in reality he had done little more than dump a cask of salt on a puddle of bubbling ooze. By comparison, her accomplishment seemed much more significant.

So he told the story, but he was careful not to aggrandize his exploits. He was beginning to lose some of his faith in heroes. The penurious and choleric old man they had encountered bore no resemblance to the valiant, if somewhat deranged, figure of legend. Even Roscoe and Torgul were not what he expected. They were bold enough, certainly, and cunning in their way, but their actions stemmed much more from workmanlike efficiency than high ideals.

Yet he genuinely liked and respected them both—even, to his surprise, the dwarf. He enjoyed Roscoe's good humor and frequent jests. He appreciated Torgul's unlooked-for sensitivity. They had teased him unmercifully for his nervousness while salting the slug. He knew, though, that this was not prompted by unkindness but was part of his initiation into the Brotherhood. So he had submitted without complaint and in the end had laughed along with them.

Back at the boat, Sod had declared that if they worked through most of the night, they could proceed the next morning. Having removed the old caulking from the damaged area on the hull, the crew was now busy tapping new twine between the planks and then sealing the seams with melted pitch.

The oats arrived as promised, in two medium-sized sacks. Once again Roscoe had conversation with Charles's men, and once again some coins changed hands. Late that night they returned, this time more heavily burdened with a variety of containers and casks. Thurmond pondered Red Charles's reaction when he discovered the plundering of his larder. Would it provoke another frenzy of liver-eating madness?

As soon as it was light enough to see, Roscoe roused the crew and announced their immediate departure. He too, it seemed, had little desire to face the wrath of Liver-Eatin' Charlie. It required all their strength to heave the boat back off the shingle, but it was at last accomplished, and the journey was again underway.

✝

Their departure was noted with keen interest by an unseen observer hiding in the bushes directly across the river. As soon as the riverboat left the shore, the scout sprinted through the surrounding trees, back to where another boat lay concealed behind one of the river's many prodigious bends. It was larger, faster, and altogether better appointed than Scrymgeour's vessel, almost a small ship. Bartholomew Staynes had spared no expense in providing his party with the finest river craft he could find.

Because of Gregorio's psychic connection with the map, Bart could track the movements of Scrymgeour's boat. Sarah's cloaking spell still denied him a clear picture of the boat and its passengers, but Gregorio's information allowed him to keep pace with his quarry as they proceeded downriver.

After several days of being confined on board with Gregorio, Bart had come to despise the man once again. He had no social graces and was forever presuming on Bart's forgiving nature by neglecting to show proper deference. He gloated about his knowledge and his ability to read. He once went so far as to clap Bart on the shoulder while attempting to make some stupid jest. He snored. He chewed with his mouth open so that food often fell out. His night farts were ghastly foul.

On the other hand, Bart had come to feel somewhat reconciled with Artos after the unpleasant episode on the practice field. He was a simple soldier who took orders well and asked no questions. He kept his men in a good state of discipline and was unfailingly deferential, holding himself and his men at a respectful distance from their master.

The scout, one of Artos's men, emerged from the trees above the riverbank. He was running and obviously bore tidings. He was yelling something as he ran, none of which Bart could understand. It would be necessary to bring him aboard with the small dory tied alongside the larger craft. Two boatmen were already climbing down into it. The scout reached the riverbank, where he began gesturing wildly and shouting unintelligible words.

The dory retrieved its passenger and started back. As it approached Bart's boat, the scout jumped to his feet and began waving more frantically than ever.

"Milord! Milord! They've taken ship! They're on the river!"

†

Just as the scout had watched Scrymgeour's boat get underway, another pair of hidden eyes was peering through the foliage as Bart's boatmen thrust out oars and took up the stroke. A bit farther upriver, just around another bend, a third boat lay hove to, waiting for word of its quarry. It was smaller than the other two—low, slim, and sleek—obviously built for speed rather than for comfort or cargo.

More than a dozen men loitered on the riverbank, glad for the opportunity to stretch their legs. Rupert and Plutonius were pointedly ignoring each other. Sims and six of his henchmen lounged in the shade of an ancient oak, passing a bottle and speaking in low tones. Four oarsmen and a tillerman comprised the boat crew.

They too were ready to depart the instant word came that Bart was again on the move. Rupert knew they had to be careful to maintain just the right distance between his craft and that of Staynes. Before embarkation, Renata had shrouded the boat in a mist spell. It was not invisible, but its outline had been rendered blurred and indistinct. It was very difficult to spot against the background of riverbank and trees as long as they did not get too close.

Like all illusion spells, the mist spell could be broken if disbelieved. If the boat approached too near, Staynes's lookouts might see something to make them suspicious, which could leave Rupert prematurely revealed. He was not yet ready for a direct confrontation with his enemy. He wanted to pick the time and place so that the advantages would all lie on his side.

Rupert had almost despaired when Renata announced that she did not intend to accompany him on this adventure. He had always just assumed that she would come, that he would have her magical abilities to back him up, so this had been a serious complication. At first, he thought she just needed some coaxing. He was used to wheedling to get his way with things. But this time she had been adamant. He recalled that conversation with some bitterness.

"Has my darling Rupert completely lost his reason? It must be so if he could even imagine that I would go camping. I wasn't born to spend my days cramped in a dreadful, little boat with a crew of stinking churls. Nor have I any intention of ever sleeping rough. So sorry, my dear, but you have completely missed the mark this time."

"But surely milady must recognize how completely indispensable she is to this venture…and to me. Without her boundless skills as an enchantress, we might well lose the treasure to Staynes. Your entire investment could be lost. I, your loyal Rupert, could meet his end."

"Then my most loyal Rupert is well advised to take great care, for I do not look favorably on the prospect of losing either the treasure or my investment— nor my loyal Rupert. But come, look not so hangdog. I gave you the good friar Plutonius. He is versed in spells."

So he had been saddled with this vile, quarrelsome friar who still carried a grudge for the incident with the troll hand. As if it had been his fault! From Rupert's viewpoint, it was the friar's shoddy workmanship that had caused the problem. The damned hand still did not function properly. It was so vicious and unpredictable that Jasper had to keep it bound most of the time.

A shout from Sims drew Rupert's attention. He looked up to see his man approaching through the forest. It was time to go.

CHAPTER TWENTY-FIVE

THE OLD TREE

For two more days, the three boats continued downstream at the slow pace of the current. No one in Roscoe's party had any inkling of the existence of Bart's craft, which lurked just out of sight behind the last bend. Bart, like everyone else on his boat, kept his attention focused in the direction of travel, or else along the riverbanks lest they be ambushed. So he never suspected that Rupert followed behind, still enshrouded in a magical mist. And Rupert had no awareness of Roscoe and company in Scrymgeour's boat. To the best of his knowledge, this was a contest between Bart and himself alone.

The river widened as the countryside flattened out. This was wilder country now, with little sign of settlement even on the eastern side. From time to time, they passed the dilapidated ruins of villas, temples, and monuments, for the ancient Etrusians had developed the area extensively, and the remnants of their efforts still dotted the hillside. But the Etrusians had been driven out centuries ago, and the land had returned to wilderness.

As they traveled, Thurmond strove to improve his fighting skills, sparring with Roscoe and Torgul on the riverboat's flat roof. The space was small, but no worse, as the Adventurers pointed out, than the cramped confines of an underground passage. Sometimes Thurmond and Sarah shot arrows at pieces of wood floating in the water.

Sarah applied herself to her new book and pored over the as-yet-undecipherable scrolls she had taken from the dead druid's hut. Notations in the book's margins seemed to reference a list of runic symbols in one of the scrolls. As she skimmed the list, she suddenly recognized one of these arcane symbols.

Sarah let out a shriek that brought the others running. She yelled excitedly to Roscoe.

"Hey, where's the map? I've got to see the map!"

The old Adventurer produced it, and Sarah fumbled impatiently as she attempted to unroll it.

"Help me with this damned thing, please. Thurmond, hold down the other end. Look here, see that rune we thought might mark a back door? Well, I figured out what it means. It doesn't mean *door*, it means *tree*."

There was a moment of silence as each party member considered this revelation.

Thurmond had an idea.

"Could be there's a door next to the tree—or even *in* the tree."

Torgul, wise to the way of runes, interposed.

"We want to be careful not to take the meaning of runes too literally. Runes are like poems. They tell the truth, but they keep it hidden. Each rune is a powerful charm in its own right. So there may not even be a real tree for us to find—only something the tree rune stands for."

No one had any idea what that something might be. After a few moments, the others wandered off and left Sarah to her studies.

†

On the third day, Nod and Sod kept their eyes skinned for familiar landmarks. They were getting close. Although the rivermen were by now far beyond their usual area of operation, they had been down this stretch of river enough times to keep their bearings. The river narrowed, and the current grew stronger. Both sides were lined with high rocky banks.

Roscoe, Torgul, and Thurmond lazed on the cabin's flat roof. Sarah was, as usual, at her studies in the cabin, her magical implements strewn at her feet. All was quiet and peaceful in the warm afternoon until Sarah again let out a shriek and then a whole series of shrieks.

She came pelting out of the cabin, shouting.

"Roscoe! Roscoe! We're being followed! There's another boat back there that's tracking us with magic."

The others quickly climbed down to where she stood. Roscoe's voice carried a tone of deep concern. They had all learned not to underestimate Sarah.

"What is it, lassie? What have you learned?"

"Like I said, there's another boat back there that's following us. Tracking us."

"And how would you be knowin' such a thing?"

"From a new spell I just mastered, from my new book."

"The one you stole from the dead druid?"

"Aye, that one. It's filled with really good spells. There's the whole process for shooting the bone and a charm for summoning a plague of locusts—even a recipe for a homunculus."

"Now I'm sure that's all very fine, and I'd like you to tell me all about it at another time. But right now I'd especially like to hear about this boat you claim you saw."

"Not *saw*—I didn't actually see it."

Roscoe was dubious.

"Then how do you know it's there?"

"Through its psychic emanations. Look, I've been worried—worried about two things. First off, that they could use the map to find us. Its previous owner had to have left his psychic imprint all over it. That might be enough for a skilled diviner. The other thing is the imp. Maybe it's still in psychic contact with the witch who sent it after us."

"And how would it know where we are at the moment?"

"Because it's here with us. It's in the cabin with my other stuff."

Horrified, Thurmond jumped into the conversation.

"You brought that demon? Have you gone daft? By God's webbed fingers, why?"

"Because it's mine! I caught it! Besides, it may prove useful somehow. And anyway, what was I supposed to do—leave it behind for some poor idiot to find and open? I'm not exactly sure how to properly dispose of a jugged imp."

Roscoe gave both bickering teenagers a stern look.

"Peace! Stop this foolish claptrap! Now, Sarah, finish your story. What did the new spell show you?"

"All right, sorry, Roscoe. I was trying to cast a new cloaking spell, a much more powerful one then before. That's when I felt the psychic vibrations coming at us, so there must be a magician back there trying to penetrate our cloak. And—this is the weird part—the vibrations are curving, matching the bends in the river, so they have to be coming from a boat. That's when I yelled out."

"You think it's the witch you saw in the mirror?"

"Maybe. I don't know. Quite possibly."

Torgul now spoke up, a degree of urgency in his voice.

"Missy, are we cloaked now? Has your new spell blocked their vision?"

"Aye, I'm fairly certain. At least to a point."

"Then we got a chance here, but it won't last long. We gotta make all speed down this river and put some distance between us and them. When we get to the goblin cave, we'll shoot by at full speed. But at the next likely spot, the boat's gotta slow for just a wee bit and we'll jump off and wade ashore just as quick as we can.

"Once we're off, the boat can go on downriver, and with any luck, the other boat will just keep followin' along. After dark, our boys can hide up some little creek somewhere."

Roscoe nodded in agreement.

"They're followin' for a reason, so they are. If they know about the map, then they're just sittin' back and lettin' us lead 'em to the treasure. So we don't' em see us jump ship. Wouldn't do at all. We'd best be gettin' our things together."

There was a flurry of activity as they ran to secure their equipment. In addition to their personal items, provisions, armor, and weapons, each party member had to carry some of the heavy tools that might prove essential. There was an iron pry bar, a small spade, a coil of rope, a grappling hook, a hamper of surgical supplies, and Red Charles's hatchet.

Roscoe handed Thurmond a bundle of torches and once again made him the designated torchbearer. Torgul wanted to bring a pick, but his burden was already too great. Sarah packed her occult gear in a wicker pannier she strapped to her back. The rest of her belongings went into a leather shoulder bag.

Nod and Sod joined the group, both dressed in leather armor and iron caps. They carried small crossbows and wore shortswords. The other boatmen hoisted the sail and then began to row with all their might so that the craft leaped forward in the water. Within a few moments, Sod pointed at the far bank. His knowledge of the common tongue had returned. He shouted excitedly.

"Looky! There be it—there—the first of the turnin's just afore the cave mouth. Stand by!"

The boat shot down the center of the river through the two small bends indicated on the map. This was a prime location for an ambush, but no goblins appeared on the riverbank. Indeed, the cave mouth was entirely invisible from their position on the water. They saw no sign of any habitation. Torgul looked over at Thurmond and sensed his uncertainty.

"Don't fret, lad, we're in the right place. The goblins—they're up there somewhere. I can smell 'em."

They continued downriver. Within about a mile, the high banks gave way to a gentle beach. This time it was Nod who revealed that he, like his brother, could also use the common tongue when need be.

"There be!"

The boatmen brought the vessel into the shallows until the keel scraped bottom. At Roscoe's command, the party immediately jumped over the side, landing in water up to their thighs—that is, all except Torgul, who was almost entirely submerged. This, however, proved no serious impediment to the doughty dwarf, who plowed forward until his head cleared the surface.

Once ashore, the party moved quickly inland to the cover of the nearest trees. It was agreed that the boat would return upstream in three days. A broken branch hung in a certain way from an overhanging limb would be the signal to land and retrieve the party. If no such branch was present, the boat would return once a day until so signaled.

Roscoe appointed Thurmond, the lowly hang-around, to be the lookout. He was to conceal himself in the underbrush and report back as soon as the following boat passed by. Strangely, it never did. He waited far longer than it would have taken for their pursuers to appear. It was obvious that something had gone awry, that things were not as they imagined them. Most likely, Sarah had misread the signs, or whatever it was that magicians misread. In any case, no boat appeared.

Thurmond returned to the group and shared his information. Torgul and Roscoe were quiet and thoughtful. Sarah got mad and adamantly defended her assessment. However, they all agreed that their best course was to follow the map to the location indicated by the tree rune and try to discover what its significance might be. The scale of the hand-drawn map was impossible to judge, but Roscoe guessed their destination was perhaps a mile from the river.

It was a long, tedious mile. So heavily burdened by the impedimenta of adventuring, the party struggled through the dense woods with the greatest difficulty. Thurmond was certain Roscoe must be lost as he led them through a series of apparently random turnings along narrow game trails and into thickets of brier and bramble. From time to time, they paused so Torgul could sniff the air, but his nose detected no trace of goblin. Indeed, there were no traces of any form of civilization.

Roscoe's injured leg pained him badly. He limped along as best he could, determined to show no sign of weakness, but the trek across such uneven ground was obviously growing more agonizing with every step.

Finally, with the expression of a man who had lost a bitterly disputed argument, he took a long swig from a small silver flask carried in a pouch on his belt. His eyes at once grew bright, his step steady and sure. He said nothing to the others, but resumed the trek at an increased pace. Whatever was in the flask had done its work.

Thurmond was trying his best to shoulder his burden without complaint, but he too was suffering. His armor chafed terribly, and the combined weight of all the items strapped to his body was becoming unsupportable. He was fast approaching the point where he would be dragged to the ground. He longed for a swig from Roscoe's silver flask.

Their march came to an end at a large clearing dotted with the ruins of ancient houses. Very little remained but the outline of foundations, broken columns, and the scattered tiles of mosaic floors. Roscoe declared it to be the remnant of an Etrusian settlement or perhaps a large villa.

Upon closer inspection, one skeletal ruin stood out from the rest. It was larger, and many of the tumbled facing stones bore elaborate carvings. Sarah examined these keenly.

"These are Goddess symbols. The moon, the cowrie shell, the serpent. This had to be a temple to the Ancient One. She Who Abides. This place must be very old."

For many centuries before the coming of Charonism, it had been the Goddess to whom people prayed and made sacrifice. Though the church had officially suppressed it, Goddess worship continued at hidden shrines in secret glens. Particularly by country folk and especially by women.

It was then that they noticed the tree, or what had once been a tree, in the temple's shattered courtyard. The blasted, fire-blackened shell of an ancient oak. The few remaining limbs were twisted and devoid of leaves. A single green root sprout, pushing itself up from the base, was the only evidence that any trace of life remained in the withered hulk.

Thurmond was thrilled. He dropped his rucksack and immediately started toward it.

"Come on! It's hollow! That's got to be the door!"

But Torgul grabbed him by the belt and hauled him back.

"Not so fast, laddie. Might be better to wait for an invitation. There's a wee brown man sitting in that tree."

No one but Torgul could see the wee brown man, who he claimed was poised on one of the tree's pitiful leafless limbs. He again credited his ability to see the unseeable to the second sight inherited from his great-grandmother. The wee brown man vanished soon after the dwarf discovered him.

CHAPTER TWENTY-SIX

THE CONVERGENCE

Gregorio's efforts were unexpectedly rewarded. He finally caught a clear vision of the boat they had been trailing for so many days. The sorcerer aboard it had cast a different cloaking spell, and in the ephemeral moment between the old and new spells, the craft stood revealed. It was just ahead, around a bend or two.

Yet he was also filled with trepidation. The powerful sorcerer who had cast the spell might use their psychic connection to send a terrible retaliation. For all his ability as a diviner, Gregorio possessed neither the skills nor the temperament for magical combat. He shuddered, knowing his unseen adversary had the power to command infernal entities. He would be powerless against demonic attack.

Gregorio was loath to share his concerns with Bartholomew, fearing another of his childish tantrums. But this information was too important to hold back, and so he announced that contact with their quarry had been made. To his surprise, Bart instructed the tillerman to bring their boat to shore as soon as possible. He then turned to Artos, his mercenary sergeant.

"I've been expecting something like this, Artos. They don't fool me. This trip down the river has been entirely too easy. They knew we were behind them from the start and have just been leading us along until the right moment. Now they've deliberately revealed their location. But I know what they're up to. They're trying to spur us on. They've stopped up a little way ahead and are waiting to ambush us at some narrow point in the river.

"Get your men ready. We'll go overland and come in behind them. We will ambush our ambushers. Neat trick, don't you think?"

Whatever Artos might have thought, he kept it to himself. He issued some low commands, and his men began to arm up.

The boat was large. It had a much deeper draw than Scrymgeour's riverboat and could not pull up on a shoal. In order to land, it was necessary to drop anchor in an eddy and ferry the men ashore in the dory. This required several trips, and no little confusion ensued as the inexperienced soldiers gathered their equipment and prepared to disembark. Several came close to drowning in their heavy armor when they fell while climbing into the dory. Luckily, they were saved by the strong hands of the attentive boatmen. In the end, only an unbuckled helmet and a sack of dried meat were lost in the Mad River's murky depths.

Eventually all were ashore—Bart, Gregorio, Artos, and twelve soldiers. The rivermen were ordered to disguise the vessel with branches and remain at anchor until Bart and his party returned. With that, Bart led his landing force into the forest. He would proceed inland just far enough to approach his foe from the rear. Then he would send scouts to locate their pathetic ambush. When they were found, he would bring up his main force for a savage rush from behind.

But this all came to naught because once out of sight of the river, the city-bred lordling became completely disoriented. He had no idea whether he was taking his men upriver or down, toward the water or away from it. His armor became unbearably heavy and confining. The pointed toes of his custom-fitted sabatons kept catching in the dirt. He finally took them off and threw them aside in disgust. They were quickly scooped up by one of his soldiers and secured in a shoulder bag.

Both Gregorio and Artos knew that their leader was lost and knew the direction they should be taking. But both had learned better than to draw attention to his folly or to suggest they were in any way more knowledgeable or capable than he. So both remained silent as Bart led his group in a big curving circle upstream, exactly the opposite direction he intended.

†

Still hidden beneath a magical mist, Rupert and his party were just rounding an oxbow bend when the lookout spotted the large mast of Bart's ship sticking up through the trees ahead. Theirs was a nimble craft, which was quickly turned and brought to the shore. The disembarkation came about with much aplomb. Soldiers and boatmen were soon over the side and set to manhandling weapons and supplies. It was decided that the boat's complement would accompany the party, so it was necessary to drag the craft onto the tiny shoal.

They were in the midst of this laborious task when Bart's party appeared quite unexpectedly on the bank above them. Without armor, shields, or even weapons, Rupert's men were at a decided disadvantage. Several dove back into the boat, grabbing bows and sheltering behind the gunwale. Others seized whatever weapon came to hand from the pile of off-loaded supplies. Rupert stood with this group, as did Sims. Plutonius splashed back into the water, seeking cover behind the grounded boat. This now stood in plain view, the mist spell broken in the confusion of the sudden encounter.

Bart was equally surprised, equally unprepared. He had been glad when he finally found the river again and was coming down to get his bearings when he stumbled upon the other party. He was not expecting to meet his adversary in this manner. That this was his adversary, he had no doubt. There was the well-groomed gentleman with long, curled hair exactly as Gregorio had described him. And he had caught a glimpse of a figure in a dark robe disappearing behind the boat—no doubt the master magician in the service of Lady Renata.

Bart had intended to launch an immediate attack, but now he hesitated. The two parties were nearly equal in size. Their magician was vastly more powerful than his own. He no longer enjoyed the element of surprise. His men were incompetent and unreliable. Under such circumstances, attack would be foolhardy. No honor would be lost in holding back and assessing the situation.

While Bart stood and tried to think, Rupert drew his men back from the bank and formed them into a defensive battle line along the shoreline. He called out.

"Holla! Holla on the riverbank! Is that you, Bartholomew Staynes? If so, show yourself—I would have words rather than blows."

Bart's suspicions were at once confirmed. These were the very people he had followed down the river, the ones who had sent a sneak thief into his home to steal his mirror and map, the ones who would deprive him of his chance for glory and self-respect. What words would he have for such despicable scum? Still, common sense argued for caution. He shouted down over the edge of the bank.

"Say your piece, sirrah!"

"Sirrah nothing! My quality is the equal of yours. Show yourself if you're not afraid, so that we may converse in proper manly fashion, face-to-face. I dislike shouting at unseen skulkers."

These words had exactly the intended effect. Bart came charging to the very edge of the embankment. His visor was raised, showing a face empurpled with wrath.

"I fear no man, least of all you! I'm no damned skulker! I'll meet you face-to-face all right, with steel in my hand, you shit-swallowing peasant bastard. Come on!"

But Rupert's voice at once grew oily and ingratiating.

"Forgive me, Lord Staynes. I wasn't certain that it was really you, and I only spoke so to draw you out. I knew that the genuine Bartholomew Staynes would never stand for such calumny."

"Who are you, sirrah?"

"As I said, not one to countenance being called *sirrah*, even from your distinguished self. My name is Lord Rupert de Pugh, and I am, as previously stated, of a rank equal to your own. My father holds a rural fief in fee."

"Blackguard! Thief! You are perhaps noble of blood but not of deed. You have already stolen that which is mine, and now you mean to take more."

"My good lord, while I cannot claim to be wholly innocent in this matter, your angry accusations fall mostly on the wrong head. I am but a humble vassal of a much greater personage."

"You speak of Lady Renata? The witch? You are her man?"

"In a manner of speaking. But I would be willing to reconsider my loyalties if certain conditions were to arise. Such conditions that might well be to our mutual advantage, Lord Staynes."

"What are you speaking of? Be plain, man."

"Then let us be frank. We both came here in search of treasure. Instead of fighting each other and thereby so reducing our forces that our goal becomes impossible, can we not join forces and in so doing greatly enhance our chances of success? Together we are twice as strong as separately. What say you?"

"I say that this is my adventure and that I do not intend to share the glory or the treasure with anyone, especially an upstart from some shithouse country fief."

"Nay, good Lord Bartholomew, disparage not my lineage. I would be your friend, not your foe, but such affronts are not to be borne. Hear me out. I will place myself and my men at your command, so the adventure and glory will remain entirely yours. I ask only the two-eighths fee that is the lieutenant's share by custom. My men are already well paid, so they require no additional remuneration."

"Who's the magician in the black robe?"

"Plutonius? He is Renata's creature. Regard him not."

"If I agree, do you swear as a nobleman to abide by our bargain?"

"I so swear. And yourself, do you likewise swear to abide by it?"

"Aye, I so swear as a nobleman by birth and deed."

And so the bargain was struck, and the two parties joined forces, each wrongly assuming that the other had the map that had led them to this location. Each wrongly assuming that the other was accompanied by a master magician wielding awesome occult powers. Each correctly assuming that the other would betray their sworn oath as soon as it was advantageous to do so. And each secure in the knowledge that they would have to be the first to take that step.

Initially, all went well. Rupert's men finished unloading the boat and lugged their gear to the top of the bank to join Bart's contingent. These were simple, straightforward soldiers who took things as they found them and did not question this new alliance. They were soon talking and laughing together. One of Sims's henchmen had previously served with Artos in Hawkwood's great company. A flask of uisge passed surreptitiously from hand to hand.

The problems started when Plutonius finally appeared and Bart recognized his vestments as belonging to the Black Friars. He was livid.

"Hey! I thought you said you had a magician in your party. This one's just a cleric."

"I said no such thing. I said only that he is Renata's creature. Which he is."

"Then you willfully allowed me to deceive myself, which is the same as lying. What else might you be lying about? You have my map in your possession—the one your agent stole from my own home. I would have it back. Immediately!"

"Addle-pated wretch, has your brain softened? I have no map of yours. 'Tis you that led us here. If any map exists, you have it already."

"Churl! Dissembler! Curly-headed fop! Draw your sword."

"Callow boy-man! I am for you!"

Only the prompt intervention of Artos and Sims kept the two noblemen from slaying each other then and there. They were compelled to lay rough hands on their leaders, pull the weapons from their grips, and wrestle them to the ground. Such behavior would, under normal circumstances, be considered such an affront that only the death of the underlings would suffice. But in the intense heat of this moment, the offense went unnoticed.

Greater still was their outrage when it was discovered that neither party possessed the map. Both Bart and Rupert were furious, each believing he had been somehow duped by the other. And their fury mounted to greater heights with the realization that without the map, they had no idea how to proceed. Rupert again launched a verbal assault.

"Dolt! You came down here with no idea of where you were going?"

"I was following you, you soft-bellied arse-licker, you flaccid—"

"Following me? It was me following you, you dung-eating maggot spawn..."

They were about to fly at each other again, though this time with only bare hands because their minions had carefully placed their weapons out of reach. They may well have slain one another if an entirely unforeseen circumstance had not occurred. Arrows began to land in their midst. The goblins were upon them.

CHAPTER TWENTY-SEVEN

THE WEE BROWN MAN

Thurmond and his party were unsure what to do next. The wee brown man had vanished and not returned, so they subjected the rune tree to a thorough examination. Torgul crawled inside the hollow trunk and probed with his spade. He found nothing. The remaining limbs were assayed for openings, the bark for carved inscriptions. Their efforts were fruitless. An exploration of the temple's courtyard was similarly unproductive.

Roscoe sat down on his rucksack and mopped his brow with a rag.

"Now, as the party leader, I am ashamed to say this, but I'm stymied, so I am. We've been over every bit of this old tree. No doorway, no wee brown man, nothin' that signifies."

But at that moment, a voice spoke to them. It was thin and reedy, pitched somewhere between the chirp of a bird and the sigh of a breath of wind.

"Why do you intrude here? What brings you to this place so long abandoned by such as yourselves? Why do you disturb this piteous wreck of a tree?"

The voice emanated from above their heads. Looking up, they saw that the wee brown man had returned, visible to all this time. He sat on a broken remnant of limb well above their heads.

It was Sarah who spoke first. She kept her voice girlish and friendly.

"We certainly mean no harm, sir. I apologize with all my heart if we have disturbed or offended you."

"I hear your words. Why come you here?"

Sarah thought quickly. She had to be careful not to reveal too much of their real intentions.

"We come at the bidding of our master, a great and terrible wizard. This tree holds the key to some arcane secret that he would discover. Perhaps there is a hidden niche with a parchment scroll or a cryptic message carved in the bark."

"Nay, the tree holds no such secrets. You have come in vain. Now begone."

"But, good sir, we have come ever so far upon this errand. You cannot just send us away. Surely there is something you can tell us."

The wee brown man shifted position so that his legs dangled down from the limb on which he sat. He seemed to be considering something.

"I've got woes enough of my own. I cannot concern myself with the comings and goings of humans. I tell you true, this tree holds no such secrets."

That being said, he vanished.

"What was he?" Thurmond blurted as soon as it seemed safe to do so.

Sarah's reply was quiet and measured.

"I think he's some kind of dryad—a tree spirit. If he is, then his existence is tied to the life of the tree. He's like the soul of the tree and can never leave it. Did you see how sad he looked? Did you not tell hear him say he has woes of his own? This tree is ancient, but it is obviously about to die, and when it does, he dies too. That's what's making him so sad."

"How can you know all that?"

"Call it my female intuition. And don't forget, we're standing in what used to be a temple of the Goddess. Maybe some of the old magic still lingers."

"What do you think we should do?"

Sarah gave a small shrug.

"At the moment, I'm out of ideas."

†

The day was coming to an end, and it was decided that the party would bed down at the far end of the temple courtyard. The tree spirit did not appear hostile, but no one was eager to sleep right next to a haunted tree. The courtyard's broken walls offered a modicum of protection, and Sarah was hopeful that a floating remnant of womanly night magic might yet linger here and lend her an inspiration. Torgul took up a water skin and went off in search of a spring, but only a short time elapsed before he returned, the bag full and dripping. He went straight to Sarah.

"I ain't sayin' this is important, missy, but I thought you might wanna know. There's a spring over behind those bushes there, but it's no ordinary spring. Got a lot more of these carved stones layin' about it, like maybe it used to be a temple or a shrine. Looks like it used to be somethin' special, anyway. Want me to show you?"

Sarah grabbed Torgul's arm and began pulling him along as if it *she* was guiding *him* to the spot. They threaded their way through the complex of weed-choked ruins and around an immense growth of bramble. The spring was just as Torgul described it, a gurgling pool of clear, sweet water surrounded by the broken vestige of an ancient shrine. A carved stone depicted a rotund female figure with a snake suckling from each of her pendulous breasts. Sarah knew at once that this spring had been sacred to the Goddess. She knew what to do.

"Torgul, could I trouble you for the loan of your helmet?"

Sarah, of course, had a helmet of her own, but she disliked wearing it and had left it at the campsite. Torgul handed her the requested item.

"Now could I beg you for a few moments alone here—just a few?"

The dwarf backed away until he was out of earshot but could still keep the girl in sight. He watched as she knelt by the side of the pool as if in prayer or meditation.

And Sarah was indeed in prayer. She prayed to the Great Goddess, the All Mother, the Ancient One, She Who Abides. Such devotion was directly at odds with the Charonite doctrine in which she had been raised. The church condemned such old beliefs as heresy. But at the moment, it just felt right to do so.

Her prayer complete, she filled Torgul's helmet with sacred spring water and returned to the courtyard. The others watched as she approached the tree, knelt beside it, and after a moment gently poured the water on the single green root sprout growing from its base.

If Sarah expected some miraculous result for her efforts, she was disappointed. The water spread out on the ground beneath the tree and was gradually absorbed into the dusty soil. Nothing more. She stood and returned to the group. They all stared at her in expectation. She shrugged.

"I dunno…it just felt right, that's all. Maybe…"

Her voice trailed off, and she left the thought unfinished.

Thurmond, the humble hang-around, began to distribute the evening's rations. Roscoe announced that they would stand watch in teams of two. Nod and Sod would take the first shift, followed by Sarah and Torgul. He and Thurmond would stand the final and most dangerous watch.

It seemed to Sarah that she had not yet been asleep when Torgul roused her to join him on watch. Taking up her bow, a quiver of arrows, and her shoulder bag, she followed him to a secluded nook in the temple's fallen masonry. The moonlight was very bright and made the rune tree in the courtyard's far end appear as silver.

"This be a good place to bide. You can see the entire yard from here, but nobody can't see you in the shadow of these stones. Can't nobody sneak up on you neither. Just stay awake and keep your eyes open. Yell real loud if you see anything, and I'll come runnin'. I'll be out front of the ruins. Just remember—stay awake. And keep a watch on that haunted tree."

Torgul disappeared into the darkness, leaving Sarah on her own. She knew, of course, that her friends were close by, that a single shout from her would summon them with weapons in hand. Yet she felt extremely small and vulnerable as she huddled beneath that mass of broken stone.

The night grew chill. It was impossible to find comfort in the confines of her niche, and her legs began to cramp. In desperation, she lay down on her side and wrapped her cloak around her like a blanket. This was better, warmer.

Her body, perhaps aware of the approaching presence, gave a sudden start, restoring her to consciousness. Her mind was groggy, disoriented. She had not been asleep…had she? She looked out on the tree and the courtyard. Both seemed somehow altered, unreal. Was she really awake now, or was this but a dream? She was aware of her surroundings, she certainly felt awake, but…

The wee brown man stood before her. When he spoke, his voice had a melodious, lilting quality it had previously lacked.

"You've done me a good service. Been many and many the year since girls brought the Goddess water to my tree. It nourishes and gives healing. Your gift allows me to abide a bit longer. I thank you for that."

"Who are you?"

"You may not be told my real name, for such telling conveys too much power. Long ago, young girls such as yourself called me Whisper."

"Whisper, like the soft sigh of wind through a tree—I like that, I think. Is there any other way that I can be of service to you?"

"I fear not. My time is drawing nigh, even with your kind gift of Goddess water. But I have a curiosity as to your real purpose. I read well the deception in your eyes this afternoon. Why are you and these others really here? You have no aura of evil about you. You prayed at the sacred spring. And yet your purpose here is not devotional."

Sarah told him the real reason for their adventure. She spoke of the map and the mirror, of the goblins and the treasure, and of the boat that had trailed them down the river.

Whisper listened intently. When she was finished, he replied.

"There is indeed a goblin den down by the river. The birds speak of it. I would like to see them come to destruction, for they are great killers of trees and haters of all things pleasant and good. You are but a novice sorceress. I can feel your power, and it is still very low. But I may be able to aid you in your quest. Some of my old magic still remains. Have you a wand?"

She sat up, drew her wand from her shoulder bag, and showed it to him.

"Place a hand on either end and hold it forth."

She did as instructed. Whisper gripped the wand in the middle, with both of his small brown hands between hers. He said something she did not catch, and a tremendous surge of energy shot through her arms. She felt as if a bolt of lightning were rushing through her in a circle, up one arm and down the other. Her ears filled with a great droning hum. Her eyes rolled up, and she felt herself slipping backward.

He leaned over her and began to speak softly in her ear. She could not make out the words. They seemed to be in a language of which she had no knowledge. And yet she felt them penetrate into her mind, into her soul, as no words had ever done before. She lost all sense of time. Did he speak thus for only a moment or for days on end? Sarah could not tell. Then he was gone, and she lapsed into a swoon.

Thurmond woke Sarah by gently shaking her shoulder. He was quite thoroughly displeased.

"Damnation, Sarah. You fell asleep on guard. You better be glad it was me that found you and not Roscoe. I don't know what he would have done, but I do know that Adventurers really frown on this sort of thing. You could've got us all killed if goblins had come over the back wall. They love sneak attacks like that."

"I'm sorry, Thurmond. I know you're right. It was stupid and irresponsible. I'll apologize to Roscoe and suffer the consequences."

"Nay, say nothing. Let this rest between you and me. The others think so highly of you, and I wouldn't have one mistake sully their opinions. Just don't do it again."

"You're a good friend, Thurmond, and I thank you for your care. All right, let it remain between us alone, and I promise never again to fail in this manner. But listen, I don't believe it was a normal sleep that claimed me. I think I was bewitched."

Thurmond grew dubious.

"Bewitched? How so?"

"By Whisper—I mean by the wee brown man. The tree spirit. He came to me."

She told him of her conversation. She tried to explain the episode with the wand, but he began to look doubtful.

"Aw, Sarah, this sounds kind of fantastic. I think you probably just dreamed this stuff."

But she knew better.

CHAPTER TWENTY-EIGHT

THE STING OF BATTLE

The goblin bows were lightweight weapons. They possessed no great range, nor could they propel an arrow with any particular accuracy. The penetrative power of their small missiles was minimal, so they could be stopped by leather armor. But what the goblin archers lacked in power, range, and precision, they made up for with speed. They could discharge their missiles with the quickness of a striking snake, relying on the sheer quantity rather than the quality of their fire. This is what the combined parties of Bart and Rupert now faced on the riverbank.

Utterly distracted by the brawl between their leaders, the soldiers and boatmen remained unaware of the goblins' stealthy approach until they were deluged by flights of their arrows. Happily, most missed. Others bounced harmlessly from iron helmets or failed to penetrate the tough leather that protected most of their bodies. But a few found their mark, and men yelled in outrage as they saw the color of their own blood.

Rupert's men were professionals and immediately returned the goblins' fire. They all carried shortbows or crossbows in addition to edged weapons. Bart's crew, on the other hand, began to edge backward toward the river. Artos stopped them in their tracks. Sword in hand, he swore to kill anyone taking one more step in that direction. More afraid of him than of the goblins, his men turned about and formed a line of battle.

A horn blew a single thin, piercing note, and with a shriek of pure hatred, the goblins dropped their bows and charged. They came on in a dark wave, for they were many. Artos sheathed his sword and picked up his glaive. This was his favorite weapon, essentially a sword blade on a six-foot shaft. Holding the weapon horizontally, he pushed it up against the backs of the men in the line. He knew how they were feeling as they faced this onrushing tide of death. The pressure of his weapon against their backs reassured them, reminded them that their sergeant was always behind them and unafraid.

In truth, not one man in the entire group had ever faced a goblin charge before. Some were experienced soldiers, but they were not Underworld Adventurers, and so their combat experience was strictly limited to human foes.

But Artos had kept his ears open and had heard a thing or two about goblins. He knew that their initial charge could be terrible, that they would thrust themselves onto their enemy's weapons with suicidal courage, that if they broke his line in the first moments, the entire party would be engulfed and slain in a maelstrom of goblin swords and axes.

Yet if his line held and repulsed the first attack, the goblins would lose impetus and begin to mill aimlessly. This was a moment for a brisk countercharge that would slay them in great numbers and send the survivors into headlong flight. Artos kept his glaive pressed up against his men and waited.

Bart and Rupert were still trying to fight each other when arrows struck around them. It took them several seconds to realize that their situation had taken a dramatic turn. Both simply stood, completely dumbfounded by the sudden assault. Neither had led men into battle before. Indeed, neither had ever been in a battle before. Uncertain and confused, they remained stationary for several more critical moments while Artos and Sims marshaled their men into a defensive formation.

Finally, it was Rupert who retrieved the sword Artos had previously wrenched from his hand. He plodded slowly to a point well behind the newly formed battle line. Bart, seeing this, followed suit, choosing a similar position on the far end of the line. During the ensuing battle, neither leader issued a single command nor delivered a single sword blow.

Plutonius immediately took to his heels, scampering down the embankment and sprinting toward the grounded boat. Gregorio saw this, hesitated, and followed as fast as his long legs could carry him.

The goblins hit the line and hit it hard. Some leaped upward as if trying to climb over the shields of their human foes. Others dropped low, striking beneath the shields with their short, curved swords. Of the two tactics, the latter proved more successful, and several men fell with wounds to the knee or lower leg.

Artos watched in dismay as the battle line buckled backward under the onslaught. He placed his glaive against the backs of his men and pushed them forward. To his relief, the line straightened and held. His men were fighting well, as were Sims's. Dead goblins were piling up before their shields, impeding the next wave of attackers. Reaching between his men, he lashed out savagely with his glaive. He smashed the point into a leering goblin face and then, in one fluid motion, turned the blade and caught another in the neck.

On the other end of the line, Sims and his men began to advance. They slew all who stood before them and then turned to make a flank attack. A goblin chieftain and his retinue, all very large and well equipped, came forward to check the advance, but Sims was not to be stopped. He slew the goblin lord with a single blow that took arm and shoulder from body. His men stampeded over the others, thrusting and chopping. The goblins were down and dead before Sims could throw another blow.

Sims led his men with cool proficiency, but the real hero of the moment was Jasper—he of the troll hand. He had entered the fight in his customary fashion, a shield in one hand, a sword in the other. Imagine his dismay when the grafted appendage began to quiver and shake as if to rid itself of the weapon. Try as he might, he could not prevent the opening of the fingers from around its hilt. As the sword slipped from his grasp, he resigned himself to an inevitable death.

But lo! The hand itself at once became a killing tool far superior to the lost blade. It lashed out of its own accord, left and right, tearing the arm from one goblin and slashing the throat of another. It struck again and again so that goblin eyes, lips, and noses hung impaled on its talons.

Disheartened by the death of their leader, the goblin right flank now began to move backward. Seeing this, Artos called for his men to advance on the opposite side and encouraged them with another push with the shaft of his glaive. As the line advanced, the goblin host lost all semblance of formation. Many threw down their weapons and waited patiently to be slain. Others tried to flee. Some, losing all reason, began to fight among themselves.

Rupert's boatmen sheathed their swords and, taking up their bows, began to shoot down those attempting escape. The soldiers continued to advance, an indomitable wall of death. Goblin heads were sent spinning from goblin shoulders. Goblin guts went slithering to the ground. The survivors ran shrieking, scattering into the woods.

The battle was over.

✝

Two of Bart's novice fighters were dead, as was one of Rupert's boatmen. This last with an arrow through his throat. Many carried wounds of greater or lesser severity. Again the experienced soldiers proved their worth, inspecting injuries and applying appropriate remedies. It was rumored that goblins routinely smeared their blades with their own bodily wastes. This would cause a wound to putrefy and bring a slow, agonizing death.

The goblin dead went unlooted. The smell of a goblin, live or dead, is innately repugnant, and the men soon abandoned this endeavor. Besides, no self-respecting human would ever covet an item of goblin manufacture.

The one person who could have been of real use at this point was nowhere to be seen. As a cleric, Friar Plutonius possessed healing spells that could restore even a badly injured man to health. But he and Gregorio remained huddled in the bushes down by the boat. Both had fled in a blind panic into the shallows of the river, but then, realizing that it afforded no refuge, had sought cover in a large patch of bracken.

Sims now dragged Plutonius back to the battlefield by the hair, slapping him with his free hand all the while. The cleric screamed and struggled, trying to explain that he was conserving his healing powers for more critical occasions, but his protestations did him no good. Sims gave him a simple choice—tend the wounded or have his skin slowly stripped from his body. Plutonius got right to business.

Gregorio also returned, sheepish and obviously afraid that his cowardice would bring recrimination. He stood well apart until the irate Sims motioned him to assist Plutonius. He too got busy. Bart and Rupert remained entirely uninvolved in all that was going on around them. It was Artos who finally approached Bart.

"Milord, if we're going to move against these stinking turds, the time to do so is right now. We've broken 'em, sure enough, and there ain't no more fight left in 'em. But if we linger, they're sure to reform, and then…"

Bart silenced him with a look of pure disdain. He was quite aware of his own disappointing performance, aware that Artos had stepped in and led his men forward while he stood helpless in the rear. But it was not his fault. He had never been in battle before, so this peasant bastard had no right to judge him.

"You presume to tell *me* what *I* must do? Do I have to remind you of *your* position here?"

Artos caught himself, realizing that in the excitement of the day, he had said exactly the wrong thing to this pompous little lordling. He took a different tack.

"Oh…nay! Please forgive me if I have offended, milord. I am sure that you have a much better understanding of the battle than I. I only meant to point out that you have won a great victory here. Your martial acumen has led to the destruction of the goblin host. Should we not, therefore, seize this moment to enhance still further your fame and glory? The men are eager. They only wait for you to lead them."

Bart's vanity was somewhat assuaged by Artos's obvious toadying, but a need to demonstrate his authority still consumed him.

"I will lead the men forward only when it pleases me to do so. Is that understood?"

Artos saw the futility of further discussion.

"Aye, milord."

"Very well. We must first see to the wounded to determine how many are no longer of use. And send someone to fetch the crew from my boat. We need reinforcements."

Artos nearly balked at this last order. Fetching the boatmen would take time, and that would squander the precious advantage their victory had bought them. Moreover, if the goblins found and burned their boat, it would be a very long hike back to Gorgonholm. But Bartholomew Staynes would have his way.

In fact, Bart was afraid to pursue the goblins. The carnage of battle had taught him to fear for his own life. Never before had he witnessed the terrible wounds inflicted by the weapons of war. He felt sickened, shaky, and was deeply ashamed for having such feelings. And for the first time, he doubted his ability to be the war leader he wanted to be. What if he led his men into an ambush? They would despise him for being an incompetent fool.

The more Bart considered it, the more he saw the wisdom in proceeding very slowly. There must still be hundreds of goblins to replace the ones they had slain. They would be mustering their forces at this very moment, preparing for the next assault. It would be dark before very long. They could not risk being caught unawares by those darkness-loving creatures. Bart felt some of his old confidence returning as he realized what they must do next.

"You, Artos! I told you to dispatch men to bring the crew of my boat. Do so at once! And you, Rupert! Organize a work party. We need a defensive barrier in case the goblins come upon us in the night. We will proceed inland in the morning."

Bart's men were not the only ones busy that night. The surrounding woods abounded with goblin stragglers, who gradually recovered from their panic and began to creep back to their lair. Goblin eyes peered through the darkness as the men strove to erect a crude barrier of sticks and rocks. These unseen eyes steadily increased in number as the night wore on. Goblin messengers were dispatched to summon additional forces from outposts up and down the river. Spears and swords were sharpened. Crude war engines were disassembled and prepared for transport. The chieftains held a midnight council.

CHAPTER TWENTY-NINE

INTO THE GOBLIN CAVE

"Fine—don't believe me then. I'm just a stupid girl, so what do I know?" Sarah was in high dudgeon. Roscoe, Thurmond, and Torgul stood around her in a semicircle. Nod and Sod squatted on their heels several yards away. They were seemingly oblivious to the conversation, but Thurmond suspected they were listening to every word. Sarah exploded yet again.

"I know what I know. Just because I can't prove it to you arrogant men doesn't mean…"

Roscoe extended his hands palm forward in an effort to sooth her.

"Sarah, darlin', it's not like we're sayin' you're wrong. We just want to make certain. There's nothin' at all wrong with makin' sure when our lives are at stake. And some of the stuff you've been tellin' us, it…well…sounds like maybe you was sleepin' on guard and had a little dream."

"I told you already, I was bewitched not asleep."

In spite of her agreement with Thurmond not to reveal that she had fallen asleep on duty, the story had all come out as she tried to explain her nocturnal visitation. She knew that her story sounded feeble, but she truly believed the tree spirit had empowered her, and she was determined to make the others believe it as well.

Now it was Thurmond's turn to challenge her belief.

"Sarah, you said yesterday that dryads—isn't that what you said he was?—are bound to their trees, that they cannot leave them. Is that right?"

"Aye, to the best of my understanding."

"Then how could this Whisper come to you last night? You were at the far end of the courtyard from the rune tree. He would have had to leave it to come to you. Can you explain that?"

"Aye, I can. I didn't see the real Whisper. I doubt he even has a real body—he's just pure spirit. What I saw was his *fetch*—it's like a double he can send out to run his errands. That's what was sitting on the limb yesterday. He used it when he decided to talk to us. But I don't think even the fetch can stray very far from the tree."

"And you know this how?"

"Because I just know. He touched me, and it gave me a lot of knowledge and a lot of power. I can do things now I couldn't do before. If I give you a demonstration, would you believe me?"

She did not want to have to do this. She had no idea how much psychic energy it would require. Her wand was so heavily charged that she could hear a low hum emanating from it, but she must be careful to conserve that power for the ordeal that loomed just ahead. If she maintained the spell for just a brief duration, maybe it would not be too costly.

The men agreed that a demonstration of her new power would be sufficient proof.

"Fine, I'll do it, but you must realize that this is a first. I haven't done this before."

And then Sarah was no longer there. She had completely disappeared. Several moments passed.

"Here I am!"

She materialized at the far end of the courtyard. Then she disappeared again.

"Now here!"

She was behind them, but only briefly, for she again disappeared. And then she quickly reappeared in her original position.

"Convinced?"

Roscoe laughed out loud.

"I can't speak for the others, Sarah, my girl, but I found your exhibition a profound inducement for belief. How did you do it?"

"I'm not sure. I think it's an advanced illusion spell. I don't know if I was really invisible. Maybe the spell made you think you couldn't see me. I wasn't transported to those different spots. I just walked to them while you thought I was invisible."

Sarah was greatly relieved that the others finally took her at her word. She was also delighted to discover that the spell had not seriously depleted the energy level of her wand, which continued to throb with concentrated power.

Torgul had been silent during the previous questioning, but now he spoke up.

"What you just showed us will be mighty useful against the goblins. Is there anything more, missy, that might aid us in our quest?"

"I believe I can cast this spell over our entire party, for a certain period anyway. I'm not sure for how long."

All five, in unison, made low, inarticulate sounds expressing approval.

They followed the map as best they could in the direction of the goblin den. It was not particularly accurate, and their steps were at first tentative. As they drew closer to the river, Torgul raised his hand to signal a stop. He spoke in a subdued voice.

"We're gettin' close. I can smell 'em. I think they're on that little hill on the left, the one that overlooks the water. See all them boulders? Looks like a likely place for a cave mouth."

None of the humans could as yet smell anything. Though their natural aversion to goblins was strong, it was nowhere near the atavistic hatred between dwarf and goblin. Generations of warfare between the two races had resulted in a sharpening of the dwarf's ability to scent the presence of his ancestral foe. This was an advantage of incalculable value. It would be very hard for goblins to take Torgul by surprise.

Yet in spite of their mutual antipathy, dwarves and goblins actually had much in common. They were nearly the same size, though dwarves tended to be somewhat taller and more robust of frame. Both had a decided penchant for the subterranean and were expert tunnelers, though dwarven excavations were much more precise. Both enjoyed excellent night vision and an inborn sense of direction that allowed them to function normally in the labyrinthine windings of the underground.

Dwarf and goblin both loved beautiful things and had an instinctual need to gather valuable items of treasure. Dwarven craftsmanship was, of course, legendary. Their smiths produced the finest gold and silver jewelry.

Their weapons and armor were lavishly embellished with skillful embossing and inlay. Goblins, on the other hand, were capable of only the crudest efforts. They hammered simple weapons and tools from badly smelted iron when they had to, but mostly they preferred to steal the goods of others rather than go to the effort of producing their own.

The abundant similarities between the two races led some scholars to posit a common ancestor. But anyone suggesting to Torgul that he was in any way related to a goblin would have found himself immediately engaged in a duel to the death. To suggest such a thing to a goblin would have most likely resulted in a knife in the back.

The party followed Torgul's nose, always careful to stay under the cover of the trees and rocks, with which the sides of the slight hill were thickly strewn. They were getting very close. Even the humans could sense it. Roscoe pulled the group together in the shadow of a great tumble of boulders that offered good concealment.

"It's time for a bit of scouting, so it is. Sarah, would you put the invisibility upon Torgul so that he might ascertain the exact location of the cave we're seekin'?"

"Aye, I can. But it might be better to use my old glamour spell. It would use up a lot less of my power. If I made him look like a goblin, he could…"

Torgul exploded in an outburst of wrath none of them had seen before.

"Nay! I am willing to suffer many appalling indignities for the welfare of this party! By my ancestors' glorious bones, I already have! But none shall say that Torgul Bonelip, twenty-third of that name, ever suffered himself to be made up as a goblin. Missy, that is just too much to ask."

Invisibility, they decided, was the better option. Sarah produced her wand, wove her spell, and cast it on the dwarf. His body immediately faded from view, but his voice remained unchanged.

"Can you see me? Is everything as it should be?"

Sarah replied.

"We can't see you at all, but be careful. I'm really not sure how fragile the spell might be. Don't do anything that draws attention to yourself. Be as quiet as you can. And stay focused. Don't let yourself get distracted. Also, I don't know how long the spell will last."

Dwarves could move quite silently when they needed to, and Torgul, an experienced Adventurer, was skilled at stealthy action. As he moved around to the western side of the hill, the river came into view below him. The location of the goblin den was well chosen. The hilltop commanded an excellent view of the river in both directions. Goblin lookouts could keep a close watch on river traffic and have their pick of likely targets.

Torgul wondered how many lookouts were on the hilltop, how many pairs of eyes were staring in his direction as he made his way through bare patches on the hillside. Actually there were none, for they had all been withdrawn for that day's assault on Bart's party downstream. That fight was raging at that very moment, but Torgul had no way to know this.

Finally he saw the entrance to their cave. On the map it was depicted as a large, yawning mouth with menacing fangs. That portrayal, he realized, was not altogether fanciful. It was an ugly cave, exactly the kind that goblins delight in. Creeping closer, the dwarf discerned a squad of goblin sentries lounging about the entrance. None seemed particularly attentive to his duties. In fact, they were all drunk, swilling steadily on their beloved onion wine. Their leaders were all gone to the battle, so there was no one left to say them nay. Some were fast asleep with their scattered on the ground at their feet.

Sarah had been adamant that Torgul should do nothing that might reveal his presence, but this opportunity was just too good to resist. He stepped forward, drawing his scramasax just as a goblin lifted his chin to swig from his skin of wine. The invisible blade slashed across his throat and then did the same for the companions sitting on either side. These deaths went largely unnoticed by the other goblins, who were absorbed in their own inebriated bantering. Then it was too late, and the rest shared the fate of the first three.

Roscoe and the others waited anxiously for Torgul's return. They were surprised to see him coming back across the hillside, fully visible and splashed with blood. He apparently had no idea that his invisibility had dissipated.

"All right, I'm back and standin' right before you. And missy, this is a most gratifyin' spell you put upon me."

Roscoe looked grim.

"Torgul, we can all see you. The spell has failed. You're drippin' with blood. What happened?"

"There was this group of guards by the entrance, and I thought to make it easier for us by…"

Sarah jumped in, livid.

"Didn't I tell you not to do anything that might give you away or break your focus? But then you had to go and…"

At this point Roscoe hushed her with a gesture and a stern look. He understood about dwarves and goblins.

"It's all right, Torgul. I'm sure our progress will be much easier for your efforts. And now we know what we should *not* be doin' while under Sarah's spell. We'll all have to be a mite more careful from here on, so we shall. How many did you get?"

"Nine, but all were given to drink, and three were asleep on the ground."

"Well done, nevertheless. Congratulations!"

Sarah recast the spell, this time over the entire group. As she did so, she felt a significant ebb in her psychic energy. The spell was expensive.

Torgul led them out, followed by Roscoe, Thurmond, and Sarah. Nod and Sod brought up the rear, bows at the ready. They skirted around the hill and climbed up to the cave, trusting in their invisibility and yet all too aware of its fragility. The dead guards lay just as Torgul had left them. The goblins inside had not yet discovered that they had unexpected guests.

They stared down into the gaping, uninviting cave. The exterior was festooned with moss and creepers. Inside, the floor ran straight for several yards and then plunged downward at a severe angle. It was easy to imagine a monster residing in such a cave. The goblin stench was hideous, though not quite so bad, as Thurmond recalled, as that of trolls.

The party paused at that forbidding opening, summoning their reserves of courage before entering the sinister lair. Roscoe picked up a spear from among the fallen goblins. It was obviously of human make, with a long, leaf-shaped head on a smooth ash shaft.

"Here, Thurmond, take this. Sling your bow on your back and take this in both hands. Torgul and I will keep 'em real busy, so we will. You just stand behind us. Hang back and wait 'til you spot a target, then stick this right into it, easy as you please. Got it?"

"Aye, I got it."

And with that they entered the cave.

CHAPTER THIRTY

THE FIGHT ON THE RIVERBANK, PART ONE

During the night, Bart's men raised a crude breastwork of dirt, rocks, and logs. An abatis of prickly tree trunks and branches provided an additional layer of defense to the front of this work. Severed goblin heads, blood trophies from yesterday's victory, were displayed on sticks along the top of the barrier as a warning against further onslaught. Both Sims and Artos recognized the shabbiness of their defenses, but goblins were small, and they prayed it would be sufficient.

They all knew another attack was pending. The drums had started in the early hours of morning, long before daybreak. First the tinny-voiced *tonbak*, then the deep-throated roar of the kettle. Next goblin bugles began to blow, shrill and frightening. Finally came the guttural war chant of the goblin soldiers, reverberating through the dark of the forest and gradually increasing in volume as more and more joined the assembling host.

Sleep was impossible. The cacophonous bellowing of their unseen foes and the continual atonal blatting of their horns unnerved even the veteran soldiers. The boatmen and Bart's novice fighters were ready to bolt, to board their boats and sail for home. Here Bart demonstrated leadership for the first time. He stood by Rupert's grounded craft, a sword in one hand and a torch in the other, and promised to burn it if anyone attempted to board. Rupert remained nearby, watching intently but saying nothing. No one knew what he would do if Bart actually attempted to ply the torch.

The goblin host continued to swell, and the chanting grew louder. Their chieftains led them in a monotonous call-and-response to excite them to battle frenzy. The timbre of their voices, the pattern of the drumming, and the wailing of the bugles were all somehow offensive to human sensibility. The clamor went on and on and on. The soldiers crouching behind the earthwork longed desperately for the horrible din to end, but they were all too aware that its cessation would signal the coming of the goblins. It was a rough night.

The goblin plan had called for a predawn attack, when the humans would be at their sleepiest. These creatures disliked daylight and preferred the night attack when their natural ability to see in the darkest caverns gave them a tremendous advantage over night blind humans.

But such an attack was, on this occasion, not to be. The host was too slow in assembling. Rounding up the fugitives from yesterday's abortive attack took too long. There was not enough time to summon reinforcements from outlying garrisons.

This was to be a maximum effort. Every able-bodied goblin warrior would take part. The hilltops and riverbanks were stripped of their lookouts. Untried youngsters and lamed old-timers were given weapons and assigned to improvised war bands. A mere handful of warriors was left behind to guard the entrance to their lair. It was not expected that anything more would be required. All the humans, they believed, were penned by the river.

The first streaks of light were appearing in the sky as the final contingents arrived and the various units were marshaled into position. Goblin tactics are almost always the same—a furious rush intended to overwhelm their enemies in a single blow. But the warlord of this group, the high chief of an amalgamation of several clans, possessed a greater imagination than most of his fellows. He had something special in mind for the despicable humans who had intruded on his demesne.

It was time. He raised his heavy, hook-bladed sword and brought it down hard.

The goblin attack opened with a barrage of darts from the half-dozen crude ballistae they had positioned on a slight rise overlooking the human position. These were sufficiently powerful to drive their projectiles right through the breastwork and into the defenders behind it. One of Sims's men was struck squarely on the shield, which the dart penetrated and pinned to his chest. Other darts flew high to carry far beyond their targets and splash into the river.

Then the goblin archers let fly, and the sky was dark with their arrows. These did less damage than on the previous day as the men were hunkered behind the breastwork. Seeing this, the goblins began to shoot high up in the air so that their arrows plunged almost straight down, and the men began to take casualties. A boatman was struck in the neck, just where it joined his shoulder. He collapsed without a sound.

When their supply of arrows and darts was expended, the goblins dropped their bows and surged forward with sword, spear, and axe. The drums beat with even greater expectation. The horns blared louder than ever. Bart's archers opened on the onrushing horde. They could not miss, so densely packed were their ranks. Dozens fell, but the loss was negligible due to the sheer size of their host.

Many in the first ranks were impaled on the sharpened branches of the abatis, pushed to their deaths by ranks behind. This obstacle effectively slowed the headlong charge, forcing the goblins to clamber over or dodge around the entanglement of interwoven tree trunks and boughs. Bart's archers continued to take a deadly toll.

At last the goblins began to penetrate the abatis and strike the human shield line. But they did so in separate handfuls rather than in a single, overwhelming wave. In addition, the breastwork, scarcely the height of a man's hips, proved a formidable barrier to the goblins. It afforded complete protection to the men's legs, allowing them to keep their shields raised against head blows. Those goblins who did manage to assault the line were slaughtered.

But now more and more of them were finding their way through the abatis. Others were pulling away the troublesome barrier so that subsequent ranks could attack the breastwork unimpeded. Their lines surged forward, undeterred by the initial setback. The horns blew, and the drums beat. The great goblin warlord, surrounded by his bodyguard, personally led the assault.

On their side of the barrier, the men drew together, aware that the real battle was about to begin. Artos kept his previous position on the right, holding his glaive hard against the back of his men. Sims was on the left. He had sheathed his sword in preference for a pike on a very long shaft he had taken from the riverboat. Its extended reach allowed him to hit the goblins long before their weapons came into range. He slew them one after another, their bodies adding an additional impediment to their attack.

But there were just too many to hold off. Soon goblin warriors were climbing to the top of the breastwork, striking down at the men behind it. Some launched themselves bodily at their foes, grasping at their shield rims in an attempt to bear them over backward. The shield line began to waver as men stepped back to make room to ply their weapons.

The warlord and his bodyguard came on in a flying wedge. They struck the lightly armored boatmen standing in the center of the line. Several went down. The others fell back, and the shield line was broken. Goblin warriors began to pour through the opening. Artos was forced to pull his men back to keep from being taken in the flank. The remaining boatmen continued to step back, further widening the hole in the line.

It was at this moment that the second phase of the goblin war plan came to pass. Their warlord was a wily one. He understood that the full attention of the humans would be devoted to the frontal assault, so he had ordered a waterborne attack from the rear. While the attack on the breastwork was at its height, a flotilla of stealthy dugout canoes had landed on the shoal by the grounded boat. A force of fifty or more goblins was at this moment climbing up the bank behind the line of men.

Rupert, standing far behind the line, was the first to see this new threat. He glanced about. Sims was occupied trying to stop the retreat of the boatmen. Luckily, on the left, his own soldiers seemed to be holding far better than the boatmen. He grabbed two of them by the arm and pointed at the new emerging danger. He beckoned frantically to Plutonius and Gregorio, who stood frightened and useless, well away from the fighting. His message was clear. If the goblins made it to the top of the embankment, the magician and the cleric would be among the first to die.

Rupert and the soldiers sprinted down the hill to counter this attack.

Two boatmen, disheartened but not defeated, joined them. Surprisingly, Gregorio did the same. With a sigh of resignation, Plutonius drew his sword and followed.

Rupert reached the edge of the embankment just as the first goblin head appeared above it. He gave it a hard kick that sent the creature sailing backward. Other heads appeared, and his men slashed down with their swords. The goblins thrust up spears to drive the defenders back and give their comrades a chance to scuttle to the top of the bank. Others shot arrows that struck their shields with a hollow *thunk*.

The men were for a time successful in holding the line of the embankment, though the number of goblins against them continued to increase. But then a new peril appeared. A unit of a dozen or more goblins came charging in from their left. These had moved down the shoal away from the humans on the bank above. They had then been able to scale this impediment unopposed and could now attack their foes on an equal footing.

Rupert was sure he was viewing his own death. He and his handful could not fight this new group and at the same time keep the others from climbing up from below. They would inevitably be swarmed over and slain. The goblins were too many.

When Rupert had pulled men from the line to meet the rearward threat, he had done so at random, grabbing whichever bodies were close at hand. Fortunately for him—fortunately for them all—one of these had been Jasper. His troll hand again proved a terror to the goblins, striking out with a will of its own. He had long abandoned any attempt to control it and simply allowed the lethal talons to do their work. His companions stood in awe as they watched Jasper turn on the second group and rip the face clean off a goblin swordsman. It slashed left and right—dismembering, disemboweling, dissecting.

The goblins stalled, dismayed by the horror wrought by the hand. And in that moment, Gregorio strode forward, gawky and inelegant in his ridiculous orange robe. He positioned himself directly in front of the onrushing goblins and began to read from a parchment scroll. They stopped as one, suddenly enveloped in a swirling purple mist that evaporated as quickly as it had appeared. Then they fell in a heap—dead or asleep, it did not matter. Plutonius plunged his sword in each one, just to make sure.

Now Gregorio turned to those still fighting their way up the bank against Rupert and his men. He read again, his voice high pitched and cracking, and another group of goblins was seized by his spell. The swirling mist was a pale green this time, and the effect was different. The goblins began to writhe, clutching at their throats as if choking. Their eyes bulged, and they fell down, squirming and kicking into death.

This was more than the remaining goblins could endure. They broke off their attack and fled down the bank toward their dugouts. Gregorio stepped to the edge of the bank, scroll in hand, preparing to blast them with yet another spell. But he never had the chance. A goblin archer standing on the shoal proved more skillful with his weapon than most of his comrades. His arrow tore through the unrolled scroll and struck the magician in the arm. For a brief moment, Gregorio stared down at the injury as if uncomprehending, but then a second arrow entered his left eye and penetrated his brain.

This clever shot was not enough to stem the rout of the goblin river force. Once the momentum of their attack was arrested, they lost all zest for battle. They fled back to the river in a panic. Some managed to board their canoes and paddle away. Others flung themselves into the water and promptly drowned.

Rupert instantly gathered his men and started back to the main fight at the breastwork.

CHAPTER THIRTY-ONE

THE FIGHT ON THE RIVERBANK, PART TWO

The goblin onslaught carried the center of the breastwork, pushing back the boatmen who had held it. But years of journeying through a danger fraught wilderness had toughened these men. They did not scare easily nor give in readily. Though their line was ragged and badly bowed, they continued to resist with grim tenacity.

The offensive spirit of the goblins, however, seemed to lag after they achieved their initial objective of the breastwork. Rather than pushing forward and breaking through the badly weakened line before them, they paused to allow others to cross the barrier and swell their ranks. The drums and horns abruptly ceased as the musicians dropped their instruments and ran to join their comrades. A second great charge was in the offing, but the goblin host needed a minute to catch its breath.

And in that moment, Artos struck back. He turned his men at an oblique angle and struck at the goblin flank. He met little resistance, for in pausing, the goblin formation had deteriorated into a disordered mob. As had happened on the first day, some simply stood and waited to be killed. But then the warlord and his guard came plunging forward to revitalize the stalled assault. He spied Artos, recognized him as a leader, and knew that were he to be slain, his men would be easily dispatched.

Though much smaller than the bulky Artos, the warlord was quite large for a goblin. He ran straight for his chosen foe, intending to slay him in one quick pass. Armed with a small, round shield and a short heavy sword, his best chance was to come in very close, well inside the effective range of Artos's glaive. If he hesitated at a distance, he would be at the mercy of that longer weapon.

Artos aimed a hard blow at the warlord's head, which was blocked by the goblin's shield. Then the warlord was in close. But Artos also knew a thing or two about close combat. He gave the goblin a powerful shove with the shaft of the glaive, hoping to knock him off his feet. The warlord was too nimble. Though thrown backward, he did not fall. This gave Artos another chance with the glaive, a fake to the head followed by a blow at the shinbone. The warlord dodged back—but only for a moment—and then came on again. He parried Artos's next blow, another head shot, with the blade of his sword. Its iron was much softer than the fine steel of the glaive and was badly notched. He howled in rage and pressed in.

Curiously, the warriors of both sides now drew apart and ceased fighting to watch this battle of champions. Goblins lined the top of the breastwork, sitting and standing to get a better view. Artos's men held their sergeant in awe and cheered loudly as he rained blows upon the warlord. The goblins were not to be outdone and began to applaud every parry and riposte of their leader.

Then a bad thing happened. The head of Artos's glaive had two stout metal strips running down the shaft to prevent it from being cut off. The cunning warlord saw this and, stepping even closer than before, aimed an extremely hard blow at the shaft just below those strips, snapping it in twain and leaving Artos with nothing more than a four-foot wooden stick. The warlord leaped in to finish the job with a victorious cry.

Quite unexpectedly, Bart rose to the occasion. He had been, like the others, standing back and watching the fray. The sight of Artos weaponless and about to be slain awakened in him a terrible anger. He came in from the left, hoping to blindside the warlord, but the goblins clustered atop the breastwork saw his intentions and shouted a warning to their chieftain. Turning from the momentarily harmless Artos, he rushed at Bart in a fury.

Bart certainly had the finest armor of anyone on the field that day. But any experienced warrior could tell he was a novice to battle. There was just something in the way he carried himself. The warlord saw this at once and was determined to slay him quickly before his real opponent, the battle-hardened Artos, could rearm. He came on with a wild flurry of blows that caused the goblins on the wall to cheer and cheer.

Bart did his best. He was well versed in the fashionable fencing maneuvers so popular with the young dandies with whom he sparred at Einarr's Academie of Fence. These moves were considered elegant, graceful, almost a form of dance, but there was nothing elegant or graceful about what he was facing at the moment. The goblin's attack was brutal and tenacious. He just kept battering away. His blows were very hard, and Bart bit his tongue after a solid shot struck his helmet.

Luckily for him, Bart's fine armor was for the most part proof against the warlord's sword. Bart was struck again and again. The blows were painful but did him no real injury. He began to gain confidence, and as he did so, he began to fight back, striking at the goblin with very little thought given to defense.

This, Bart discovered, was what he had been looking for all his life. Sparring matches with his cronies could in no way compare with actual life-and-death combat. This was the explosive outlet for the bottled rage that seethed within him—the perfect remedy for the years of humiliation and frustration at the hands of a cruel father. For the scarcely concealed scorn of his inferiors. For the condescension of his so-called friends. The desire to kill consumed Bart.

The warlord, however, was by far the superior swordsman. He came in low and quick but then rose and snapped a fast blow to the head. As Bart raised his shield to block it, he saw to his dismay that he had been faked. It one fluid motion, the goblin's sword changed direction and snaked in under the shield's tip. It was a powerful blow that smote Bart squarely in the ribs, shearing through the links of his mail and the thick quilting beneath. It sliced into his body, and his blood began to flow. Bart gasped. His eyes began to lose focus, and his shield began to droop. He was aware of the warlord again closing in, his hideous grinning face only inches from his own.

Bart, however, was not yet fated to die. Sims appeared as if from nowhere.

With the battle in a lull, Sims had crossed from the far side of the line to lend a hand in whatever way he could. With the whole force of his body behind it, he now drove his pike through the skull of the warlord, who dropped his sword and flung his arms wide, as if suddenly offering to take Bart in a friendly embrace. Then he dropped like a bundle of rags.

Sims cared nothing for chivalry or fair play. He had taken the warlord entirely unaware, which was, for him, always the best way. The goblins on the breastwork, though, were outraged and at once leaped to the attack.

Nonetheless, the goblins' efforts were doomed, squandered when they had failed to press forward earlier and complete the victory they had almost won. They now lacked momentum, and their most capable leader was slain. The men, on the other hand, had taken the opportunity to rest and reorganize, so when the goblins surged forward as an unruly rabble, they rushed into a deadly trap.

Artos, armed now with sword and shield, called a charge. This was risky. His men had never been adept at this particular maneuver. But he need not have worried, for these were no longer the raw recruits who had fumbled and stumbled on Einarr's practice field. They jumped forward in a solid, unstoppable mass. The foremost goblins were simply bowled over and slain as they lay on the ground. The line pressed on, forcing their enemies back and pinning them against the breastwork.

On the other end of the line, Sims ran to rejoin his tiny force of soldiers and boatmen. They were too few to advance but continued to provide an impenetrable barrier against which the goblin assault was futile. At that moment Rupert and his men returned from their fight on the riverbank. Combining with the small knot of boatmen still holding the center, they launched a savage attack straight into the middle of the goblin mob.

Lacking effective leadership, penned in on three sides, and pushed back against the breastwork, the goblins again began to lose their will to fight. Those who could scampered back over the breastwork and fled into the woods. The vast majority were pressed so closely together that they could not raise their weapons. These were readily slain. Some few continued to resist. The warlord's bodyguard fought to the last. But as is often the case, the goblin's lack of staying power proved fatal, and most of their vast host was soon strewn lifeless on the battlefield.

This time there was no holding the men back. As the goblin survivors took to their heels, the remaining men were hot behind them, striking down the stragglers and the wounded. These men had come for loot. They had fought two horrific battles, and victory had come at a terrible price. They were not now to be denied the fruits of that victory. They vaulted the breastwork and surged through the woods. The men, like the goblins, had become a leaderless mob.

Some of the fleeing goblins fled blindly into the underbrush, but the largest group beat a path straight back to their lair. Their track was easy to follow, being well marked with blood trails and discarded weapons. The men arrived at the same cave mouth into which Roscoe and his party had descended shortly before.

✝

Every person remaining alive on the battlefield was unhappy. The wounded, of course, were in agony. Abandoned by their loot-hungry comrades, they were left to bind their own wounds. Some were taking their last broken breaths. Bart sat stripped to the waist against a rock. He had somehow managed to wriggle out of his mail and padding, which now lay on the ground in a heap. His linen undershirt was rolled into a thick pad, which he kept pressed against the bleeding wound in his side. He was furious with Rupert, who stood before him. Rupert was equally angry with Bart.

As soon as the goblin host had been dispatched, their previous animosity had immediately flared, though this time over a new issue. Rupert insisted that Bart's wounds had rendered him incapable of leading their expedition. As the lieutenant, it was now his responsibility to assume command.

He sneered at Bart.

"You are nothing more than a foolish child and a blundering lummox. You were never fit to lead men, especially not now when death is so obviously coming to claim you. If you want to retain your command, come then and wrest it from me."

Bart was in no condition to renew their earlier fight. He was sure two of his ribs were broken, and there was a long, deep laceration across his left side.

It was painful to breathe and far worse to move. Arguing with Rupert was like being stabbed with a dagger.

"Cowardly dog! You taunt me when you know I cannot rise and thrash you like the lowborn villain you are. Fetch your friar! Have him heal me with his spell casting, and we will see who leads this group."

Rupert laughed, knowing there was nothing Bart could do to oppose him.

"Nay, the good friar's holy power is limited. I have instructed him to use his spells to heal several of the more lightly injured men. We will need them should the goblins return. He has nothing extra to waste on a broken fragment such as yourself. You should be thankful that I don't just put you out of the way like a lamed mule."

This provoked an outburst of rage from Bart that, in turn, induced a spasm of violent coughing. Rupert laughed again, turned, and walked on.

Friar Plutonius was well aware of the cause of their dispute. Rupert had adamantly forbidden him to restore his wounded rival, so he now stayed well away from both, moving across the blood-soaked ground where the dead lay sprawled with the injured. He could draw on only so much holy healing power each day, and this amount had dwindled over the years as Plutonius fell more and more into corruption. So it was essential that he help only those men whose wounds were such that they could be restored to duty with only a minimal expenditure.

Some of the goblins continued to squirm or twitch. He passed his sword through them all, living and dead, a task he did not find particularly onerous. Plutonius had grown into a spiteful old man. Motivated mostly by envy and avarice, he resented the great advantages bestowed on nobles, even minor ones like Rupert and Bart. Why should they enjoy what he had been denied?

But he had fallen in with them readily enough. That asinine business with the troll hand had paid extremely well. And this expedition, if he lived, would bring him more gold than he would normally see in a year. Perhaps enough for the rest of his life. So he had joined on, in spite of his loathing for Rupert.

Friars of all denominations were strictly forbidden to join adventures on a freelance basis as he had done. A cleric belonged to his church, body and soul. So any remuneration he might receive was to be turned over to his ecclesiastical exchequer.

Friars were often assigned by their superiors to accompany adventuring parties in exchange for a set percentage of the profits. The Black Friars' standard price was fifteen percent off the top. The Blues, being more prestigious, demanded a whopping twenty percent. The other clerical orders asked for less, the specific percentage depending on their standing in the hierarchy.

Plutonius had entered the service of Lady Renata—and Rupert by extension—without the knowledge or approval of his superiors. Were he to be found out, he would face severe punishment—most likely imprisonment, whipping, and finally excommunication. This last would strip him of his holy powers and leave him an old man with no special talents.

But he was also a cagey old man who was always alert for ways to turn awkward situations to his advantage. He thought he saw one now. He watched as Rupert stepped over the breastwork and disappeared in the direction of the woods, perhaps looking for his departed men or scouting for goblin stragglers. He quickly made his way over to Bart, who was sitting with his eyes closed and his jaw clenched.

"Be of good cheer, Lord Staynes. I have come to help you. I am more mindful of my obligations than to squander all my power on mere commoners when my noble lord is in need of succor. Fear not, milord, I will have you hearty soon."

Bart opened his eyes but said nothing. He distrusted this creature, but he was too much in pain to care overmuch. He gingerly removed the blood-soaked shirt that served as a bandage and allowed the friar to examine his wound. Plutonius bent close.

"'Tis a right grim cut, surely, but not mortal unless it putrefies. And two ribs are stove in and pressing on your lungs—right painfully, I'd imagine. Most of this I can mend with a healing prayer. Not all of it, but the pain will ease and the bleeding stop. Tomorrow when my powers are sufficiently renewed, I can..."

Bart interrupted. He'd heard enough foolish talk for one day.

"Just fix me. Do whatever you can, but make me able to walk again—and fight if I have to. Just do whatever it takes, but get me on my feet."

Plutonius began to pray, and Bart immediately felt sleepy. He slipped back into a pleasant doze and could actually feel the pain ebbing away as the chant continued. Within a few moments, Bart came out of his doze and discovered that he felt much improved. His side still hurt, but the pain was now bearable, and the excruciating pressure on his lungs was gone. He looked at Plutonius, who grinned at him slyly.

"Lord Rupert forbade me attend to you, milord. Should he discover my defiance, he will make me pay for it, most probably with my life. He despises me already, though I know not why."

Bart well understood Rupert's feelings. Plutonius was a despicable old man. But he had just proved himself to be very useful, so Bart was not inclined to see him slain by a wrathful Rupert.

"You may be easy on that score, old man. You will have nothing to fear from Rupert once I attend to him. Where has he gone?"

"Straight off into the woods. I think he seeks the others."

Bart began to rearm. He pulled on his padding and mail. This hurt, but he could bear it. He then attached the various plate pieces to his arms and legs. Some of the buckles and ties were difficult to reach, so Plutonius lent a hand. The friar carefully lifted the helmet onto Bart's head and strapped the shield to his left arm.

Bart still felt a bit shaky as he lurched to his feet, but he was not to be deterred from his purpose. He gathered up the half-dozen newly healed soldiers and boatmen, and led them off in search of his hated adversary. Plutonius continued his previous business of tending to the remaining wounded and skewering the occasional twitching goblin.

PART 4

UNDERGROUND

CHAPTER THIRTY-TWO

THE GOBLINS AND THE SHADOW

Torgul went first. He could see quite effectively in almost total darkness, so it was logical for him to lead the way. Goblins could be flagrantly stupid in so many ways, but they could also demonstrate great ingenuity when it came to devising death traps to safeguard their lairs. The dwarf kept a wary eye open. He knew of more than one luckless adventurer who had lost all after plummeting into a concealed pit of spikes.

Within a short span, the cave mouth narrowed to a tunnel about as wide as a tall man could spread his arms. And there they found the trap, a small, flat, seemingly harmless stone lying in the middle of their path. The dwarf recognized it at once—a solitary stone placed in the middle of an otherwise bare tunnel floor, where an unwary passerby would almost certainly kick it. Torgul gestured for the others to step carefully around it. Whatever it triggered would be unpleasant.

Their way angled steeply downward as the tunnel twisted into the depths of the hill. They could all smell goblins now, thick and foul, and it was getting steadily more difficult to see as they progressed away from the entrance. Thurmond was thinking of lighting a torch when Torgul held up his hand in a signal to wait. He disappeared around a bend but was back in a moment.

"We're in luck. The walls ahead are covered with *steg*. That's going to make things easier."

Thurmond turned to Roscoe.

"What's *steg*?"

The old adventurer silenced him with a quick shake of his head. Moving again, the party rounded the bend, and Thurmond got his answer. The tunnel walls were matted with a thick layer of moss or mold that emitted a soft luminescence. The light was dim but sufficient enough that he could make out the shadowy shapes of his companions. Torgul could see perfectly.

Most importantly, the glow of the moss would allow them to proceed without the necessity of a lighted torch. Sarah was relieved. She had no idea whether their cloak of invisibility would cover the light of a torch. If not, it would surely reveal their presence to the inhabitants of the cavern complex.

Torgul made a gathering gesture with both hands, signaling that the party should draw close together. He spoke in a low tone, scarcely above a whisper.

"Something ain't right about this. There shoulda been a stronger guard at the gate, not just a handful of drunk idiots. And there should be goblins comin' and goin' along this passage. And we should be able to hear 'em screechin' away in that horrible language of theirs. And other sounds too. But instead it's all quiet and empty. Somethin' ain't right here."

Roscoe responded.

"I was just thinkin' the same thing, so I was. It's plain to see that the goblin army ain't at home at the moment. They're off on some errand of mischief, bringin' woe to some poor, undeservin' souls. It's providence for us, most certainly it is. But we best proceed most carefully, for even if the warriors are away, I'd bet that their wives and brats are here in great numbers."

Thurmond was surprised to hear this. He had never before considered that goblins might have families, let alone wives. And in truth, they did not, at least in the sense humans recognized. Goblin society was more akin to a dog pack. It was a stark communal existence that placed no value on ethics or compassion. The strong dominated the weak. The females, being of smaller size, were subjugated to the caprices of the males. Juveniles were left to fend for themselves from the time they could toddle and were forced to earn their survival in an indifferent and often hostile surrounding.

At the moment, several hundred of these females and their offspring—goblins were prodigious breeders—were assembled in a series of large caves below the feet of the adventure party. With their males away, they had drawn together in large defensive groups. Noise and movement were kept to a minimum. Goblins were not wise, but their survival instincts could be strong.

The map indicated a small chamber marked with a rune representing gold or wealth. It was toward this that the party now advanced. There was no need to consult the map. Each member of the party had committed the relevant parts to memory. This was no small feat, for twistings and turnings complicated their way. The passages diverged and converged, passed over, under, and around. Perhaps this convoluted warren had been dug with the strategic intention of confusing and frustrating intruders, or perhaps it simply reflected the random workings of the goblin mind.

The party dropped deeper, the tunnel descending in a series of steep switchbacks. The goblin stench grew worse, and for the first time, they could hear the murmur of high-pitched voices. They moved as softly as possible, huddled together in a single, compact mass—Torgul in the lead, followed closely by Roscoe, Thurmond, and Sarah. Nod and Sod came last, always keeping a wary eye open against an attack from the rear.

The passage widened, then opened into a huge natural cavern. Here was one of the large communal dens in which an entire goblin clan went about their daily lives. All was cluttered and filthy. Crude tools, broken weapons, random bits of wood, and gnawed bones littered the floor. Piles of fetid animal skins seemed to serve as nests.

A large group of females and juveniles were gathered around a smoky fire that vented with only limited success through a crack in the ceiling. They were fully engrossed in the antics of an ancient female, who pranced before them, waving a large bone and apparently enacting in pantomime a tale of engrossing import.

As quietly as possible, the stouthearted adventurers began to move past this assemblage but stopped in mid-step when one precocious goblin brat suddenly turned in their direction, suspicion written plainly on his face. They watched in dismay as his nostrils dilated with a deep intake of breath. He looked about, wary, and opened his mouth as if to shout a warning. To their great relief, he instead sped off in the direction from which they had just come.

Torgul signaled, and the party moved a little faster now. Should the brat continue all the way to the entrance, he would discover the slain guards, and all would be up. They moved through two more huge caverns, very much like the first, with dozens of females and brats living in collective squalor.

The fourth and final room was the Great Hall or throne room of the goblin warlord. No actual throne was in evidence, but the furnishings here were superior to the foulness and disarray of the common rooms. Spears and swords were neatly stacked. The floor boasted what had once been fine carpets, though they were now sadly soiled and frayed. Tarnished silver platters held remains of some bygone goblin feast.

The room was deserted—the warlord and his bodyguard had just been slain in their abortive attack on the breastwork. In one corner, Torgul came upon the warlord's snake pit. All goblin leaders maintained such pits for the entertainment of certain favored guests. Thurmond peeked inside and then looked away in revulsion.

This was the room they had sought. This was where they would find the door to the treasure chamber. Even the correct section of wall was indicated on the map. But either the map was in error or the portal was well concealed, for, search as they might, nothing of the sort was to be seen.

Torgul continued to search and search, his face and fingers pressed against the wall's blank surface. Roscoe turned to Sarah. He was getting desperate, well aware that they must make haste. The goblin soldiers could return at any moment, or the precocious brat might carry back word of the slain gate guards. He loomed over her.

"Darlin' girl, might you know a wee spell to reveal the whereabouts of that cursed door? Maybe something to detect the presence of gold? Or something to change a stone wall into a window of glass? Anything at all, girl?"

Sarah was a little frightened of Roscoe at that moment. She saw in him a grim determination that had not been present in the jolly vendor of fruit and vegetables.

"I'm sorry, Roscoe, but I don't know such spells. They would be divination spells. They're not the kind I'm good at, and they'd be more advanced than…"

"Stand back!"

Thurmond's voice was shrill with excitement and dangerously loud.

"Please, stand away from the wall."

He had discovered a full pail of the goblins' onion wine, which he splashed against the wall just at the point where they guessed the door should be. Miraculously, a thin crack appeared in the stones as the noxious beverage seeped away. That was enough for Torgul, who began scratching out the portal's outline with the edge of his scramasax.

When the entire outline was exposed, he spoke to the others.

"This isn't goblin work. It's much too fine. Nobody but my people makes hidden doors as excellent as this one. That means that these were dwarven halls long before these stinking little biters took over.

"Now that's both bad and good for us. Bad because the keyhole is still hidden, and even if we find it, we have no key—if an actual key is required. It's good, because I know something of such matters and may be able to figure things out, though it's likely to take…"

Sarah interjected.

"Try drawing the wealth rune on the door. See what happens."

Torgul was prepared to be offended by the rudeness of the girl's interruption, but he paused, impressed by the ingenuity of her suggestion. He took a piece of charcoal from a nearby brazier and sketched the symbol. Nothing happened. He added a few words in the dwarven tongue, but the door remained impassive. He tried again, repeating the words, and when they failed, he gave the door a heavy, frustrated kick. It swung silently open.

Torgul's features spread in a broad grin. This was the first time any of the others had seen such a sight. He actually chuckled as he spoke.

"I knew it had to be something like this. Had to be real simple, or the brainless goblins couldn't open it. It's usually something like this, only…"

He turned to Sarah.

"only I might never have thought of adding the rune. That was indeed a worthy inspiration."

She demurred.

"A lucky guess, that's all. What about Thurmond? His bucket of wine was no less inspired."

At this point Roscoe intervened.

"Certainly the three of you have proved your worth, both at this moment and many times before. But now ain't the moment to stand about singin' our own praises. Let us pillage the treasure room and abscond before our good hosts reappear."

Torgul was the first through the doorway with Roscoe close behind. Both stood in silent awe of what they saw in the flickering torchlight. It was indeed a treasure room. There was gold, so much gold. Gold coins overflowed from chests and spilled from sacks on the floor. Gold bars and ingots sang a siren song of greed. Gold jewelry and gewgaws. Golden crowns and scepters. Golden spurs and golden goblets. A coffer of newly minted sovereigns winked seductively. Gold-filigreed weapons and armor called to their eager fingers.

It was then that Torgul spotted the axe, a large, two-handed weapon on a stout wooden haft. The head drooped down in a long beard embellished with delicate interlaced knotwork of inlayed silver and gold. It was clearly dwarven work and a magnificent piece even by their high standards.

Torgul stepped forward, intent on seizing the axe for his own, and this thoughtless act nearly cost him his life. As he lifted it, an immense black shadow suddenly rose up before the dwarf and dealt him a blow that sent him spinning senseless to the floor. It hovered above him, slightly hunched, human in shape, but much taller than any man. There were no features visible, just a silhouette so black that it seemed to absorb light.

Its huge hand was raised to finish the fallen dwarf when Roscoe moved forward to cover his friend with his shield and body. The creature was slow to react, allowing Roscoe time to aim a powerful blow at the center of its head. He was aware of a slight resistance as the weapon passed through the target, but the creature suffered no discernible effect. It then returned a buffet so powerful that Roscoe was knocked back out of the doorway.

The creature emerged from the treasure room in pursuit of the stunned Roscoe. Thurmond stepped in from the side and thrust his spear into what ought to be its face. Unfazed, the creature lashed out with a backhand that was more a push than a blow, but it was sufficient to knock the young man from his feet. Nod and Sod sent crossbow bolts whizzing into its chest, but these too had no effect, passing though the shadow form and striking the wall behind.

It struck Roscoe again, catching him on the side of the head. His helmet was sent flying across the chamber, and he went down in a profusion of blood. Next it turned on Sarah. She had long since realized she would be of little help in physical combat. Her bow, therefore, remained on her back, her sword in its sheath. She held instead the spell scroll Thurmond had stolen from Staynes's library. Her studies aboard the riverboat had, she believed, provided her with the requisite knowledge to at least read and thereby activate the spells written upon it.

What she was about to do was highly risky. Not only was the nature of the scrolled spells entirely unknown, but Sarah's very limited magical ability would not allow her to aim them at the proper target. Such rogue spells were dangerous and unpredictable. They might strike friend as well as foe and could even turn against the spellcaster.

But with the shadow creature now lurching toward her, Sarah knew they had little to lose, so she read the first of the three spells inscribed on the scroll.

CHAPTER THIRTY-THREE

FATAL AMBUSH

When Bart caught up with his men, they were still gathered at the mouth of the goblin caves. Rupert had removed his helmet and was holding it under his arm. His mail coif was thrown back onto his neck, so his head was protected by only a padded arming cap. He was standing before this group, exhorting them to form up and follow him into the underground. The men sat motionlessly, ignoring his commands, with neither Sims nor Artos making any attempt to force them into action.

Rupert had no idea that Bart was stalking up from behind. And none of the men present—not even Rupert's henchman Sims—shouted a warning, though they all saw Bart as he approached with his sword raised. The men had seen too many childish antics from the two nobles and no longer cared what they did to each other.

Bart dealt Rupert a tremendous blow that left him motionless on the ground. He then delivered a passionate kick to the head of his fallen foe and, witnessing no sign of life, stepped over the recumbent form and issued a series of commands. The men cast surreptitious looks at Artos and Sims, who nodded and climbed to their feet. The others followed their example.

Of the thirty-odd soldiers and boatmen who had fought the goblins on the riverbank, only eighteen remained under arms.

Bart examined the pile of dead goblin guards. It was clear to him that, for reasons unknown, they had been slain by their own comrades. The foul little beasts were obviously in a complete panic, utterly defeated, and in full retreat. So there was nothing to do but advance with all haste. They would corner the remaining goblins in their den and destroy them. Then they would reap the rewards of victory.

Bart led his men into the cavern, moving along quickly with the rear ranks holding torches even in the mellow glow of the steg. He was in the best of spirits, supremely confident in his ability to bring his adventure to a happy conclusion. This optimism continued just until he marched his men directly into the goblin deadfall.

A torrent of head-sized rocks came crashing down from a hidden niche far above. His men screamed when struck, the heavy, jagged missiles breaking their shoulders and fracturing their skulls. The torches dropped to the floor as the bearers attempted to cover themselves. Trodden underfoot, they soon went out. Their eyes were accustomed to torchlight, and the men were left blind in the dim illumination of the steg.

From somewhere deep inside the caves, a gong began to sound, echoing along the tunnel with a hellish resonance. This was the signal for the goblin counterattack. Like most feral creatures, goblins are ferocious when cornered and will fight to the death in defense of their dens.

The survivors of the riverbank fight now came charging out of the dark, many bearing open, bleeding wounds. All were overflowing with hatred and thirsting for revenge. The gong was struck again and again, its reverberations growing louder and louder as if a frenzy of madness had taken the beater.

The attack was now joined by a limitless swarm of wives and brats, whose viciousness and determination matched that of the goblin warriors. They came armed with heavy cleavers, wooden clubs, or crude stone knives. Others fought solely with claws and teeth, clinging to the arms or ankles of their foes, biting, scratching, gouging.

The men did their best to defend themselves, but battered by the avalanche of stones and blind in the dark, they stood little chance. Many, especially the more lightly equipped boatmen, went down in the first assault, and once off their feet, they were not allowed to rise. Others stumbled backward, tripping over their comrades and the large rocks that had fallen from above.

A few fared better. Bart, in his superior armor, remained unscathed.

Jasper's troll hand once more proved a formidable weapon as it summarily crushed the skulls of the goblin brats that teemed about his feet. Though both were injured, Artos and Sims remained on their feet and fought desperately to hold back the deluge of swords and spears and knives and teeth.

The men retreated step-by-step, stabbing and chopping, stomping young goblins underfoot. Their ears rang with a cacophony of shrieks, howls, screams, and the incessant pounding of the horrible gong. They continued to die in ones and twos, while goblin fingers poked at their eyes and clutched at their throats. The tunnel floor, largely invisible to the night-blind men, was slippery with the blood of friend and foe.

Then Artos and Sims went down. For a brief moment they continued to struggle on the floor, but they were soon buried beneath the writhing mass of goblins. More and more of the vile creatures surged forward in a relentless wave. Bart's men broke ranks, and there was nothing left to do but flee.

The few survivors, Bart in the lead, finally emerged from the cave mouth into the blessed daylight. They scampered frantically down the hillside in the direction of the riverboat. A barrage of arrows flew from the opening and landed among them, but it was of brief duration and did no further damage. The goblins, decimated and exhausted, offered no further pursuit. With their warlord dead and their warriors almost annihilated, their aggressive spirit had waned.

The fleeing men, however, remained unaware that the assault had ceased and assumed the goblins were hot on their heels. They plunged through the woods in a blind panic, casting away weapons and armor, their one objective being to reach the boat and sail away from this accursed spot.

Bart strove to remove his cumbersome armor as he ran, but there were too many buckles and ties connecting too many separate pieces. Armor must be donned and doffed in a systematic fashion and cannot be discarded while dodging trees and bushes in a state of horror. As a result, Bart was left far behind as the others sped to safety.

Exhausted and disoriented, he could go no farther. He sat down and removed the heavy helmet. The relief was immediate and wonderful. Next, he discarded the greaves that encased his lower legs. These had been a constant hindrance to walking. The rest of his harness soon followed. Rather than struggle with the myriad of buckles, he simply cut the straps with his dagger.

Bart discovered that he no longer had his sword but could not remember losing it. He considered keeping his mailshirt. It was flexible and comfortable, and its weight was sustainable, but in the end, it too was left on the ground in a heap.

This frenzy of disarming, however, was little more than a welcome distraction from the much greater problem now facing the young lord. His grand adventure had ended in disaster. He had led his men to their destruction. He had botched his chance to win treasure. He was a failure.

There was no possibility of returning home and resuming his old life. His father—and he had no doubt that the old man still lived—would be well aware by now that he had squandered a substantial portion of the family fortune. Worse still, his failure would indelibly confirm his sire's estimation of his worthlessness.

He was in debt to a multitude of craftsmen and merchants, whom he had no prospect of repaying. He owed the ruthless Black Friars a tremendous sum. He cringed when he contemplated the methods they were said to employ when collecting bad debts.

Then there was the mob of spoiled lordlings he had once called friends. They would make him the butt of their coarse jokes, deriding his aspirations as a warrior and leader. Even the peasant scum would hear of his shame. They would whisper and laugh behind his back. He had lost his honor.

But these considerations were not the greatest problem. His much more serious and immediate predicament was that he had once again become completely lost in the woods. As he sped from the goblin cave, he had taken no notice of distance or direction, but merely followed the others in a blind dash for survival. Now, lacking even the most basic woodcraft, he had no idea how to find either boat or river.

Alone and armed with only a dagger in a forest undoubtedly overflowing with vengeful goblins, Bart could feel the stealthy approach of his own death.

†

Friar Plutonius continued to tend the injured men on the riverbank. Four were deemed worthy of helping and dragged down to the grounded boat. In a day or two, after a period of meditation and rest, his holy energy would be sufficiently replenished for him to lay healing hands on their wounds.

He did not intend to be left alone in a hostile wilderness. The boat would require healthy rowers, and he wanted to make sure he had them. Several others were beyond usefulness. Their wounds were too severe and would require too much time and holy energy to restore. These he dispatched with his sword just as he had done for the injured goblins. They would have been nothing but an impediment.

Consumed by his work, he gave little thought to what was going on beyond the corpse-strewn breastwork. He knew the soldiers had gone off in search of treasure and that Bart was looking to revenge himself upon Rupert, but none of that was of much concern at the moment.

Plutonius just wanted to live. He was ready to make whatever deal was necessary with whoever came back to the boat from the woods. If treasure came his way, he would certainly accept it, but his greed had succumbed to his will to survive. The corrupt old friar grew so desperate that he even began to pray, but being so well schooled in the protocol of financial transaction, even his supplication took the form of a bargain.

Let me live, and I'll be a better friar, a good friar, a perfect friar. I'll cease my sinful ways. I'll tithe just like I'm supposed to. Better yet, I'll give you all my money. Just let me live, damn it, and I'll do whatever you want.

He picked about the battlefield, looking for anything that might be useful. There was a pouch of small coins on this one's belt, a sturdy pair of boots on that one's feet. Assorted weapons and foodstuffs were gathered and brought to the boat—anything that might expedite a successful escape. Then he found the torn remnants of a spell scroll Gregorio had dropped when the arrow pierced his eye.

Plutonius was well aware that he had no business dabbling in magic. The holy power of a cleric is of an entirely different nature than the psychic energy of a magician. But as his desperation continued to grow, he was more and more ready to take any chance that might give him an edge. He was, after all, a caster of spells. How dangerous could it really be to merely read one from a scroll?

He continued to putter about the slain. Here was a warm cloak, there a broad-bladed knife in a sheath. He came upon some scraps of food and suddenly discovered how hungry he was.

The friar was just preparing a small cooking fire when Rupert stepped out from behind a large spread of broom. He was drenched in his own blood. His long curled hair was stiff and matted with the stuff. It had run down his face and neck and sopped into his mailshirt.

Plutonius recoiled in surprise. He had hoped never to see this man alive again. He had defied his master's explicit command not to cure Bart's wounds, and he did not imagine that such offense would be readily forgiven. Knowing he would have to strike a quick bargain, he filled his voice with gentleness and concern.

"Lord Rupert! You're hurt! Let me help you at once!"

He approached the injured man, his arms extended, eager to provide all possible aid. In fact, the friar's healing powers were entirely depleted, but he was willing to wager that the injured man was in no condition to defend himself. His real intention was to cut his throat with the broad-bladed knife.

But Rupert was far too experienced in deception and betrayal to be taken in by so simple a ruse. He drew his sword and stepped closer, an expression of cold hatred stamped on his blood-clotted features.

"You've needed killing for many a long day, old man. And now you've given me the reason."

"Nay, hold thy hand! You've need of a cleric! Your wounds scream for my healing hands!"

"Too late. I'm sped. I can feel my death upon me. So we'll go nearly hand in hand to whatever hell awaits us both. Your time, like mine, has come around at last."

With nothing else for it, Plutonius unrolled the scroll and read the third and final spell.

CHAPTER THIRTY-FOUR

THE FINDING OF TREASURE

Sarah read the first of the three spells on her scroll and then winced as she was immediately struck by what felt like a whirlwind of needles and pins. They lashed her face and hands, stinging cruelly. She screamed and ducked down, the shadow creature momentarily forgotten.

The spell had summoned an ice storm—a puny blow compared to those tempests provided by nature to enliven a midwinter evening, but confined as it was to the cavern's interior, it reached an intensity of violence seldom equaled by anything found out of doors.

Those still standing found themselves blown backward. The howling of the wind and the density of the ice needles rendered sight and hearing impossible. Sarah was pushed hard against the wall. She sank to the floor and raised her arms to shield her eyes, thankful for the helmet and armor that protected her head and body.

And then the storm was over, the spell being of very short duration. The ice and the wind departed as quickly as they had arrived, leaving no trace of cold or moisture. Sarah whirled around, expecting at any moment to be struck down by the shadow creature that had been looming so close above her.

To her relief, it now stood several feet apart from the group, casting about as if befuddled by the sudden storm. This boded well. The creature might be immune to the bite of steel weapons, but it could be affected by magic.

She took a quick look at her companions. Torgul had been struck down in the treasure room and could not be seen. Thurmond was on hands and knees as if attempting to rise. Nod and Sod had been bowled over by the wind and blown to the far side of the chamber. Roscoe lay flat in a pool of blood. She was on her own.

Its senses at last restored, the creature resumed its slow but deliberate approach toward the girl. Her feet instinctively began to back away as she attempted to summon sufficient concentration to read the second spell. Whatever it was to be, she knew she was unleashing a force entirely beyond her control. Her thoughts were too scattered, her will unfocused. But come what may, she would not merely stand and let the shadowy treasure guard kill her.

The second was also a cold spell, but not as dramatic as the first. The temperature of the room suddenly plummeted to an unimaginable depth. Sarah's lungs burned like fire as she breathed in the freezing air. Her body began to tremble uncontrollably, but whether from cold, fright, or both, she was not sure.

The creature seemed unaffected by the cold and continued to advance upon her, at least for the first few steps. But as it closed in, its pace grew markedly sluggish, as if it could scarcely lift its feet from the floor. This was Sarah's chance to dodge, to fight back, but she found herself utterly incapable of moving beyond its reach. For the first time in her life, she was stricken with abject terror. She just stood there and watched as a great black hand or paw or whatever it was rose above her head. Slowed though it was, the creature possessed such tremendous strength that its blow could crush her skull like a sparrow's egg.

But thankfully the blow never landed, for Thurmond, rising to his feet, grasped the axe that had tumbled from Torgul's hands. He smote the shadow thing squarely between the shoulders, and as he did, the blade flashed red fire—surely there was magic in it.

The creature reacted much as any mortal man might do if an axe struck him in the spine. Its back bowed in a terrible arc as if it were trying to move away from the offending blade. It then pitched forward onto its face and made no effort to rise.

The cold spell ran its course, and the chamber returned to its normal temperature. The naturally cool subterranean air seemed, by comparison, as hot as the blast of a furnace.

As reason began to return to Sarah's eyes, she began to sob.

"Oh, Thurmond, thank you! Oh! What was that horrid…?"

But the young warrior made no move to comfort the weeping girl. There was no time for such things at the moment. Instead he interrupted sharply.

"See to Roscoe! At once! Go to him now! He may be badly hurt."

Torgul had regained his feet and now joined his friends. He immediately reclaimed the axe. Thurmond's spear was gone, having been blown away in the ice storm. Nod and Sod also emerged, for all appearances unhurt. Their attention elsewhere, none of the party noticed as the fallen shadow creature gradually evaporated and returned to the ethereal abode from which it had been summoned.

Roscoe had sustained a mighty blow that dented his helmet deeply, broken its leather chinstrap, and knocked it flying from his head. The old Adventurer lay on his side as if asleep, his face sticky with the blood that seeped from his mangled scalp.

Sarah had no experience as a surgeon and no real idea what to do first. She was just happy to discover that the old Adventurer still breathed. After posting Thurmond and the brothers to keep watch against inquisitive goblins, Torgul joined Sarah at Roscoe's side. Together they removed the shield from his arm and rucksack from his shoulders. Then they rolled him on his back.

Torgul spoke softly and firmly.

"Fetch one of the water bottles and somethin' to wipe away some of this blood. I have to have a look at the wound. Then get the parcel of surgeon stuff outta his backpack. Off you go!"

Sarah had never been one to submit to being ordered about in such fashion. Her pampered existence as Master's favorite had exempted her from any such indignity. But she understood that Roscoe's life was at stake here and that it was not the moment for a display of vanity. She immediately did as she was told, bringing the water flask and a wide strip of cloth she had worn as a headband.

She was digging through the rucksack when Torgul made a sound equally indicative of delight or dismay. She turned to him alarm.

"What?"

"Not nearly as serious as I feared. A bad gash, but I can sew it up, and it'll mend. His skull ain't mashed in. If it was, you'd be decidin' whether to carry him or leave him."

"Would you really leave him?"

"Nay, not me. I'd never run out on a brother Adventurer, but I can't speak for you and the others."

Sarah now allowed a bit of her indignation to show through.

"I would never consider such a thing, not for a minute. Nor would Thurmond, I'm quite sure. We're of more substance than to abandon a friend to the mercy of horrid goblins."

Torgul said nothing. Having heard a great deal of bold talk in his time, he knew the validity of her sentiments could be demonstrated only with deeds, not words. He also found it probable that her convictions would very shortly be put to the test.

His worse fears were soon borne out, for at that moment there commenced the booming of the goblin signal gong. They were unaware that Bart's company were now making their incursion on the goblin den and assumed they themselves were the cause of the commotion. Thus a moment of panic seized them.

Torgul again proved himself a calm and sensible leader. His orders were clear and succinct.

"You'll all get a chance to grab whatever gold you can carry, but not quite yet. I've gotta try and get Roscoe on his feet first.

"Sod and Nod, cover the tunnel where we came in. Shoot anything comin' through it. Anything! Got it? Good—go!

"Thurmond, I don't know if we're still invisible, but I don't think so. That black thing could see us for a fact. So I don't want to chance goin' back the way we came. Go find us another way out. Light a torch if you have to.

"Sarah, dig around in Roscoe's pouch and find the silver flask. Pour whatever's left down Roscoe's throat and see what happens."

"What is it?"

"A special dwarf potion. It ain't exactly good for him, but it should get him up and movin'."

By this time, all party members had shucked off their rucksacks, which lay strewn on the cavern floor. Torgul began to empty them of all nonessential items—tools, extra weapons, cloaks, even food. He paused to consider Sarah's pannier of magical supplies but then left it untouched. He then went to the treasure chamber and filled his own bag with as many gold bars as he thought he could carry.

Sarah found the silver flask as instructed and dumped its contents down the throat of the unconscious Roscoe. He began to choke and then gag violently. Afraid that he would expel whatever it was, she pinched his nose closed with one hand and held his mouth closed with the other.

The old Adventurer gagged a couple of more times and then, to her relief, swallowed and lay still. The results were nearly immediate. His eyes popped open as if he had awakened from a frightful dream. As she looked down on him, she saw recognition come into his eyes.

"Well now, if it isn't Sarah, so it is. I'm afraid you have the advantage of me, darlin', as I seem to be off my feet at the moment. Let's see now...I must have had a grand time, for I don't recall a moment of it. A tad too much uisge, I'd imagine. Hey now, where am I? What is this place? How'd I get here?"

Sarah wanted to try to explain, but Torgul was summoning her to come and take her fill from the treasure hoard. The dwarf took her place and began to talk quickly to his injured friend. A moment later he was struggling to pull the big man to his feet.

Thurmond now returned, breathless and wild-eyed.

"We're at the end. No more passages. No escape."

Torgul was dubious.

"Nothin' at all?"

"Just a small wooden door, and it's locked. Looks more like another treasure room than a way out."

The dwarf handed him his rucksack.

"Go fill this with whatever you can carry. Then go relieve Sod and Nod so they can come and take their share."

Thurmond ran to fulfill these tasks, and Torgul went to see the small door. Soon there came the splintering sound of an axe chopping through wood. Sod quickly filled his sack, and his brother took his place. Sarah fashioned a rough bandage around Roscoe's bloody pate.

Lady Fortune's capricious wheel seemed to be turning in their favor. Their sacks were filled with treasure, and as yet no goblins had discovered their presence. Torgul returned to announce that the small door led not to another storeroom but to a low, narrow crack in the rock that offered their only chance to escape. No steg grew on the walls, so it was pitch black inside. It would be rough on Roscoe, big, lame, and wounded as he was, but it was imminently preferable to the hospitality of the goblins.

The gong ceased to pound as abruptly as it had begun. In actuality this marked the defeat of Bart's company and the rout of the few survivors. But to the party, wholly unaware of the goings on in the outer passages, the silence was ominous.

Then the first goblin emerged from the passage on the far side of the chamber. It was the same precocious brat who had sniffed them out when they crossed through the first den. He saw them and froze, his mouth falling open in surprise as he raised an accusing finger in their direction. The spell of invisibility was indeed broken.

Nod and Sod raised their crossbows and fired almost simultaneously. The first arrow entered the goblin's open mouth and exited the back of his neck. The second took him in the chest. He went down, dead, but not before emitting a piercing squeal that echoed along the cavern walls.

Now the inexorable wheel of fate turned against them, for a multitude of shrill voices farther down the passage took up this cry. The remaining goblins, flush with victory, had just returned to their lair when they heard the death shriek of the stricken brat. They rushed headlong into the throne room to contend with this new outrage.

Mustering her willpower, Sarah cast the sleep spell she had been studying so diligently on the trip down the river. It failed completely. She either did it wrong, or the goblins were immune, or perhaps they were just out of range. Her heart sank.

"Oh shit, now we're in for it."

The brothers shot goblins one after another as they pressed forward.

Thurmond unslung his bow and joined in, firing shaft after shaft into the oncoming mass. Their combined fire was enough to drive them back into the passage from which they had come.

Torgul now turned to Sarah.

"Quick, get Roscoe through the little door. It's gonna be rough on him, you'll have to help him."

"I can't, Torgul. He's too big, and I'm not strong enough."

"Thurmond, help her with Roscoe. Hurry up! The goblins will be back any moment. We'll hold 'em off while you get Roscoe through that crack."

Thurmond was loath to turn tail while his comrades stood and fought, but he was sworn to obey the commands of the experienced Adventurers. He looped his bow over his shoulder and did as he was told.

The words of the dwarf were indeed prophetic, for the goblins reemerged from the passage and charged across the throne room in a berserk fury. Nod and Sod shot off the last of their quarrels and drew their shortswords. Torgul stepped up beside them with his new axe. He grinned broadly, which was an aberrant and altogether unpleasant sight.

"What do ya say, lads? Shall we give the bards something to sing about? Maybe for a hundred years? All we have to do is make sure the others live to tell the tale."

CHAPTER THIRTY-FIVE

A JOURNEY THROUGH THE DARK

The trip through the crack was indeed rough on Roscoe. Thurmond and Sarah pulled and pushed him along as best they could, but his game leg did not bend properly, and his big belly kept catching on the ragged surface of the walls. Dazed and bewildered as he was, he was mostly unable to help himself as they forced him along.

The trip was hard on Thurmond and Sarah as well. Encumbered by their heavy rucksacks, armor, and weapons, they were scarcely better off than Roscoe. Thurmond was tempted to discard his bow, but he wisely forbore.

In the throne room, Nod, Sod, and Torgul held the goblins at bay while the others pushed through the narrow crack. Luckily, the goblins' fighting spirit was greatly diminished. The bulk of their warriors were slain, and the population of females and juveniles decimated. But it did not seem so to the companions as they fought for their lives.

There was a brief lull as the goblins drew back to catch their collective breath. Torgul deemed the time was right and ordered the brothers into the crack. Lithe of build and lightly armed, they slipped easily into its narrow confines. The dwarf stood for a moment amid the shattered remains of the wooden door. Then, with a rude gesture in the direction of his ancestral foes, he ducked into the crack.

The goblins howled in rage, but none dared follow the dwarf into that dark hole.

Sod, Nod, and Torgul soon caught up with the others. Sarah and Thurmond were doing their best to squeeze Roscoe through, but the going was slow. The floor was slippery and uneven. Sharp protrusions jutted from wall and ceiling. As they inched along, there was much bumping of head and rasping of skin.

Thurmond suddenly had a horrible thought—what would happen if the way became too narrow for Roscoe to pass? Sarah was in the very front, on the far side of the old Adventurer, so she could proceed. But she would be trapped in a hostile subterranean labyrinth. He and the others could only turn around and face the wrath of a fully aroused goblin population.

Then an even worse thought came to mind, a possible resolution to be sure, but one too awful to contemplate. But contemplate it he did, nonetheless. Should Roscoe become stuck in the fissure, or if it became too narrow for him to pass through, it would be only possible to clear the way by knifing him and dismembering his body. Thurmond shuddered, disgusted with himself. How was it possible that he could even think of such a thing?

There were no sounds of pursuit, nothing to suggest the goblins had followed them into the crack, which was certainly a comfort, but might they not at that very moment be racing along some parallel tunnel, preparing to ambush them as they emerged on some other side?

Entombed in the constricting confines of the dark crack, Thurmond felt far greater fear than he had ever known when facing an actual foe. It became difficult to catch his breath, and his stomach began to churn. As his panic worsened, it became increasingly hard not to push back through the boatmen and the dwarf and take his chances in the other direction.

Finally, he noticed that the pervasive goblin stench had markedly waned. There was a new smell, certainly not pleasant, but somehow not as unnatural and instinctively loathsome. More like, perhaps, the sickly-sweet smell of decaying dung. He heard Torgul mumble under his breath.

"Kobolds."

Fear clutched Thurmond by the throat. His one prayer was that the narrow crack would be their deliverance. But now, trapped between a mob of enraged goblins and this new peril, it was to become his grave. He fought desperately to keep his terror under control.

"Torgul, what are kobolds? Tell me about 'em."

"They're small and can be pretty nasty."

"Nasty how?"

"Kobolds are kinda like goblins' little brothers. I dunno, there's not much else to tell you."

In fact, there was a great deal to be said about kobolds. Torgul's observations were not incorrect. There were many similarities between a kobold and a goblin, and the two races might well have shared a common ancestor. Certainly there was a degree of natural affinity between them, resulting in frequent alliances and joint forays. Kobolds, like goblins, were avid tunnelers, and the two often established adjacent lairs with connecting passageways.

Calling the kobold the *little brother* of the goblin also had some merit. The creatures did, in fact, resemble goblins, though the largest kobold stood no taller than the average gnome, coming to about the hip bone of a man. The openings of their dens were typically of a corresponding size and thus largely inaccessible to humans. For this reason, they were seldom bothered by intruders from above.

But there were points in which kobold and goblin were at variance. The former were neither as avaricious nor as innately brutal as the latter. Certainly kobolds were capable of offensive action and would sometimes combine with goblins to attack those humans or dwarves unfortunate enough to enter their territory, but they were just as often willing to remain in their dens, ignoring potential victims. And they seemed far less interested in amassing great piles of stolen treasure.

The psychotropic mushroom played a significant role in kobold culture. Their warrens invariably boasted extensive growing beds where such mushrooms were cultivated in great quantity. All other aspects of kobold society remained woefully primitive. They tanned no leather, wove no cloth, fired no pottery, worked no metal.

The cranial cavity of the average kobold was astonishingly small. As such, they were creatures of instinct rather than reason, their actions being determined by the same innate telepathy that guides the movement of a flock of birds or a school of fish. If goblin society resembled the dog pack, kobolds lived in something more akin to a nest of wasps.

Thurmond and company were about to become well acquainted with the kobold and his culture. Their passage through the dark fissure finally came to an end, and they found themselves once again in a chamber softly illuminated by steg. The ceiling was high enough so that even Roscoe could stand erect, but much lower than the spacious caverns inhabited by the goblins. All was preternaturally quiet.

Relieved as he was to be free of the crack, Thurmond remained uneasy. The air was heavy, damp, and infused with that sweet smell of decay he had noticed earlier. Or was it the reek of some other shadow creature stalking them unseen, biding its time, laughing at their pitiful efforts to escape? Perhaps death itself creeping along behind.

They stood for a moment, weapons drawn, scarcely willing to breathe as they assessed the new location. Roscoe was doing better. Whatever had been in Torgul's silver vial was bringing him around. He had sustained a serious wound, and he was still shaky on his feet, but he was now able to stand without assistance, and his mind was clearing.

Torgul gestured that the others should stay put and then glided off into the darkness. He returned almost at once and beckoned for them to follow. For one so heavily encumbered, the dwarf was amazingly light on his feet. Thurmond could detect no sound of movement as he came and went across the chamber.

Then they could all discern why Torgul's interest had been drawn to that side of the cavern. There was a light ahead, still quite dim in the distance, calling to them like a beacon of salvation. Its source was of no consequence. It did not matter what its illumination might reveal or whatever fell creatures might huddle around it. The dark subterranean world was fundamentally foreign and terrifying to humans, even to experienced underworld Adventurers like Roscoe. Light promised a degree of normalcy and safety.

The chamber they crossed was quite large, its walls invisible in the distance. The steg-covered ceiling offered just enough radiance for them to make their way. Torgul, in the lead, kept an eye skinned for unseen pitfalls in the floor. Roscoe steadied himself with a hand on Sarah's shoulder. The sweet smell waxed stronger as they grew closer to the light.

This light was not, they discovered, nearly as bright as it had initially appeared, being little more than a subdued glow. But it was at least greater than the feeble illumination of the steg. It drew them forward, a token of sanctuary. Where there was light, they might find warmth and rest, perhaps a chance to refresh themselves with the meager remnants of food and drink that remained in the bottoms of their rucksacks.

Thurmond recalled with dismay that most of their comestibles had been thrown out to make more room for gold. Were they doomed to wander these black halls until they starved? And why had the goblins declined to chase them through the crack? Was there something here that even they feared, that they had been holding at bay with the stout, little wooden door?

Drawing nigh, they saw that the light emanated from a tunnel opening. Unlike the crack, which was obviously a natural formation, it had been cut through the cavern wall with great skill and precision. The sides were perfectly aligned, and the top was round like the top of a castle gate.

Roscoe ran his hand along the arrow-straight line of the entrance.

"Dwarf work, Torgul?"

"None other. Strange, though. I know nothin' of my folk ever dwellin' in these parts. Must have been very long ago. It grieves me that these fine halls have fallen into the hands of such vermin who lives here now."

Thurmond was greatly relieved that Roscoe seemed to be returning to his old self. He piped up, hoping that the taciturn dwarf might be willing to expand on his frustratingly brief description of kobolds.

"Tell us more about kobolds, Torgul. What can we expect? What should we do?"

"They're chaotic little buggers, so you can expect just about anythin'. If Lady Fortune is on our side, we might be able to slip through without stirrin' 'em up. Even if they see us, they may not attack. But if we provoke 'em, they'll swarm, and then look out! There'll be a great lot of 'em, and they'll be after us like a hive of angry bees."

"So you've fought kobolds plenty of times before?"

"Nay, I've just been close enough to smell 'em. I had the good sense to shy away after that."

Roscoe now joined the conversation.

"Here's something else to consider. These chambers and passages are spacious enough for us to move about. But kobolds are famous for making the entrances to their burrows very small. Torgul might be able to wriggle through, but the rest of us might face a bit of a dilemma."

Torgul nodded in agreement.

"Could be a problem. But my people like wide passages and high ceilings, so we need to stay in sections built by dwarves and hope to find one of the original gates."

Sarah, silent to this point, finally spoke up.

"How about the map? I memorized the passages leading to the treasure room, but I didn't pay much attention to the rest of it. Couldn't there be something on it that might help us?"

Roscoe shook his head.

"Doubtful, most doubtful, I'm sorry to say. I studied the map at some length, so I did. No wooden door in the throne room. No crack. Nothing to suggest that these parts even exist. Still, not a bad idea to take a wee peek when we get up into the light."

And so the party proceeded in that direction.

CHAPTER THIRTY-SIX

THE KOBOLDS RECEIVE THEIR GUESTS

The dwarf tunnel was short, no more than a dozen paces. It opened into an expansive chamber with finished walls and a high vaulted ceiling obviously of dwarven construction. There was light enough that even the humans could see quite normally. Long stone tables ran the length of the room. They were very low, no more than a foot from the ground, and covered with a dark, sticky substance that was obviously the source of the sweet smell.

Here the source of illumination was finally revealed. The tables were the growing beds for an infinite variety of mushrooms. Some had stems as long as canes and caps as broad as a noble lady's parasol. Others were tiny, scarcely the size of a child's thumb, while still others had plump spherical caps poised on dangerously thin stems. One variety boasted delicate scalloped projections resembling wings that fluttered as if wanting to fly. Another was the size and shape of a man's prick.

There were shrooms with red caps and black stems, red stems and purple caps. Some were as translucent and ephemeral as jellyfish, others as stark and white as a corpse. There were spotted shrooms, piebald shrooms, and shrooms with weird zigzaggy lines. All throbbed with a powerful intrinsic energy expressed in the form of weird light. This permeated the cavern and spilled out along the tunnel through which they had entered.

Captivated by the strange sight, Thurmond reached out to touch a lumpy green specimen that squatted almost in the shape of a toad. But Torgul at once struck down his hand.

"Don't be touchin' 'em. Some of 'em might be poison—probably most of 'em are. And just touchin' 'em might be enough to kill you. So hands off!"

Thurmond did not need to be told twice.

Moving deeper into the chamber, they became aware of a low droning coming from somewhere up ahead. It was sonorous yet not deeply pitched, a sound such as a child might make if humming far down in their chest. The further on they went, the louder it became, until at the room's far end, they came upon the kobolds.

There were a dozen or more standing in what appeared to be some type of formation, though its exact nature was impossible to determine. They stood rigidly upright, arms straight down with hands pressed tightly against their legs, eyes wide open, staring straight ahead, yet glazed and unseeing. They offered no awareness that strangers had invaded their domain. They simply stood and droned.

Each wore a cap composed of what seemed to be a nest of twigs smeared with the same reeking substance in which the mushrooms grew. Indeed, small shrooms sprouted in profusion from the crowns of these caps. Thurmond wondered whether the roots extended down into the creatures' brains.

Torgul had been right, they were ugly little buggers. A lot like goblins, only smaller. This bunch was naked except for their stupid caps. There was one—a bit uglier than the rest if that was even possible—who sported a high conical hat instead of a cap. He looked older and more wizened than the rest and was perhaps their leader.

Thurmond remembered Torgul's irresistible need to slaughter the goblin guards at the cave mouth and silently prayed he would not find it necessary to repeat the performance. By the knobby knees of God, he wanted to escape this place without further bloodshed. He just wanted to go home. *So please*, Thurmond thought, *let us not provoke them by killing these who seem so content to ignore us.*

Happily, Thurmond's apprehension was not realized. Dwarf though he was, Torgul desired nothing more than to reach the surface and be done with kobolds and goblins. Roscoe shared these sentiments entirely, though he also longed for a cool draught of ale. Sarah had been so frightened for so long that she was, for the most part, emotionally numb, yet such feeling that was left to her was a yearning for the peace and solitude of the books in her old master's library. Sod and Nod, being simple souls, wished for nothing beyond a return to their boat.

It looked for a while as if their collective wish for escape might be realized. They crept noiselessly by the formation of entranced kobolds, who still declined to acknowledge their existence. But then Lady Fortune laughed and gave her wheel a spin, causing the luck of the party to plummet to the bottom. A pulpy, evil-looking shroom twisted on its stalk as if regarding the intruders. A puckered orifice opened on the apex of its black and yellow cap, and it spat a cloud of spoors directly into Thurmond's face. He began to cough and sputter, and in doing so, drew the spoors deep into his lungs.

He was at once as entranced as the kobolds, whose droning chant seemed to clutch at his soul. He looked into the face of the kobold leader, who, for the first time, displayed awareness of his presence. The shroom's magic had put them on the same plane. Anger blazed in the kobold's eyes as he raised a short stick that had until now rested at his side. Made of some dark, gnarled wood, it was undoubtedly a wand or rod of power. It seemed to writhe in his hand as he extended it toward Thurmond's face.

Though lamed and battered, Roscoe was quicker. He smote down with his sword, and the kobold's hand, still clutching the stick, flew from the wrist. His next shot took the creature across the face and sent the little body sprawling to the floor.

The other kobolds began to stir, but Roscoe and the others didn't hesitate. They piled on with weapons swinging, and within an eyeblink, the entire formation was dead and dismembered. His brain addled by the enchantment of the spoors, Thurmond could only stand and watch. With their Keltin blood aroused, Sod and Nod did a brief victory dance and gave the traditional war shout of their mother's clan.

But this celebration was not long lived. A high-pitched howling from somewhere deep within the cavern complex answered their shouts. With no better option available, the party sprang in movement, exiting the grow room through another dwarf tunnel on the far side of the chamber.

Under the mushroom's spell, Thurmond saw the world in a whole new way. Time slowed down. Solid matter became plastic and insubstantial. The tunnel walls began to undulate, and he paused, fascinated, to watch them. He found that he could *see* the smells in the air around him and *hear* the colors that streaked before his eyes. He reached out to catch one.

Whack! Roscoe reached out and slapped him on the back of the head, making him grateful for the light helmet he wore. It was nevertheless sufficient to bring him out of his reverie.

"Keep sharp, boy! This ain't no time to be driftin' off into a mushroom dream."

Thurmond gave a prodigious sneeze and felt his brain clearing. The spoors' effect was intense but beginning to wane. The howling was louder and closer now. With a sinking feeling, Thurmond realized it was going to be impossible to outrun the kobolds. The party was exhausted, wounded, and overloaded with gold. They had no chance. They would die forgotten in this disgusting crap hole. He saw very little glory in such a death, only the inevitability of paralyzing fear and terrible pain.

He knew Sarah must be feeling the same terror and dismay that was gripping him, but her face showed none of it. She looked as confident and determined as ever as she continued to help Roscoe shamble along. His bad leg seemed to be hurting him terribly. He signaled her to move aside, that it was his turn to bear the big man's weight on his shoulder.

Sarah gave him a grateful nod and complied, then at once drew her bow from her back and nocked an arrow. How he admired her at that moment! She could be bossy and impatient, but for courage, intelligence, and steadfastness, she was nonpareil.

Thurmond realized these were masculine virtues and not usually considered becoming in a young woman, but the many dangers and deprivations they had endured together had swept away such considerations. They had faced kobolds and goblins, hired murderers, a sinking boat, a liver-eating madman, unknown pursuers, and an invisible demon.

She was a great girl! If they ever got out of this cave, he would have to tell her how…

Whack! Roscoe's hand again found the back of his head.

"Stop moonin', boy. That damnable mushroom has turned your brain. Pay more attention to what you're doin'. You keep steppin' on my foot."

They exited the tunnel and entered another large chamber. The howling was quite loud now, coming from a number of passages that branched from the sides of the room.

Suddenly Torgul gave an excited shout.

"Light ahead! Real daylight. There's a big hole in the wall, and light's streaming in."

They could all see it now, and with hope renewed, the party lurched along. But they did not get far before the side tunnels disgorged a deluge of maddened kobolds. They surged forward in a solid mass. Sarah immediately started shooting arrows. She could not miss, so densely did they press together, but her efforts in no way deterred the onrushing horde. She dropped her bow and pulled out her spell scroll. There was only one spell left on the parchment. She turned to Thurmond, who was also firing arrows as fast as he could pull them from his quiver.

"Take Roscoe and get out through that hole! Go on! Everybody, go on. I'll give these little bastards one good shot of magic, then be right behind you. Now run for it!"

This time Thurmond refused to run. He was willing, if need be, to abandon the gold, but he would not flee danger a second time, especially if it meant leaving Sarah behind.

"Nay! Nod and Sod, take Roscoe out! I'll hold them off while you get him away!"

The brothers, evidently eager for sunlight, dumped their rucksacks and set off at once with the big man. Torgul, however, never moved. He stood solidly beside the girl, feet spread wide, axe in both hands. He gave her the same insane grin he seemed to save for moments of imminent death.

The wave of kobolds was almost upon them as Sarah read the spell. She could see them quite clearly. Some wore the shroom caps they had seen in the grow room, a few sported the tall, pointed headdress denoting rank.

The first two spells on the scroll had summoned cold. Sarah was hoping for another ice storm, or anything that would blind and confuse the kobolds long enough for them to escape. The results she got caused her hopes to soar. A wall of ice began to grow before her, a wall that would shield her and her friends from the berserk flood that was almost upon them.

A dozen or so kobolds, more fleet than the rest, managed to climb the wall before it achieved any significant height. The first ran straight at Thurmond. So blind was his charge that he impaled itself on Thurmond's extended blade, stopping only when his ripped stomach slammed into the crossguard.

Thurmond had barely cleared his blade from the welter of guts when a second attempted to brain him with a stone-headed hammer. Fortunately, his sword arm seemed to move with volition of its own, delivering a sharp lateral blow to the side of the creature's head that sheared off the top of the skull and sent his tiny brain spilling to the floor.

Thurmond pivoted, expecting another attack, but to his surprise none came. He shot a glance toward Torgul and was shocked to see a great heap of kobold dead strewn beneath his feet. He moved to help the dwarf but was able to claim only one more, skewering it in the neck as it circled wide to take Torgul from the side. And then it was over, at least for a moment. The hard-chargers had paid the price for their recklessness.

Sarah was screaming something. She had drawn her shortsword and was using it to point toward the opening. It was time to run. The ice wall continued to grow in height, and with each inch, so did their hope of escape. Thurmond and Torgul dropped their packs and sprinted for the opening. Sarah had already dropped the leather wallet she had filled with gold but retained the light wicker pannier that held her occult paraphernalia. Even with this burden, she was able to keep pace with the short-legged dwarf.

Thurmond's heart sank when, looking back over his shoulders, he saw that the ice wall had stopped rising, topping out at a height barely above his thighs. Kobolds were already beginning to climb over its top.

Yet even this diminutive barrier proved to be a more formidable obstacle than it seemed. Many of the kobolds were either unable or unwilling to surmount it and stood milling aimlessly, the pursuit apparently forgotten.

Their more determined brethren were delayed, forced to hoist themselves over the wall on their stomachs. These then rose and resumed the chase, their fury unabated.

Roscoe and the brothers had by this time made it out though the hole and into the world of light and air. Thurmond, Torgul, and Sarah had almost made it, were on the very threshold, when the kobolds caught up with them.

Sarah cast her sleep spell right in their faces. The first half dozen fell into an ensorcelled swoon. She cast again, but the spell fizzled, and none felt its effect. Her psychic energy was expended. The power of her wand had been used up.

Torgul caught her arm and shoved her roughly through the hole. Thurmond tried attempted to stand behind him, but the dwarf gave him a mighty shove with the haft of his axe, which sent him sprawling out into daylight. There was a crazed gleam in his eye, and his mouth hung open in a carnivorous leer.

"Run, both of you! Run! I'll hold 'em back while you get away."

There was nothing else for it. They found themselves on a narrow ledge on the face of a high, steep, rocky precipice. Thurmond wagered a quick glance over the edge. It was a straight drop down to the river, a very long way below. Scraggly pines clung to tiny projections in its nearly vertical cliff-face. Clasping hands, he and Sarah moved along the ledge as quickly as they dared. They saw Roscoe and the brothers a bit ahead.

At that moment Torgul emerged from the hole, a dwarven war song on his lips, his enchanted axe blazing with magical fire. Bits of kobold rained through the air. But the courage and skill and fighting spirit of the doughty dwarf was not enough.

He was overborne by a bevy of frenzied kobolds that latched onto his arms and legs with their teeth, shaking their heads to and fro as if trying to rip him apart with the power of their jaws. He fell backward and tumbled over the edge, his foes still locked to his extremities.

Thurmond and Sarah watched helplessly as he struck the water far, far below. Clad in his heavy mail, he sank like a stone.

CHAPTER THIRTY-SEVEN

RETURN TO THE RIVERBANK

When battling the goblins, Gregorio had read the first two of the scroll's three spells. They had both summoned deadly mists—one purple, one green—that had knocked the attackers from their feet. Now, with Rupert bearing down, sword in hand, Plutonius was hoping for more of the same. He unfortunately met with only partial success.

The spell did indeed invoke a mist, a black one this time. But instead of a swirling, robust cloud, it was but the merest puff, a meager wisp. And instead of enveloping and suffocating the intended target, Rupert, it landed at Plutonius's feet with a subdued *poof*, the sound of someone stepping on a puffball.

Nonetheless, results were immediate and impressive. A single curl of black mist wafted up from the ground and sought entrance at the cleric's nostril. It continued to climb, tickling slightly as it climbed into his brain. Plutonius uttered a single weak groan and died on his feet, his eyes rolling back to the whites.

Rupert was immensely gratified by the outcome of this encounter. This was the first time something had gone his way since they landed on this forsaken riverbank. First there had been the unexpected confrontation with the swinish Staynes, whom he had expected to take by ambush. Then that oaf had so bungled things that both their companies had been nearly annihilated during the goblin attack. Only his own quick thinking had saved them from being slaughtered from behind.

Plutonius had betrayed him, had healed Staynes despite his explicit instructions to the contrary. And then, just when Rupert had been about to lead the men to victory, he had been struck down from behind.

He had regained his senses by the cave mouth only to find himself completely alone. Even his most devoted henchman seemed to have deserted him. There had been nothing for it but to return to the boat.

Rupert gingerly touched the great gash Bart's sword had made in his scalp. He was sure it was a mortal wound. But if he must die, he would first take his revenge on Bartholomew Staynes. He was quite willing to devote whatever fleeting life that was left in him to that purpose.

As he stepped past the fallen Plutonius, he pushed the tip of his sword into his abdomen. He was sure the old friar was already dead, but mangling his remains gave him pleasure.

Rupert looked down at the cooking fire Plutonius had been building as his last earthly act. The flames had taken hold and were beginning to snap and spark. He threw on more sticks from a small pile nearby, then larger pieces, and waited until the flames rose as high as his waist. Catching up a blazing brand by its unburned end, he strode down to the boat grounded on the shingle.

Rupert could accept the fact that he was fated to die a miserable death in this goblin-haunted wilderness. But he could not accept the possibility that Bart might escape, might actually live through this absurd adventure and return to civilization—perhaps with untold riches. Well, return he might, but he would not do so in Rupert's own boat.

He thrust the fiery brand into a coil of tarred rope stored in the boat's prow. The flames found this meal most toothsome and then, their appetite far from satiated, began to gnaw at the pitch used to caulk the seams of the wooden hull. Rupert threw on several more brands, and the prow became an inferno as the flames gorged themselves. Its gluttony still unappeased, the fire ate its way toward the stern, where Plutonius had placed the four wounded men he deemed worthy of healing.

Seeing the approach of a terrible death, these began to scream for help and tried to drag themselves out of the boat. Badly injured as they were, this was no easy feat. Their torn limbs and slashed flesh made movement exceedingly painful and climbing almost impossible. Yet they did their best to haul themselves and each other over the gunwales to the safety of the shingle. One of the four died soon after, his extreme exertions bringing on a swoon from which he did not awaken.

Rupert looked on impassively. He had made no effort to assist their escape and offered the survivors no aid or compassion as they lay panting at the water's edge. He recognized the man who had just died. He had been one of Sims's hired mercenaries and had come downriver with Rupert in this very boat. He had been a big fellow with a loud laugh, but that made no difference now. Nothing mattered now but avenging himself on the loathsome Staynes.

With the boat attended to, Rupert moved to the goblin dugout canoes lying along the shoal. They were small and crude and could be of no real use to humans seeking passage up the great river, but he wanted to make sure. He procured an axe from among the discarded items scattered about the battlefield—it would do nicely—and then chopped a hole in the hull of each canoe.

Rupert knew Bart's own boat was concealed a short way upstream. All he had to do was follow the river until he came upon it. He would burn it, too, depriving Bart of his last chance to escape by water. Let him walk back to civilization if he could. The wilderness was vast, trackless, and fraught with enemies. He would never make it. Once his boat was burned, Bart would be doomed to suffer the same nameless death he had brought upon Rupert.

A wave of nausea and dizziness suddenly swept through Rupert. His knees began to tremble, and he felt his strength waning. As much as he hated to postpone his vengeance, he was forced to rest. He sat down in the shade of the broom bush, hoping to regain his strength and move on.

He began to remove pieces of his armor. His helmet had been left in the woods where he had been struck down. He now cast off his shield and gauntlets, then unlaced the splinted leg defenses of iron and leather.

Rupert's greatest fear was that he would die before he could destroy the other boat, but he need not have worried overmuch, for it was already alight. Even as he prepared to take his ease, the first small flames were taking hold on its hull.

†

When Thurmond and company fled the kobold stronghold, their pursuers had been content to break off the chase and allow the intruders to go their way. One could never tell with kobolds. Maybe Sarah's magic and Torgul's ferocious axe had disheartened them. Or maybe they had just lost interest. Or perhaps even forgotten what all the fuss was about. In any case that particular group returned to their cave and resumed their normal business.

Not so the other clans that shared the huge cavern complex. Once roused, these went swarming from the many small openings that lay concealed on the surrounding hillsides. They descended like a hive of enraged bees, intent on wreaking blind vengeance on any unfortunate creature they might encounter. Even the goblins knew to seek shelter when the kobolds swarmed.

Luckily, the mad rush of the kobolds carried them in all the wrong directions. They came upon none of the surviving humans, who were wandering about the woods or lying on the riverbank. And these, in turn, remained blissfully unaware of the presence of the kobolds, their howls and yips muted by the dense underbrush.

One rampaging group, however, combing the bushes along the river, did manage to find Bart's boat, which the crew had moored in a backwater a score of feet from the shoreline and well beyond their reach. These men were all dead now, either upstream on the riverbank or on the floor of the goblin cave.

The kobolds hated the boat on sight. Vile abomination! It was the accursed thing that had carried the intruders who had violated their sacred mushroom den. Many of the kobolds carried short flint-tipped darts. These were now wrapped with moss and spread with a thick tarry goo that burst into flames when struck with a spark.

Their position on the riverbank placed them well above the vessel. The wooden deck below was an easy target. Soon a second column of smoke joined that of Rupert's still-burning craft.

Had Rupert seen this second column, he might have taken some comfort. He might have guessed its source and thereby felt a degree of relief, secure in the knowledge that even if he had to die, his greatest enemy would still suffer. But Rupert was not to have this satisfaction. From where he lay beneath the broom bush, the surrounding trees blocked his view of the smoke rising from Bart's vessel.

The smoke from Rupert's boat was far less concealed and thus served as a guidepost for those few men who had survived the abortive attack on the goblin cave. After losing Bart in their headlong flight from the cave, they continued downhill in the general direction of the river. Seeing the smoke rising above the treetops, they headed for it without considering what it might portend.

Arriving at the riverbank, they stood in unspeaking horror at the sight of the boat, now in the final stages of conflagration. They saw the other survivors stretched scorched and bleeding on the shingle. These raised their hands and wailed pitifully for succor. The newcomers rushed forward in response to their pleas, unaware that Rupert sat watching them from the shade of the broom.

The men sat on the ground in a huddle—silent, unmoving, unthinking. They were weaponless though the area was still strewn with swords and spears from the goblin assault earlier in the day. Their fighting spirit had so evaporated that arming themselves did not occur to them. If their bellies were empty, they felt no hunger. They did not recall that Bart's boat lay concealed a short way downstream, though some of Bart's soldiers were among their number.

All were wounded to a greater or lesser extent. They bore deep contusions from falling boulders, penetrating wounds from spears and arrows, and ragged gashes from swords and knives. Their faces were gouged by the claws of goblin wives, their ankles chewed by the teeth of goblin brats. The survivors were used up and at this moment could do no more than simply sit, take the pain, and await the next spin of Lady Fortune's fickle wheel.

Rupert continued to sit and observe. He felt no need to make himself known to these men. He, like they, was in a state of desolation, for he had come to believe he was not going to die of his wound. But it was extremely painful. A large section of his scalp had been sliced open and now lay like a great loose flap against his pate. He had believed his brainpan to be cracked, but his exploring fingers could find no sharp edges of exposed bone.

His queasiness and vertigo were slackening, and his strength seemed to be returning. His knees had stopped shaking, and he felt certain he would soon be able to rise without difficulty. But he was not yet ready to rise.

Indeed, his returning health had driven the young blackguard into a severe depression. Inexplicably, his premonition of death had been a comfort. He would have escaped the painful reality of his own supreme failure, both in this current adventure and in his life as a whole. He would have avoided the arduous journey back to civilization, now made almost impossible by the premature firing of his own boat. And he would not have had to face a showdown with that bitch Renata, who would probably demand that he repay all her expenditures. Nay, better just to die and be done.

But now, if he was destined to live, he would have to make himself known to the small group of broken men who squatted in the mud by the river. He would have to muster enough force of will to command their obedience and bind them to him. He would have to play the leader, to pretend to know what to do. But Rupert was not yet ready for any of this. If he could not die and be done, he could at least rest in the shade a bit longer.

†

By the time the first smoke column crested the treetops, Bart had gotten himself more lost than ever. He could not even find the river, which he believed had to lie just in front of him. In fact, he was too far upstream, and he was moving parallel with the river rather than toward it. So every step took him farther away from either of the burning boats.

Bart climbed a small rise in the hope of getting his bearings. From this point, he finally spotted the black columns from both boats. He had no idea what might be ablaze but assumed the smoke to be the work of prowling goblins. Perhaps they were burning whatever doomed captives they had taken in his ill-fated raid. With a tremor of revulsion, he turned away and continued to trudge in the opposite direction.

CHAPTER THIRTY-EIGHT

A CONVERSATION IN THE WOODS

Roscoe and company continued along the treacherous cliff-face as rapidly as they dared until it became obvious that the kobolds had broken off their pursuit. They then stopped, every bit as shattered as the pitiful survivors who huddled on the riverbank. They were covered with scratches, cuts, and bruises. Sod had an especially deep laceration running nearly the length of his forearm, which his brother now bound with a strip torn from his tunic. The left side of Roscoe's head was a disgusting crust of clotted blood, and his scalp wound remained oozy. They sank to the ground, exhausted and dispirited.

Many of their weapons had been lost or broken in their frantic retreat through the caves. Most of their food had been left on the throne room floor to allow their rucksacks to be stuffed with gold. And then this gold—the treasure they had risked their lives to win—had been abandoned to the abhorrent kobolds. This was a bitter blow, indeed.

But most terrible of all was the death of their boon companion Torgul. Roscoe had said from the first that the doughty dwarf would prove a good friend and valuable ally, and he had been correct. Torgul's courage, loyalty, and good common sense had saved them again and again. He had even displayed—especially in moments of desperate peril—a good humor, a most unusual characteristic for a dwarf.

Now he was gone, sunk to the bottom of the Mad River with his axe in his hand and his foes tearing at his throat. Thurmond suddenly had an intense need to say something reverential, but he held his tongue. There was nothing to say. He knew each member of the party shared his feelings. Better to swallow his grief and just rest. There would be time for a eulogy later, if they managed to survive.

Roscoe at last arose and began to take his bearings. He easily recognized where they were. Their flight through the goblin tunnels and kobold caves had brought them upstream from where they had originally come ashore. Here the river ran between high embankments that fell off to gentle slopes not far below. He spotted the high hill that held the cave mouth where they had entered the goblin realm. Then he saw a column of black smoke begin to rise above the trees from somewhere a bit downstream.

"Looky there at that pillar of smoke down by the river. That's no wee campfire."

All eyes snapped to that direction. Sarah spoke to the old Adventurer.

"What could it be, Roscoe? Kobolds? Goblins?"

"Aye, mayhap, or it could be whoever was followin' us down the river."

"Serve 'em right if the kobolds got 'em."

"Well, I suppose so, but right now just about any bunch of regular human people would be a welcome sight to my eyes, so they would."

Thurmond joined in, his voice tense with restrained excitement.

"Maybe it's Scrymgeour's crew sending up a smoke signal to attract our notice. I'll bet they're down there waiting for us."

Sarah remained skeptical.

"I doubt it. That's not what they're supposed to do. If it's them, something's gone wrong. They're in trouble. Maybe the kobolds are burning their boat."

This last bit drew dark, nervous scowls from Sod and Nod. Roscoe put an end to the banter and debate.

"Well now, we are all aware of what we must do. We'll take it slow and easy, not makin' any noise, and when we get down close, Thurmond will scout ahead and see who it is. Is that agreeable to you, lad? If it's people you find, we're lookin' to talk, not fight, and you're possessed of a fine eloquence when it's needed, so you are."

Thurmond was well aware that he was being tested again. This was another of those moments when he must prove himself if he ever wanted to join the Adventures' Brotherhood. Somehow the shining appeal of that dream had tarnished a bit, but he nodded his agreement. It made perfect sense for him to take point.

"What do I do if it's a pack of kobolds and goblins?"

"Then you fall back as quick and quiet as you can, boyo. You come back, and we hunker down under a bush until they all head back to their lairs. It grieves me to say it, but we're in no shape to take 'em on at the moment."

Thurmond certainly agreed with that—so did Sarah—so did the brothers.

They continued their journey down the cliff-face in the general direction of the smoke. The path gradually widened and leveled out. The going got easier. Nod found a long, straight stick he brought for Roscoe to use for a walking staff. This allowed him to make his way unassisted, though at a painfully slow pace over the uneven ground.

It was at this moment that the kobolds fired Bart's boat even farther downstream, sending a second smoke column into the air. But the party had by then moved too far down the hill to see it, their view blocked by primal forest around them.

It took them a long time to reach the river. By then the kobolds had all returned to their dens, and Rupert was asleep in the shade of the broom. The bloodied survivors still sat listlessly by the edge of the river. Some dozed. Others simply stared off at nothing. No one spoke.

Thurmond, hiding in a thicket that grew along the top of the riverbank, looked down on the scene in amazement. He saw a little group sitting clustered on a battlefield strewn with abandoned weapons and the mutilated bodies of men and goblins. He saw the remains of the boat, which was now reduced to a skeleton of blazing timbers. There was the broken breastwork with goblins still impaled on the makeshift abatis. There was the corpse of a tall man in an orange robe, and another in the habit of a Black Friar.

He wasted no time in returning to his friends, who, as Roscoe had suggested, were concealed in a little gully a short distance around the hill. His findings seemed to confirm Roscoe's supposition that these dispirited men had once belonged to the group that had followed them down the river. The old Adventurer seemed encouraged by their presence and questioned Thurmond closely.

"So, laddie, you say there was less than a dozen?"

"Aye, I counted seven. They were too bunched up to be certain."

"And they looked to be cut up somethin' frightful?"

"Aye, that they did."

"The friar and the sorcerer were down and dead, you say. You saw no others who might be spellcasters or some such?"

"Nay, all looked to be simple fighting men. And no one seemed to be in charge. They were all just sitting together like they were too badly hurt to move."

"And the boat—burnin' fierce and hard?"

"Aye, almost nothing left."

Roscoe turned from Thurmond and addressed the group.

"You all heard the lad's story. It explains a great deal and bodes very well for us indeed. So, let's proceed to the river and pay our respects to those unfortunates."

Thurmond's face clouded with concern.

"You think we should attack them?"

"Nay, lad, nay, you mistake my meanin'. We'll go introduce ourselves—try to make friends and recruit 'em into our party."

Sarah was on her feet in an instant.

"Why, Roscoe? If they were the ones following us down the river, they don't mean us well. Why would we want to meet them?"

"Why, lassie, you surprise me. Those is human men down there, hurt and stranded in a heathen wilderness. It would go against custom to just abandon them, so it would. And besides, whatever their original intentions were, they've done us no injury. Rather, they've done us a great service, drawin' off the goblins so we could sneak in more easily. And they've done a heroic deed in killin' off so many of the nasty buggers. Nay, we can't just leave 'em."

She retorted.

"Well, Roscoe, in case you haven't noticed, we're pretty much stranded in the same damned wilderness. And just about as cut up and used up as they are. There are more of them than us. What's to stop 'em from turning on us and stealing Scrymgeour's boat—if not at first, maybe later when they're feeling better?"

Roscoe's voice assumed a tone of authority as he slipped into his role as captain.

"Looky here, lassie, we need them as much as they need us right now. Some of 'em must be real fightin' men with sand in their gizzards if they knocked off as many goblins as Thurmond says. It's a long way home and a different kind of journey goin' upstream. No more floatin' nice and safe down the middle of the river. We'll be meetin' locals, and some of 'em might not be so nice. We could really use those men."

Now he softened, the twinkle returning to his eye.

"I don't think you need worry so much, Sarah. Thurmond says they look lost and confused. That tells me their leader's dead—probably he was the dead magician or that friar layin' toes up on the beach. They're plenty scared 'cause their boat's burnt and they're feelin' trapped. Not one of 'em knows what to do 'cause they ain't use to thinkin' for themselves, so they just sit.

"I'll put on my best commandin' air, then just step in and take charge and start givin' orders. I'd wager they're used to takin' orders and will be happy to cooperate. I'll give them a purpose, and they'll be most eager for that. And I think those men will be fallin' down with gratitude when I offers 'em a boat ride, won't they now.

"And if my imposin' presence ain't enough to keep 'em in line, one sight of you will scare 'em so bad they won't think of disobeyin'."

"Me? They'll be scared of *me*?"

"Aye, scared near witless. 'Cause you'll be playin' the part of a demented witch. Rollin' your eyes, snarlin' and showin' your teeth, wavin' your wand about. You'll scare the shite from their bowels. Plus, we'll all act afraid of you and warn 'em how powerful and evil you are."

"I guess I look the part. I'm filthy and all splattered with your blood—some of it's my own, too."

"Aye, the nastier the better for you. But I better clean up a bit if I want to make an impression. Got to look imposin'—not like a fat old man with a broken pate and a bum leg."

Thurmond rejoined the conversation.

"Roscoe, you know where we are, right?"

"Aye, pretty much so. Just a bit upriver from the goblin cave."

"And you can find our way back to the place where we landed, where the boat is supposed to pick us up?"

"Of a certainty, lad. It's just down there, where the river makes that slow bend around that hillock."

As their eyes moved in that direction, they saw for the first time the second column of smoke, the one from Bart's burning boat.

"Roscoe, what's that?"

"I…uh…couldn't rightly say, boyo."

"It couldn't be our boat, could it? Burning like the other one?"

"Don't see how. It ain't supposed to pick us up 'til day after tomorrow. So I…"

Sarah interrupted. Her lips were quivering, and her voice was shrill fraught tension.

"The smoke looks just the same. And it's right along the river where a boat would be. What else could it be? Suppose something went wrong and they came back early?"

Roscoe laid a hand on her shoulder.

"Hush now! No more! No time for that. Now we're gonna go down to that beach and brass it out. Proceed accordin' to plan. If it turns out our boat has burned…I'll have to give that problem a good think, so I will. Come on now."

As they marched down to the beach, Roscoe discarded his walking staff. He straightened, and his steps became brisk, with hardly a trace of his normal limp. They paused briefly at a small stream, and he washed away most of the blood. Sarah bound his head with a fresh cloth that disguised the seriousness of the wound.

The others, too, did their best to mask the terror and defeat they felt so deeply. Such weapons and equipage as remained were cleaned and put to order. Injuries were bathed and bandaged. Only Sarah remained dirty and bedraggled, wanting to appear as crazed and dangerous as possible. She twined leaves and sticks in her hair. Occult designs were added to her cheeks and forehead with dabs of Roscoe's blood.

CHAPTER THIRTY-NINE

A DUEL TO THE DEATH

When all was ready, the party stepped out of the trees and approached the deserted breastwork. The ground was littered with spent arrows and dead goblins. They looked over the breastwork and saw the knot of men squatting on the beach below just as Thurmond had described them. Roscoe made a trumpet of his hands and bellowed, "Holla! Holla on the beach! Hey there, you men! I would speak to your lord!"

Those who were able climbed to their feet and stared blankly at the newcomers. When none spoke, Roscoe continued to harangue them.

"Who is in charge here? You, I'm speakin' to you, the tall fellow in the rusty mail. Are you the captain here?"

He was addressing Jasper, who was self-consciously hiding his gruesome troll hand behind his back. Shreds of goblin meat still stuck to its claws. The man was a brave and capable soldier, to be sure, but he did not possess qualities of a leader. He answered as best as his slow wit would allow.

"We serve Lord Bartholomew… or maybe Lord Rupert. But we don't know where they are."

This was good news. The men were, as Roscoe had surmised, bereft of leadership. He had hoped their captain was dead, which would make things easier. But this Bartholomew—or Rupert—was maybe only lost. He had to move quickly before one or both returned. He shouted down at Jasper.

"Both of those are slain by the goblins. Before they died, they gave you over to my command. You men now belong to me."

A stocky, squint-eyed fellow named Drax, smarter than Jasper, took up the conversation.

"And who might you be exactly?"

"Captain Roscoe Appleman of the Brotherhood of Underworld Adventurers, Gorgonholm chapter. My troop and I are comin' down. Leave your weapons in their sheaths or on the ground if you value your lives. I come as a friend, but I will tolerate no dirty business. Understood?"

The men made no response, but neither did they begin to arm themselves. They stood empty handed as Roscoe and company made their way through the riven breastwork and climbed down the riverbank to the shingle.

Once again all was going according to plan. The men on the beach seemed calm and compliant. Such moments are, however, fraught with peril, for it is exactly at such moments that Lady Fortune delights in giving her wheel a devious spin. Had Roscoe been listening closely, he might have heard the whir of its turning.

Awakened by the shouting, Rupert now appeared on the beach. Remarkably, he felt much better. His wound, he decided, would not prove fatal after all. Now was the moment to reveal himself to the survivors and take charge of things. But first he would have to put an end to all their damnable caterwauling.

He stopped short. A group of strangers were descending the riverbank, while his men just stood and watched. There was an awkward moment as he paused and considered. He grew even more confused when he recognized Thurmond, the peasant stable boy he had hired to steal Bart's magic mirror. How came he to be here?

That little shit had always been a problem. He had disappeared right after the theft, frustrating his best efforts to have him finished off. Renata had sent her demon after him, but it never came back. Neither did the three murderers Sims had sent. Who was he really?

And then the pieces suddenly fell together, and Rupert finally grasped how mistaken he had been from the start. He had always assumed this adventure had been a contest solely between Bart and himself. But there was a third party—there had always been a third party. And it now stood before him on the beach.

Now he understood why he and Bart could never agree about who had followed whom down the river. That thick-headed lout had always maintained that it had been he who had stalked Rupert, which had made no sense at all. He understood why Bart had so strenuously denied having the treasure map yet had come directly to the correct location.

The stable boy had the map, had had it all along. It was he whom Bart had followed, with Rupert trailing behind, unaware of the first boat's existence. It was this basic miscalculation that had somehow brought his plan to grief. Well, he could find some satisfaction in the destruction of the stable boy and his friends. He called out to the men—his men—who stood sullenly on the shingle with empty hands.

"You, Jasper, pick up your weapon! All of you, draw your swords! These men will kill us all unless we get them first. Get cracking!"

The men just stood, ignoring his commands. They all knew by now that he had burned the boat with his own people inside. Had they not been so completely broken in spirit, they would have given the heartless nobleman an excruciating demise, one involving fire.

When they failed to obey, Rupert barely paused. He was beyond caring, consumed by recklessness and fatalism. He gave a flourish with his sword and moved on the fat old man who stood at the head of the newcomers. Rupert would finish that one off first and then go for the stable boy. Baring his teeth in a snarl, he lunged.

†

Thurmond did not at first recognize the man who emerged from the broom bush, sword in hand. His head and face were encrusted with clotted blood, worse even than Roscoe's had been. Yet there was something in his carriage that was familiar, and when he spoke again, Thurmond knew the voice. It was the well-groomed gentleman, though not nearly so well groomed at the moment. He was coming at Roscoe with his weapon raised.

The old Adventurer was trying to draw his sword when his bad leg gave out and down he went. He had walked too far without the aid of a staff, and his strength finally failed him. Thurmond saw a sardonic smile crease the bloody face of the attacker as he prepared to smite the stricken man.

In an instant Thurmond pulled his sword from its sheath and stepped between Rupert and his friend. To his surprise the attacker paused and then laughed.

"Well met, stable boy. I've been wanting to see your blood for some time, but you've been hard to find. So I'm going to enjoy this."

Rupert exuded a supreme confidence. He was, as a nobleman, a trained swordsman. What chance did a lowborn dung-shoveler stand against him?

"I want this to be fun, stable boy, so we mustn't end it too quickly. You and I will fight it out just like two real gentlemen. What do you say? Sound like fun?"

With his sword, he pointed toward a small round shield lying near Thurmond's feet.

"Go ahead—pick it up. I'll stand back and give you space to get ready. Word of honor."

He moved back several paces, allowing Thurmond to retrieve the item in question. As he was buckling the shield on his arm, Rupert picked up his own larger shield from where it lay beneath the broom. He thought about replacing some of his discarded armor pieces but decided against it. His opponent was not worth the effort. Then he came gliding back.

"All set, stable boy? Lay on!"

He gave another fancy flourish and jumped to the attack. Thurmond was far from all set. His feet were out of position, and his shield strap was too loose. Nor was he ready for the suddenness of Rupert's onslaught.

He managed to deflect the first blow with his shield, but it was followed immediately by a shot to the other side of his head. Only luck allowed him to get his sword up in time to block that one. He pivoted awkwardly, trying to align himself for a riposte, but Rupert slammed him hard with the edge of his shield, striking his right shoulder and knocking him back a step.

Had Rupert closed in then, he could have easily slain the confused and battered stable boy. But instead he stood back and laughed his dark laugh.

"You liking this, peasant bastard? You told me you wanted to be a warrior—is this what you had in mind?"

He moved in even faster than before, easily getting inside Thurmond's poor defense. One blow struck his helmet. It did not penetrate but landed with a painful, stunning impact. The next struck his left leg, cutting through the leather armor and opening the flesh beneath. Thurmond gasped in shock and staggered back. He was again wide open and completely vulnerable, but Rupert elected once more to drift out of range and bait his adversary.

"I'm finally getting to see your blood, just like I told you. It's red, by the way—just in case you want to know."

Rupert swooped in again, but this time his face was twisted in a cruel expression that said he meant to bring the fight to a rapid conclusion. He aimed a hard, slow roundhouse blow at the left side of Thurmond's head. It was an obvious fake, but the novice swordsman fell for it, moving his shield too far in that direction. Rupert than pivoted slightly, spun the sword over his own head, and delivered two swift strikes to this opponent's right shoulder. Thurmond's coat-of-plates lacked metal reinforcement on the shoulders. There was only thick leather, so both blows drew blood.

Rupert continued to press forward, intent on finishing the job. But his strenuous movement had opened his scalp wound, and blood began to ooze into his eyes. He backed away in an effort to clear his vision.

Thurmond saw his opportunity and at once launched his own attack, striking furiously and repeatedly while his foe was in disarray. Unfortunately, his ill-aimed blows landed directly on the face of Rupert's shield and did him no harm. Weakened and out of breath, he was forced to pull away. The two fighters remained apart, resting, glaring at each other in mutual antipathy.

Thurmond's mind raced as he tried to devise some tactic that might save his life. Experienced swordsmen know a wide array of tricky moves and feints to create a hole in an opponent's defense. Good fighters can conceal their real intensions with a shift of a foot, the drop of a shoulder, or even the glance of an eye. They throw blows in a flurry that always seem to land in the place their opponent least expects. Thurmond knew none of these advanced techniques. In their lessons Roscoe had always stuck to the very basics, the first steps that had to be mastered before moving on to more the complex aspects of fighting.

As Rupert came into range, he remembered a simple fake Roscoe had frequently used on him during their practice sessions. Holding his hand high, he threw a quick snap at the side of the nobleman's head, but at the last moment, he pulled the sword almost straight down toward the left leg, just above the knee. Not expecting such a move from this raw beginner, Rupert was caught off guard. The leg shot sliced through his unprotected flesh at an angle that almost severed his kneecap. He screamed and dropped. Following Roscoe's instructions, Thurmond did not hesitate. He delivered another horizontal blow that landed straight across the bridge of Rupert's nose.

The nobleman was carried over backward by the force of the impact. He lay supine, squirming in agony, his scream replaced by a muted whine. Thurmond looked back at his friends. Sarah was kneeling beside Roscoe, who had raised himself to a sitting position. The old Adventurer spoke in a gentle tone.

"Finish him off, Thurmond. It's the merciful thing."

Without another thought, Thurmond pushed the point of his sword through the eye socket of his fallen foe.

He began to walk back to his companions but became aware of wobbliness in his legs. Things around him began to get dreamy and unfocused. The world seemed somehow muted. He was dimly aware of Sarah's voice, sounding as if coming from far away.

"He's going to swoon. Oh, he's going to swoon."

†

Meanwhile, back in Gorgonholm, Lady Renata was jolted from her afternoon nap, stuck by an epiphany as sharp and sudden as the sting of a serpent. Rupert was dead. Even in her sleep she had felt it—the psychic link that bound him to her had been abruptly cut. There could be no doubt, he was dead. This fact was, in itself, not a serious concern. But it was grievously annoying that someone other than she had chosen the time and method of his demise.

And she knew—somehow she just knew—who that somebody was. It was that dreadful little thief, that horrid stable boy who had obstructed all her plans. Who had stolen her dear Aborax. From whence had come such audacity? How could it be that such a one could so thwart her power? How could he dare challenge Lady Renata de la Pole?

That damned stable boy—may he be eaten alive by some vicious beast in that dismal wilderness! Her rage building, she opened her mouth to scream but then did not. There were worse deaths than being eaten by wild beasts, were there not? She calmed as a plan began to take shape in her mind.

The stable boy would be returning to Gorgonholm by the same road he had left it, on the river, so he would have to stop at riverside villages along the way. And she knew of one in particular that could offer him a most gratifying reception. She need only summon a small sprite to carry a message to a certain priest.

CHAPTER FORTY

SARAH'S SOLITARY MISSION

When Thurmond finally regained consciousness, he immediately regretted it. He hurt all over. Head, shoulder, and leg seemed to be in competition to see which could inflict the most agony. A myriad of small cuts and abrasions added such torment as they were able. Contusions, not to be left out, did their bit.

He opened his eyes, shut them again, and then opened them once more. The pain was too great to permit the blessed oblivion of sleep. He did not know where he was. It was dark, and he could not get his bearings. He remembered the fight but nothing beyond it.

Sarah appeared beside him. She wiped his brow with a cool, wet cloth and poured a sip of water between his lips. She picked up her witch's wand and began to murmur something. He was at once filled with an irresistible fatigue and drifted back into a dreamless sleep.

When he next awoke, the sun was up. He tried to raise himself slightly, trying to look around, but wincing with the attendant pain. He was still on the shingle by the river, but downstream from the site of battle where the bodies had begun to bloat and fester. He lay upon a pallet of folded cloaks and blankets. Others were spread over him.

Sarah and Roscoe were gathered at a nearby campfire with a group of men, the same ones they had found on the beach yesterday. They all seemed to be in deep consultation. He did not see the brothers. Then Sarah happened to glance in his direction.

"Oh, he's awake! Roscoe, did you hear me? Thurmond's awake."

She came over and sat at his side.

"How do you feel?"

"Like to die. I've never felt pain this bad before."

"I'm sure it's dreadful. But I've got good news. You're not badly hurt. Nothing's broken inside. You're cut up, but everything will heal, and you'll be okay."

"How can you be so sure?"

"Roscoe looked you over while you were out cold. He knows a lot about chirurgery—how to treat wounds and things. He sewed up the cuts on your shoulder and thigh. Said the scars will make you look like a real Adventurer."

"What did you do to me last night?"

"You started moaning and rolling around in your sleep. You finally woke yourself up. A little of my psychic power had come back by then, so I used a sleep spell to put you back under. Worked perfectly."

Roscoe now came over and carefully lowered himself on Thurmond's other side.

"Well, boyo, it's about time you were up and around. We've a big day ahead of us, and we can't be held back by any slugabed hang-arounds. So get up and get your gear together."

This wholly impossible command took Thurmond aback.

"Look, Roscoe, I don't think I can."

The older man exploded in a great peal of laughter.

"Thurmond, laddie, I did but jest. Just lay easy. I've sent Sod and Nod downriver to meet their boat at the appointed time and place. They'll be back tomorrow to this very spot. Then we'll go aboard and start the journey home.

"Those lads over there, the ones sitting by our fire, have had the good sense to join our cause. Seems they had no great fondness for that nobleman you slew. They called him by the name of Rupert de Pugh. And the other one, some pompous ass, is either dead or has made off somewhere. No one knows where.

"So I've assumed command, just as I said I would, and they've agreed to be my loyal minions. Of course they'll bear watchin', at least until they've proved themselves, so they will."

Thurmond was consumed with curiosity about the new recruits.

"Who are these new men, Roscoe? What are they doing here? Were they the ones following us down the river?"

"'Tis a strange and twisted tale, filled with error and false assumption, so it is. As it turns out, there were two parties behind us, wantin' our gold. One came in the boat you see burned there on the beach. It belonged to the man you slew. The other landed a bit downstream, where they tried to hide it in some bushes. But it was found and burned by somebody. Most likely goblins or kobolds."

"That man I slew—he was the well-groomed gentleman I told you about. Remember? The one who hired me to steal the magic mirror."

"Is that a fact? Well, I can't say it's surprisin' news. And here's another strange turn of events. Two of our new recruits is wearin' the livery of a noble of Gorgonholm—Bartholomew Staynes. Sarah says this Staynes was her very own brother, the shit-heel she was tryin' to escape from when she ran away with you.

"And guess what else? That pretty boy you killed was workin' for a witch by the name of Lady Renata. Ever hear of her?"

"Nay, the name means nothing."

"Me and Sarah never heard of her neither. They say she lives in a tower south of Gorgonholm. Sarah thinks she's probably the dark-haired witch she saw in the mirror."

"This is too strange. My brain feels like it's filled with scorpions."

"Just rest as easy as you can. There'll be plenty of time to sort things out on the boat ride home."

Under Sarah's direction, those less injured scoured the battlefield for whatever useful items were to be found. She had them erect a makeshift awning to protect Thurmond and the other badly wounded men from the heat of the sun. Rations were meager, for most had been stored in Rupert's burned boat.

The new recruits were docile and cooperative. As Roscoe had anticipated, they were too defeated to contemplate insurrection. They needed his confidence and authority.

It was during these comings and goings that Thurmond noticed the scaled and taloned hand attached to Jasper's wrist. There could be no mistake. Here was the very troll hand he had retrieved for the well-groomed gentleman, the man he had slain. The one Roscoe had called Rupert de Pugh.

He thought of calling the man over and questioning him about how and why he had acquired such an unwholesome appendage, but then decided against it. Maybe on the way home. Maybe when he felt more capable of conversation.

The day passed quickly. Sarah apportioned such sustenance as they had, but there was little enough to go around. She made sure the wounded—Thurmond, in particular—received the largest portions. In the late afternoon, the man lying next to Thurmond, a severely injured boatman, went into convulsions. A goblin arrow had pierced his lung, and he had been badly burned while trying to escape from Bart's blazing riverboat. He died shrieking, his moral outrage articulated in incoherent gibberish.

As the shadows grew long in the late afternoon, Sarah became more and more agitated. She stomped about camp, slamming things to and fro. Roscoe, fully aware of her unsettled state, finally approached her.

"Sarah, darlin', whatever is the matter? You're stormin' about like a banshee with a bellyache. How can I help you?"

"You can't. This is my business alone. It's hard to explain, but I have to tell you. I have to leave here for a while."

"What's that? Leave here? And go where? Why?"

"Back to the temple of the Ancient One, where we spent our first night."

"And why would you be wantin' to do that?"

"I made a bargain, and I mean to keep it. When I made it, I never imagined that there would be no one fit to go with me. I thought that you or Thurmond...or Torgul... But it doesn't signify. I have to go back."

"Has your most excellent brain turned to mush? These woods abound with fell beasties. Who knows what may be peeking through the bushes even as we stand here? You can't be serious."

"I am very serious. I have to do the right thing. I learned that from you.

You wouldn't abandon those men over there, even though they came here as our enemies. And we all trust that Sod and Nod will show up here and pick us up instead of just sailing away. Why?"

"Well, because they're honorable men who gave their word."

"Women can have a sense of honor, too! And I gave my word, so I have to go."

"You've made a pact with the wee brown man—correct?"

"Something to that effect. Listen, Roscoe, this may take longer than I want. I promise I'll hasten, but if I'm late, please wait as long as you can for me. Please don't get angry and leave without me."

"Wouldn't dream of it. We'll wait—my word of honor."

Sarah got ready in short order. She still had her helmet, sword, and mailshirt. The wicker pannier, though battered, still held her occult paraphernalia. By this time, the battlefield was imbued with a hideous reek, but she braved it to search for additional gear. She picked up a lightweight bow that had once belonged to a slain boatman. She then gathered a quiver full of arrows, pulling them from the ground and the bodies of dead goblins.

Once fully prepared, she approached Roscoe again.

"I don't think you know this, but Sod and Nod took some mushrooms from the kobolds. I made them give me some, and I brewed a tea from them. It's in that little pot over by the fire. If those two badly burned guys start hollering again or thrashing around, give them some. Maybe it's good for them…maybe. Anyway, it quiets them down. And if Thurmond gets restless, dose him too."

She gave the old Adventurer a quick hug and disappeared into the woods, wanting to get as far as possible before the daylight failed. Roscoe was left with an appalling sense of doom. In his prime he would have been apprehensive of a hike through those woods alone and at night. What chance would she have should she encounter the denizens that lurked there?

†

It was a bad night. Roscoe hungered, but there was not much to eat. He was too worried to sleep, and his wounds ached unmercifully. The burn victims began to moan, so he dosed them as instructed. He considered taking a sip of the tea himself, but he did not like the glassy stare of the men to whom he fed it.

He posted two sentries atop the riverbank but assumed that they were still too exhausted to stay awake. He should go and check on them, but climbing the steep bank would hurt his leg something awful.

His thoughts turned to Thurmond, who appeared to be sleeping soundly. The kid had saved his life when he challenged that hotshot nobleman. He thought of Sarah wandering alone through the woods. And then he thought of Torgul—those were some dark thoughts indeed.

When the first hint of morning gray first appeared above the trees, Roscoe was not sure whether he had slept at all. He must have dozed a little, he decided, for the fire had burned down to a bed of coals. One of his men was also beginning to stir, aroused by the meager light. Then a sharp recollection of the previous afternoon came to him, and he sprang up, fully awakened.

Sarah had not returned. Roscoe tried to catch his breath and calm himself, to slow the hammering of his heart. He knew she would not yet have had time to reach the ruined temple, conduct her business, and return. Yet his reason was unable to overmaster his fear.

There was nothing else for it but to bundle their gear and make ready for the boat. He kicked his sleepy men into wakefulness. One was tasked with rekindling the fire, another was sent off to relieve, or perhaps awaken, the sentries. The rest began to gather their scant belongings and pile them at the water's edge. When Sod and Nod arrived, they needed to be packed up and ready to embark.

CHAPTER FORTY-ONE

AN ANXIOUS DELAY AND A JOLLY SURPRISE

Their preparations were quickly completed, so there was nothing left to do but wait and worry. Time dragged ever so slowly. If Roscoe had had an hourglass, he could have watched the individual grains of sand drop one by one through its neck. Still no Sarah.

As a young man, Roscoe had been on many reckless adventures but never with a female as a member of the party. And especially with one so young and pretty. The world was indeed changing when pretty young girls started fighting goblins and going off in the woods alone in the dark on who-knows-what chore. No, sir, he did not like it. When he was young, girls knew better than to try to act like men. Did not *want* to act like men.

Yet he had to admit that Sarah had done her part. More than her part. She was whip-smart and as brave and loyal as any of them. Without her they would never have deciphered the rune that led them to the tree sprite. And without that creature's power, she could not have turned them invisible, which was the only thing that had allowed them to enter the goblin cave.

Her magic had slowed the shadowy treasure guard so Thurmond could kill it. Before the adventure had even begun, she had saved Torgul from that murderer by throwing her ink pot. She had saved his own skin as well, dragging him along when the shadow creature's blow had left him half addled.

The problem was not with Sarah herself. She had proved herself entirely capable. The problem was with his own feelings. Had Torgul or even Thurmond gone off by themselves, he would not have suffered the torments he was now experiencing. He had sent Sod and Nod off to find their boat with scarcely a thought. So the problem was his instinctive need to shield the girl from harm, even though she quite obviously did not require such protection. This was all so bloody confusing.

The sun climbed high in the sky as the morning wore down. The men sat on the baggage and watched for the boat. No Sarah. Roscoe was just about resolved to go after her, to take a couple of his most able-bodied minions and try to pick up her trail. He could only hope his leg could stand it. And then Thurmond stood before him, looking drawn and pale, but obviously on the path to recovery.

"Where's Sarah?"

When he tried to explain the nature of her errand, Thurmond pitched a fit.

"You let her go? Why didn't you stop her? Don't you care what happens to her? Those woods are full of goblins and kobolds. By God's arse, Roscoe, how could you allow this?"

Roscoe held up his hand for silence, and surprisingly Thurmond obeyed. He was still too weak from loss of blood to continue his complaint.

"You're right, laddie. I must concede that. I never should have let her go, but in sooth, I didn't know how to prevent it. I was in no condition to chase her down. Could you have stopped her?"

This brought Thurmond up short. Even if both of them had been in the best of health, it was doubtful that they could have held the strong-spirited girl against her will.

"My apologies, Captain Roscoe. I spoke out of turn."

"Let it go, boyo. We're none of us at our best right now."

There was a commotion among the men sitting by the river. Several jumped to their feet and pointed excitedly downstream.

"The boat! Here it comes! Here it comes! Holla! Holla!"

And sure enough, Scrymgeour's boat was moving slowing toward them, forcing its way against the current by means of four long sweeps, two to a side. Some of Roscoe's men were so transported that they began to dance a merry jig. All laughed, even those with serious hurts. But neither Roscoe nor Thurmond could share their joy. Sarah had still not returned.

The boat pulled ashore. The men stood ready to toss the pile of equipment aboard and clamber in behind it. Roscoe was in a quandary. He knew everyone, soldier and boatman alike, wanted nothing more than to depart this fetid place of death. Wanted to return to the comforts of civilization. Wanted to go home.

But there would be no departure until they found Sarah. This could be a serious problem. These men were bound to him by no particular sense of duty or loyalty. How would they respond when, with the boat waiting on the shingle, he announced a delay? Would he and Thurmond be able to keep them in line?

How would Nod and Sod react? They had been hired to provide transportation and join the party in their raid on the goblin nest. They might not feel obliged to help suppress an insurrection among the new recruits. So the situation might get dicey.

Then something unforeseen occurred that put this problem, for a while at least, entirely out of Roscoe's mind. Sitting in the stern of the boat, with his feet propped up and a mug of ale in his hand, sat a familiar figure. Torgul!

Roscoe was struck dumb for a moment but then hobbled down to the boat and reached over the low gunwale to embrace his friend.

"Torgul! You're alive! Damn your eyes, man, you live! Ha!"

Thurmond was right behind him, a little hesitant because he thought he might be confronting a ghost. Roscoe's large form mostly blocked his view, but at last he managed to reach across and touch the apparition's shoulder. It was, he was relieved to discover, quite solid.

"Torgul, by the bloated belly of God, 'tis you. In the flesh—not some phantasmal form. 'Tis really you."

He felt as though a great weight of stone had been lifted from his heart.

The dwarf gave them both a hard stare.

"Of course it's me. I'm not so easy to kill as you seem to think. Let me remind you that I am Torgul Bonelip, twenty-third of that name, and as such..."

Roscoe chuckled.

"Aye, aye, prithee, spare us the saga of your lineage. We're just so happy to have you back that all proper decorum escapes us."

He stepped aside to allow Thurmond to catch their resurrected companion in a bear hug

And then, as if out of nowhere, Sarah joined them. They had been so occupied with greeting Torgul that no one had seen her approach.

Roscoe had expected Sarah to return, if she returned at all, even more exhausted and disheveled than before. But to his surprise, she looked exceedingly refreshed and healthy. Her eyes gleamed, and her step was sprightly. She was clean, too. Her hair looked washed and combed. How could this be?

She still wore her mailshirt, but with none of the mud and blood that had caked it yesterday. But her helmet was gone. She had left camp with the small, round casque buckled securely under her chin. Where could it have gone?

Sarah joined the others at the boat. Her greeting was quite matter of fact, as if she were entirely unaware of the anxiety she had caused him.

"Hey, Roscoe, I'm back. Everything went better than…"

Then she squealed with utter delight at the sight of Torgul. She too launched herself across the gunwale and clasped him with both arms. The dwarf was visibly uncomfortable with all this display of raw human emotion but permitted it nonetheless. He patted her shoulder as she clung to him, speechless and sobbing for joy. When his embarrassment grew too great, he took her gently by the shoulders and removed her to arm's length.

"I'm glad to see you too, girl. Glad you escaped from them nasty biters as was chasin' us. Sod and Nod learned me about things as best they could—hard to follow their jabberin' tongue though. I at least knew you was all safe."

Sarah finally got herself under control.

"We never thought to see you again. I saw you go over…into the river…and…"

Roscoe could restrain his good humor no longer.

"And we thought for a fact that the fishies were nibblin' on your innards, so we did. Now then, there's many a story to be told here, but would it not be better to hear 'em as we're wendin' our way home? So let's get in the boat and be on our way."

Sarah held up a finger in a gesture requesting patience.

"Of course, we must be off. But just one moment—I have to get something."

Without waiting for a reply, she turned and trotted up the beach. Good to her word, she was back almost at once. In her hands was her missing helmet, which was now filled with dirt. In it was planted a single small, green root sprout.

Roscoe gave her a strained look.

"I've always thought that gardenin' was a fine pastime for a young lady. But I have to wonder if this is really the best moment to devote yourself to the tendin' of a houseplant."

Sarah smiled slightly, signaling that she understood his sarcasm. But she was adamant in her response.

"You know this isn't a houseplant. It's a root sucker from an oak tree. And you know I'm not bringing it along just to while away the hours."

Roscoe became more serious.

"Sarah, as captain of this company, I have to be told about any and all things that might affect our success or failure—even our survival. Is the wee brown man inside that slip of a plant?"

"Aye, he is. And I call him Whisper."

"Well then, please inform me as to what is going on."

"He's a dryad, a spirit that lives in a tree. And you saw his tree, how ancient and sick it is. If he's inside when it dies, he dies, too. When he came to me and charged my wand—that really helped us, didn't it? So I promised that I'd help him if I could. I have to take this sprout home and plant it where I can water it and look after it until it can survive on its own."

Thurmond was just getting ready to climb into the boat but halted midstep upon hearing Sarah's story.

"He can do that? Switch trees? That's allowed?"

"I think so. I don't really know. I was just an idea I had. I mean, the sprouts grow from a tree's roots, so they're part of the same tree, aren't they? So why not? It has to work. He said he'd never heard of such a thing before, but it's at least worth a try, isn't it?"

"How do you know he's really in there?"

"I can feel him somehow. He gives me a nudge once in a while, like an unborn baby kicking inside its mama's womb."

Roscoe continued in a serious tone.

"You've come back to us remarkably clean and refreshed, lass. Can you explain that?"

"Aye, a dip in the Goddess pool and a bit of help from Whisper."

"Should we have occasion, on the way home, to need a bit more of his kind help, would he oblige us, do you think?"

"I don't think he can. As I said, he's become like a babe in the womb. I don't think he'll get his power back until he's properly planted and his roots take hold. Right now he's about as helpless as an infant. I guess I'm the mama. You and Thurmond and Torgul are going to have to play papa."

With that she handed the improvised flowerpot to Torgul, stepped over the gunwale, and sat down beside him. Roscoe started to follow her, but his bad leg hindered her. Finally, with Thurmond pushing from behind while Sod and Nod pulled from the fore, he was hauled aboard. Still smarting from his wounds, Thurmond had even greater difficulty boarding the boat. Reaching down, Roscoe and Torgul lifted him as gently as they could. The other men were long since stowed amidships and waiting impatiently.

And with that, they cast off and headed for home.

PART 5

THE HARD JOURNEY HOME

CHAPTER FORTY-TWO

TORGUL'S TALE

The Mad River was grossly misnamed. It could by no means be fairly described, as the appellation implied, to be either angry or insane. Its rapids were brusque but not ireful. No deadly cataracts riled it to frothing frenzy. For the most part, it sauntered at its own stately pace through a landscape smooth and even, the surrounding countryside punctuated by nothing more provocative than rolling hills. It was a dignified river, magnificent in its length and girth. A regal river that changed its pace for no mortal creature.

It was small wonder then that so many of the inhabitants of its shoreline worshipped the river as a living god. It was a benign and generous deity that granted a bountiful existence to the myriad of villages and farmsteads that dotted its banks. These simple rustics, mindful of their good fortune, raised shrines to their river god to which they offered sacrifice and made obeisance. Yet they remained a dour, self-sufficient people who seldom ventured beyond their own isolated villages.

The river must have loved the villagers as they loved it, for it remained steadfast in is congeniality and placidity. In very few places did it narrow, grow agitated, and pick up speed. Thus our intrepid heroes enjoyed a much-needed period of recuperation as they made the long, long journey back to Gorgonholm and civilization.

As Roscoe had warned, the voyage upriver was more difficult than the passage down. Though the current was gentle, constant physical exertion was needed to make headway against it. Occasionally, when the wind was just right, the boatmen raised the square sail on a mast that rose just behind the vessel's cabin. But mainly, the boat had to be propelled by the four massive oars known as sweeps that projected from its sides like the legs of a water bug.

The veteran watermen could row for hours, making the arduous task appear effortless. They sang while they rowed, belting out their lines in a regular four-beat rhythm, perfectly matched to the rise and fall of the sweeps. Their intonation was nasal and sing-songy, their dialect so thick that only Roscoe could understand the meaning of their words. Most, he told the others, were old songs that had to do with ancient sea battles or romantic conquests. He refrained, for Sarah's sake, from being more explicit. Drax was less circumspect. He belted out a seemingly endless array of utterly filthy soldier songs that Thurmond found delightful.

Two of the new recruits had served as crewmen on Bart's boat. Nod took one look at their callused hands, recognized them as watermen, and pressed them into service. They were soon taking their turn at the sweeps and joining in the singing. They seemed entirely satisfied with their new situation, happy to be back on the water and away from the accursed goblins.

Wounds healed with remarkable rapidity. These were all robust individuals who were inured to hardships. Their bodies seemed to understand they might soon be needed for the next desperate enterprise and that healing must proceed with all possible haste. So bruises quickly faded, cuts closed, and skin regrew. Their spirits lifted, and soon they were all trying to sing along with the rowers.

Even the most badly wounded men, the ones burned when Rupert fired his own boat, were able to rise. Thurmond's leg and shoulder stopped aching and began to itch as the offended flesh mended. When his strength returned, he joined the rowers at the sweeps, eager for a chance to demonstrate his prowess.

To his dismay, he failed utterly. He could neither control the heavy sweep nor maintain a steady, even rhythm. His sweep would often miss the water altogether or collide with those of the other rowers. Watching the seemingly tireless rivermen, he had assumed the task would require little effort, but rowing proved to be backbreaking work. He was quickly left gasping and out of breath. The young man flushed with anger and humiliation as the entire party broke into loud guffaws. But Roscoe drew the sting from the moment by slapping him heartily on the back.

"It's all right, laddie. We're all your friends here and mean you no ill, so there's nothin' to be gained by gettin' grumpy. You set yourself to an impossible task, that's all. Old Nod over there fiercely maintains that no one masters the sweeps but what he were born on the river. Sod is more generous, holdin' that a landsman might make a decent rower after ten or twelve years of steady practice. You've just got a few years to go yet, so you do."

Thurmond felt his ire fading away, and in the end, he laughed as heartily as anybody.

Many of the riverside villages had narrow paths running along the top of the adjacent riverbank. For a modest sum, a local boy with an ox or a mule could be hired to tow the riverboat up against the current. During such episodes, the entire crew was able to take its ease.

The brothers were already familiar figures in some of the villages, having stopped on previous journeys to buy provisions or to arrange for a tow. In these locations, the reception was cordial. In those where they were unknown, the residents remained wary and sullen. Certainly they were eager for the coins the outsiders offered them, but long experience had taught them to remain on guard with strangers.

Roscoe and company did not come equipped for trade, with knife blades and bolts of cloth to swap for salted eels. They were obviously a party of dodgy Adventurers, so when they hailed from their boat and called for a parley, the village men assembled with their bows and fishing spears. The young boys ran to fetch their slings and gather a pouch full of smooth stones. Women and girls ran to hide in the surrounding thickets.

Negotiations were terse, and even Roscoe's good humor, normally infectious, failed to inspire trust and warmth in the river people. Torgul and Sarah remained unseen in the boat's cabin. Many humans displayed a strong aversion to dwarves, and Sarah…well…she might prove a temptation. Thurmond and the others stood by with their weapons concealed but close at hand.

Happily for all involved, nothing dire occurred during any of these encounters. A few coins were produced, an ox or two were yoked, and a lad was dispatched to drive the team up the towpath. Such paths were never very long. At the end, the boatmen untied the towline and prepared the sweeps. The boy gathered the line, turned his ox or mule about, and returned to his village.

The journey afforded the company much time for talk, and the most pressing topic of conversation was of course Torgul's escape from the depth of the river. Scarcely were they aboard and underway before they were all pestering him for details. They had seen him plummet from a high cliff, clad in mail and helmet, axe in hand. A half-dozen kobolds had him gripped in their jaws. So how could he be sitting with them now in the stern of the boat?

Torgul was in his element. He was a born teller of tales. Among dwarves, storytelling was deemed a high art. The dwarven bard crafted his story within a complex set of conventions that must be diligently observed. Torgul was sufficiently well acquainted with human tastes to know his companions could find his style a bit tedious, but he was not going to violate the venerable traditions of storytelling.

Such tales always began with a recounting of the deeds of one's ancestors

"Hwæt! Much have you heard of the triumphs of the dwarves of Spear Mountain, how Torgul the Great, first of that name, the bane of goblin and terror of troll, the winner of treasure and giver of gold, glorious his fame and long his beard as he battered his foes—of his greatness I sing. Cast out from his clan, luckless and lonely, wandering the earth, friendless and..."

Sarah interrupted, her voice pleading.

"Torgul, please, we want to know what happened to you in the river. Can't you just tell us that story now, and about your family later?"

The dwarf paused, rose to his feet, and stretched himself imposingly to his full height, which was somewhat short of Sarah's chin.

"Missy, I am not to be hurried. Our poetics must adhere to proper form. This is a time-honored custom. To do otherwise would bring dwarven civilization down in a crashin' ruin. I will not be the one to so undermine our most treasured art form."

Thurmond pitched in, using his best diction in an effort to both placate and sway their touchy companion.

"Honored bard, while we all maintain naught but the highest regard for your poetical formalities, I fear we may be unable to pay sufficient heed to its subtle niceties, to the artful turns of phrase, while yet consumed with questions regarding your own self. Plus my wounds pain me like fire."

Roscoe, too, added his bit.

"As an adventurin' brother and your boon companion, prithee, show mercy. Sweet as your poesy is to your people's ears, it's pure sufferin' to mine. No offense intended."

But Torgul was not to be moved. He instead became more formal and loftier in his indignation. He could speak most eloquently when he chose to.

"I am not offended. My only regret is that you humans lack the cleverness to appreciate the depth of complexity of my verse. You are sadly missin' one of life's sublime joys. But fear not, for as your true brother and boon companion, I will persevere in your education. To my joy, we have an abundance of time to devote to it."

The others gasped out as one.

"What do you mean?"

"I mean that lessons will commence at once with the recital of my entire verse. You will attend carefully and take note of the aesthetic minutiae. You could not possibly appreciate the significance of my small deeds without those of my ancestors to provide a complete context. Listen and learn."

"Cannily conniving those monks of the moorlands, beguiling the gate guards to pillage and plunder, stealing the monies locked in their storerooms, ill-gotten gain of clerics unworthy, grown fat in their greed, their faith betrayed…"

Just before sundown the next evening, the story had progressed to the point where Torgul fell from the cliff. Unable to follow the convoluted syntax and tortured diction, the listeners began to interrupt the narration with a barrage of questions. Torgul finally relented. The sustained attentiveness of his audience had satisfied his injured honor, so he lapsed into the common tongue.

"You will recall, Sarah, how them nasty little biters was about to swarm over us."

"Of course, the ones who came sliding over my little wall of ice."

"Aye, those ones was on me as I tried to back out of the cave. Got their teeth into me and kept bitin' and shakin' their heads like a dog with a rabbit. Mighty weird it was. Anyway, there was too many of 'em, and they pushed me backward over the edge, with them still hangin' on and waggin' their little heads. 'Twas my good fortune they let go when we hit water."

"But, Torgul, why didn't you drown with all your armor on?"

"You wouldn't think it possible, would you, to wiggle out of a mailshirt while deep underwater, but I did it. One handed, too, because I wouldn't let go of my axe. I first had to unbuckle my helmet, but then I got kind of upside down and then the whole thing slithered off.

"I kicked up to the surface just where a dead log was floating by, so I sunk my axe into it and hung on while it carried me down the river. I was still hangin' on when I spotted Scrymgeour's boat pulled up on the bank somewhere downstream. I started yellin', so they threw out a line, caught the log, and pulled me in."

The others just stared at him in open-mouthed awe. Finally Thurmond spoke.

"It's a really nice axe, Torgul, but why didn't you just drop it? You were almost drowned. I know dwarves are supposed to be fond of axes and everything, but it's not that important. You could always get another one."

"Nay, lad, that I could not. Not another like this one. Here now, have a look."

He drew the weapon from beneath his seat and held it before their eyes.

"Behold the Axe of Lodbrok the Thunderer."

It was a truly beautiful piece of work. The head was large, but thin and light. Its cutting edge described a graceful curve ending in a pronounced beard. The polished sides were inlaid with intricate interlaced figures in gold and silver. Grotesque warriors pulled each other's beards. Fearsome beasts gripped their own bodies in their claws. Torgul gave them a moment to gaze, then continued.

"This is one of the great treasures of my people. It has been lost for many years, but now it is found. I would as lief shave the beard from my face as leave this on the river bottom."

This axe, he claimed, was one of the fabled Lost Treasures of Lodbrok, all of which carried a potent enchantment. There was also a helmet, a horn, a shield, a mailshirt, a scramasax, a war belt, a brooch, a wolf skin, a mattock, a harp, and a cauldron. They had been lost for centuries, but their recovery, it was believed, would signal the return of dwarven civilization to its former power and glory. The return of the axe was therefore of the greatest cultural import.

The other great topic of conversation was, of course, money. Captain Roscoe called the party together and demanded that any and all treasure recovered from the goblin hoard be turned over to a communal fund for evenhanded distribution at adventure's end. Because the party had been forced to abandon the bulk of their winnings in the kobold cave, no one expected the collected total to be substantial.

But they were pleasantly surprised when an unlooked-for amount was amassed on the deck of the riverboat. Gold kept emerging from hidden repositories—from inner sleeves and concealed pouches. Sod and Nod upended their boots, releasing a small torrent of coins. Sarah produced a handful of ingots from the bottom of her pannier.

Thurmond suggested that an investigation of body orifices might unearth further revenue, but this idea was so soundly rejected that he let the matter drop. Sod and Nod offered the shrooms they had stolen from the kobolds, but these were turned away.

For all this, the pile of gold was woefully small. They had hoped that wealth of life-changing proportions would compensate the hardship and danger of their adventure. Roscoe longed for a stately home in which to retire in a grand style. Sarah wanted a fully appointed magical workshop and occult library. Thurmond saw himself clad in custom-made armor and astride a great warhorse.

Unfortunately, none of these aspirations could be brought to fruition with the quantity of gold that lay on the deck before them. Their disappointment was great. Even the brothers, usually so quiet, began to jabber excitedly to each other. Roscoe translated.

"They're worried what their old dad will say when he sees the scantiness of his share. He's likely to be a bit put out. He would have, you see, earned substantially more by runnin' uisge over the river."

In his frustration, Thurmond exploded.

"He'll be put out? We're the ones who almost died while he sat at home having a holiday. By the great balls of God, *I'm* put out! I'm downright peeved, I am!"

CHAPTER FORTY-THREE

STRANGE CREATURES
AND SAGE ADVICE

One hot afternoon, Thurmond and Sarah sat on the cabin's roof eating apples, a basket of which they had purchased in a village while stopped for a tow. Suddenly, something brown and fast dropped from the sky, snatched the fruit from Thurmond's hand, and was gone. More swift brown creatures descended on the boat, seizing whatever was lying about the deck—a freshly caught fish, a random glove, a ballista bolt. One made a grab at Sod's sheath knife, missed, and then spread its leathery wings to rise, circle, and try again.

"Eeeeyahh—Thurmond! Get it off me!" Sarah began to scream hysterically when one of the creatures became entangled in her hair. She began to run, beating frantically at the thing as it struggled to free itself. Thurmond started to draw his shortsword, then thought the better of it and went after it with his bare hands.

As he fought to rip the creature loose, it pummeled his face with its wings and sank sharp little teeth into his thumb. Finally it came loose, together with a generous hank of Sarah's hair. He threw it upon the deck and stamped on it as hard as he could. It squealed once and died.

Another of the flying fiends made a dive for Roscoe's wide Adventurer's hat, but the leather laces tied under his chin thwarted it. It received, for its trouble, a mighty smack from Roscoe's beefy hand, which sent it spiraling out of control into the river. Torgul removed his hat and was using it as a swatter, fending off the swooping things that seemed intent on his beard. Then the attack was over. The last creature grabbed the end of a coil of rope and sailed away, seemingly unaware of the great length of line that trailed out behind him as the coil unwound. He sank lower and lower as the weight of his burden grew, and he was at last forced to drop it and soar away.

Sarah was crying, her scalp scratched and bleeding. Thurmond wanted to sooth her, but he was distraught as well, his face and hands covered with welts and bites that burned like the bite of a horsefly. Once again, it was Roscoe who restored order.

"Thurmond, lad, be so kind as to help poor Sarah down the ladder so I can see to her injuries. And then bring yourself down as well—you're lookin' a mite tattered. And bring whatever it is you killed, so we can all have a gander."

Thurmond got Sarah started down the ladder and then took a look at the dead thing at his feet. In general shape it resembled a person, but its height was only the length of a man's forearm. The face was round and pinched, with a weak chin and sloping brow. The body was mostly bald, though there were patches of coarse, bristly fur. From its rump sprouted a short, naked tail.

The creature's most singular aspect was its large, membranous wings, rather resembling those of a bat, growing from the middle of its back. The spindly bones were visible through the translucent skin. Several were fractured, broken either during the tussle for Sarah's hair or by the subsequent stomping. Three short, hooked claws projected like fingers from the front of each wing.

Roscoe called again.

"Bring it down, Thurmond. We're all wantin' a look-see."

Thurmond was unwilling to touch the thing, even dead, so he nudged it off the cabin roof with his foot to land with a *plop* on the deck below. He then skinned down the ladder and joined the others. Sarah had stopped crying and was holding a cloth to her head while kneeling over the mangled remains. She looked up at him as he joined the others.

"Thank you, Thurmond. You are so brave, taking hold of that horrible thing. I thought I might have gone mad with it caught in my hair. Oh…your face is scratched, and your thumb is bleeding. I am so grateful for what you did. If I can ever repay you, you know I will."

With that, she embraced him and then kissed him full on the lips.

Thurmond was a mite surprised. He had come to Sarah's aid the same way they had all done for each other throughout the journey. Of course he would help her. The dead creature was disgusting, to be sure, but its attack had not been life threatening. In fact, he was pretty sure its entanglement in Sarah's hair had been accidental. So why was she acting as if he had done something heroic? He did not know what to say.

He looked over at Roscoe.

"What is this thing?"

Roscoe had no idea. Neither did Torgul. Neither did Sarah. It was Nod and Sod who finally offered an explanation, speaking rapidly in their twangy dialect. Roscoe translated.

"These boyos call this thing a *witch bat*, while them folks livin' on the wild side of the river calls 'em *flying horrors*. They never seen one before, but all the rivermen knows of 'em.

"The story goes that in the olden days, a witchwoman had a castle somewhere in these parts, and she used to spawn these beasties. Kept a whole flock of 'em to do her biddin'. Used to send 'em out to steal children or livestock or whatever else she was wantin' at the moment. And used 'em as guards to keep local fisherfolk from risin' up against her. They was much bigger and more fearsome in those days, it seems. Smarter too. Could follow her speech and obey her commands.

"But somebody finally killed that old witch in spite of her flying vermin, and they been on their own ever since. Over years and years, they went wilder and wilder, and got smaller and stupider until this thing here is all that's left. They still try to steal, same as in the old days, 'cause stealin' is rooted in their blood, don't you see. But they ain't big enough to carry off children or lambs no more, so they just grab whatever they happen on. At least that's what these laddies are tellin' me.

"Now, Torgul, can I trouble you to heave that disgusting offal over the side? And Thurmond, let's see to your bites and scratches. We can't have you comin' down with a fever from an untended bite from a devil bat. And one more thing, Sarah, the boys claim that if one of them things gets tangled up in your hair, he'll never come out."

†

Their injuries were slight, and life on the boat quickly returned to normal. Sarah, however, found herself restless and distracted. She needed solitude to sort out her thoughts and feelings, but this was close to impossible on the crowded riverboat. The cabin was too hot and airless for comfort, so she settled herself on the deck directly abaft the cabin, with her back against its wall. At that moment, the only other person nearby was Sod, who was manning the tiller, and being with Sod was as close to being by herself as she could hope for.

She intended to resume her occult studies, but her mind kept wandering from the book she was holding to another subject—Thurmond, of course— and to the kiss she had given him. She could not get over the intensity of feeling that it had inspired. A delightful glow had coursed through her body as if her veins were suddenly filled with warm honey. It had been more subtle but every bit as powerful as the charge of energy Whisper had put in her wand.

Of course everyone likes a nice kiss. Do they not? But who could have guessed that Thurmond would be capable of inspiring such an intense feeling? She could not deny that she had liked it and had to admit she would not be opposed to another. But that did not mean she wanted Thurmond slobbering on her every chance he got. And would he even want to?

He seemed to have forgotten about the whole episode. He had not approached her since, nor did he offer any indication that things might have changed between them. Males were such dullards! Yet she absolutely loved his shining eyes.

Sarah tried to return to her book, but it could not hold her attention. She had always prided herself on her ability to focus her mind, to learn quickly and easily, but she was quite unable to do so at this moment. Was she losing her wits?

Roscoe appeared before her. She had been so absorbed in her thoughts that she had missed the telltale thumping of his bad leg on the deck boards.

He settled down beside her with his back to the cabin wall, and to her surprise, reached out and placed an arm around her shoulders. He had never before attempted such an intimacy. What could it betoken?

"Sarah, darlin', I've been wantin' to speak with you on a matter of some delicacy, but there was always others about, and so I was forced to bide until I could find a private moment, as it were."

Sarah found herself growing uncomfortable. What was this leading up to?

"You know, lassie, that I've grown very fond of you, so I have. And the time has come for me to declare something I know in my heart to be a true thing, even at the risk of offending you."

Sarah pulled away from the hand resting on her shoulder.

"What are you trying to say to me, Roscoe? Please tell me straight out."

"Well, with all due respect to your female sensitivities, I've seen how you been lookin' at Thurmond, and it's not hard to guess that you've come to have feelin's for the lad."

Sarah felt herself blushing from the top of her bat-gouged pate to the tips of her toes. How could he know this? Nobody was supposed to know this! She opened her mouth to reply, but when no words came.

Roscoe continued.

"Now, Thurmond's a fine laddie. He's loyal and honest and has lots of sand in his gizzard. He'll make a fine Adventurer after he learns a thing or two. But good Adventurers don't usually know how to talk to a young lady. They're all the time thinkin' of travelin' to strange lands and fightin' monsters, so they don't give much thought to things like marriage."

"Marriage? Do you really think I want to marry Thurmond? Has your brain gone soft? I'm not about to tie myself to him or any man! Are you daft?"

"Nay, lassie—now hear me out. I know you're not like those girls who think they have to have a man to do their thinkin' for 'em. You're different, and I like that about you."

Sarah remained silent, but her countenance expressed her growing unease with the subject and direction of his words. Roscoe proceeded nonetheless.

"I ought to know. I was married before. I guess I still am if you get right down to it, at least if she still lives. But I made a piss-poor husband with all my adventurin' ways."

This got Sarah's attention, and she finally spoke.

"What happened, Roscoe? With your wife, I mean."

"Oh, I was always off somewhere, slayin' fell beasts or carousin' with my adventurin' brothers. I were a vulgar and reckless young profligate in them days, to be sure. Never gave much thought to what she might be thinkin' or needin'. Just figured that as long as I was bringin' home the coin, she should be satisfied."

"How did it end?"

"I come home to find her packed up and gone. Not a word was said—she just left. Folks told me she run off with a travelin' knife grinder."

"Did you go after her? Try to find her and bring her home?"

"Nay, lass, I knew that wouldn't do no good."

"So what did you do?"

"Went down to the Severed Head, got drunk, and beat the livin' hell out of the first person I could pick a fight with. I was disappointed, though, 'cause I was intendin' to lose that particular tussle. You see, I wasn't mad at the guy I was fightin'. I wasn't even mad at her, 'cause I couldn't much blame her. I was just mad at myself and was lookin' for someone to beat some sense into my thick skull. Trouble was, I was a pretty good brawler back in them days, and my natural instincts kind of took over."

"What was her name?"

"Her name was Rose, so it was. She was pretty and plump, with blue eyes and fair skin. Used to tie up her hair with pink ribbons. She were a fine lass and did her best to be a good wife to me."

"Why are you telling me all this?"

"Because I think all the world of you and Thurmond, and it's plain to see that the pair of you could stand a bit of instruction right now. Thurmond's smart, not as bright as you perhaps, but plenty smart and a merry companion. But he's a fumble-fingered dolt when it comes to serenadin' a young lady. I don't want for him to let you slip away through damned foolishness as Rosie did from me."

Sarah's blush came hastening back, eager to demonstrate the depth of her embarrassment. Her face grew hot from the onrush of blood, going from red to magenta to purple. She again lost her ability to speak.

"So, lassie, if you're dependin' on him to say the first word, you might be in for a long and disappointin' wait. It's not that he doesn't want to, he just doesn't know it yet. So he's needin' your help to figure it out. Understand?"

Roscoe rose and returned to the prow of the riverboat.

Sarah, most decidedly, did not understand. But she knew sure as hell that she would never tie pink ribbons in her hair.

CHAPTER FORTY-FOUR

THE CALM BEFORE THE STORM

With the more serious issues settled, the party finally had the chance to discuss the many narrow escapes and harrowing encounters they had had in the course of their adventure. Thurmond found it quite odd that each recalled specific details so differently from the others.

Roscoe remembered the kobold priest's tall, pointy hat as short and round. Torgul and Sarah could not agree as to the height of the ice wall she had summoned with the final scroll spell, he insisting it had been hip height, while she maintained it did not even reach to her knees. The relative statures of humans and dwarves might have been the cause of this discrepancy.

It became somehow very important to Thurmond to determine the accuracy of their various points of view. He needed to know with certainty what had happened to him, what he had lived through, and what challenges he had surmounted. Roscoe and Torgul were scarcely interested in estimating the number of kobolds who had chased them from their lair. Such minutia had, for them, become irrelevant many years ago.

Sarah was more helpful, and he questioned her on many things. He was, for example, quite curious about the nature of the shadow creature that had attacked them in the goblin's treasure room. None of them had ever seen or heard of anything like it. But Sarah consulted her book and eventually arrived at a theory.

"At first I thought it was some kind of demon. You know, a bigger, meaner version of the imp in the ale jug. But now I don't think so. It didn't fit the description of demon behavior as described in my book. I don't think a demon would be hampered by cold.

"So my best guess is that it was some kind of spectral creature that was summoned to guard the treasure. Maybe some goblin shaman called it up, or maybe some other priest or magician before the goblins took over. I don't know.

"Anyway, he wasn't made up of flesh and blood like a living being. That's why regular weapons couldn't touch him. But he was material enough to be affected by magic, so the spells and the enchanted axe worked fine."

Thurmond was stunned that such a creature could even exist. He was even more disconcerted that he had overcome a thing that was not of this earth. The simple village boy was by now a long way from home.

Sarah continued.

"Anyway, I don't think you really killed it, even with Torgul's axe, because I don't think it was ever actually alive—at least, not what you and I think of as alive."

Thurmond found this very confusing.

"Well, if it didn't die, what happened to it? It sure hit the floor like it was dead."

"That's true, but remember later? It was just gone. As if it had dissolved or something. I don't think you killed it. I think you released it, set it free from whatever was binding it to the treasure room."

"So you think that thing is maybe someplace out there? Maybe wanting revenge?"

"It could be out there, but I'm guessing it's as brainless as a tadpole and has no recollection of us. Probably can't even enter our world without being summoned. So don't worry."

But, of course, Thurmond *did* worry. He asked Torgul and Roscoe whether they knew aught of such a creature, but they could tell him nothing. Moreover, they exhibited a pronounced disinterest, maintaining that the world was filled with strange and unexplainable creatures and that any attempt to understand such things was futile.

This was not reassuring.

As the boat made its way slowly upriver—rowed, towed, sailed, and poled—things gradually settled down, and the party began to address themselves to more routine daily chores. Sarah resumed her occult studies, having somewhat regained her power of concentration. From time to time, she watered the young tree potted in her helmet. Torgul repaired the various rents and dents in their armor and scoured their weapons clean of accumulated rust, gore, and grime. Thurmond renewed his plea for Sarah to teach him to read.

She was agreeable and set about to teach him the letters of the alphabet. Thurmond, always a quick study, learned his letters with great speed and was soon duplicating them with a charred stick, to the dismay of Nod and Sod, on the clean deck of the riverboat.

Their lack of basic instructional materials hampered his learning. There was no parchment. The only pen was Sarah's designated Pen of the Art, and to use it in such mundane fashion would have been to render it useless for occult purposes. The only book they had was the grimoire Sarah had taken from the dead shaman's hovel at Red Charles's stronghold. Its language was so cryptic as to defy any attempt at literal interpretation.

Thurmond had indeed set himself to an arduous task, but spurred by his enthusiasm, he made rapid progress that exceeded Sarah's expectations. If he did not fully comprehend the content of the book, he could at least make out many of the words. The more he read, the more he wanted to read. Not bad for a dung-carrying village boy.

At Roscoe's suggestion, the Adventurers also took pains to become acquainted with the new members of the party—the ones Roscoe called the recruits, the survivors of Rupert's and Bart's ill-fated companies.

Thurmond realized that their loyalty would be entirely dependent on their own self-interests and where they believed their best chance of survival might lie. He began to engage them in friendly banter, to ask innocent questions about their previous experiences and future aspirations, anything that might throw light on their thinking.

Drax had come downriver as one of Sims's hired henchmen. He, like troll-handed Jasper, was a mercenary willing to sell his sword to whoever paid his price. Drax was short and stocky, his dark hair beginning to recede. His eyes were drawn in a perpetual squint that lent his expression a sinister, deceitful cast. Of all the new recruits, Roscoe was most leery of that one.

Two of the recruits, Lars and Bodo, were the sole survivors of Bart's contingent of trainees. All the others, soldiers and boatmen alike, had fallen. Both had sustained painful wounds and remained very docile and unassuming, as if eager to put their grim experiences behind them and return to their original positions as servants or laborers.

Rupert's two surviving boatmen blended seamlessly with Scrymgeour's crew. Once on the water, they were already at home.

Jasper was, naturally, the most intriguing of the lot. Though at first reticent, he eventually explained that his proper hand had been severed in a barroom brawl and that Rupert had commanded that the troll hand be grafted in its place. He told of how the Black Friar Plutonius had performed an elaborate ritual that magically bonded it to his own stump of an arm.

In the beginning Jasper had had little control over the hand. One of its first deeds was to try to strangle Plutonius. Little by little, he had gained control over it, except on occasions of extreme stress. It had, for instance, functioned in a wholly independent fashion as Jasper and his companions had fought their way through the several waves of enraged goblins. It had crushed and slashed and bludgeoned as if guided by a mind of its own. Jasper credited the hand with his survival during an ordeal in which the vast majority of his company had perished.

Thurmond was pleased to learn why Rupert had hired him to retrieve such a loathsome article, but he did not reveal his involvement in the affair. He saw no advantage in making known his connection with that dark business. So he had told no one. Not Sarah. Not Roscoe. No one. The grafting of troll parts to a human man was a vile and blasphemous deed, not something to be bantered about, not something to tell one's closest friends.

Jasper's voice was low and deep, a soldier's voice. As he told his tale, Thurmond pressed in close so as not to miss any interesting details. Suddenly the hand sprang to life, jumping up from Jasper's lap like a bird taking flight. Thurmond was the undeniable target. It clutched him, not by the throat as it had to Plutonius, but by the upper arm. It then began to wriggle upward toward his shoulder.

The young man leaped back, tearing himself from its horrible grasp. The other bystanders, Roscoe and Torgul included, erupted in laughter, but Thurmond did not share in their amusement. The hand continued to twitch and hop as if under the influence of a powerful stimulant.

Jasper was nonplussed.

"I dunno what's happenin'. It ain't acted like this 'cept right at first."

He looked at Thurmond.

"Man, it sure wants to get at you, don't it? Why do you suppose that is?"

Thurmond fled to the far end of the ship, putting as much distance between himself and the hand as possible.

CHAPTER FORTY-FIVE

THE VILLAGE IN THE REEDS

The days drew on, and despite the slow upriver progress, journey's end was finally approaching. The countryside, at least on the eastern side of the river, was no longer a howling wilderness. Farm fields and vineyards dotted the rolling hills. Occasional castles and strongholds sprouted from rocky outcroppings. River traffic increased, and villages grew more frequent as they got closer and closer to the city of Gorgonholm. It became much easier and less risky to hire a team of oxen to tow them toward their destination.

The afternoon was hot and muggy. Mosquitoes buzzed in their ears, and flies licked at their sweat. There was no wind, and the usually uncomplaining oarsmen were tired and quarrelsome. Thus all were pleased to see a towpath beginning its run along the eastern bank. They moored on a wooden post set into the mud of the shallows. Sod rang the iron bell suspended from its top to summon the tow team.

Strangely, no one appeared. Villagers were by necessity quite suspicious and often observed their would-be customers from some point of vantage before descending to barter for a price. Thus, they were sometimes slow to respond to a summons. But there had not yet been a village in which they had refused to answer a call. Something seemed wrong.

Sod made a gesture, and four crewmen sprang to man the ballista on the cabin roof. The others drew spears, axes, and short heavy-bladed swords from beneath the rowing benches. Nod retrieved a crossbow from the cabin, donned an iron cap, and stepped over the gunwale into the shallow water. Torgul and Roscoe were right behind him. The latter turned and spoke quietly to Thurmond and Sarah.

"You two stay put. We're goin' to have a quick look-see, but we'll return in a twitch of a donkey's tail. Maybe they didn't hear the bell. So we'll just pay our respects quick like and come right back. Thurmond, you watch out for her now."

The shore party then disappeared into the thick growth of reeds that grew heavy and verdant in the rich black soil. The departure of the two experienced Adventurers made them acutely aware of their own vulnerability. Thurmond strung his bow, as did Sarah.

The moments plodded slowly along. No sound came from the riverbank. No clang of weapons, no war cries, no screams of mortal agony. Not even a bird chirped or sang. It was as if the reeds had swallowed up all sound and had perhaps swallowed the shore party as well.

Sweat dripped down Sarah's face. She was edgy and itchy. Something was weird here. Then Thurmond laid a hand on her shoulder, giving her a small start.

"What is it?"

Her friend did not reply but only stared intently into her eyes.

"What is it, Thurmond? What's wrong?"

Again, there was no answer. Instead, he moved his hand to her back and attempted to draw her to him. Sarah suddenly realized what he wanted, recognized the unfocused look in his eye. He was after another kiss.

"God's lungs, Thurmond! Not now! I'm all hot and sweaty, and besides, something's amiss about this place. We're supposed to be keeping watch."

Sarah pushed him away and moved to the other end of the boat. She cared for him deeply, but he could be such a child at times.

After an interval that seemed much too long, there was a rustle in the barricade of reeds and Roscoe appeared, Torgul and Nod close behind. With them came a young girl of about twelve summers and two even younger children, a boy and a girl of perhaps eight and nine respectively.

Roscoe stepped up to the boat and spoke across the gunwale.

"These wee bairns are in a spot of trouble, so they are. Seems their village has been raided by the people across the river. They carried off their mamas and papas as slaves, but these and some of the other children were saved because—and bless God's hairless pate for it—their village priest was quick thinkin' enough to hide 'em in the woods.

"We can't just go on and leave 'em here. They'll starve sure come winter. Or the raiders will come back and take them too. You two know where I stand on this kind of thing. We have to take the honorable path."

These words were, of course, all that was necessary to ensure Thurmond's immediate agreement. And Sarah was no less willing to acquiesce. She took one look at the girl, saw herself, and gave her assent.

Roscoe pressed the point.

"There's a power more of 'em back in the village. A mite distraught, as you might imagine. It's gettin' toward dark, so I'm thinkin' it's best if we spend the night here and give 'em a chance to gather their things and be ready to shove off at first light. Maybe we can find 'em places that'll take 'em as we pass other villages along the way. Are you agreeable?"

They were. Sarah and Thurmond began to gather those things that might prove wanted during a night ashore. They packed extra rations, medicines, and cloaks—anything they could think of that might bring comfort to distressed children. When all was bundled, they climbed over the side and splashed down into the shallow water by the shoreline.

Drax joined them, as did Jasper—his unruly hand concealed by a rag bound around his wrist. After a moment's hesitation, Lars and Bodo followed suit, though their wounds were still stiff and painful. Soon they were following Roscoe down a narrow path through the sea of reeds. Sod, Nod, and their crew did not join them. The brothers were not needed at this venture and so preferred to remain with the boat.

The village lay surprisingly close to the river, but the reed barrier was so dense and imposing that it seemed much farther away. It was in most respects a typical village, a compact collection of wattle and daub huts thatched with reeds. A trim little church sat at its center. Chickens and pigs meandered between the houses in search of scraps.

Yet the village possessed some indefinable quality that set it apart from so many others of similar size and layout. Perhaps it was something in the air, a cleanliness produced by the filtering properties of the reeds. Perhaps there was something in the late afternoon light that lent the scene an appealing clarity and crispness. Perhaps it was just a nice village.

Thurmond found himself quite drawn to it. The warm, homey ambiance put him at ease, suggested a life of quiet contentment as his own native village had never done. This was a place where a man could settle down and be happy. Could get married and raise a family. Could enjoy the simple pleasures of a sunny spring day or a warm summer rain shower.

Roscoe seemed to read his thoughts.

"Aye, it's pretty nice, ain't it, boyo? A right fine place, so it is."

But all was not well in that right fine place. There were no people, so all was silent. No ringing blacksmith hammer. No creaking oxcart. No chattering housewives. No laughing children. It seemed wrong that such an appealing place should be devoid of human activity.

The three children led them to the big doors at the front of the church and knocked on it with their small fists.

The oldest, the girl of about twelve, called out.

"Father James, please open the door. It's all right! These are good people, and they want to help us. It's safe to open the door."

Almost at once, the door swung slowly inward, and Father James emerged to meet his rescuers. He was dressed in the robes of a White Friar—a young man of middle height, spare of build, with a thick crop of dark hair. His eyes were warm and pleasing. He offered a smile of relief and grasped Roscoe's hand as if assuring himself he was really there.

"I'd just about worn out my knees praying for deliverance. You can't know how happy we are that you've come. Bless you all."

He turned to the three children standing at Roscoe's side.

"Lynd, take Sal and Ugo inside and wait for me. Tell the others that God has sent people to help us. That everything is going to get better now. I have to talk to these men for a little bit."

His face clouded as he told the story of the raid.

"They hit us three days ago, Keltin renegades from out of the west. We've always got along with the river clans, but this wasn't a proper tribe. Just a bunch of broken men who've banded under an outlaw leader called the Tyree. They took us entirely by surprise, so we had no chance to defend ourselves. They gathered up the adults and such children as they could find, grabbed anything of value, and went back across the river.

"I'd taken most of the young ones into the woods to hunt for acorns, so we escaped. I heard the screams and shouts, saw what was happening, and led them far back into the trees to hide. We came back after the raiders left. I have forty-seven children in the church now. We have enough food for the present, but we won't make it through the winter. And we're entirely defenseless if they come back. Please, we are desperate for your help."

Roscoe removed his Adventurer's hat, smiled hugely, and offered a deep bow.

"Captain Roscoe Appleman and company are at your service, holy father. We would be delighted to assist you in saving the lives of these poor, little unfortunates. What do you require of us?"

"I presume you have a boat. We heard the bell ring, which is why I sent Lynd to meet you. Can you carry us to Gorgonholm? My holy order, the White Friars, maintains a prosperous temple in that city. If we can reach it, my brethren will feed and shelter us."

"Certainly we will aid you in this, but our boat is a tad small for so large a group—near fifty? Alas, you won't all fit aboard. But here's what I propose. We'll take as many of the wee babes as the boat will hold. My men and I will accompany the older ones on foot. The countryside twixt here and the city is flat and even, so we can follow along the river and keep the boat in sight. We'll never be too far apart. We can meet up at night and make a merry camp on the riverbank. What say you?"

Father James smiled.

"I think it an excellent plan. Can we start at tomorrow's dawn?"

Roscoe nodded.

"Aye, holy father, that would be my choice as well."

"There are a few pigs and chickens in the village that escaped the raiders. If your men could slaughter and dress them, we could all have an excellent repast before commencing our journey."

"My men are experienced soldiers, every one, so they're well-schooled in the preparation of village livestock. And we could do with a bit of fresh meat ourselves, so we could."

At this point Sarah could stand it no longer and pushed forward. Though Father James had failed to notice her, she was already smitten. He was undoubtedly the most handsome man she had ever seen.

"Captain Roscoe, you seem to have forgotten that your company is composed not entirely of men. Nor are we all soldiers."

Then she turned to Father James.

"I am Sarah Staynes."

She had never before taken her father's name as her own.

"And I too offer you my services."

Her self-introduction took the priest by surprise. He simply stared for a moment, but then graced her with a broad, warm smile. His teeth were white and perfect.

"I thank you, Sarah Staynes. Dressed as you are, I took you for a youth. But I confess that I find it somewhat irregular that such a young and, if I might say, attractive lady would be found in the company of rough soldiers, especially so far away from her home and family."

Roscoe gave a chuckle.

"You mustn't underestimate Sarah, Father James. She's proven time and again that she can take care of herself. And Sarah, I must apologize if my ill-chosen words made you feel slighted. Such was never my intention."

She threw him a slight smile.

"Thank you, Roscoe. I know you meant no insult."

James studied Sarah intently, as if really seeing her for the first time.

"And I, too, must apologize for any inadvertent insult. Your captain's endorsement convinces me that you are a young woman of remarkable ability. The children and I are most fortunate to have you for a protector, Sarah Staynes."

Sarah said nothing. She was extremely gratified to have such a charming man acknowledge her in such grand fashion. But as always when embarrassed, she could find no words, so she stepped back behind Roscoe before the rising blush revealed her inner turmoil.

Father James suggested that the party spend the night in the house of the village headman. It was the best in town, but now it stood empty, the residents having been carried off by the raiders. Several children were sent to lay a fire and make it ready. The priest and his charges would remain in the church. There was a bustle of activity as the older children began gathering and packing for their early departure. Roscoe, Torgul, and Father James sat discussing the details of their plan. Jasper and Drax, with Lars and Bodo in tow, set off to slaughter the village livestock. Thurmond and Sarah tended the smaller children, tickling and teasing them in an effort to raise their spirits.

The evening meal was of gargantuan proportions, with far more meat than could possibly be consumed. Loaves of bread, still warm from the oven, were slathered with honey and freshly churned butter. Great wheels of strong, blue-veined cheese were cut into thick slices. Lynd kept the tankards brimming with ale.

Over dinner, Father James turned his attention to Sarah.

"You are indeed a most remarkable young woman. Do you not miss the enticements of the city? The fine clothes? The lavish banquets? The attention of handsome young men?"

Sarah did not care to explain that she had been trapped with her lecherous brother in the home of her aged and ailing father. As such, she had known none of these things. Instead, she shook her head demurely, scarcely daring to raise her eyes.

"Nay, Father, the things that entice other girls mean little to me. I have sought the adventuring life…for reasons of my own."

The conversation was cut short when the boy Ugo arrived and whispered into the priest's ear. James rose at once.

"Pray forgive me, milady. Duty calls—one of the children is frightened and requires some reassurance. We must speak more on the morrow."

He followed Ugo out of the room.

Once the meal was finished, large wooden platters were filled and sent down to the boat crew. The remainder was wrapped in clean cloth for their journey. Everyone ate enormously, and all were suffering from bloated bellies as they waddled through the night to the headman's house. The full moon bathed the village with a silvery sheen that presaged good fortune on the morrow.

Though it was just a simple half-timbered structure with a dirt floor and a thatched roof, the headman's house exuded the same inviting coziness that permeated the village. They lit the fire that the children had laid in the heath, filling the room with a golden glow. The homemade furnishings were not remarkable in any discernable way, yet they possessed a rustic appeal that betokened the love and decency of the family that had lived there.

In such a place, and with their bellies so full, they were all soon sound asleep.

CHAPTER FORTY-SIX

THE HORROR IN THE NIGHT

Maybe it was all the greasy pig meat in his stomach, but Thurmond had a restless night. He had fallen asleep readily enough, but his rest was disturbed by vague and displeasing dreams. He awoke with a violent start, aware that something was not right. A disturbing cry had pulled him from slumber—something like a shrill screech of mortal agony. But nay, surely it was nothing more than the call of some bird, some night-haunting predator. Yet had it not come from the direction of the river?

Thurmond was suddenly very certain that he and his comrades were in terrible danger. The Keltin raiders might even now be attacking the riverboat, butchering its crew. The village, the children, would be next. He ran to the door for a look, but it refused to open. Had they been deliberately locked in, or had it somehow jammed? He tried one of the shuttered windows, but it too was fastened shut. He was, however, able to open a crack wide enough to afford a view of the moon-bright village square. Everything looked normal. Too normal.

Confused, scared, and frustrated, Thurmond murmured under his breath.

"By God's holy arse, I don't believe what's happening."

And with that everything changed.

Although his harried antics had caused much clang and clatter, the others continued to sleep soundly. The men were snoring. Sarah was curled up like a little girl with her hands beneath her head. He gave her arm a gentle shake and softly whispered.

"Sarah, wake up."

She continued to slumber, unaffected by his efforts. He shook harder, and his voice grew louder.

"Sarah, wake up. I need you. You have to see this."

But again she did not stir. He then took her by both shoulders and gave her whole body a forceful jolt.

"Wake up! Damn it! What's the matter with you? Wake up now!"

That did the trick. She finally opened her eyes, but remained disoriented.

"Why did you wake me up? I was sleeping."

"Get up! Come on. You have to look at this."

"Look at what? What's so impor...?"

He did not wait for her to finish her sentence but pulled her to her feet before she could become coherent enough to resist. Drawing her to the window, he again forced open the shutter, allowing her a view of the village square.

"Just look!"

She did as he demanded and instantly became fully awake.

"Oh shit! Thurmond, what's happening here?"

"Remember back in Gorgonholm when I turned our gold sovereigns to river rocks? You told me I should never disbelieve—remember that? Well, I disbelieved again, and that's what happened here."

"We've been charmed! We're under some sort of glamour. That's what made the village seem so lovely. None of it was real."

"We've got to wake the others. I think they put something in the food to make us sleep. I had a difficult time getting you up. Come on, help me. We must get out of here."

Sarah snatched a jug of water from a nearby table and threw it directly in Roscoe's face. She then delivered several hard kicks to the soles of his feet. He awoke with a sputter followed by a bellow of outrage.

"Gaagghh...what are you...?"

But Sarah did not stop to hear to his complaints. She moved to Torgul and gave his beard a vicious yank. He howled and jumped to his feet, ready to fight. Sarah jumped out of his reach and addressed them both.

"We are in great danger. We must leave here at once."

The two Adventurers spoke with one voice.

"What danger? What has happened?"

"Look out the window."

Thurmond held the shutter open as they did so.

They looked upon a structure that was vastly altered from the tidy little church where they had met Father James. That had been a simple one-story, rectangular building with a low bell tower, the kind of church one might find in any number of small rural villages.

That congenial edifice had now been replaced by a monstrosity of dark stone. Its exact shape and dimensions were impossible to calculate, for there was something in its basic architecture that was obscenely amiss. The angles of the walls were just wrong. The sweep of the buttresses inspired an instinctive disquiet, while the jutting spires aroused unnatural sentiments and unwholesome thoughts. Whatever rites were carried out within such a monument could only be horrid and degrading.

Roscoe exploded.

"God's holy bones! Let's go! Sarah, wake the others."

He headed toward the door, but Thurmond grabbed his sleeve.

"The door has been fastened shut. So have the shutters. We're locked in."

"Locked in? What is happening here?"

Thurmond quickly explained about the scream he thought he had heard and the breaking of the glamour spell. Meanwhile Sarah tried to rouse Jasper and the others, who continued to snore in spite of the commotion. Torgul began exploring the room for some other avenue of escape. He probed the dirt of the floor, the thatch of the ceiling, and the wattle and daub walls.

When they left the boat, none of them had really expected to do battle. They all bore weapons as a matter of course, but no one wore armor. Sarah had left her pannier of occult items behind to bring more relief supplies to the children. Then she remembered Whisper. He had been left behind on the roof of the vessel's cabin. Was he safe?

Torgul called them together, his exploration complete.

"We're in trouble. This room ain't what it seems neither—it's a trap. There's a layer of flagstones under the dirt of the floor to keep us from tunnelin' out. The walls ain't really wattle and daub. There's stones hidden under the mud. I'm not sure about the ceiling, but I think there's heavy timbers embedded in the thatch. Whatever it is, it's solid. We ain't gettin' out any time soon."

Thurmond, who had been keeping watch at the window, suddenly cried out.

"Here comes Father James. Maybe he'll explain things."

The others crowded around the narrow opening between the shutters, and indeed it was Father James, looking as handsome as ever. A tall, gangly, somewhat stoop-shouldered man followed him. He had a crop of dark hair so thick that it looked like a hat.

The prisoners began to clamor, demanding to be released, but James silenced them with a raised hand. He produced his warmest, most endearing smile.

"Friends, I am sorry it has proved necessary to detain you. It is an unthinkable rudeness, especially after your kindness and generosity—coming to our rescue and all. But it is an unfortunate imperative that we hold you here while we attend to certain vital details."

The prisoners interrupted his speech, some asking questions, others insisting on their freedom, but James only smiled and shook his head. He gestured to the taller man at his side.

"This is Derkyn. He will stay here with you to ensure that you do not inconvenience yourselves by attempting escape. If you can quietly bide your time, we will release you in a day or two, and you can be off on your journey. But it will go badly for all of you should you try to leave this building. You're safe enough inside, but there are *things* outside that you wouldn't care to encounter. Trust me."

Roscoe shushed his companions and thrust them aside so he could speak clearly to James through the crack in the shutters.

"What of my boat crew? Have you taken them too? Bring them here so we can all be together."

James's face grew sad. He held his palms up in a gesture of resignation.

"Alas, it's all over for them now. I am truly sorry, but we couldn't get to them in time to save them. You must now look to your own well-being."

With that James turned and departed, leaving Derkyn to stand sentry. He shot them a grin that was anything but the warm and reassuring smile of James. He looked depraved.

Thurmond stood watch at the window, while the others began discussing what James's words might portend and what they might do to save themselves. Roscoe was the first to speak.

"I'll tell you what I'm thinkin'—that we can't believe a word that damned priest says. And we can't be sittin' here on our jolly arses, just hopin' they'll really let us go. And I ain't believin' the whole boat crew is dead. Nod and Sod are too canny for that. Nay, they're out there hidin' in the reeds and figurin' how to help us. That's what I think."

Sarah spoke up.

"What about those children? I don't really think Father James would hurt them. He was so concerned for our safety. Obviously he is trying to protect us from something. He must be doing the same for them."

From his post at the window, Thurmond broke in.

"I think Father James still has you under his spell, Sarah. That guy outside, that Derkyn, I recognize him and you should too. Though he looks a tad older than when we were playing horsey with him this afternoon."

Sarah ran to the window to scrutinize Derkyn, who was now sitting, slouched with his back to a tree. He leered and winked when he saw her at the window.

"Oh, Thurmond, that *is* him. That's Ugo. He's got the same smirk, the same strange eyes. I didn't like him this afternoon either. There was just something wicked in his face. That's definitely him, just older."

"So the children were under a glamour spell too. They're not real children at all."

The party began to discuss their best course of action. All were frightened, no one was listening, and their voices rose into a frenzied hubbub until Thurmond silenced them by again calling from the window.

"Come and see! Look there, up in the sky."

A red blaze was beginning to illuminate the sky over the landward side of the village. It waxed in intensity, and soon the tops of flames could be seen above the trees. Then drums began to pound with a steady, even beat, followed by a low, mournful chant—or, more properly speaking, a dirge. Derkyn saw them at the window, and his face split into a wide, evil grin.

And then the screams began—doomful screams like the one that had snatched Thurmond from his sleep. Such screams as should never be made by human voice or heard by human ears. As each scream died away, a pitiless howling arose. Not the howling of the ravenous wolf pack nor even that of a moon-frenzied madman. It was too deliberate, too intelligent, too satisfied, as if signaling some deep desire at last fulfilled.

They counted eight screams in all, then the howling ceased, and the chanting began anew.

Eight screams, Roscoe thought but did not say. Eight screams for eight boatmen.

CHAPTER FORTY-SEVEN

THE PLIGHT OF PRISONERS

The new day was bright and warm. Birds sang cheerily in the trees and flitted across the clear blue sky. The village was peaceful and calm, still wrapped in a blanket of early-morning silence. Save for the appalling church, it could have been any riverside village basking in the pleasant morning sunshine.

The prisoners had taken turns watching throughout the night but had observed nothing untoward. There had been no sleep, there could be no sleep. They sat and waited in dumbfounded terror, trying to envision the true intentions of Father James.

But the friar had made one serious miscalculation. He had not considered a dwarf's innate capacity to dig and delve. Torgul had been at work on the back wall for hours and had made considerable progress in loosening the mortar around several of the stones. It was a slow process of scraping carefully and quietly with the point of a dagger. A more robust effort would have produced undue noise and attracted the attention of watchman Derkyn.

Their watchman was fast asleep under the same tree when the sun first rose through the trees. But he soon stirred, pissed, and became attentive to his duty. Gradually other people began to appear in the square, and the scene assumed the semblance of normal village life. They laughed, called to one another, and whistled while they worked.

Through the crack in the shutters, Thurmond could see the corners of several houses. All looked just as he remembered them. The only thing that had changed was the church, which continued to dominate the community with its evil majesty. Just to be sure, Thurmond tried his trick.

"I disbelieve. I disbelieve."

But nothing changed.

Finally Roscoe called the group together for a morning meeting.

"I've given our plight a power of thinkin', so I have, and I've concluded that we have no chance at all unless we can break ourselves out of this accursed house and escape from this filthy village. I assume you have all figured out the meanin' of those screams we heard last night."

Squint-eyed Drax spoke up. He was usually dour and withdrawn, but he was now agitated and seemed eager to speak.

"Aye, we got it. 'Twas our boatmen makin' them screams, or I'll be damned. And if them is gone, we ain't got nobody but ourselves. So what are we gonna do? We gotta act quick, 'cause maybe tonight it'll be us doin' the screamin'."

Sarah had been sitting silently for a long time as if deep in thought. Now she joined in.

"I've got an idea. That Derkyn—he kept looking at me in a way I don't like. I know that look. My brother Bart used to look at me that way—ugh. But if Derkyn likes me, maybe we can use it. If I stand at the window and call to him, I bet I can lure him over. Then maybe I can cast a spell.

"I'll bet he's protected from illusion spells, at least the little ones I know. They're highly skilled in illusion here. But I've read about something that might help us. It's a truth spell, and it works differently, almost like a possession. For a few moments at least, a person under the spell will answer any questions with complete honesty. I've never used it before, but it's worth a try. Maybe we can discover their real intentions."

Roscoe brightened and almost smiled.

"Glory be, girlie, that's a fine idea. I knew there had to be some reason I like you so much."

But then Thurmond brought unwelcome tidings.

"I hate to say this, but it's not Derkyn out there. Now there's a nasty-looking old gaffer with a warty face."

Sarah and Roscoe pressed into the window. She ducked down a bit so he could look through the crack above her head.

"I could still try it. It might work on him."

Roscoe thought otherwise.

"Nay, best to wait. I'm thinkin' that Derkyn is the night watch, and this ugly yokel's got the days. This one's too old to be lured by your female wiles. Derkyn will be along when the sun goes down, so he will. Then…"

Drax interrupted, his voice thin and bitter.

"When the sun goes down, they might be takin' us out to their balefire in the woods. Didja think of that?"

"Aye, friend Drax, I did indeed think of that, so I did. But we're trapped here, sealed inside this tomb of stone. So a few hours, give or take, are of little consequence, don't you see?"

"Nay, I don't see. I say we gotta do something now."

"I'd be honored to hear your ideas."

"Do somethin' now to make 'em open the door. Holler for food—or maybe tell 'em one of us is sick. The girl—we'll tell 'em the girl is sick. That might do it. Or maybe let on that we're havin' a fight among ourselves. Throw things around, yell, make it real loud. Or if none of that don't work, maybe set the thatch on fire and burn our way out."

Roscoe knew Drax was entirely correct. They had weapons, and even a slim chance was better than no chance at all. If they could only trick the guard into opening the door, maybe… He did, however, utterly reject the idea of setting the thatch alight. If death by fire was to be their lot, he did not want it to come by their own hands.

Then Thurmond had an idea.

"How about your invisibility spell? If they open the door, we can just walk out."

Sarah shook her head.

"I can't. It takes too much energy. I used all the power Whisper put in my wand. Plus it's an illusion spell, and I don't think it'd work on these people."

Drax got tired of waiting and pushed his way to the window. He yelled harshly to the old watchman.

"Hey you, grandpa! Aye, you! We're starvin' in here. Go get us some grub.

Hey you, I'm talkin' to you. You deaf? I said we need somethin' to eat. Go on, wart-face, get us somethin'. Damn your eyes! Damn your mother's eyes! I need food, you old turd. Move!"

But the old man was unmoved. He made a single dismissive gesture toward the window and then just sat as if entirely unaware of the prisoner's abusive harangue. This continued for some time before Drax finally got tired and gave up.

Churlishness having failed, Roscoe next tried gentility, though he had little hope that his honeyed words would achieve any better results than Drax's crude ranting. His tone was courteous and amiable as he called out through the window.

"Good sir, you must pardon my companion. He's the best of fellows, really, but his mind is wandering at the moment for lack of nourishment, so it is. It's been ever so long since we've had even a morsel. And the young girl, sweet little Sarah, is feelin' it somethin' bad. Can scarce hold her head up for want of a bite of bread. Could you not see fit to fetch her a wee snack? Just something to tide her over 'til we clear up this misunderstandin' and are on our way once again. What do you say, good man that you are?"

The old man simply ignored him, did not even offer the gesture of dismissal with which he had honored Drax. It was like talking to a man without ears.

Thurmond inquired.

"So, shall we stage a fight?"

"Nay, laddie, they're not interested in aught we have to say, and I don't think we'd fool 'em by thrashing around and makin' a fuss. Better to wait until tonight and try Sarah's plan."

And so they waited. No one brought them food or drink. No one called them to the window or approached the prison house in any manner. Save for the warty watchman, the villagers did not so much as glance in their direction. There was no sign of Father James.

They waited some more. Torgul continued to scrape away at the wall. Bodo and Lars joined in his effort. These men dug without respite, as indefatigable as the dwarf. They had remained uninvolved during the myriad of discussions and arguments, but their will to survive was evident in their grim determination to dig free. Drax sat and glowered, angry and frustrated that his ideas had come to naught. Jasper, never much of a thinker, curled up and went to sleep. Sarah meditated to clear her mind in preparation for casting the truth spell. Thurmond kept watch on the window. Roscoe took station by the door and sharpened his sword with a stone.

For a while, no one spoke. Then Drax ended the hush.

"It strikes me, it does—eight was took last night. Eight men and eight screams. The boat crew. I counted 'em on my fingers so to make certain. And there be eight of us here. Same number—eight. I counted us too, just to be sure. Eight and eight. Only we're the next eight. Sure as shit, we are."

The silence was much preferable to such dire arithmetic.

†

The gentle cloak of night descended slowly on the village. The bustle in the square slowed and then stopped as the inhabitants completed their day's work and returned to their homes for their evening meal. The night was warm, and rich, golden candlelight spilled from open doorways. Nightjars began to sing in the reeds. Locked in the stone hut, the prisoners prepared for what they were certain would be a night of unyielding horror.

The moon rose, large and dazzling, bringing a luminescence that was almost as intense as the light of day. Thurmond needed a breather from his post at the window, and Sarah took his place. She could see the aged watchman clearly in the moonlight. He sat motionlessly in the same place and position where he had spent the entire day. Then she saw something that gave her a bit of hope. Perhaps Fortune's Wheel had touched bottom and their luck was on the rise.

"Hey! Derkyn's back! He just sent wart-face home to supper."

She thrust her face into the crack between the shutters as far as it would go. She wanted Derkyn to get a good look. Then she gave a slight girlie sneeze, a delicate little *chewww*, to draw his attention. That was all it took. He saw her looking out at him and immediately gave her that same penetrating leer as before. This time, however, she smiled at him. Her best shy, modest, maidenly smile. His mouth fell open like that of a fish.

It did not take long before he strode to the window. His expression remained slack and blank, as if his feet were drawing him toward it without this brain willing them to do so. He stopped before the narrow crack, his face just a few inches from hers. That was good. Proximity was important in spell casting. Sarah went into her act.

"Greetings, sir. I know your name is Derkyn. Do you remember mine? I'm Sarah."

"You're real pretty."

"Derkyn, won't you help me? I'm trapped in here with these terrible men, and they…well…they keep bothering me."

"Real pretty…real pretty."

"Derkyn, I have to tell you a secret. Something I've never told before, even to my mama. Can I trust you, Derkyn?"

He reached out a hand and tried to worm it through the narrow opening. Happily only his fingers could squeeze through.

"Wanna touch your hair. Real soft and pretty."

"All right, I'll let you touch my hair, but first you have to let me tell my secret. Put your ear up to the crack so I can whisper it."

"Touch first."

Sarah's face suffused with revulsion as she realized what must be done. She turned her head and allowed her long brown hair to spill into the crack. She felt Derkyn's fingers take hold, entangling themselves in the strands. He caressed the tress against his palm and then took a long sniff. With her head turned, she could not see him, but she was certain he had buried his face in her hair. His voice grew soft and mewling.

"Soft…soft."

All the while, Roscoe stood beside her, hidden behind a shutter, dagger drawn and ready to cut her free should Derkyn lose control.

She slowly began to pull away. He held on at first, and panic filled her eyes. Roscoe raised the dagger. But then Derkyn allowed the stands to slip through his fingers without resistance.

"Now Derkyn, I know you are my friend. That's why I let you touch my hair. That's why I have to tell you my secret. Won't you let me? Tell you what—put your ear up to the crack, and I'll let you touch my hair again. Maybe for longer next time. Please?"

Such temptation was too great to resist. James had given Derkyn strict instruction not to speak with the prisoners, but he could not hold back. He placed his ear to the crack, and Sarah whispered the truth spell directly into his brain. His body went rigid for a moment as the spell took effect.

Sarah stepped away from the crack, and Roscoe took her place. His voice was low and smooth as he too spoke directly into Derkyn's ear.

"Friend Derkyn, why are we bein' held here? For what purpose?"

"Feed River Folk."

"And who might they be, pray tell?"

"Come from river. Help us. Give us things."

"What kind of things?

"Nets full of fish. Good things from river bottom. Gold maybe."

"And you feed 'em in return? Is that right?"

"Feed 'em. Feed 'em."

"And what type of food do they enjoy?"

"Blood. Man blood."

"So James will use us to feed these River Folk?"

"Aye."

"When might this be set to happen?"

"Big feed last night. Three days more, then big ceremony."

"And what is the best way for us to esca...?"

But Derkyn's body stiffened again, and this time he stepped back from the window. He stood, vacant of countenance, as if he could remember neither coming to the window nor speaking his words with Sarah. He shook his head as if to clear it, looked guiltily from side to side, and then slunk back to his spot beneath the tree. The spell had obviously run its course.

CHAPTER FORTY-EIGHT

A DESPERATE UNDERTAKING

Derkyn's words were devastating. All activity ceased. Even Torgul and his helpers abandoned their excavation. They looked to Roscoe for answers and then, as one, exploded in a barrage of questions and accusations. Once again Drax forced his way to the center.

"That guy's a simpleton. Maybe he don't know nothin'. Maybe he's just talkin' big."

Sarah countered.

"Nay, he was under the spell. His information might not be correct, but it was the truth as he knows it."

"What he said don't make no sense. They wanna feed our blood to some buncha people what lives down the river? Are they cannibals? Why would they want our blood?"

Sarah shook her head in disagreement.

"I wouldn't assume the River Folk are people exactly."

Drax was obviously uninterested in her explanation.

"This ain't gettin' us nowhere. It don't matter who they are. How are we gonna get out of here? That's what I want to know."

Sarah turned to the others, ignoring the loutish mercenary.

"I've read about something like this. I think they're some kind of water demons that like the life force in fresh human blood. It's hard to say. Maybe they're something else, some kind of fish men. I don't know."

Thurmond brought up another point.

"Derkyn said our turn will come three days after last night's big feed. Correct?"

Roscoe and Sarah nodded in assent.

"That means we've got tonight and tomorrow night to get away from here. Maybe we can…"

Drax was uninterested in anyone's ideas but his own.

"I say we wait 'til they open the door to take us, and then we rush 'em. Fight our way out, those of us what can. We got weapons, so we'll use 'em. They might get us, but we'll kill a passel of 'em first."

The interruption had clearly peeved Thurmond, and Roscoe saw this. He stepped between them at once to head off any brewing confrontation. After so many stressful hours, nerves were raw, and tempers were growing short. He smiled and played the role of peacemaker.

"Drax, my friend, you have once again cut straight to the heart of the matter, so you have. If that is the only option left to us, then we must take the dreadful path you suggest. But could we not, perhaps, hope for a happier outcome?

"Now is it not likely that they would already have some plan for bringin' us out without risk to themselves? I don't believe that they're new to this game, so they must have somethin' in mind. Someone in this village, perhaps Father James, is a skilled magician. I wager that they'll charm us again, charm us with a spell so powerful that we'll walk out of here as if on our way to a jubilee. Maybe we'll smile and say *thank you* as they cut our throats."

Drax was not convinced.

"So whatta we do? You ain't done nothin' but talk, *captain*."

He emphasized the final word to express his frustration and contempt. Roscoe did not rise to it.

"You and I are experienced soldiers, as is Torgul. Sarah and Thurmond are young but smarter than any of us. Surely one of us will hit on some clever plan that will at least give us a fightin' chance. Give me that, and I'll be satisfied. The day a party of armed Adventurers can't roll over some bumpkin villagers…well…that's the day they can go ahead and feed my blood to some devilish fish man."

These words, dark as they were, cheered Drax up immensely, cheered them all up. Then Torgul, silent for so long, stepped forward.

"I can tell you what to do—dig! Maybe we'll make it out, maybe we won't, but you won't go anywhere sittin' on your arses. Like Thurmond was tryin' to say, we ain't got much time, so come help us dig."

With that the dwarf and his men returned to their task. Jasper joined them and discovered, to everyone's delight, that troll claws made an excellent tool for scratching out mortar. Everyone took a turn, affording Bodo and Lars a chance to rest. Even the sullen and uncooperative Drax did a stint. Torgul worked as if driven by demons. Anything was better than just sitting and waiting to die.

Thurmond and Sarah were kneeling side by side, chipping away with the blunted points of daggers. Without taking his eyes from his work, Thurmond asked a question.

"Hey, have you still got that demon bottled up in the ale jug?"

"Certes, back on the boat."

"What happens if some of these villagers open it? I'm sure they must have picked through all our stuff. They must have found it. What happens if they look inside?"

"In that case, whoever opens it will wish they had been fed to the River Folk. Imps are nasty things, and they hate being confined, at least that's what I read before. So he'll come out extremely pissed and vent his spleen on whoever is handy. They're stupid—all emotion, no brains."

The night drew to a close as it invariably does, and the sun rose in the east as it inevitably will. Thurmond resumed his post at the window. He saw the warty gaffer arrive and relieve Derkyn as watchman. Villagers began to appear, going about their daily routines.

Then, for the first time since their initial imprisonment, Father James entered his range of vision. He was laughing, obviously delighted, as he conversed with an elderly woman. Her back was so bowed that Thurmond wondered how she kept from toppling forward.

The bent old woman was clad in the same long, white robes as Father James. Thurmond was certain that White Friar nuns did not wear the same ecclesiastical vestments as the priests. So what was she?

Thurmond tried his favorite trick.

"Disbelieve, disbelieve, disbelieve."

But nothing changed. The old woman remained bowed, and James was as handsome and charming as ever. Disbelieving was a good and useful trick, but sometimes it just failed.

In midmorning, Lady Fortune finally gave in and spun her wheel a couple of notches toward the top. Torgul emerged from the hole in the wall, his dark hair and beard so powdered with mortar dust that he looked aged and venerable. He was almost smiling.

"I have glad tidings! We've hit mortar that didn't set right—all chalky and crumbling. Must have been badly mixed. Jasper's tearing right through it. We should have an escape hole ready in a couple hours."

The prisoners began to cheer, but Roscoe immediately called for quiet.

"Your raisin' such a joyous din is like to bring an investigation of our situation. You're not supposed to be happy in here, so if you go cheerin', they'll probably want to know why. And Torgul, dig through as much as you can without makin' a hole clear through the wall. We'll wait 'til dark for that last bit."

They spent the rest of the day plotting the details of their escape. The first priority was to reach the riverboat. If any of the boatmen still lived, and there was always a chance that they did, they were lurking in the reeds around their vessel. At the very least, the party would be able to recover whatever food or supplies the villagers had left on board.

If they found the boatmen, they could escape on the river. Otherwise they would be forced to flee on foot—none of them had any knowledge of sailing. If this was the case, they would head due east, away from the river, before swinging north toward home. They assumed any pursuit would follow the river straight north.

With their plans laid, there was again nothing else to do but wait for dark.

†

"All right, Torgul, lead us out."

The party gathered around the escape hole, while the dwarf dug the last of the mortar from between the stones. Within moments a draft of cool night air streamed in through the opening. He pushed the last remnants of blockage outward and wriggled out to freedom. Jasper came next. His valiant efforts against the mortar earned him a place of privilege in the queue. Bodo and Lars followed Jasper. Drax was next.

Roscoe had intended to go last, but Sarah and Thurmond prevailed on him to follow Drax. They were concerned that his considerable girth might lodge in the small opening through which he must squeeze. If so, better to have someone behind him to push as well as those in front to pull. Thankfully, neither was needed.

The fresh air smelled wonderful after the close confines of the locked room, but there was no time to stop and enjoy such simple pleasures. They set off toward the boat as quickly as they could, almost at a run. The moon was no longer quite at the full, but still cast sufficient light for them to make their way through the surrounding reeds.

To their relief, the boat was still there and intact, though the removal of the rudder and tiller had rendered it inoperable. Some of their equipment had been unloaded and stacked on the beach. The rest was still on board.

They hastily gathered whatever they thought they would need for a trek through the wilderness—food, cloaks, weapons, armor, chirurgical supplies, and a few simple tools. Sarah slung her pannier on her back and cradled the potted tree sprout in her hands as one might carry an infant. Roscoe retrieved their small store of goblin gold from its hiding place in the bottom of a cask of rye meal.

Jasper stepped into the craft and was bending for a coil of rope when a dim figure emerged from behind the cabin and struck his head with a heavy cudgel. He collapsed as if his bones had all turned to jelly, the only sound being the hollow, almost musical, *thonk* as his skull shattered.

Upon arriving at the boat, Drax had immediately selected a crossbow from the various weapons piled on the beach. He was ready, therefore, when Jasper was struck and immediately let fly at his assailant. The bolt struck the dark figure just below the breastbone, burying itself up to its fletching. Drax then leaped into the boat, sword in hand, and stabbed the squirming man repeatedly in the chest, belly, and face.

It was one of the villagers, obviously assigned to guard the boat. He had most likely been asleep when the party approached, awakening just in time to brain the ill-fated Jasper, who was now quite dead.

Thurmond joined Drax in a quick search of the boat, but they failed to discover any other lurking menace. He then examined the fallen Jasper, who was sprawled facedown, the back of his head strangely misshapen by the savage blow. Yet the troll hand still lived, quivering and leaping at the end of his arm as if afflicted by St. Vitas's dance.

Disgusted, Thurmond struck with his sword, cutting the hand free at the wrist. It immediately came scuttling crab-like across the deck and attempted to clamber up his leg. He squealed in shock and horror, dropped his sword, and began batting at the thing as it ascended to his sword belt and fixed its iron grip on the buckle.

Thurmond took the thing in both of his hands and tugged with all his might, but he was unable to pull it free. He tried prying loose the fingers one at a time, but with no luck. He jabbed it with his dagger, but it refused to let go. In desperation, he used the dagger to cut through the heavy leather of the belt.

The hand seemed to read his intentions and made a leap for his shoulder, but Thurmond was able to knock it away in midair. He skewered it with the dagger as soon as it hit the deck and then flung it into the river. He heard a splash and saw a ripple of moonlit water. At least the hand was gone for good. Food for fish. Let the River Folk have it.

CHAPTER FORTY-NINE

HEADLONG FLIGHT

They gathered their gear as quickly as they could. Thurmond carried a makeshift rucksack fashioned from a blanket. He found his bow and slung his quiver of arrows over his shoulder. Then they headed inland, away from the obvious direction of flight, away from the expected direction of pursuit. Travel became more difficult after the setting of the moon, but they kept up a rapid and steady pace nonetheless. Beyond the village, the dense stretch of forest was an imposing barrier, especially in the dark, but it proved to be quite narrow in width, and they soon emerged on an open plain.

There they found a small flat-topped hillock, which was so symmetrical in shape as to appear to be formed by human hands. Roscoe led them to its base and then stopped and addressed the group.

"Unless I miss my guess, this is where the ritual took place, where our friends were fed to some river demons. I'm going up to have a look, so I am. I can't face Scrymgeour without I try to make certain what became of his boys.

"The rest of you wait here. Don't be followin' me—captain's orders. This is somethin' I want to do alone. So don't interfere. I'll only be a moment, so I will."

With that he disappeared into the night before anyone could raise an objection. No one was comfortable with this turn of events, but having no option, they formed a defensive circle to await his return.

True to his word, the old Adventurer returned after a much shorter period than expected. They could hear him huffing and puffing as he approached, clumping down the hill on his bad leg. His countenance was set and grim when he rejoined the group. They clustered about him, demanding to know what he had seen on the hilltop.

"There's no time now for the tellin' of tales. Nor am I of a mind for it. Now's the time for fast walkin' and plenty of it. All will be revealed in good time, but I'm not up for it just now."

And so he led them off to the east.

The night grew darker, and the going was slow. Their one comfort was that the darkness would make pursuit all the more difficult. Still, they strained their ears for any sound that might indicate the presence of their enemies.

As she trudged along, Sarah had time to think. A random thought struck her.

"Thurmond, when you were watching the village square, did you see any dogs? I don't remember seeing any. There were always dogs in the other villages we stopped at."

"Dogs? Ohhh…"

Thurmond had not considered the possibility of dogs. If the villagers had dogs, they could track them through the darkness. But he could not recall seeing dogs, though he knew villagers always kept them for hunting, herding, and guarding.

"I don't think so. Nay, no dogs, I'm pretty certain. But it doesn't make sense—why wouldn't they keep dogs?"

"There's something deeply strange going on in that village. I bet they can't have dogs because dogs won't abide the place. Maybe things there don't smell right."

Thurmond remembered his own experience with village dogs when he was covered in troll stink. She was right—there were things a dog just would not stand for.

"Better for us in that case. If they had dogs, they'd use 'em to track us. But how about magic, Sarah? Couldn't they use spells to find us?"

"Certes, at least if they have a diviner."

"Couldn't you block it like you did on the river?"

"No time. I can't prepare a spell while I'm running for my life."

There was nothing to do but keep moving and to pray their pursuers had neither dogs nor diviners.

†

In far-off Gorgonholm, Lady Renata was jolted from her sleep. A sprite sat on her chest and was tickling her nose with one of its nails. She batted at the small creature, but it faded into nothingness, and her hand passed through empty air. Still invisible, it whispered Father James's message in her ear. By all the demons in hell, nay! The stable boy thief had escaped again.

†

The encounter occurred just before dawn. It was during that strange interlude when the emerging light of the almost-risen sun turns the sky milky white and casts the landscape as a black silhouette. Drax, who had taken the point position, came upon a narrow path, which led them through a jumble of boulders and underbrush, then went up the side of a low knoll—and right into an ambush.

The villagers, as it turned out, needed neither dogs nor diviners. They knew well those hills and vales and woody groves. They knew the paths and game trails, the creeks and bogs. They knew the rough impassable places and the clear ones through which passage was possible. So it had not been difficult for them to anticipate the likely avenues of escape and dispatch armed groups to intercept the fugitives.

The site of the ambuscade was well chosen. The hilltop was for the most part bare, leaving the fugitives fully exposed and visible in the new morning light. A large rocky outcropping, however, provided perfect concealment for a squad of village boys armed with slings. From there they could remain in complete concealment yet have a clear view of the path. So the party was taken entirely by surprise when a barrage of stones came buzzing around their ears.

The sling is a difficult weapon to master, but it is highly effective in skilled hands. These slingers were only village boys, and they had only river rocks to hurl, but they had had much opportunity to develop their expertise. As a result several members of the party were struck in the first seconds.

Thurmond received a clanging blow on his helmet and another on his leather armor. The first was not painful, just loud. The second hurt, but not too badly, with the leather absorbing the impact.

Sarah was struck on the unprotected leg and went down with a yowl. Roscoe pulled her to her feet and covered her with his body and shield, while Thurmond rescued her potted plant. Drax, somewhat ahead of the others, was struck repeatedly, but his small, round shield deflected many of the stones.

Driven back in disorder, the party was entirely unaware that a second group of villagers had come out of the brush behind them and was about to hit them from the rear. This would certainly have been the end of things, but Torgul sensed the approaching danger and shouted a warning.

This group was well armed, mostly with swords and spears, but luckily wore no armor. Roscoe did not hesitate. He called a charge and was thankful when his group sprang forward as if launched from a catapult. He had not expected his command to be so promptly and smoothly obeyed.

The villagers had expected an easy victory over a confused and unsuspecting foe. Instead they were on the receiving end of a determined and cohesive assault that enjoyed the added impetus of moving downhill.

Torgul struck first, Lodbrok's axe severing a leg at the knee. Roscoe held his shield high and smashed straight into a tall young man who seemed to be the leader, sending him sprawling over backward. He simultaneously cut at a skinny man on his right, forcing him to spin sideways to avoid the blow. This clumsy move exposed the man's side, and Lars skewered him with a spear. The prostrate leader attempted to rise, but Roscoe pushed him back down and then stomped hard on his face.

Thurmond had shot goblins and battled maniacal kobolds, but this was his first experience with mass combat against humans. It was quite different than the one-on-one fighting he'd been trained in. There were too many things going on around him. He saw openings—an exposed belly, an overextended arm, a vulnerable leg—but by the time he could react, the window of opportunity always seemed to close. He was determined to do his bit and so kept jabbing and slashing with his sword. He finally managed to drive its point into the thigh of a bloated fellow on his left.

Thurmond turned just in time to find a rangy, snaggle-toothed villager about to knock out his brains with a heavy, two-handed flail. The blow was slow and clumsy—an easy block. Thurmond raised his shield and waited for the impact, but he had not considered the weapon's flexible shaft. The shield indeed stopped the haft, but the flanged head kept right on going, the short chain looping right over its top edge.

It slammed into his helmet, denting it and sending the young man to his knees. He could only sit there, stunned, expecting to be slain by the next blow, but it never came. Instead, he was bowled over as the body of the flail wielder came crashing down on top of him, covering him with blood. Then Sarah was by his side, bloody sword in hand. She had used the weapon to open the flail-man's throat. She stood in staring open-mouthed shock as her victim gave a last convulsive kick.

Thurmond shook off his confusion, stood, and put an arm around her shoulder.

"Oh God! He had me for sure."

She did not seem to hear him, her attention was riveted on the dead man at her feet.

The fight was apparently over. Roscoe and the others chased the survivors a short way down the hillside. Thurmond and Sarah remained behind, as did Drax, who kept an eye on the slingers in the boulders behind them.

He gave the alarm, "Behind you—here come the slingers!"

No sooner was this said than another barrage of stones struck them. The slingers had been forced to suspend their attack for fear of hitting their fellow villagers. Now that their friends had been driven off, they resumed their efforts.

A half-dozen boys of various ages had left their position in the rocks to form a line along the crest of the knoll. They worked their slings furiously, sending down their painful missiles in a steady stream. Drax was hit again and again, but protected by his shield and armor, he was not seriously injured.

As the stones continued to pelt him, he calmly sheathed his sword and dropped his shield. He unslung the crossbow from his back and then, ignoring the painful impact of the stones, cocked, loaded, aimed, and fired the weapon. One of the slingers, a blotchy redhead of perhaps twelve years, was taken just below the throat. Drax then repeated the process and hit another, a tall, gangly youth maybe two years older. Sensing that they had no chance against such an indomitable enemy, the others faded back over the top of the knoll.

The party caught their breath, regrouped, and took stock. The slingers were only boys, but their stones could break bones and even kill if they struck in the right place. The villagers had been well armed, so they were extremely lucky to emerge from the fight with only an assortment of lumps and bruises to show for it.

Drax suffered most of all, having endured the strikes of many sling stones that left bloody swellings on his unarmored arms and legs. Luckily, the stones had missed his face and neck. Sarah could feel a hard, hot lump rising on her left thigh. Thurmond's head ached horribly.

There could be no pause for binding their wounds or celebrating their victory. More villagers might appear at any moment, and the fleeing boys would no doubt report the party's location to Father James. Their only hope lay in moving quickly and keeping under cover.

†

It was past midday. The party was moving through a narrow defile between two hills when they spotted another line of villagers moving along a ridgeline above them. They dropped to the ground and remained immobile until the last one had disappeared from sight. That last one had been Derkyn—his tall, gawky form was unmistakable.

They kept walking, staying in the shadows, avoiding clearings and open hillsides. As it grew dark, fatigue dictated that they must at last stop and rest, so they huddled in a dense stand of dogwood and ate such scraps of food as they had brought from the boat. As night fell, the air grew cold, but they dared light no fire lest they reveal their hiding place.

Thurmond found that as bad as he needed it, sleep would not come. He was too agitated by the events of the last few days. He recalled every frightful details of that accursed village. Finally he sought out Roscoe who, like himself, was sitting in the dark with open eyes.

He whispered, "Roscoe, are you asleep?"

The old Adventurer's voice was worn. "Obviously not, laddie, you're talkin' to me, are you not?"

"If you don't mind telling me, what did you see on top of that hill, the one where they had the big bonfire?"

"To tell you true, I don't much like thinkin' of it, but I guess you got a right to know. The place was what I expected, and I found Scrymgeour's boys and the others, so I did."

When paused, as if not wanting to envision the scene, Thurmond pressed him.

"What was up there? What did they do to them?"

"The top of the hill was all flattened out and clear of brush. Like it was special made for their ceremonies. Right in the middle the villagers had lit a great bonfire."

"Did they burn them, the boatmen?"

"Nay, didna burn 'em. Their throats was cut, and they was bled into a big bronze bowl. It was all crusted black with dried blood, but empty now."

"So whatever comes out of the river...the River Folk...emptied the bowl."

"Looks like."

Thurmond was decidedly sorry that he had initiated this conversation. He never did manage to go fully to sleep, and terrible dreams interrupted even his light doze.

†

Thurmond finally gave up on trying to sleep. He could barely make out the dark shapes of his companions, who lay curled on the hard, stone-strewn ground, their exhaustion having overcome the discomfort of their resting place. In dire need of a pee, he forced himself to his feet and moved off, as quietly as possible, a short distance from the group.

As he was relieving himself, there came the sharp snapping of a twig, then the scrape and rustle of underbrush. Something was approaching their sorry little camp. Father James and the villagers? Goblins? A monster? The sounds grew louder as the thing grew closer. Then a stag stepped into view from the shadows. It lifted its head, snorted—perhaps it was offended by the reek of Thurmond's urine—and moved off again into the dark.

When Thurmond returned to the others, he found Torgul awake, axe in hand. He too, unable to sleep, had been aroused by the snapping and crunching in the night. Thurmond held up a hand in a calming gesture.

"Just a stag."

Torgul nodded and sat down, abandoning, as had Thurmond, any further attempt to sleep. Lars and Drax, equally restless, soon joined them. Bodo and Sarah rose next, and they all sat silently in the dark. Only Roscoe continued to snore. The old Adventurer had had a difficult time the day before and needed his rest. Their cross-country trek over steep and uneven ground had been extremely painful for his bad leg.

The new day was equally demanding. Sarah awoke Roscoe just after sunrise, and the party set off at once. They were all hungry, exhausted, and footsore, but there was nothing to do but keep walking. The countryside was trackless and almost devoid of human habitation. This was the great expanse of wasteland stretching between the Mad River and the Royal Highway running up to Gorgonholm from the south.

Legitimate people had no reason to come to that dangerous region. There were no proper towns, only isolated farms and tiny hamlets. The residents of such secluded places had very compelling incentives for removing themselves from the company of their fellow man. They might be broken men, outlaws, escaped bond servants, or the followers of some forbidden religious practice.

Fell creatures abounded in such desolate areas. One could encounter roving bands of goblins. Trolls or ogres might lie in wait along the rocky hillsides, and Thurmond had heard Adventurer's tell of worse things. There were tales of living corpses, stinking of rot, climbing at night from ancient, forgotten barrows, of vampyres that would hold you down and take your blood, of ghouls and nightghasts that delighted in human flesh.

And who could say what gargantuan beasts might stalk or slither through these woodlands. Perhaps the ferocious cave bears of lore and legend. Adders and vipers of monstrous girth and length. Blood-sucking insects grown beyond any sane proportion. Perhaps the cyclops, the werewolf, the hydra. Or even the most feared of all creatures—the dragon.

The party kept heading east, their objective the Royal Highway that would take them north to Gorgonholm. Once on the road, their way would be much easier and safer. Wayside guard stations would offer a degree of security, and frequent villages could provide food and shelter. So there was nothing else but push on and put this blighted expanse of seething wilderness behind them.

Sarah remained downcast and withdrawn. Thurmond assumed she was wrestling with the fact of having killed a man. He remembered how he had felt after knifing the assassin who had burst through the door of their lodging. That man had been trying to kill him, and yet he, the intended victim, had felt a terrible guilt after taking his life.

Torgul had remained unaffected by that encounter. They had dragged out the bodies of the three assassins and dumped them in the river as if removing the muck from a stable. The dwarf had commented on the warmth of the night air but never on the proximity of death. Never on what it might mean to take a life. Roscoe's attitude, when he heard the story, had been much the same. As much as he liked and respected the Adventurers, it frightened him that they were such hardened killers.

Thurmond strove to reconcile his very conflicted feelings. Perhaps he should talk things over with Sarah. She was no doubt as upset as he had been. Or perhaps it was better to keep silent and create the happy illusion that the slaying of one's foes was unworthy of further thought. He did not know.

CHAPTER FIFTY

THURMOND'S HAPPY DISCOVERY

The hillsides were steep, rocky, and hard to climb. The sun was merciless, the wilderness endless. By late afternoon their collective strength was expended, and they flopped down to rest in the shade of a grove of alders. Fraught with fatigue, disappointment, and despair, even the normally garrulous Roscoe remained silent.

Yet it was at this unhappy moment that an unlooked-for incident dispelled the cloud of gloom that hung so heavily above them. Intending to check their fletchings, Thurmond pulled the few remaining arrows from his quiver. With them came a packet about the size of a man's fist. It was wrapped in brown leather and bound with cord.

"Hey, Sarah, look at this! I forgot all about it. Let's see what it is."

She rolled over and looked at him without much interest.

"What have you got?"

"I don't know. It was lying on the floor in the goblin treasure room. I nearly tripped on it while I was filling my rucksack with gold coins. It looked, I dunno, interesting somehow, so I picked it up. I was already wearing my ruck and didn't want to take it off again—it was too heavy anyhow—so I just dropped this into my quiver. Then with all that happened, I never thought about it again."

The words *treasure room* attracted the others. Their complaints momentarily forgotten, they now crowded around, eager for a look.

Thurmond drew his dagger and cut the cord that bound the packet. He laid it on the ground and tried to unroll the leather covering, which was stiff and brittle with age. The layers had, over time, bonded into a single mass, and it was necessary to snap small pieces off one at a time. Finally the contents were uncovered.

They looked down on a clutch of green and red gems, each about the size of an elf's testicle. Roscoe whistled softly.

"Bugger the gold. I think this'll do it, so it will."

The light twinkling from the many facets enchanted Sarah. She spoke slowly, distractedly.

"Are those real, do you think? They look like…"

Torgul completed her thought.

"Emeralds and rubies. Aye, they do indeed look real enough. Leave me have a gander—I know a thing or two about gems. Dwarf, you know."

He plucked a red one from the clutch and held it to catch the light.

"Aye, real. I can't really tell the grade without a larging glass, but cut and clarity look to be exceptional, mayhap first water."

He returned the red and selected a green.

"Now here's a pretty one. Nice color and very clear. And see here, it's engraved with a rune. I'll bet this one has quite a story to tell. Might be magical."

The group had become preternaturally quiet while Torgul conducted his examination. Roscoe finally broke the silence.

"And what are you thinkin', brother Torgul? How much would you guess this bonny little nest is worth? As much perhaps as the gold we left lyin' on the kobolds' floor? More?"

"Impossible to tell. Without a larging glass, I can't see the details. The cut looks very good, but I can't be sure. There may or may not be imperfections."

"Damn it, my brother, just say it as true as you can. No equivocatin', by God's holy bones. Do you think we're rich?"

"If we get back alive and we can manage to keep these safe, and if they're truly of the quality they appear to be, then, aye, we're rich."

Roscoe rose without a word and commenced an awkward one-legged caper. Thurmond threw his arms around Sarah and then, caught up in the moment, kissed her on the lips. Taken by surprise, she stiffened for a moment and then returned his kiss with gusto.

✝

Thurmond was, of course, proclaimed their blessed savior, whose brilliant foresight and enlightened wisdom had saved the party from financial ruin and brought them instead to a life of position and prosperity. He was fawned upon and praised, congratulated and adored. The wilderness no longer seemed so bad.

Roscoe and Torgul at once fell to arguing over the division of the treasure. This was another time-honored tradition of adventuring brothers—haggling over the spoils. Their debate was not a casual wrangling one undertakes to beat down the price of a merchant in a market stall, nor was it the vociferous argument of drunken bravos. Rather, it was a polite and orderly ritual that allowed two heavily armed and dangerous Adventurers to come to accord instead of turning on each other when tempted by the lure of treasure.

Custom demanded that the treasure would not be divided until the captain declared the adventure officially over. Until that moment, any winnings would remain in common ownership. All necessary expenditures would be drawn from this common store prior to division.

The customary shares had been agreed to long before the party had left Gorgonholm. Roscoe, as captain, was to receive three-eighths, a captain's rightful share. Torgul, his lieutenant, was to receive two-eighths, also as per custom. Scrymgeour would collect one-eighth for the use of his boat and sons. Thurmond and Sarah, mere fledglings that they were, would get the remaining two-eighths.

Their small hoard of gold, being of established value, would be quite simple to divide. The gems were going to be more difficult. They had first to gain a fair assessment of their value—no small task in a world acrawl with grasping and unscrupulous types—and then to locate a buyer willing to pay something approaching a reasonable price. So it was resolved that the adventure must officially continue until these two tasks were completed.

The real issue was placing a market value on Torgul's axe. All agreed that it was an enchanted weapon. It had readily dispatched the shadow creature, against which their regular weapons had proved useless. Torgul stipulated that it was exceedingly fast and agile. When employed against the kobolds, it seemed to jump in his hands as if possessed of a life of its own. And it sheared through their tough little bodies with remarkable ease, leaving a streak of red fire in the air as it did so. So, aye, there was magic in it.

Such weapons commanded a high monetary value, and the customary procedure would be to have it assessed by a reputable dealer in such items. If Torgul wanted to keep it for himself, and if the others had no objections—which they did not—the value of the axe would be deducted from his share and divided by the others.

But a dispute arose because the axe in question was not just an enchanted weapon. It was, as Torgul professed in a transport of joy, one of the Lost Treasures of Lodbrok, a legendary dwarf king who had ruled in ancient days before the encroachment of human civilization had pushed the dwarves from their ancestral homes into the wilds of the north and east. Every dwarf child, he claimed, had learned of these revered items before his or her beard began to sprout.

Because he, Torgul, had actually recovered Lodbrok's axe from the goblins, his immortal fame was assured. Dwarven bards would herald his praise as long as they had tongues to sing with. Its cultural significance far exceeded its value as a weapon, even an enchanted one. It was not to be used as a mere tool for killing goblins and kobolds. It must be enshrined and venerated in the halls of Spear Mountain.

And this was the source of the dispute. Roscoe maintained that the monetary worth of such a piece must be many, many times that of a workaday magical axe. To compensate, Torgul must be willing to forgo the bulk, perhaps the entirety, of his two-eighths share. Torgul countered that the axe's enhanced value was sentimental, not fiscal, and, as such, could not be accurately assessed. Therefore, it could not be considered when establishing value.

So the two Adventurers began to haggle as they walked. Neither was motivated by greed or even much by self-interest. What most inspired them was arriving at an equitable settlement in accordance with the established traditions of their brotherhood. This was a slow and tedious process, and the debate went on for days. Sarah and Thurmond quickly lost interest and moved off, leaving the two old hands to work things out.

Torgul and Roscoe eventually arrived at a satisfactory compromise. Unable to establish a befitting monetary value, they agreed that the axe would count for one-half of Torgul's two-eighth lieutenant's share. Both were pleased with this arrangement. The extra eighth would be added to the general hoard and divvied among the party members. Torgul would be compensated by the great honor and financial rewards he would receive when he restored the venerated item to his people.

Roscoe called the party together and announced that a solution had been reached. Since there were no objections, the old Adventurer broached another subject.

"We must be holdin' onto these lovely jewels for a while, so I propose that we choose a guardian to keep 'em hale and hearty until we can find a willing buyer. I could, as captain, just assume that role without askin' your leave, but I thought it proper to discuss the matter."

"I propose Thurmond! He was the one who brought us the gems."

Sarah blurted these words even before Roscoe had finished speaking and then immediately regretted them. Roscoe and Torgul were much more formidable fighters and would obviously make more effective guardians. Any debate over qualifications would by necessity prove humiliating to the young man.

But to her surprise, Roscoe seconded her motion.

"I think that's a fine idea, Sarah, so it is. Any objections to Thurmond as guardian?"

There were none.

"Well then, that's settled. Looky here now, this is what I'll do with our bright little stones. I'll sew them all up in a nice leather pouch, so there's no way to get at 'em save for cuttin' it open, and we won't do that until we're back to Gorgonholm. I'll put it on a stout leather thong so Thurmond here can wear it 'round his neck. Just keep yourself alive, boyo, and the stones will stay right where they should be."

Thurmond was amazed that such a serious responsibility should be offered to him. Nay, not offered, *thrust* on him. Later, when the pouch was ready, he dutifully hung it around his neck and dropped it inside his shirt.

Then Torgul, standing at his elbow, spoke to him in a low voice.

"'Tis custom that the hang-around holds the goods. Kind of a test of faith. If Sarah hadn't proposed you for it, I would have. Just don't get curious about the contents of that pouch, and all will be well. You guard the gems, and we guard you."

CHAPTER FIFTY-ONE

A PAINFUL BETRAYAL

Unfortunately, rich or not, the party was still many days' walk from any town or village where their newfound wealth could purchase provisions. By the next day, their food supply was exhausted. Hungry bellies began to growl. Sore feet barked like angry dogs. Roscoe's leg was a continual source of misery.

On the fourth day, they spotted a thin white column of smoke rising above the treetops. It was the kind of smoke that might have drifted up the smoke hole in a cottage roof. Creeping through the trees, they looked down from a low bluff upon a small farm lying in a narrow glen. There was a ramshackle hut of logs and branches, an equally decrepit structure that might be a barn, and several dilapidated outbuildings. Pigs wallowed in the mud of a sty. Chickens wandered about the yard, pecking at the ground. A kitchen garden spoke of vegetables.

After their last encounter with villagers, no one was eager to meet the denizens of this hinterland. So instead of approaching the farm, they watched and waited, lying on their stomachs as they peered over the edge of the bluff.

They didn't like the place. There was something bad down there, an undeniable ambiance of unwholesomeness. It was not the general squalor or the stench of the pigs—those were common enough features of every farm. What was it?

Torgul sidled up to Roscoe. Thurmond could hear their conversation.

"You see any dogs down there?"

"Nary a one."

"Not a good sign, certainly not. Every farm has dogs."

The young man tried to identify the cause of their ill ease. And then it came to him—there was a smell. A distinctly displeasing and unsettling smell. Not the pong of human or animal dung, nor the fetid reek of troll, but something more subtle. Something more like the pungent stink of insanity.

No one appeared until late afternoon, when three women came from up the glen. Two were middle aged, the third younger, perhaps just entering her teens. All were large and robust. They carried hoes on their shoulders and had obviously been at work in a field somewhere up the glen.

They returned their tools to one of the outbuildings and retired to the hut. Soon the volume of smoke increased and carried the smell of cooking to the famished watchers. One of the women came out to draw water from a well. Another, the young one, fetched firewood from a stack behind the hut. This was nothing out of the ordinary. Their actions were those of farm women everywhere.

And then the men returned—an older one, obviously the patriarch, and three younger ones, about the same age as the girl. They too carried tools that they stacked in the shed. The women emerged from the hut with wooden trenchers of food, which the men consumed while sitting in the dirt of the farmyard.

Drax rolled over next to Roscoe and Torgul.

"Listen, if there's one thing I learned bein' a soldier, it's how to steal food from a farm. I don't see no reason to go down there beggin'. That's just askin' for more trouble. There's somethin' wrong with 'em—anybody can see that.

"I'll go down when it gets good and dark. Bring back some chickens. I figure one of them sheds is a smokehouse, so maybe bacon. Whatever I can grab, see?

"Let Thurmond come with me to help carry back. He's smart, so he won't do nothin' stupid. Plus if he wants to be a soldier, he needs to know how to feed himself when he has to."

It was a reasonable plan. The farm smacked of some indefinable weirdness, and no one wanted to reveal their presence to its inhabitants. Roscoe assented, and they all hunkered down to wait until it got good and dark.

†

The hut was quiet, the residents having retired as soon as the sun set. Thurmond's job was to keep watch while Drax searched for food. He would whistle softly at any sign of danger. Neither wore armor nor carried weapons other than knives. They were grateful for the absence of dogs.

Thurmond was impressed by how smoothly Drax glided from one patch of shadow to the next. He had perfected a crawl that allowed him to scoot along, propelled by his elbows and knees, with his belly flat to the ground. He tried to emulate the movement and found he could do it without great difficulty.

He also admired how stealthily Drax moved, silently lifting the crude homemade latches of the various outbuildings and slipping inside, bringing out two large smoked hams, a sack of milled grain, another of dried peas, and another of dried apples. He gathered in three chickens and wrung their necks without a single telltale squawk. Best of all, he found a large stone jug of what proved to be a potent apple cider.

Drax sidled up to Thurmond with two fresh eggs in his hand. He offered him one while he cracked the other into his own mouth. He whispered with a chuckle.

"That's your reward for comin' with me."

Thurmond smiled and followed Drax's example. He was impressed with the soldier in other ways as well—the coolness with which he had withstood the pelting of the sling stones and the skill with which he had dropped the bothersome slingers. He liked how promptly he had avenged the unfortunate Jasper. Drax might be hotheaded and blustering, but those were admirable traits in a soldier.

As he waited for Drax to finish up, he dipped into the bag of dried apples. He knew he should wait, that the food should be shared evenly. But what real difference did it make? There was plenty to go around. Anyway, had he not earned a few apples? And they were so good! He kept on dipping.

When Drax had brought as much as they could carry, Thurmond crept over to the well and placed a small gold coin on a bench where it would be sure to be found. This was done at Roscoe's insistence. A true Adventurer, he had said, did not steal from innocent farmers unless driven by necessity. Further, he did not want to provoke their wrath. The single coin was worth many times the value of food they took, but it would be worth it if it kept them from giving chase.

Roscoe had been very specific in giving the coin to Thurmond and instructing him in its placement. He did not give it to Drax, who would, he assumed, simply keep it for himself. There was something in his squinty eyes and brash manner that suggested deceit and duplicity.

The old Adventurer did not approve of the camaraderie he saw beginning to bud between Drax and Thurmond. The man was a mercenary, for whom the concepts of honesty and loyalty meant little or nothing. Adventurers strode a higher path, one on which honor was valued far more highly than gold. Drax's influence could only be a hindrance to the lad as he learned to walk this path.

Still, Thurmond would have to learn for himself. Roscoe had no intention of trying to shield him from every negative influence that came his way. Adventurers had to learn to solve their own problems and overcome their own inner weaknesses. And if Thurmond gave into the temptations Drax might offer, then he was not of the right material to join the Brotherhood.

Nonetheless, Roscoe was relieved when the pair returned without incident, and he was delighted with the quantity of food they had gathered. This was neither the time nor the place to eat, of course. They must put some distance between themselves and the farm before satisfying their gnawing hunger.

Later that night, while the others slumbered with sated bellies, Thurmond was forced to rise again and again to step behind the bushes—the victim of too much dried fruit. But other than that, their heist had gone off without a hitch, for which they were all duly grateful.

†

On the afternoon of the seventh day, the party finally set their feet on the Royal Highway, the great trunk road that joined the northern city of Gorgonholm to her sister cities in the south. Built to facilitate the rapid movement of royal troops to the volatile north, it was employed primarily for commercial purposes. Along it, the raw materials of the northern territories flowed to the markets and factories of the south, while manufactured goods and luxury items went north.

The Royal Highway was famous for its amenities. Massive stone bridges spanned rivers and ravines. Guard stations and mounted patrols discouraged highway banditry. Inns and villages offered food and shelter. Roadside wells provided fresh water. All of this had to be paid for, of course. So there were also frequent toll stops, and the mounted Road Guards were authorized to tax anyone found without an official toll receipt.

The Road Guards were universally disliked. They routinely bullied the travelers they encountered, often demanding payment far exceeding the proper toll. They molested women and helped themselves to the inventories of merchants. They had been known to take over roadside inns, consuming the entire stock of comestibles, smashing the place, and then departing without payment. No one wanted to see the Road Guards approaching.

And there could be other dangers as well. Outlaw bands sometimes waylaid travelers or attacked lightly guarded caravans. Goblins staged an occasional raid. There were stories of evil innkeepers who murdered their guests for the value of their belongings. None of these untoward occurrences happened very often, but it was always wise for travelers to stay together, be well armed, and remain wary.

Compared to their travels up to this point, though, the highway was indeed a welcome sight. They would soon have real food. There would be village markets with garden produce and fresh meat. Inns with casks of foaming ale, loaves of warm bread, and fat geese turning on spits.

Perhaps they could join a merchant caravan, mayhap even get paying jobs as guards. As bona fide Adventurers, Roscoe and Torgul would be recognized as skilled warriors as well as honest and dependable men.

Their provisions were again exhausted, but they were not yet ravenous with hunger. Indeed, fatigue trumped the need for sustenance, and Roscoe decided to camp for the night in a clearing just out of sight of the road. They even chanced a small fire, and Sarah brewed a tea from some herbs she thought she recognized. It tasted foul and gave them all an itch.

Drax pulled Thurmond to one side.

"What say me and you scout down the road a little? Maybe there's a farm or somethin'—maybe do a little foragin'. We shouldn't have to starve just 'cause the old guy's leg hurts. What you say?"

That suggestion sounded good to Thurmond. He might be slender of build, but his appetite had always been mighty. Hunger pangs seemed to bother him far more than they did his companions. Without telling anyone, they set off down the road toward the south, the direction a completely random choice. As before, neither wore their armor, though Drax brought along his crossbow, just, he told Thurmond, in case.

They had not gone far when they heard voices and loud laughter coming from a glade on the road's far side. Then came the tantalizing aroma of roasting meat. They looked at each other and without a word crept forward to investigate. The night was dark, so approaching unseen was not difficult.

A squad of six Road Guards was in the process of getting grandly drunk. They were just finishing their evening repast, toasting the last pieces of meat on sticks over a bed of glowing coals, all the while passing a large jug of what, considering their sputtering and whoops of delight, could only be uisge. They grew louder and more raucous as the jug passed from hand to hand, but then suddenly the whole group seemed to collapse in a heap and began to snore.

Thurmond recalled his precarious encounter with a similar group on his way back from his dealings with the Trollkeeper. He touched Drax's arm and whispered.

"Those guys are a bunch of poxy bastards."

Drax gestured him to silence and drew him aside where they could speak.

"Them be Royal Road Guards, and we don't wanna tangle with 'em—drunk or sober. But I got me an idea—their horses."

Thurmond loved the proposal. If they could steal the horses, the guards would be left stranded and unable to pursue. The party could ride in fine style, making much better progress than slogging along on foot.

They crept in a wide circle to where the animals were picketed for the night. Following their previous routine, Thurmond kept watch while Drax did the actual stealing. And as before, he was swift and silent as he went about his business. Thurmond heard a few low whickers from the horses and a bit of nervous stomping, but nothing was loud enough to rouse the drunken guardsmen.

Drax was back in good time with the horses in tow. One was even saddled and bridled. The others wore only the halters by which they had been tied to the picket line. No outcry came from the guardsmen, whose slumber remained undisturbed. The moon was rising, and it was easier to see as they crossed the road and made their way back toward camp. They passed through a screen of trees and bushes, and entered a small clearing where the moonlight shone down brightly.

Thurmond was elated. He and Drax, of their own initiative, had accomplished a deed that would bring much joy to the entire party. Everyone was tired of walking. Roscoe could give his leg a much-needed rest. They would be home soon and could start enjoying all the good things that came with wealth. Drax's low voice, however, interrupted his reverie.

"Hey, kid—"

Thurmond turned, smiling, eager to share his excitement. But his smile froze and his excitement died when he saw Drax was aiming the crossbow straight at his chest.

"Sorry, kid—just business."

He squeezed the trigger. The shot was at point-blank range, so he could not miss. The bolt struck Thurmond square in the breastbone, knocking him off his feet. Then he was on the ground, unable to move, powerless to breathe, consciousness ebbing away. Aware only of a terrible burning pain in his chest and Drax bending over him, knife in hand.

"I'll be havin' those jewels, kid."

But then it was Drax's turn to be taken by surprise. A crossbow bolt suddenly appeared in his left shoulder. He gave a shout more of outrage than of agony and rose to face his attacker. Roscoe stood on the far edge of the clearing, feeding another bolt into his own crossbow. Torgul was already halfway across the clearing, his axe raised above his head, its blade gleaming red in the moonlight as if eager for blood.

Drax knew he stood no chance against the two Adventurers, especially with a bolt in his shoulder and his left arm hanging useless. He ran to the one saddled horse, vaulted onto its back, and drove his heels sharply into its sides.

It reared slightly and then plunged toward the road and the cover of the trees. Roscoe fired again, missing Drax's neck but by the width of a finger. Then horse and rider were gone, lost in the darkness. Its hoofbeats echoed through the night, pounding down the road to the south.

Both Adventurers ran to their stricken comrade. He lay flat on his back, the shaft of the bolt standing straight up from the center of his chest, testifying to the accuracy of Drax's shot. He groaned and gasped as if trying to catch his breath. Though he still lived, both old warriors knew a shot to the heart must bring death.

Frantically, they tore away his blood-sopped tunic to try to gauge the severity of the wound. Then Roscoe, quite inexplicably, started to chuckle.

"Why looky here—looky what happened! This boyo must be one of Lady Fortune's most beloved. There can be no other reason. I do believe, brother Torgul, that this laddie might yet live to see the sunrise, so I do."

Drax would have been better served had his aim been a little less true. The bolt had hit Thurmond dead center, and in so doing had struck squarely on the small pouch of stones—their cache of gems—he wore suspended about his neck. The bolt's force had been sufficient to drive its head clean through the pouch and pierce the young man's chest, but the wound was not fatal. The hard stones of the pouch had so slowed the missile that it penetrated no deeper than the length of its square iron head.

The punch of impact had been enough to knock Thurmond from his feet and drive the air from his lungs, but he was already regaining his breath. The injury was painful, to be sure, and he yelled lustily as Roscoe pulled the bolt from his body. A fragment torn from his tunic staunched the bleeding.

Just then, a chorus of angry shouts erupted from the direction of the road. The inebriated guards, awakened by all the commotion, had finally discovered the theft of their steeds. This was no time for delays.

Torgul rounded up the remaining five horses, which had remained remarkably undisturbed by the violence going on around them. They loaded Thurmond onto the back of one and then led the whole herd off toward their camp. The wounded lad could scarcely keep his seat. He held onto the steed's mane with his right hand and clamped the bandage to his chest with the other.

So few were their possessions that breaking camp was but the work of a moment. Everything not absolutely essential had been discarded during the long hike through the wilderness. Sarah started to make a fuss over Thurmond's injury, but Roscoe emphasized the necessity of haste.

They were unavoidably delayed by the sad fact that neither Sarah, Bodo, nor Lars—having lived their whole lives in a city—had ever before been astride a horse. They had no idea how to mount or control such a beast and were, in fact, rather afraid of them. So it took some time to get them on their backs and moving. And then the pace was frustratingly slow.

Thurmond had, as a boy, sometimes ridden the large work horses of his village. But these were no more than short jaunts around the village green, not desperate flights through the dark with an arrow wound in his chest. He too had a hard time keeping up. Roscoe and Torgul were experienced riders, though the latter's short legs made him look like a child sitting on his father's horse.

The horses themselves were neither powerful warhorses nor prancing thoroughbreds, but tough, thick-legged cobs bred for endurance rather than speed. They were ideal horses for the ride back to Gorgonholm, which made it all the more frustrating that they could not keep them. Each bore a brand identifying it as the property of the Road Guards—royal property. There would be a reward for their recovery, and that would inevitably tempt some busybody wayfarer or villager to raise the hue and cry as soon as dawn broke.

PART 6

THE TURNING OF FORTUNE'S WHEEL

CHAPTER FIFTY-TWO

ABOUT THE GEMS, PART ONE

The party rode until the sun began to push itself above the hills in the east. They then dismounted and sent the horses off with a slap on the rump. The herd started back south as if heading for breakfast in their barn.

Thurmond could see the thatched roofs of a village just around a bend in the road. That was a most welcome sight. His wound pained him so badly that he could scarcely stand, and walking was a jolting agony.

Roscoe led the others into town and banged on the door of the inn, which had not yet opened for business. An upper window opened, and a woman's head appeared, her hair bound in a kerchief. Roscoe once again played the charmer.

"Terrible sorry to trouble you at this hour, goodwife, but our friend is in sore need of a leech. We're a company of honest travelers bound for Gorgonholm. We was campin' by the roadstead when we was set upon by footpads in the night. Young Thurmond here has been shot and will surely die, so he will, unless your village boasts a leech of considerable talent."

That was all it took. The door was unlocked and the leech sent for. Thurmond was given a vigorous bleeding to cool his feverish blood, followed by a sleeping draught. A special room was designated as an infirmary, where Sarah appointed herself to sit with him. The others meanwhile enjoyed a lavish breakfast and retired to the sleeping loft.

When Thurmond came around, it was early evening. He saw Sarah dozing in a chair and reached to touch her hand. She awoke with a start.

"Oh—you're awake. How do you feel? Can I fetch you something?"

"Perhaps a mug of ale—my throat is parched. Thanks."

He hesitated. There was a question he had to ask, though he was loath to do so.

"Can you ask Roscoe to step in a moment?"

When the old Adventurer arrived, Thurmond got right to it.

"Did Drax get the gems? I can't remember what happened after he shot me."

Roscoe gave him a dire look.

"You mean the gems we trusted you to hold for the party? Those gems?"

"Aye."

"You mean the ones we all risked our lives to win—and that some of us died for?"

Thurmond felt a lump catch in his throat.

"Aye, I do."

"The gems that you put at risk by carousin' with that sneakin' mercenary? Those gems?"

Thurmond turned his face away, unable to look his friend and mentor in the eye.

"Aye, Roscoe, those gems."

Roscoe reached into the leather wallet hanging at his side and withdrew the pouch that had once hung around Thurmond's neck. It was bloodstained and still pierced by the crossbow bolt that had been pulled from his chest.

"You're meanin' the stones that are in this pouch, are you not? The ones that I gave to you for safekeepin'?"

He tossed the item into the young man's lap. It was badly torn, and the contents spilled onto the blanket. Thurmond was flabbergasted.

"These aren't gems—they're just pebbles."

"Aye, laddie, pebbles scooped from the ground when no one was lookin'. Do you really think we'd allow a damn fool hang-around to hold such a grand treasure?"

Now the old Adventurer smiled for the first time.

"Torgul and me...we thought it best, so we did, to employ a bit of misdirection. We knew the whole crew had their ears open wide, so better if they thought they knew where the gems were, even if they didn't. And it was a nice little test for our new hang-around—a chance to see if his judgment is everythin' we want it to be."

Thurmond almost died of shame. He had failed his friends. It was not often that he was rendered speechless, but this was one of those times. The kind and charitable Roscoe read his thoughts perfectly and spoke in soothing tones.

"Look you, we don't expect perfection. You're bound to make mistakes, so you are, and you've made one. But it turned out all right because Torgul saw you slippin' off with Drax, and we followed along. We lost you for a tad, but then, by sure dumb luck, you two came right back to us. Lady Fortune must really love you, boyo."

Roscoe grew more serious.

"We don't expect perfection, but we do expect that you learn from your mistakes. What lesson did you learn from this one, hang-around?"

"I learned not to trust every slick-talking arsehole that comes around. And that I need to listen to you and Torgul because I don't know enough yet."

"Well said. But you still don't yet see the bigger concern here, I'm thinkin'. Still, you're on the right path. You're a fine lad, Thurmond. Just don't get too full of yourself."

"I won't, Roscoe. Hey! What happened to the gems? Who's got them?"

"They're safe, laddie, never fear."

Roscoe heaved himself up from the stool and left the room. Thurmond decided to keep the bolt and impaled pouch as a memento of the incident and as a reminder to be more circumspect.

†

As uplifting as this news was to Thurmond, his day was darkened when he learned that Torgul was to leave them on the morrow. Anticipating a hero's welcome and a substantial reward, the doughty dwarf was most eager to carry the Axe of Lodbrok to his ancestral homeland of Spear Mountain, there to be enshrined as a sacred relic. He promised to return to Gorgonholm as quickly as he might, for he was almost equally keen to collect his share of the party's treasure.

Later in the evening, he came to Thurmond's chamber.

"I must be off for a bit. Be quick in your healing, lad. Roscoe will have much need of you before this adventure is done."

That was all he said. In the morning he was gone before cockcrow.

They remained in the village a week, though their stay grew tedious after the first few days. There was a constant temptation to spend their gold wantonly on such frivolous luxuries as the village offered, but caution prevailed. They could only invite trouble by making a display of their wealth. They did, however, acquire those articles as seemed essential for the rest of their journey.

Roscoe purchased a horse for himself, another stout-legged cob. He assured the others that the cost of their steed would be charged against his personal share, not to the general fund. He also bought a two-wheeled farm cart and a mule to pull it. The others had demonstrated such a pronounced lack of horsemanship that a cart was unquestionably the best option.

After a week, Thurmond was deemed fit for travel. He was sufficiently recovered from both this arrow wound and the frequent bleedings administered by the leech. Bodo and Lars took turns driving the cart. It was not a smooth or pleasant ride. The springless vehicle jolted and bounced so violently that Sarah often chose to walk rather than sit inside. Thurmond was made as comfortable as possible, either lying on a thick bed of straw or sitting propped against a folded quilt.

The last leg of the journey was uneventful—boring even. The miles fell away without incident or excitement. As they grew closer to the city, Thurmond tried to amuse himself by watching for familiar landmarks. He knew they were at last getting close when he recognized the Old Forest Road, the path he had taken when in search of the Trollkeeper. At least he thought it was the same path, but that episode seemed so long ago that he could not be certain.

He finally got his bearings when, a couple of hours later, he spotted the top of the old watchtower far off on the south side of the highway. Next came the Gray Friars' monastery. He recalled the long-winded conversation he'd had with their gate porter and the miserable night he had spent in the rainy woods. Next, he saw the small, round hill in which he had met with the well-groomed gentleman—not a real gentleman, as is turned out, but a contemptible blackguard he had been forced to kill with his own hands.

Then Gorgonholm's South Gate rose before them, its massive gatehouse and proud heraldic banner betokening their return to a world of order and stability. There were the gatekeepers, busily collecting a toll from any who would enter the city.

In his jug the imp suddenly awakened after a long period of dormancy. He could hear his old mistress calling to him and feel the surging of her magic. She could not be far off. Great was his hunger and terrible was his wrath after so much time in the jug. Trapped he was, but he was not without certain abilities.

†

During the ride home, Torgul and Roscoe had debated long and hard about how best to transform the pouch of gems into a mountain of gold. They knew they had to exercise extreme caution. If word of their good fortune got out, every grasping civic official and voracious self-entitled noble would be clamoring for a share. Earl Ralf would undoubtedly enact a new tax, the church a new tithe. The Brethren would either demand an exorbitant cut for their protection or they might attempt to steal the entire treasure.

None of the city's several gem merchants possessed the astronomical sum of gold they expected to realize. So what were they to do? When Roscoe suggested that the dwarves of Spear Mountain, Torgul's relatives, might buy them, his friend demurred. The dwarves, he said, could not be expected to deal fairly with humans, even if they were his own relatives. And they would not, under any circumstances, be willing to pay even a small fraction of the gems' actual value.

Roscoe knew he must call on the one man in Gorgonholm who might come to their aid. Only Jarvis trafficked in such high-end, clandestine merchandise. His shop was a big, rambling affair of brick, stone, and half-timbering, almost hidden among the long warehouses in the city's Merchant Quarter. A simple signboard proclaimed simply USED AND UNUSUAL ITEMS, JARVIS, PROP. No further advertisement was required—the people who required his services knew where to find him.

Jarvis had the reputation as a businessman of great acumen. He was infallibly honest and dependable, and he always maintained the highest level of personal dignity and reserve. His customers were not his friends, and his dealings with them were strictly professional.

Jarvis, Roscoe knew, would be the only man in Gorgonholm who would be capable of arranging the sale of their gems. Moreover, he believed they could trust him. He was the frequent recipient of exotic and expensive items brought by Adventurers from the underground. Roscoe had had various transactions with him over the years. He knew Jarvis's fees would be painfully high, but he was the only one with the right contacts to make the sale possible. So Jarvis it had to be.

The first item of business upon arrival in the city was to secure a flat over a warehouse on a narrow bystreet. Bodo and Lars begged to be allowed to stay on as Roscoe's personal retainers, so the old Adventurer formally received them into his service. Their first task was to unpack the gear and arrange their accommodations. Roscoe, Thurmond, and Sarah left to call on Jarvis, whose shop was conveniently located just around the corner.

Though the shop was quite large, it was stacked to the rafters with the accumulated miscellanea of decades. There were shelves of books and rolled parchments, racks of weapons, and huge glass jars in which indefinable body parts floated in oil. Helmets and shields of all configurations hung from the rafters. A lidless sarcophagus held a wrapped mummy. Carved furniture was stacked higher than a man's head, while a jumbled multitude of barrels and boxes and casks and bales left only narrow pathways through which the party was forced to squeeze. The place was dark and permeated with the pungent aroma of odd and discordant smells.

Jarvis was small, round, and gray. He sat behind a high counter within a cage of wrought iron bars. These were extremely stout and ran floor to ceiling. Perched upon a tall stool, he looked down on his customers as if from a great height.

Jarvis's security measures were impressive. There were many stories of the terrible consequences visited upon those foolish enough to try to pilfer his treasure. Not only had they all failed, but their physical remains had borne evidence of torments exceeding even those inflicted by the Brethren, who were usually content to cut out an offender's guts.

According to local legend, those who trespassed against Jarvis had been found torn into small morsels. One housebreaker had been turned entirely inside out. This was not the work of human hands. The merchant clearly employed creatures of the netherworld to protect his premises.

Jarvis was writing in a ledger as the party approached. Roscoe cleared his throat to draw attention but received no acknowledgment. He stood unmoving until the merchant, his writing completed at last, condescended to notice him. His voice was flat and surprisingly high pitched.

"Can I help you?"

Roscoe knew better than to glad-hand Jarvis, so he did his best to restrain his usual prolixity.

"Friend Jarvis, we are just returned from a most desperate adventure, so we are. We have won great treasure, and we are now in need of your ability to—how shall I put it?—render it into a more serviceable form."

"And the nature of this treasure?"

Roscoe pushed the sack of gems through the bars of the iron cage. Jarvis drew the drawstring and spilled the contents onto his countertop. The set of his face never altered, but his hitherto expressionless eyes began to burn. Nonetheless, his voice remained unchanged.

"Where did you acquire these?"

"Goblin hoard. Down south."

Jarvis climbed down from his stool and exited the cage. He crossed to the front of the store, drew the bolt on the door, and returned. His voice was now tense, his face serious.

"Come into the back. We must discuss this. I know these gems."

CHAPTER FIFTY-THREE

ABOUT THE GEMS, PART TWO

Roscoe, Sarah, and Thurmond sat around a table in Jarvis's parlor. It was, if anything, more crowded with outlandish bric-a-brac than his storefront. Every available space was crammed with chairs, chests, tables, or trunks. A huge stuffed bird of prey was suspended from the ceiling. A collection of ragged battle flags hung on the walls. All was coated with a thick layer of dust that made Thurmond sneeze again and again. In a wooden box fronted with wire mesh, a spotted snake lay at rest, cold evil in its eyes.

Roscoe did not waste a second on unnecessary chitchat.

"You know our jewels? What, pray tell, might you mean by that?"

"I recognize them—know them well enough to tell you that you can never sell them."

All four party members exploded with one voice.

"What?"

"If you attempt to do so, they will be recognized and seized. You will be questioned, tortured. Then the four of you will be hanged—probably worse."

Again four voices echoed as one.

"Why?"

"Because these are the Mortimer gems. They're quite famous."

"Mortimer...surely you don't mean..."

"Surely I *do* mean. This is the heirloom jewelry of the Mortimer family. The family of our own Earl Ralf Mortimer. They were stolen from his maternal uncle some twenty years ago or more. Once it is known that these jewels have come to light, the family will demand their return."

Roscoe flushed red and began to grow angry.

"Now listen here, Jarvis, we risked our lives for these stones, so we did. Some of us died. And we all suffered terrible hurt and deprivations. Now you're tellin' me that they're worthless to us because some fancy-boy noble will just take 'em? I'll throw 'em in the river first, so I will."

Jarvis remained unmoved.

"I would advise you to restrain yourself and listen more carefully to my words. I said that you can never sell them. But I did not say that they are worthless—not to you, not to me."

"Please be so kind as to explain yourself."

"These stones once formed the basis of the Mortimer family fortune. Even without them, the family is far from impoverished, to be sure. But I doubt they have the ready funds to buy them back, even at a fraction of their real value—even if they were inclined to do so, which they would not be.

"But powerful nobles can offer compensations other than cold coin. Forget not that they are related to King Tancred. This lends special weight to their petitions. Could we show that noble blood runs in your veins, perhaps a grant of arms could be arranged. This would cost the earl nothing but would mean a great deal to you.

"It would be more realistic for you to become a wealthy franklin. The Mortimers own vast parcels of land and control many lucrative interests. They can convey the tenure of mills, quarries, docks, ferries, bridges. I can see you living a very comfortable life, enjoying the revenue generated by such an enterprise. How does that sound to you?"

The old Adventurer had to admit it sounded pretty good.

"I can undertake to negotiate on your behalf. I have had many dealings with the earl, and he trusts me. And I trust him, at least to a point. But I must not reveal that the gems have actually been recovered. If he suspects that he need only stretch his hand to take them, the temptation might well prove too great.

"So we must concoct a plausible tale to keep our beloved earl from dishonoring himself. He is a fine man, really, within the limitations of his class. Now tell me exactly how you came by these stones."

Roscoe gave Jarvis a quick summary of their raid on the goblin lair, but he specifically excluded any mention of the two parties that had followed them down the river. Rupert de Pugh and Bartholomew Staynes were nobles. Lady Renata was the sister of the most feared man in the county. Including them could only add unwanted complication.

When Roscoe was finished, Jarvis told the tale of the theft of the jewels from so many years past.

"'Twas in the time of Earl Reginald Mortimer, sometimes called the Merciless, and for good reason. A terrible and greedy overlord, he was. I am now old, but my memory is as keen as ever, and I can say truly that never was a lord more hated by his subjects. He took from them not just whatever he wanted but whatever there was to take—even the smallest things, things of no value. My business suffered terrible loss under his sway, which at least was blessedly brief.

"Such a tyrant could not last long, for he stole from his nobles no less than he did from the common folk. He was found dead in his own bed in his own sleeping chamber. His throat had been cut and his body repeatedly stabbed. His two bodyguards took the blame. They were discovered drunk and senseless in the adjoining room. Their faces were splashed with the earl's blood, and their own gore-slathered daggers lay on the floor beside them.

"The guards of course pled their innocence, claiming that someone had drugged their possets, but, unsurprisingly, it did them no good. They were condemned to die a traitor's death. They were tied to stakes in the Market Square before the assembled populace. Their bellies were slit and their entrails drawn forth yard by yard. I remember it well, for I was in the front of the crowd and witnessed every detail. It was a terrible sight and a dreadful death—a death you would not wish on your mortal foe.

"Then it was discovered that the family treasure vault had been looted. The Mortimer heirloom jewelry, these very gems on the table before us, were gone. No one apparently had even thought to check before. That was a bad time for us in the city. The Mortimers' men ransacked every house, broke things, stole things. And they took away anyone who they thought might tell them something. Most never came back. Those who did were forever broken in body and spirit.

"In the end, it was announced that the guards had fallen in with a crew of desperate outlaws who had used the confusion following the murder to effect a break-in. This, of course, was patently absurd. If the guards had been part of such a gang, why would they have remained behind? But the family was, I suspect, more interested in establishing a cover story than in discovering the truth.

"It was obviously an inside job. Many fingers pointed at the earl's wife Dorotea, others at his sister Maud. But the finger-pointers tended to disappear suddenly, so such accusations quickly came to an end.

"The lives of both women were improved by the earl's demise. His widow, Countess Dorotea, retired to a life of ease and self-gratification on an extremely generous stipend when her nephew became the succeeding earl. This was our own Earl Ralf, who was then but a child. Within a year Dorotea married a foreigner, who rejoiced in the title of Marquis de Slyme. The less said of him the better.

"Ralf's mother, Lady Maud, served as regent until her son achieved his majority. It has been long rumored that his true father was not Maud's deceased husband but her own brother, the old earl. Judge them not, for the ways of the Quality are not the ways of the common folk. In any case, the people were right glad to receive the young man as their rightful Earl. He grew into a vigorous and handsome man, who attended to his duties with a much lighter hand than his father."

Sarah, silent up to this point, suddenly interrupted the narrative.

"Why did Lord Ralf succeed his uncle? Did Reginald not have any proper sons of his own?"

"Nay, the old earl died without legitimate issue. His wife was thought to be barren."

"So Ralf was next in line of succession?"

"Aye, there are strict laws and customs that govern such things."

"Suppose the old earl had had a daughter—what then?"

"'Twould have made no difference. Only male issue may succeed."

"And if there is no male issue, none at all?"

"In such cases—which are extremely rare, I might add—a female may succeed to a title of nobility."

Roscoe now intervened with a gentle hand on her shoulder.

"Let the man tell his tale, lassie. Let's not get distracted by a bunch of blather."

"It's *not* blather, Roscoe. Please, let me ask just one more question. Master Jarvis, sir, can a title pass to a child born on the wrong side of the blanket?"

"You mean to a bastard? Aye, 'tis possible, though also very rare. And it can only happen if the father makes written recognition of the child as his own. Such a child may, if he succeeds, carry the familial arms, but differenced by *bend sinister*."

"By what?"

"A diagonal bar running across the shield from the top right corner. It indicates bastardy."

Roscoe again laid his hand on her shoulder.

"Enough, Sarah—let the man finish his story."

And Jarvis did so.

"The stolen gems were never found, which was not surprising, for where could one find a market for something so distinctive? They would have to be hidden away for many a year. How they ended up as part of a goblin treasure will, I'm afraid, forever remain a mystery. I can only surmise that the thieves, whoever they were, must have been waylaid by those malicious creatures.

"But if you now appear with the gems, claiming to have rescued them from some far-off goblin den, you will be accused of being part of the gang who stole them twenty years ago. It will not matter if you can prove your innocence—you will never be allowed the chance to do so. It would be so much easier for the Mortimers to simply kill you all. Then the gems will revert to their family, and any old suspicions that may still linger will be put to rest. You may even suffer the same fate as the unfortunate guards, who, I have no doubt, were as innocent as yourselves."

Roscoe flung up his hands.

"Then what should we do?"

"Allow me to negotiate on your behalf. I will concoct a plausible tale that will allow this strange turn of fate to bring benefit to all involved. The Mortimers will once again possess their family treasure, and you will be grandly recompensed for your considerable efforts."

"How much recompensed?"

"You cannot expect to glean anything approaching the true value of the gems—such a thought is beyond reason. It would never be allowed. But as I said before, you can anticipate a permanent improvement in your manner of life—freedom from the drudgery that has always been your lot. A life of comfort and abundance rather than hardship and want."

Despite these happy tidings, Roscoe remained wary.

"I have had dealings with you in the past, Master Jarvis, and while you have always dealt fair and honorably, you always did so for your own gain, did you not? Why are you so generous now? How will you gain from helping us?"

"The gratitude of the nobility is always of value to me. In addition, I might expect that the earl, in his appreciation, would offer some appropriate monetary consideration."

"And how much *consideration* would you expect from me?"

"None at all. Any financial remuneration will come from the earl. I ask only that you trust me."

"What story will you tell him?"

"I'm not yet certain. Perhaps I will tell him that the gems have been located in the possession of a certain Keltin chieftain who lives deep in the forest on the other side of the river. And that I have contacted a select crew of highly trained Adventurers who are willing to undertake their recovery if sufficient inducements are offered. I'll have to be careful here until I get a sense of how much he's willing to part with. Once I have a general idea, I can begin to negotiate in earnest."

"What if he's not interested? What then?"

"Worry not—he'll be interested. We'll just have to see how interested. If you agree to my plan, I will call upon Earl Ralf on the morrow."

Roscoe, as captain, gave his approval. He also agreed to leave the gems in Jarvis's safekeeping. He trusted the merchant and understood that the treasure would be far more secure locked in Jarvis's shop than in his own possession.

With that the meeting adjourned. Roscoe went off to the Severed Head to drink with his old companions and to catch up on the local news. Thurmond and Sarah returned to their new lodging. She had something on her mind.

CHAPTER FIFTY-FOUR

SARAH'S MACHINATIONS

As soon as they arrived at the lodging, Sarah gave Thurmond a hard stare. Her tone was serious.

"We need to talk."

Thurmond was a regular fellow, so these words filled him with dread. Nonetheless, he dutifully invited her to speak her mind.

"You heard what Jarvis said about women being able to inherit when there are no male heirs?"

"So?"

"Don't you see? That's me! I'm the daughter of Lord Percy Staynes, and I'm next in line."

"What? Have you gone dippy? You said he has a son, your young master."

"Bart *was* his son. But don't forget, he disappeared during the failed attack on the goblins. Drax and Jasper told us the whole story. He never came out of the cave. He has to be dead."

Thurmond paused and thought.

"You're probably right about that. But wait a minute—you said Bart had a bastard son, the one who shot at me with a crossbow. He's a male, so he'd inherit before you would."

"Nay, he shall not. For as Jarvis said, a bastard can inherit only if they are formally recognized by the sire. Gyre never received such recognition, and he can't get it now because his father is dead."

"But you've not received recognition either."

"Actually, I'm pretty sure I have. I've seen it."

"You've seen it? Seen what?"

"My father is old and in his dotage. He forgets things. There is a locked cabinet in his library where he keeps his important documents. Sometimes he neglects to shut it. Whenever I saw it open, I went through his things."

"Why?"

"I was curious. That's where I saw this big parchment document that was all about me. At the time, I didn't know what it was. Actually, I didn't know until listening to Jarvis this evening. But now I'm certain it was an official recognition of myself as the daughter of Lord Percy Staynes."

Thurmond remained skeptical.

"You're certain? Really?"

"Well…pretty certain."

Thurmond was not.

"Didn't you say that your master…your father…was always having a go with his servants? You must have some brothers and sisters."

"Most likely, but I was always favored and pampered. None of the other household children received the advantages I enjoyed. They were treated like the servants they were born to be, while I was educated and given leave to pursue my own interests. That was a form of recognition too, was it not?"

"Why you?"

"I know not. Perhaps my father held a special fondness for my mother."

"Does she yet live? Can we ask her of these matters?"

"Nay, she died long ago. I need your help."

"To do what? I know nothing of these things. How can I help with such matters?"

"You must help me sneak into Father's mansion and steal the document of recognition."

Thurmond's eyes widened, and his voice grew taut.

"What? Nay, I will not. The last time I was there, I was nearly killed by a child with a crossbow. And I had to stab one of the servants. I'm not going back."

"Fear not. We'll enter by the same secret tunnel we escaped through, the one that runs from the old warehouse to Father's library, so you won't encounter any of the servants. And if Gyre is still playing with that crossbow, I can take care of that too."

"How?"

"With my invisibility spell, the same one I used when we went in with the goblins. I think I can cast it now."

Thurmond remained unconvinced.

"This is truly daft, Sarah."

But in the end, Thurmond being Thurmond and Sarah being Sarah, he agreed to help her steal the coveted document.

†

They next morning, no one mentioned their discussion with Jarvis or what his words might portend for their future. The implications were too staggering. The possibility that Roscoe might soon be a wealthy landholder did not seem real. Only Sarah fully grasped how significantly their lives were about to change, and she spoke only to Thurmond. But she did not disclose all her thoughts, even to him. Everybody was on edge and seemed eager to get away.

Bodo and Lars, unaware of the previous evening's revelation, requested some time away to visit the former's home. Bodo, it turned out, was a married man and eager for a renewal of connubial bliss. He also had two children and a widowed sister-in-law, who Lars was eager to meet. They arranged to return in a few days.

In the meantime, Roscoe had to face the more difficult job of bringing Scrymgeour the hard news of his sons and his boat. He expected his old comrade to be angry, to perhaps demand his blood in compensation, so he did not reveal that Sod and Nod had been sacrificed to water-devils. The riverman's reaction was not what he had anticipated. Scrymgeour was silent for a moment, then spoke in a quiet, resigned tone.

"Life on the river is hard...never certain. My boys, they died well?"

"Aye, plucky to the end. True rivermen, so they were."

Then, unexpectedly, Scrymgeour gave a half smile.

"They was good sons and good watermen, too. They died doin' their duty—ain't nothin' more to say. Lucky thing I've still got the hammer and tongs to forge a new son or two. Fire in the forge too."

†

Thurmond and Sarah were consumed with their plan to enter Staynes Hall that very night. Roscoe was not told of their mission. They said only that they would out for a while. Thurmond wanted to call upon an old friend, and Sarah had agreed to accompany him.

Sarah led them to the same abandoned warehouse where she and Thurmond had had their first conversation following their meeting in Staynes Hall. That had been the night he stole the mirror. It seemed ages ago, though she knew that it had not really been very long. But so much had changed since Thurmond entered her life.

As they approached the sagging door, she whispered to her companion.

"I know this part of the city fairly well. Once I discovered the secret passage from Father's library, I used to sneak out all the time. Mostly I just wandered around. I didn't have any place to go. But it was exciting to be out on my own, especially at night."

They entered the gloomy, cavernous edifice and made their way to a certain loose brick in a back wall. Sarah pushed the hidden lever that opened the secret passage. As they were about to step in, Thurmond had a thought.

"You said that your document was locked up in a cabinet. Is there a spell that can open it?"

"Certes, a knock spell."

"You know this spell?"

"Nay, I know it not."

Thurmond felt his skepticism beginning to return.

"Then how, may I inquire, are we to open said locked cabinet?"

"With this."

Sarah produced a short iron crowbar from her shoulder bag. It was one of the tools they had taken from the boat when preparing their incursion into the goblin cave. It had remained in her pannier throughout their adventure.

She grinned.

"Time for a little invisibility. I've got enough power back to cast it."

But noticing his doubtful expression, she grew a little miffed.

"Oh, cheer up, Thurmond, this will be fun."

Thurmond did not think that any of this was fun, but he stood quietly while Sarah chanted the incantation to invoke invisibility. He felt a slight current pass over him, not unlike the tickle of a cool gust of wind. Then there was a subdued *ppffftt*, the sound of air escaping from a punctured bladder. And then nothing. The spell had fizzled, and they both knew it. There would be no invisibility that night.

Sarah frowned and exhaled a long breath through her nose.

"Damn it! I was sure it would work. I don't know why…"

Her voice trailed off. Thurmond said nothing, just nodded toward the passage. He was not going to desert her at this point. They moved quickly along its length. It was pitch dark, but Sarah knew the way so well that they had no need of light. The latch at the far end was unconcealed, being on the inside of the door. She pulled it, and they stepped into the library of Lord Percy Staynes.

The room was as dim as Thurmond remembered it, illuminated only by two small oil lamps. This was the very room where he had first met Sarah in the guise of a lopsided, little man named Spoon. She started for the cabinet but froze when a voice came out of the gloom.

"Hello, Sarah. Welcome home."

A hitherto-unseen figure was seated behind the desk, shrouded in darkness. There was grave uncertainty in Sarah's voice as she turned and replied.

"Father?"

"Is that what you call me now? Not Master?"

"Isn't Father not more fitting?"

The figure lit candles that suffused the room with golden light.

"Who is with you?"

"His name is Thurmond. He's my friend."

"Well, friend Thurmond, welcome to my home. Draw nigh so that I might see your features. I am old, and my eyes are frail."

The man Thurmond encountered was sunk far into the deepest depths of decrepitude. His face was covered with ulcerating pustules. His breath wheezed, and his hands shook with a palsy. The whole room stank of age and corruption. Thurmond felt the hair on the back of his neck bristle in fear and disgust.

"Aye, look closely, friend Thurmond. Bear witness to the inevitable consequences of a life spent in the indulgence of sin. Mark it—mark it well.

"Now Sarah, what brings you and friend Thurmond sneaking in like thieves in the night? Why not enter your home in the proper manner, through the front?"

To Thurmond's surprise, she seemed entirely unaffected by the horror of the creature who spoke to her.

"I came for that which is my own. Something that you have held for me for quite some time, but something that I now require."

The old man gave a small, dry cackle. It touched off a spasm of coughing that ended with a throaty retch.

"Will you be needing this?"

He pushed a large iron key across the top of the desk.

"Go on, take it. That which you seek is right where you saw it last.

Now Sarah was taken aback.

"Then you knew that I rifled through your papers?"

"In this house, few things escape me. My servants have remained incomprehensibly loyal. Go on, open the cabinet."

Regaining her composure, Sarah did as instructed and withdrew a large parchment document she spread out on the desk. The formal language was beyond Thurmond's ability to read, but it all looked very correct and official. He saw Staynes's signature and his heraldic seal stamped in wax. Sarah gave it but a cursory glance.

"Aye, that is what I came for. My legal recognition as your daughter."

"Then take it. Be recognized."

He rolled the parchment and presented it to her with a mock flourish. She accepted it with a grateful nod.

"I don't suppose, Daughter, that you intend to stay and reside here once again—you and...perhaps...friend Thurmond."

This was entirely impossible. She had finally escaped from the confinement of Staynes Hall and was not about to relinquish her independence. To return to this roof would place her once again under the control of this capricious old man.

"I cannot. I have many things to attend to."

"'Tis a pity, but no matter. I understand. Say, have you any news of Bart... your, um...brother? They tell me he went off on some adventure and hasn't yet returned. Have you heard anything?"

Sarah regretted having to lie to the old man but decided it was for the best.

"Nary a word. But if I learn anything, I will come and tell you. What of young Gyre? Is he hale?"

The old man gave a sly, sardonic chuckle.

"Ah, Gyre. Of course you would be concerned for his health—of course. Hale? I would imagine so, but the young man is no longer with the household. His behavior became problematic, so he is now with the Blue Friars—as a novice, I believe. I have made arrangements for his future. He will enjoy a secure and peaceful life."

Sarah realized that her father's words were every bit as insincere as her own. Gyre, like Bart, longed to be a soldier, not a churchman. Yet he had been sent off to a monastery when his presence had become inconvenient for his grandfather. It was of no concern to the old man that the child would hate the life he had been forced into.

Yet this was also welcome news to Sarah, for by consigning Gyre to the church, her father had effectively placed the boy at an even greater distance in the line of succession.

"Father, we must away. I thank you for this document that names me your daughter. I will always be grateful for the kindness I received as a child in your house. Bless you, Father."

"Your words are well received. You make me hope that perhaps I have, in some small way, atoned for one or two of my many transgressions. Would it be too much to ask for a kiss before you depart?"

"Nay, of course not. I would be honored to do so."

So Sarah swallowed her revulsion and kissed the poxy cheek.

CHAPTER FIFTY-FIVE

A CONVERSATION WITH EARL RALF

As he had promised, Jarvis departed early to make the day-long journey to Earl Ralf's castle at Norwerk. Four armed guards and a body servant accompanied him, all mounted on well-fed, long-legged palfreys. The road was in fine repair, so they made good progress.

This was the Old Eastern Road, a military highway constructed for the rapid deployment of troops in times of war. In times of peace, it functioned, like the Royal Highway, as an artery for merchant caravans and travelers to and from the city of Gorgonholm. For this reason, it was most commonly referred to as the Golden Road.

Norwerk Castle was nearly ten leagues to the east of the city, so even with a smooth road and an excellent horse, Jarvis was tired and saddle sore by the time they arrived. He was an old man and over the years had grown unused to riding, but the business in which he was currently engaged was sufficiently compelling that he had dismissed all thoughts of caution and comfort.

There had been no time to send a messenger ahead to announce his coming or to ascertain that the earl would even be in residence. So he was relieved when Norwerk finally came into view atop an approaching hilltop.

The castle was a massive construction perched atop a steep outcropping of red rock. It had been enlarged and reinforced over the years so that a series of concentric battlements covered every conceivable avenue of approach. Huge towers frowned down in disapproval as Jarvis came within their shadows. A forbidding barbican led to a drawbridge that spanned a gap cut in the solid rock. On the far side, the gatehouse leered with arrow slit eyes.

The primary purpose of such castles was of course to provide a nearly impregnable defensive position against an invading army. Over the years, Norwerk had served well in this capacity. From time to time, invaders had entered the valley, burned the village, and slaughtered its population. The castle, however, had always withstood both assault and siege. Catapults had battered its towers, rams had pounded its gate, and scaling ladders had been thrust up against its wall, but no attacker had ever fought his way inside.

But Norwerk, like all castles, also had a more routine, daily function— to remind the earl's serfs and tenants of the awesome power of their feudal overlord. They must never be allowed to forget that Earl Ralf held their very lives in his hand. Norwerk Castle's grim visage was well suited for this doleful purpose.

As Jarvis and his retainers approached the barbican, two soldiers wearing the earl's personal badge crossed their spears, denying further access. Others could be seen in the shadows behind them, quickly donning helmets and retrieving weapons in case the callers should prove less than cooperative. One came forward, obviously the sergeant in charge of the guard detail.

"State your business, my man. Why do you approach the earl's residence?"

"You will please convey to the earl my compliments and inform him that Jarvis has come on the most urgent of matters—matters that concern the entire Mortimer family. He will be most desirous of this information."

He held out a gold sovereign as an inducement for cooperation, but to his surprise, the sergeant waved it away.

"The earl is a-hunting. I know not when he might return to the castle. You will have to wait."

With no better option, Jarvis settled down to do as suggested. He sent one of the soldiers to acquire lodging at Norwerk's only inn. His body servant, a thin, obsequious man named Milburn, was dispatched to make inquiries in the village and learn who had charge of the earl's schedule of audience.

Any number of needy people might have accumulated in his absence, and Jarvis did not want to have to wait in line. It would be much better to bribe his way to the front than to have to wait who knew how long for their whining, tawdry complaints to be heard.

Three days went by, and still the earl not returned. The accommodations were verminous, and the food was appalling, but there was nothing for it but to wait, because Earl Ralf, like all nobles, loved his hunting.

†

Norwerk was surrounded by an enormous tract of forest and pasture reserved as a royal hunting park. Only Mortimer and his favorites were allowed the use of it. Large parties of nobles and ranking churchmen, accompanied by an even larger group of servants and foresters, would be off for days at a time in pursuit of deer, boar, and sometimes bear. Their trained hawks were flown against heron, swan, and partridge. Even inedible beasts such as fox, badger, and otter provided wonderful sport.

Nights were spent in one of the several lodges scattered about the park. These were great rustic structures of hewn logs, each equipped with a massive stone fireplace where great haunches of venison and sides of pork were roasted. Here the nobility gathered at the end of each day's chase for bouts of riotous feasting and drinking. So much pleasure was had by all that the hunters were never eager to return to their various responsibilities.

To be honest, Earl Ralf was never overly concerned with his official duties. He held involvement in the mundane affairs of his county to be beneath his social station, so he was therefore content to leave such matters to his staff of civil servants. His main function as a noble, he believed, was to cut a fine figure and enjoy himself while so doing.

For all this, Mortimer was not a bad earl. When called upon to fulfill his feudal obligation as a vassal of the king, he was unfailingly prompt to comply. As Earl of Avincraik, he was duty bound to present himself and eight hundred armed followers, including a contingent of forty armored knights, for forty days service every year. In this capacity, he had proved himself a capable warrior and a successful leader of men.

He was an easy man to like. Tall and muscular, with a thick crop of curly black hair, the earl cut a dashing figure that women found irresistible. The strong line of his clean-shaven jaw suggested courage and force of character. He smiled readily.

His own vassals, villeins, and serfs found him much more congenial than his cruel and avaricious predecessor. They were mostly left to their own devices, which was much preferable to the harsh treatment the lower classes often received at the hands of their lords. Taxation was not excessive, nor were his punishments unduly severe.

One notable exception was the merciless treatment of those caught poaching within the bounds of the royal hunting park. The standard punishment was mutilation. Being apprehended with a hare or grouse might entail the lopping off of an ear or the blinding of an eye. Those with a stag might lose a hand or suffer castration. On occasion, a repeat offender would be hanged and his body displayed in a gibbet as a warning to all who thought to engage in such practices.

†

On the third day of Jarvis's stay in Norwerk, Earl Ralf returned, leading a procession of mounted nobles and clerics through the lanes of the village and up to the gates of the castle. Even attired for the rigors of the hunt, their clothing and equipment were of the finest kind—fur-lined hoods with golden clasps, tunics with embroidered sleeves, and hunting swords set with precious stones.

Jarvis recognized one rider as Boniface, the Bishop of Gorgonholm and the city's spiritual leader. The toes of his red boots were extended into long points. Beside him, a beautiful woman rode sidesaddle on a high-stepping field hunter.

Behind the nobles rode a double column of foresters—men dressed in the greens and browns of the woodlands, bows and hunting horns slung on their shoulders. They were surrounded by a pack of grinning, slobbering hounds that leaped and yipped in the sheer joy of their existence. Finally came the retinue of servants and peasants, many bearing long poles from which hung the carcasses of their quarry. Others carried thick-shafted, heavy-bladed boar spears.

It was a joyous return, and the local villagers tossed their hats in the air and cheered. Though the choicest cuts of meat would be reserved for the Quality, the less desirable portions would be doled out to the villagers. There would be suet and stomachs and lungs and guts. Tonight the local wives would be hard at work stuffing sausages. These people knew well the importance of cheering the return of their lord.

Though his bribes had been accepted, it was another two days before Jarvis was finally granted an audience with Earl Ralf. It was seldom that the earl heard any of the petitions of merchants, preferring to foist them off on his lackeys. Yet Jarvis was different. There was always something of interest when Jarvis came to speak to him.

Earl Ralf, like the vast majority of his class, lived in the realm of bodily sensation. The intellect was foreign—even suspect. Books, after all, were for clerks. If something needed to be read, it could be done for him. Yet for all this, the earl was not unintelligent. He immediately realized that Jarvis would bring something worth listening to.

Jarvis eyed the earl carefully. He saw a man in his middle thirties—strong, vigorous, and still youthful. A man who had yet to embrace the inevitability of his own decline and death. Their previous transactions would, he hoped, incline Mortimer in his favor. Nonetheless, the merchant had planned his approach carefully. He had even sent the earl a magnificent dagger in a silver-mounted sheath to help smooth the way.

Jarvis knew his scheme was fraught with peril. What was to prevent this powerful noble from having him seized and tortured until he told all he knew? He would undoubtedly feel fully justified in doing so, believing that the merchant was withholding information that would restore his rightful property. Why should he negotiate with an extortionist?

But Jarvis need not have worried, for Mortimer was well disposed toward him. The gift of the dagger was pleasant but unnecessary. It was the success of their prior dealings that truly opened the door.

The merchant had proved himself able to attend to highly confidential matters with aplomb and discretion. On various occasions, the earl had both purchased and sold certain items that no one else must learn of. So he trusted Jarvis—at least to the point that he could trust any commoner, particularly a merchant.

Jarvis approached the high seat and made a deep bow.

"Your Excellency, I have been made aware of a most urgent development that concerns both your honorable self and your illustrious family. It is of such import that I dare not speak it aloud. If you will condescend to receive the note I hold in my hand, you will be informed of the matter of which I speak."

"I will receive your note."

A gentleman of the court approached with a silver tray. Jarvis laid the note on it and watched as it was carried to the earl. A herald advanced, and at the earl's nod, picked up the note and read it. He immediately began to whisper in the earl's ear. The latter spun and fixed his gaze on Jarvis.

"Clear the room. The merchant and I must hold a privy conference."

Men-at-arms immediately rushed forward to remove the servants, courtiers, petitioners, and court staff. The soldiers followed the others out, leaving Jarvis and the earl alone inside.

"So, master merchant, what exactly can you tell me of my family's ancestral jewels?"

Jarvis was nervous but hid it well. He knew he could not afford to appear afraid or unsure. To display any emotion that could be mistaken for guilt or duplicity.

"They have been located, Your Excellency."

The earl's response was curt and cold.

"Tell me."

Jarvis knew he was on dangerous ground here. Should he reveal too much, the earl might grow suspicious, might have him tortured to discover the rest. Too little, and he would be discounted as a fraud and summarily dismissed—perhaps worse—perhaps much worse.

"Word has come from the far side of the river. The gems are in the possession of a certain Keltin chieftain living far back in the wilderness. The tribe is small but well regarded as formidable warriors."

"And who brought this word?"

"Smugglers, Your Excellency. Smugglers of uisge."

Jarvis hoped to bolster his facade of honesty by making such a blunt confession of illicit dealings with smugglers. Such a minor transgression, he knew, would be overlooked, for Mortimer liked his uisge too.

"How are these smugglers called?"

"I have prepared a list of names."

In fact, all the names on the list were fictitious. Should Mortimer have them investigated, Jarvis's deception would be revealed. Yet he handed the list to the earl and then made his most daring move.

"If it would please Your Excellency, I believe I am the man best able to restore your property."

Mortimer's eyes narrowed.

"How so?"

"Smugglers are a very secretive, very elusive breed. If they heard that they were sought—and they would most certainly hear of it—they would immediately disappear across the river. Yet they trust me of old and for certain inducements would, I am certain, be willing to reveal all they know.

"Once we learn the location of said tribe, the matter grows much more delicate. You could send soldiers across the river, but the various tribes would straightaway band together to achieve their annihilation. You know how many times that has happened in the past. Or the tribe in question could simply melt away into the far west."

The earl shifted in his seat, obviously impatient with the merchant's discouraging predictions.

"So what would you have me do?"

"I would ask that you permit me to recover your family property."

"What would you do that I could not?"

"I have in my employ a party of experienced Adventurers who could successfully penetrate the Keltin frontier where an army must fail. They are highly skilled in the languages and customs of the various tribes, and they have long-established friendships with many of the chieftains. All are expert woodsmen and deadly fighters.

"Further, they are unwaveringly honest and loyal, but my hired magicians can provide a rather compelling occult inducement to make doubly sure of this. They will return with the gems or die trying."

"And what would you ask for undertaking such a mission?"

"Naught, Your Excellency, other than your goodwill. If I fail, you will be no worse off and may proceed in whatever manner you see fit."

Earl Ralf gave a slight, disbelieving chuckle.

"Then this is the first time you have been motivated by less than the clink of coin."

"Aye, perhaps that is true. But I truly ask for nothing more than your friendship."

"Help me regain my family jewels, and I will indeed be your friend."

"Those, my gracious lord, are exactly the words I hoped to hear."

CHAPTER FIFTY-SIX

A FALLING OUT
AMONG FRIENDS

"It's got to be Sarah—can't you see that? We've got proof that Lord Staynes is her father. It's right here."

Thurmond gestured toward the parchment spread on the table. He was on one side, Roscoe on the other. Neither looked down at the document because neither could read it—the language was too formal. So they had only Sarah's word as to its contents. She remained on the far side of the room, reading from her book of magic and seemingly aloof from the argument that had been going on for three days. In truth she was riveted on every nuance of every word that had passed between the men. Thurmond had never before challenged Roscoe's authority as captain, but he was doing so now, and he was adamant.

"She's got the blood, so she is eligible for a grant of nobility herself. I'm certainly not fit for it. I think my papa was the village carpenter, but I can't even be sure of that. You told me that your father sold apples and made cider, so you're not born to the Quality either. Torgul is a lord among his own people, but he's a dwarf—he'd never be accepted here. It's got to be Sarah."

They had been over this same point again and again. If Jarvis was successful in his negotiations with Earl Ralf, they might soon be awarded a valuable tract of real property. One of them would be selected to hold the official tenure, to become the pledged vassal of the earl. But who would it be? This was the point on which they could not agree. The Brotherhood of Underworld Adventurers had laid down specific rules for the dividing of treasure, but there were no stipulations for awarding mastery over a feudal fiefdom.

Thurmond renewed his plea.

"As a lady of noble birth, Sarah could hold the land in her own right. Then we'd be safe. If it's you, we'll always be peasant tenants and at the mercy of some corrupt lordling with absolute power over us. I left that life behind when I ran away from my village. I don't want to go back to it."

Roscoe was plainly tired of arguing.

"Now, boyo, it wouldn't be so bad as all that. Freeholders are guaranteed specific rights by law and custom."

Thurmond's reply was heavy with sarcasm.

"Do you think Lord Drakar cares aught for the *guaranteed rights* of freeholders? He's the most brutal lord in the county. If he decided to take our holding, nobody would stop him. And as I said before, nobles don't pay taxes, so whatever we earn, we could keep for ourselves. Isn't that better than having the earl take most of what we have?"

Roscoe recognized that these were valid points. If Sarah received a grant of arms, she could hold land directly in her own right. As a freeholder, they would be little more than the earl's caretakers. But Roscoe knew he was the best choice. He had no particular ambition to rise in social class or to play the role of gentleman. He had no desire to exert control or command others to do his bidding. And he certainly did not want to create dissention among his friends. But he saw disaster looming if Sarah took charge.

"You're a fine, stout-hearted laddie, Thurmond, so you are. But a laddie you still be. You've not been out in the world long enough to see what befalls when a woman takes charge. I'll tell you what happens—nothing but trouble. The men around her see a woman as weak, even a smart, tough lassie like our Sarah, and they always try to grab away from her whatever there is to grab. I've seen it—I know how it is. It isn't right, but it is the way of things."

Thurmond rose to the challenge.

"Let them just try! With me and you and Torgul standing behind her— let anyone try to take something from Sarah."

"'Tis not that simple, not at all. You mentioned Drakar. He wouldn't care snap about her havin' a grant of arms. For certain, he'd see an opportunity and come callin'. Or maybe the Blue Friars would decide to double or triple our tithe—what then?"

"We could appeal to the earl."

"The earl? I'm afraid not, laddie. Drakar and the bishop are his most loyal supporters. He'd not risk offending them to save a minor noble—especially a female one."

After days of arguing, Thurmond was exhausted, frustrated, and angry—he blurted out the words without thinking.

"Are you a coward, Roscoe? Shying away from what you know is right because you're afraid to stand up for your friends?"

These were indeed serious words. An accusation of cowardice was a serious affront to a man's honor. In theory, only the nobility possessed honor—it was something they were born with and something they spent their lives trying to protect. But in sooth, all men possess an innate sense of dignity, and being called a coward is universally offensive. Such a challenge to one's honor could only be washed away in blood. The conversation stopped at once. Roscoe rose, gave Thurmond a penetrating look, and left the lodging without a word.

Sarah looked up. Thurmond, she knew, had in his pique made a serious tactical error. Up to that point, without even knowing it, he had played his part well—the part she had assigned to him after the visit to her father. His arguments had been well stated and cogent—the very arguments she had rehearsed with him again and again. But he had just made a terrible muddle of things by losing control and insulting Roscoe so gravely.

Her thoughts were interrupted when the imp began to buzz within its sealed jug. It had been doing this lately, which was strange, for it had been docile during their adventure. It was an unpleasant sound, as annoying as a persistent itch.

Sarah's thoughts returned to the problem at hand. Thurmond was such a sweet boy. She cared about him, really, but lately she had begun to question those feelings. She could not allow her involvement with Thurmond and the others to keep her from what was rightfully hers.

The imp began to buzz more stridently than before. A maddening sound that broke her concentration and seemed to be digging into her brain. She forced her thoughts back to her current dilemma—what do to about Roscoe. The old man wanted to claim the reward for recovering the gems. He might argue that it would be the best course for all of them, but she saw clearly that the old Adventurer, like herself, was most interested in his own advancement.

She was undeniably the rightful heir to her father's title and holding, but she needed the earl to officially recognize her claim. The name *Lady Sarah Staynes* must be entered in the roll of the kingdom's nobility—that must be their reward, a patent of nobility for herself. Only that would bring her the independence she had always longed for.

In his jug the imp continued to buzz.

✝

Outside on the street, Roscoe struggled to regain control of himself. That a mere stripling boy would dare to speak to him in such a manner was beyond comprehension. Such disrespect could not borne. He knew what he should now do, yet how could he raise his hand to a fine laddie like Thurmond?

Roscoe was correct, of course, about the problems women faced when they assumed any position of power. There had been times in the past when a queen ruled a kingdom in her own right, but these were always periods of civil strife as greedy nobles attempted to wrest her power for their own. It was the unfortunate way of the world.

But that was not the only reason he was so stubbornly opposed to Sarah's holding sway. He had, of late, seen something about her he did not fully trust. On one hand, he knew her for a fine lassie, and he loved her dearly, but he did not believe she could withstand the corrupting influence of power. Should she gain the title of nobility she so desperately craved, she would, he believed, no longer remain the Sarah they all admired. She would become like all the other nobles—selfish, cold, and cruel. It broke his heart to think of bonnie Sarah as such a person.

There was only one possible remedy for such grim thoughts, a few pots of the Severed Head's strong ale. But as he headed off down the narrow, twisty lanes toward that sacred spot, he became aware of footsteps padding along behind him. He spun, hand on the hilt of his sword, and found himself staring into the face of Torgul. He was back! And much, much sooner than expected, and he still had the axe.

The dwarf remained silent, recognizing instantly that Roscoe was deeply distraught. He knew his comrade would open to him when the time was right. He just gestured, and they headed off toward the Head. Once ensconced inside and with a mug of ale in hand, Roscoe told his unfortunate tale. Torgul said nothing—there was nothing that needed to be said. He understood Roscoe's quandary perfectly. Instead, he explained why he had come back to Gorgonholm so directly.

"Made good time gettin' home to Spear Mountain. After I left you at that village, I stole a horse as soon as I could and rode hard. When he was used up, I stole another, then another, and so on. So I got there much quicker than you'd expect."

Roscoe raised an eyebrow.

"So you've become a horse thief now? That's a fine thing for an Adventurer in good standin', so it is."

"I was in a hurry, you see. Anyway, I left gold for the first one, and after that left a horse as good as the one I took.

"I was pretty pleased with myself and eager to show off for my relatives who look down on me for associatin' with you humans. So, imagine how let down I was when they told me this ain't the real Axe of Lodbrok at all. Just the Axe of the Pretender."

Roscoe swigged his beer.

"Who would that be now?"

"Some mountebank who came in years ago claimin' to be the reincarnation of Lodbrok the Thunderer and tryin' to pass off this axe as the original. There were more than a few simpletons who believed him and started callin' him the True King. He gained quite a following for a while.

"As you can imagine, this didn't sit so good with the aristocracy. They're a hardheaded and old-fashioned bunch, and they naturally tend to take exception to anythin' that challenges their authority. So they drove all them shit-for-brains out of Spear Mountain—sent the pretender and his followers into exile."

Roscoe seemed saddened by the story.

"Seems like dwarves is just like men—they'll try anythin' to grab some power, so they will. Sorry things didn't work out for you like you wanted. It's a nice axe, though."

Torgul nodded.

"Aye, I'm gonna hang onto it. I named it Bloodtroll."

The inn's door opened, and two familiar faces entered—Bodo and Lars. Roscoe gestured for them to join him. They had, they said, come to the Head hoping to share a mug of ale with their new master. Bodo needed a break from his squalling children, Lars from the insatiable appetite of Bodo's sister-in-law.

†

In his castle at Norwerk, Earl Ralf and Jarvis smiled and drank a toast in honor of their joint undertaking. An agreement had been reached, an agreement so secret that no one but themselves knew all the details. The earl's relatives, the myriad of Mortimers who enjoyed high station and privilege throughout the kingdom, were not informed. Even King Trancred was not to be made privy to the intimate details.

Dispatch riders were sent flying south and west. Soon after, armed troops from various feudal holdings would be marching toward Gorgonholm. But Earl Ralf's personal retinue was not mustered, and his banner remained in place above the castle gate. In Norwerk, all was to remain at peace.

Jarvis was overflowing with relief and satisfaction as he watched his servant pack the heavy chests on two mules. As he had anticipated, the earl had been generous. Jarvis protested that he would, as promised, bear the entire expense of the upcoming expedition, but the earl wanted the Adventurers to be well equipped and richly rewarded.

Earl Ralf had also provided additional men to supplement Jarvis's guard. But they had been required to doff the earl's livery and dress as ordinary hired soldiers. The earl did not want to appear directly involved in any fashion.

Jarvis would have to concoct a smashing tale of how his party of Adventurers had recovered the Mortimer treasure trove. It would have to be carefully tailored to suit the primitive tastes of the warlike earl—so lots of heroics and gory details. He must remember to include a step-by-step description of how the heroes donned their armor before the final battle. The Quality always loved such scenes. The earl, he was sure, would believe every word.

And of course the Adventurers would have to die, one by one, surrounded by heaps of their fallen foes. Only one, Roscoe, would survive to deliver the gems and receive his reward. He just hoped the old Adventurer could keep the story straight if Earl Ralf felt inclined to inquire about the undertaking.

Not that the earl was likely to be overly curious. Jarvis assumed that as soon as he had the gems in hand, he would quickly forget how they had come to be there. Such was the way with nobles. Mortimer was his friend for the momentand had rewarded him handsomely, but he could not expect their friendship to be recalled the next time they met. Such trepidations were minor—just part of doing business. So the merchant was, in his own understated manner, quite gleeful as he made his way home. It is, of course, in such moments of high expectation that Lady Fortune delights in giving her wheel a spin.

Jarvis's horse gave an awkward lurch as it shied from the wavering shadow of a windblown branch. The merchant's knee was badly wrenched, and his party was forced to put up in a roadside inn for several days while a wisewoman, summoned from a nearby cave, treated his injury with poultices and charms. Thus, Jarvis entirely missed the great, clamorous entrance of Lord Drakar into Gorgonholm—an event he and Earl Ralf had already set in motion. Even before Jarvis had departed Norwerk, messengers on swift coursers had been sent to the landed nobles of County Avincraik, summoning them and their followers to war.

CHAPTER FIFTY-SEVEN

BOWS AND BILLS

Lady Renata de la Pole was in one of her foul moods that evening. She had been having a lot of them lately. And as usual when taken by a fit of the vapors, she took it out on her tableware. One by one, a complete set of imported glass goblets—very expensive—was smashed against the stones of the hearth. These were followed by an elaborate silver service, engraved with her family coat of arms. She was well and truly pissed.

Her brother, Lord Drakar, the county's most fearsome warlord, wanted to reduce her stipend. He claimed to need the money to fund another one of his stupid expeditions, another foray over the river to take treasure from the Keltin tribes. He was always going off on some such nonsense, raiding a village or sacking a town. When would he learn that these jaunts never seemed to bring in any real wealth?

Renata suspected that he actually enjoyed his escapades—sleeping rough, eating horrible food, wearing the same clothing day after day. But please— could he not find someone closer to home to terrorize? Someone he would not need a small army to defeat? Someone cheaper to kill? Drakar was just impossible!

If he cut her income, how could she afford the things she required. Food that was fit to eat, apparel befitting her station, new tableware? Her rage redoubled. She threw a jewel-studded chalice to the floor and crushed it underfoot. It had cost more than the average worker could earn in five years of labor.

And now she had learned that the thieving stable boy had returned to the city. She had found him in spite of their cloaking spell because Aborax's psychic signature had suddenly grown so strong. He got like that when he was angry. He must be hungry, the poor little dear. He was always so cranky when he did not eat. The stupid peasant had no doubt neglected to feed him. Well, she soon enough would attend to that.

Her spies had performed well. They had asked questions, observed, listened, and finally found the stable boy and his friends huddled in a squalid tenement in the Merchant Quarter. The magician, that ugly, crook-shouldered little man, was not among them. Instead there was some silly little bitch, no doubt the thief's slut, and a fat old lummox with a gimpy leg. They all had to die.

It was said that the gimp kept company with a dwarf. A dwarf! By all the demons in hell! Had those people forsaken the last vestige of decency? The very thought of associating with such a hairy, little beast filled her with revulsion.

She had had, to date, no luck in eliminating these contemptible, lowborn vermin. Father James had failed, as had Rupert's assassins, as had her pet demon. Even her itch spell had missed its mark. Rupert had also fallen short, though he had, at least, the good taste to die as a consequence. Poor, pitiful Rupert—she would miss his long, curled hair.

She began to consider her best course of action. If this bothersome thief was to be dispatched once and for all, she would, she realized, have to do it herself. Since there was no reason to delay, she prepared to go at once and perform this not-unpleasant task. The night would be dark and cold, so she donned her long black cape, the hood trimmed with sable. Her gown was scarlet embroidered with gold. She pulled on long black gloves of the softest kid leather and caught up her staff of power.

She then summoned her guards. These had been sent over by her brother. They were not regular liveried soldiers but hired mercenaries—undisciplined, ill mannered, and slovenly. There was, however, a dozen of them, which would be more than sufficient to dispose of the stable boy's rabble.

Renata would deal with the stable boy personally. She also looked forward to her reunion with Aborax. She knew the imp would be equally delighted to return to her loving care. He might be a bit peevish at first, but she knew how to bring him around. She need only hold him back with her magic staff while she whispered the spell of binding. And then he would be happy to return to her service—especially since she knew which little treats he really, really liked.

She called for her carriage to be brought to the door. It was nearly two leagues between her tower and the dreadful slum dwelling where her target had taken up residence. Even to such a dreadful location, she would go in style, in a gilded coach drawn by four night-black horses. A noble lady must, after all, keep up appearances.

Renata had heard that some of her sister sorceresses actually flew through the air while sitting on brooms. While it would be no great feat to cause a broom to fly, she could not imagine trying to maintain one's balance on such a thing. And sitting astride the narrow handle must be uncomfortable in the extreme.

She had in her workshop a jar of special salve that would have let her sail through the air without need of a broom or any other such contrivance. But it smelled bad, and the stench seemed to linger for days on her skin and in her hair. Far better to take the carriage. It would afford her extra time to plan her attack—not that she expected much in the way of opposition. Renata was a powerful witch. The stable boy and his friends find themselves at her mercy—and she had none.

Her anger rose when the carriage took longer to be brought than she expected. Her staff of servants were well versed in their mistress's emotional upheavals. They knew that they must remain well hidden while she was on the rampage but be instantly available as soon as the period of madness passed and she called for them to come and clean up her mess.

On this occasion, the unfortunate grooms had hidden themselves a bit too deeply and missed the call for the carriage. By the time they got word, harnessed the horses, and brought the carriage to the door of her tower, Lady Renata was again in a red rage. How dare these bungling insects make her wait! They would suffer for this.

Punishing her servants always made her feel better after something aroused her ire. The giving of pain was a remarkable panacea, as if she were actually able to transfer her own torments onto these lesser creatures. It was extraordinary, but for whatever reason, seeing them writhe always cheered her up.

So the grooms would suffer. On a bad day they might have had to die before she could feel the needed relief. But this time they would probably receive nothing worse than a vigorous lashing. The death of the stable boy thief would no doubt go a long way toward smoothing her ruffled feathers, and so the grooms would get off lightly.

She mounted her carriage and settled into the plush cushions inside. The driver snapped his whip, and the horses leaped forward into the night. They too were well schooled and obeyed with alacrity. The twelve guards mounted their steeds and followed in a ragged column of twos.

†

Roscoe, Torgul, Bodo, and Lars left the Severed Head tavern and headed back toward their old lodging in the Merchant Quarter. It was Roscoe's intention as captain to declare the adventure officially at an end. He would see that Thurmond and Sarah received their fair share of the treasure, but the bond between them was to be dissolved. He felt terrible about it, but events had come to such a sorry pass that he saw no other option. He must break with Thurmond entirely or else kill him.

Their friendship had been badly damaged by Sarah's manipulation of Thurmond and the boy's blind loyalty to her. She had become so consumed by her own pretensions, by her overpowering desire to join the nobility, that she had forgotten it was friendship that had carried them through so many trials.

The old Adventurer knew Sarah was, in her heart, a good and caring person, but the corrupting influence of ambition was destroying those qualities. You could not trust such a person. And Thurmond had to learn to think for himself. He was quite intelligent, but he was far too eager to let the girl do his thinking for him. This was always dangerous, especially when the other person was as self-centered as Sarah was becoming. So Roscoe's heart was indeed heavy as they made their way up the last dark, narrow lane.

Oddly, the fancy carriage of some wealthy noble was blocking the street directly in front of the stairs of the lodging. A woman in a long black cape was descending from its open door, assisted by a groom. Behind it, an armed escort held the reins of their mounts. The woman stared at Roscoe for a moment, offered a brief smile of recognition, and pointed straight at his face.

"That's them! They're the ones you want. Kill them all!"

The soldiers began to advance. Their weapons were out, and they appeared to be in deadly earnest.

Surprised as he was, Roscoe hesitated for only a moment before springing to action. His reflexes, always keen, had been well honed by their recent adventure. A two-wheeled handbarrow stood propped against an adjacent wall, where its owner had left it after dumping a load of cobblestones. Roscoe seized it by one wheel and toppled it sideways so that it formed a barrier between himself and the attackers.

It was a pathetic barricade, but it gave his companions a chance to prepare for the oncoming rush. They had not anticipated trouble, so they wore no armor. Roscoe carried his sword on his hip, but Torgul's axe was swathed in cloth and tied across his back. There was no time to loosen it, so he drew his scramasax. Bodo and Lars carried nothing more than small belt knives.

The dwarf took a position on the right side of the upturned barrow. Roscoe stood on the other. Bodo found a wooden-bladed shovel and joined him. Lars came up with a cobblestone in each hand.

The attackers were brash, confident of an easy victory over a rabble of untrained peasants. All were well armed, and protected by leather, mail, and iron caps. Had Renata's men been more thoughtful, they would have won the battle within moments of beginning it, but their attack was sloppy and disorganized. They came on in no discernible formation, with only one or two carrying small shields.

A large, bearded man was the first to die. He came charging around the barrow's right side several steps ahead of his comrades. Torgul darted around the corner of the barricade and stabbed him deftly in the groin just beneath his mailshirt. A look of puzzlement came over the man's face. He took a step backward and collapsed.

In the next moment, two of his comrades came at Roscoe on the other side. The old Adventurer preferred, when possible, to counterpunch—to allow his opponent to throw the first blow. He would block it and then deliver an immediate riposte while the attacker was out of proper position to defend himself. It was a tactic that often worked well for him. On this occasion, however, he did not get the chance to use this trick. As the first mercenary came around the barrow, Bodo struck his upraised sword arm with the edge of his shovel, knocking the weapon from his grasp. Roscoe shrugged and drove his sword under his chin and up into the brainpan. That did for him.

The second man paused, unnerved by the plight of his companion, and this was his undoing. He caught the flat of Bodo's shovel full in the face. Bodo was a lean man but immensely strong from years of manual labor. The force of the blow sent the soldier over backward and snapped the shovel's head from its haft.

All the while, Lars had kept a steady barrage of cobblestones flying over the barrow. A loud yelp from the other side told that one of the missiles had gone home. Realizing that their foes were much more capable than anticipated, the mercenaries drew back and began to organize a battle line. The lull was brief, and they soon pushed forward again.

This time the assault was more circumspect. Two men with demi-lances began to jab furiously over the side of the upturned barrow. Lars, in the midst of throwing another cobble, was skewered just above the wrist. He stared in horror at the iron lance point projecting from the side of his forearm. Without shields, the Adventurers had no defense against these weapons and were left with no option other than to retreat back out of range. The attackers at once seized hold of the barrow and pulled it to one side.

Roscoe saw the hopelessness of their position. Their foes, in spite of their losses, still outnumbered them by two to one. Their spears, shields, helmets, and mail gave them a tremendous advantage over his own unarmored and under-armed party. Bodo now had nothing more than a broken shovel handle. Lars stood behind them, trying to staunch the blood flowing from his wound. Deprived of the feeble protection of the barrow, they were left entirely exposed.

With nothing else to do, they fell back to a recessed doorway beneath the overhanging upper story of a nearby shop. The position's defensive value was minimal, but it would keep them from being entirely surrounded. Torgul tried the door, seeking a possible avenue of escape, but it was firmly barred.

The attackers saw all this and broke into laughter. Their quarry was cornered and helpless. Their fallen comrades would soon be avenged.

Lady Renata stood on the step of her carriage, watching the battle unfold, fascinated by the drama she had set in motion. It was amazing how willingly these stupid peasants would risk their lives just for the chance to kill one another. The desperation in their faces delighted her.

But now it was time for her to act. She descended from the carriage and climbed the stairs leading to the apartment where she knew she would find the thief and his slut—and good Aborax, of course. Roscoe saw her leave the carriage, mount the stairs, and disappear through the door of their lodging. Then he saw the mercenaries lining up for another assault and forgot all about the unknown woman.

A thought struck Roscoe, and he began to bellow as loudly as he could.

"Bills and bows! Bills and bows! To me! To me, citizens! Bills and bows!"

This was the traditional rallying cry of the population of Gorgonholm, the signal against impending attack and dire emergency. When it was given, every citizen, old and young, was required by law and custom to come running to the defense of their city. But would any heed his call?

The cry was not to be given lightly. Woe be to any who roused the citizenry without just cause. Roscoe doubted that the armed mercenary band posed any threat to the city, but he was beyond caring at that moment. So he opened his mouth and bellowed some more.

"Bills and bows! Bills and bows!"

The attackers were entirely unfazed by his antics. During the lull, several had unstrapped shields from their horses' saddles. They were now forming into a proper assault formation with shields in the front and longer weapons reaching forward from behind. Their next attack would be unstoppable.

At that moment, however, windows were thrown open in the rooms just above the Adventurers' heads. A torrent of random household articles were hurled down on Renata's soldiers—pots and pans, shoes, a rotten cabbage, several onions, a live chicken, a cat. One man went down when struck squarely on the head with a heavy three-legged stool. Another was scalded by a tureen of boiling soup.

The mercenaries again stepped back, beyond the range of this unforeseen bombardment, but still holding Roscoe and the others at bay in the doorway. Two now ran to retrieve crossbows from their saddles. There would be no reason to close with their quarry. They need only stand back and shoot them down. Death was very near.

Lady Fortune has always been a fickle old girl who delights in the most fanciful acts of capriciousness. So she must have been feeling especially whimsical at that moment when the destruction of Roscoe and his party seemed as certain as a thing could be. The fact that they did not die that night can be attributed only to her direct intervention.

As the crossbows were being drawn and loaded, Roscoe was preparing for a suicidal lunge into the midst of his enemies—far better to go down fighting than to passively wait to be shot. But this never came to pass. Of a sudden, the street was filled with citizens rushing to answer the call to arms. Cooks with cleavers and toasting forks, smiths with hammers, stablemen with rakes and pitchforks. Goodwives with rolling pins, fry pans, and distaffs. Bullyboys with swords, and apprentices with stout oak cudgels. Others came with barrel staves, fence posts, and the spokes of wagon wheels.

Dogs snarled and snapped at their masters' sides. Blind beggars waved their walking staves, butchers their meat hooks. Painted doxies produced concealed daggers. The raw might of the populous was thus unleashed upon Renata's soldiers as they rushed up the street with a shrill, inhuman cry.

Roscoe immediately leaped forward, calling for the others to follow him. They did so with alacrity. He smashed directly—shield to shield—into the foremost mercenary, his great body weight knocking the man to the ground. Before the soldier could recover, Lars fell upon him, knife in his hand, and cut his throat. Torgul came in low and sliced the tendons behind the knee of another. As he fell, Bodo battered him with the shovel handle.

The mercenaries recognized the futility of their position and turned to flee, but even as they tried to mount their horses, the mob was upon them, pulling them from their saddles. A few managed to break away, but these were brought down by a similar throng of citizenry approaching from the other direction. The doomed men were bludgeoned, kicked, stabbed, and throttled. Their deaths were hard and bloody but mercifully quick.

Even before the last had fallen, the mob's attention changed from blood lust to looting. Discarded weapons were scooped up and carried off. Horses were led down adjacent alleys. The bodies were stripped of their armor, boots, belts, and pouches—then tunics, breeches, and even small clothes. Soon there was naught but a dozen nude or near-nude bodies strewn upon the cobbles.

Renata's carriage remained untouched. Its role in the incident was unknown to the crowd, and the grooms, huddling on the roof, wanted no part of the action going on around them. The vehicle was obviously the property of some great noble, so the ireful citizens were reluctant to defile it. Thus, the carriage and grooms were spared the fate of the hapless mercenaries.

With no one left to kill and no more booty to gather, the mob dispersed as quickly as it had appeared. Best not to be nearby if Sheriff Brandon and his constables arrived. Anyway, they now had more pressing business. There was loot to be sold.

CHAPTER FIFTY-EIGHT

LADY RENATA PAYS A CALL

It was a bad night. Thurmond was appalled by what he had said to Roscoe. He sat alone by the hearth fire, absentmindedly feeding small sticks into the tiny blaze. He had attempted to distract himself by practicing his reading, but his mind kept wandering. The old Adventurer was deserving of his respect and gratitude, yet he had spoken to him as if he were shit in the road. Where had those words come from?

He recalled the conversations that had passed between himself and Sarah over the past few days. Had his words to Roscoe not been the very words Sarah had been whispering in his ears all the while? What was happening to him? To her? Why was she so utterly consumed by the need to join the nobility? What would become of them if she succeeded?

He recalled her imperious manner when they were first met. Were she to become Lady Sarah, could not that girlish thoughtlessness deepen into the sneer of cold command worn by so many nobles?

When they had fled the stable and moved into their first lodging, she had summarily commandeered the backroom for her own use. He had, at the time, thought of her as a spoiled child of privilege. But could her actions not signify an inherent selfishness—perhaps the nobleman's repugnant sense of entitlement?

But most troublesome of all was that her temper was so quick to flare when thwarted. Nobles were like that. When angered, they need not restrain themselves, but they could vent their ire on their underlings in the cruelest fashion. Would Sarah act in such a fashion?

Thurmond was dismayed by the gulf that had grown between them ever since their return to the city. She was not the same girl who had kissed him after he pulled the witch bat from her hair. Nor the one who had wept so hard when they saw Torgul fall into the river. She had grown more and more humorless and withdrawn. She paced the floor of their lodging in a state of unremitting distraction. She had even taken to carrying that damnable demon jug under her arm.

He had a strange thought. He had always assumed that the most horrible monsters loitered in underground dens, but perhaps that was untrue. Was there not a loathsome beast within some people that was more horrible than a goblin or a troll? A beast that ate them from the inside until they could no longer feel friendship or loyalty or love?

Roscoe had once told him that he did not yet understand the bigger concerns of being an Adventurer, but maybe now he was beginning to see it. Perhaps it was less important to slay fell beasts in the underworld than to overcome the dark creature that gnawed within one's own breast.

He began to see that his unyielding devotion to Sarah had been foolish and destructive. Instead of helping her resist her beast, he had enabled her to serve it. As a result, she was growing cold, distant, and self-absorbed. Roscoe, his mentor and boon companion, was now his enemy—most likely a mortal foe. And his great dream of joining the Adventurers was shattered forever. But maybe there was still hope for Sarah. He rose to confront her.

Sarah was on the far side of the room, sorting through the battered pannier in which she had carried her magical supplies during their long adventure. She removed the items one by one and placed them on a table—the magical tome she had stolen from the dead shaman's hut, the wand Whisper had charged with power, her anthame, her pen, and the ink pot Torgul had given her, with her name inscribe in gold. The dried mushrooms Nod and Sod had taken from the kobolds. Here too was the root sprout still potted in her helmet. And of course the demon jug.

She mused to herself—Lady Sarah Staynes. She liked the sound of that. Was that not her true and rightful name? Bart was dead, and her father had confirmed her parentage. She had only to secure the earl's acknowledgment of that fact.

She had, as a child, always felt so helpless, so completely dependent on a father she seldom saw and rarely spoke to. He had never been cruel, but he had always remained aloof, so she had always feared that she might say or do something that would cause his favor to be withdrawn. She had never known how or where she fit in or who she really was. Not a servant, but not a daughter, either. She had always been an outsider in a household in which everyone else had, for good or ill, a defined position. But who was she?

Sarah craved the title. It would define her, and the wealth would allow her to pursue her own interests without the interference of a father, husband, or brother. Allow her to move beyond the lingering fear that a single misstep might lead to her downfall. Thurmond had created a large obstacle when he angered Roscoe. It would not be easy to bend the old man to her will, but his cooperation would be necessary if her plan was to be carried through. So how was she to get to Roscoe? What would force him to agree?

The sounds of fighting outside interrupted her thoughts. Street brawls were far from uncommon, but this one was much louder than normal and had the sound of an actual battle. It continued for several minutes. Then the imp began to buzz more loudly than ever before. Something was clearly agitating it.

Though securely bolted, the outer door swept open, and Lady Renata stood before her, magnificent in her black cape and blood red gown. Sarah looked up in shock and made the mistake of gazing into Renata's eyes. In that instant she was caught, frozen, unable to move or speak or help herself.

Hearing the screams and clash of swords from outside, Thurmond too fell victim as he instinctively turned his eyes toward the intruder. He found himself paralyzed, fully aware of all about him but entirely unable to command his own body.

Renata laughed. It had been even less difficult than she expected. She had taken them so easily. They would have no choice now but to obey her every whim, so she might as well have some fun. Thurmond, she saw, was not unattractive in an unrefined sort of way. He was no Rupert, certainly, but perhaps he would do for a while—if he could be trained. A bit of grooming would be necessary, and he would have to grow his hair so she could curl it. And he did have lovely eyes.

Her gaze returned to Sarah. She was a comely little tart if you liked them young, but a bit too tall and muscular for her taste. No matter—she had to die. She spied Sarah's anthame on the table before her. Perfect! She would have the silly bitch run its point through her own eye and into her brain. And she would make her do it slowly, as slowly as the human hand can move, so that the pain would be drawn out for an excruciating length of time. All the while, the girl would be fully aware of what she was doing but completely unable to keep herself from doing it.

Renata gave the command and Sarah obeyed. As if seized by a great languor, her hand inched along the tabletop in tiny increments, and her fingers closed with a desperate sluggishness around the hilt of the anthame. Renata was so taken with her own cleverness that she squealed with delight and gave a small skip. Now the dagger was being lifted ever so gradually from the table.

The sorceress saw the book lying beside what looked to be an old ale jug. She recognized it as a grimoire, and she wanted it. She turned again to Thurmond.

"You, boy, bring me the book."

The point of the anthame was rising steadily toward Sarah's eye as Thurmond moved to comply. But as he reached for the tome, his finger inadvertently brushed the slim stalk of the root sprout. Instantly, a surge of wholesome earth energy coursed through his body. It was the clean, natural power of towering trees and clear running springs. The witch's spell was instantly broken, but he had the good sense not to show it.

Renata had in the meantime remembered her imp and was nosing about the room in search of him, knocking beneath the furniture and poking in the corners with her magic staff. The spell with which she had originally summoned and controlled it had long since expired, but she need only whisper certain words to regain its obedience.

"Here, Aborax! Here, kitty! Come to Mama! Kitty, kitty, kitty, kitty…"

Thurmond kept his face as blank as possible as Renata bent to search around the hearth.

"Aborax! Where are you, you bad kitty? Mama has a treat for you. Here kitty, kitty."

As soon as her back was turned, Thurmond sprang into motion. He snatched the demon jug from the table, gave it a hearty shake to aggravate the thing within, and threw it with all his might against the hearth where Renata stood. It struck the stones and smashed to pieces, releasing the imp. The anthame was now but a finger's breadth from Sarah's eye. He knocked it from her hand, grabbed her by the wrist, and pulled her from the lodging, slamming the door behind him.

Sarah had been correct in her prediction that the imp would emerge from the jug infuriated by its long imprisonment and seeking vengeance on whoever was at hand. Caught entirely by surprise, Renata had no opportunity to defend herself, and Aborax gave her no chance to whisper the words of binding or to protect herself with her staff. It fell upon her with tooth and claw, exacting in its blind wrath a terrible revenge for its long confinement. Renata died there, her body slashed from head to toe as though cut by a thousand knives.

The demon's attack released Sarah from the spell that bound her. She and Thurmond fled down the steps of their lodging, while a cacophony of shrieks and growls emanated from above. A mephitic stench descended on the street as Aborax departed for the infernal realms. The people in the street groaned as a spasm of nausea passed briefly through their bellies as it sailed overhead.

In spite of the rampaging mob, Renata's grooms had dutifully waited with the carriage, anticipating their mistress's return. But the hellish reek was too much for the horses. They bolted in a panic, knocking the grooms from their sanctuary on the vehicle's roof. Befuddled and afraid, they hesitated for only a moment before following the stampeding horses with all possible haste.

Reaching the street, Sarah sat down on a doorstep, buried her face in her hands, and began to sob. They were the painful racking sobs of a soul in torment. Thurmond had never seen her in such complete distress, not in any of their dangerous encounters or desperate dealings. Not knowing what else to do, he sat beside her and encircled her shoulders with his arm. She seemed not to notice. When the sobs continued unabated, he grew concerned and whispered in her ear.

"Sarah, it's all over now. We're safe now. Please stop crying."

This seemed to get her attention. Her breath hitched, and she lowered her hands to reveal a face smeared with tears and snot. When she spoke, her voice came hoarse and ragged.

"You saved me, Thurmond, from that horrible witch."

"Aye, I'm sure she's dead. We're both safe now."

"I...that's not it...aughhh..." Her voice again broke into a gargled sob.

"I'm certain she's dead, Sarah. The imp got her."

"Nay, nay, you misunderstand. You saved me from becoming like her."

"Me? How did I do that?'

"By just being here with me. You are the only thing that stopped me from growing as cold and evil as she was. I could feel it coming over me ever since we got back to the city—the selfishness and the greed. A feeling no one else mattered. But that's over now. I think an evil spell has been broken. I'm sure I'm me again."

She once more dissolved into tears, and Thurmond, sitting at her side, began to sob just as hard as she.

Then Roscoe appeared, standing over them as they sat huddled together, as frightened and lonely as either of them had ever been before. Torgul and the others held back several paces, giving Roscoe the chance to confront the boy on his own.

"What has happened here, boyo?"

"Oh, Roscoe, I'm so glad..."

Thurmond was slipping into incoherence, so Roscoe took him by the shoulders and drew him to his feet. He stared straight into his eye.

"Get yourself under control, hang-around. What has happened here?"

These words helped to restore the boy's reason. He began to tell the story, and as he did, Sarah ceased to cry and rose to join them. When it was finished, he looked away in shame.

"Why have you come back?"

Roscoe chose to conceal the real reasons. He was reluctant to declare the adventure officially at an end. He had yet to hear from Jarvis and thought perhaps a message might have arrived at the lodging in his absence.

The real reason, though, was that he wanted to see Thurmond and Sarah.

The souring of their friendship had saddened him deeply. He missed the camaraderie and good cheer they once shared. So he lied.

"I came for the rest of my gear, but instead I found you two sittin' there, obviously in the deepest of shite."

Thurmond abruptly blurted out.

"I'm sorry. You've always been my friend, but I acted like a stupid peasant. I'm not worthy to be your friend or an Adventurer. I know you'll never forgive me—I wouldn't ask it. But I want you to know that I didn't mean what I said. I'd take the words back if I could."

Roscoe felt a great relief wash over him. With the terrible insult withdrawn, he was no longer obliged to spill Thurmond's blood.

"Laddie, you didna act so much like a stupid peasant as like a stupid noble. Sarah too. We'll have to talk this out, you and her and me. But doin' that will require a mug or two of ale. Is there any in the lodgin'?"

With that, they gathered the others, mustered their courage, and crossed the threshold. Things were not as bad as they had expected, for the lodging and the furnishings were relatively intact. The potted tree spirit remained healthy and unharmed.

Renata's mutilated carcass lay in the inner room surrounded by shards of the shattered demon jug. Her long black staff was beside her. Roscoe kicked it into the blazing hearth, where it twisted like a snake with a broken back. When the flames took hold, it burned to ash.

Only then did the old Adventurer think to ask a very important question. "Who was she?"

Sarah was the only one with any idea.

"She was the woman I saw in the magic mirror. She was talking to the curly-haired bastard Thurmond killed on the riverbank. She had to be a witch—she sent her pet demon after me."

Thurmond looked at the corpse and then at Torgul.

"River or pigs?"

CHAPTER FIFTY-NINE

LORD DRAKAR COMES TO TOWN

Several days later, Gorgonholm was awakened by a great ballyhoo. A large contingent of armored cavalry came pounding into town, the hooves of their horses casting up a shower of mud and dung from the city streets. They thundered over the drawbridge exactly at dawn and entered through the South Gate as soon as the startled gatekeepers could swing it open.

A trumpeter and a herald rode well ahead of the rest to clear the way of merchant carts or delivery wagons. Lord Drakar de la Pole was not accustomed to being delayed. A huge banner displayed the black and silver arms of the de la Poles—a viper swallowing a baby. Everyone recognized these arms and knew to keep their distance.

The cavalcade proceeded straight up Castle Wynd, the powerful war steeds climbing the steep hill without slowing. They passed Market Square, where early-rising vendors were forced to jump back or be trampled, and frantic parents pulled children into the safety of doorways.

As they passed Cathedral Square, the iron-shod hooves struck sparks on the cobblestones. At City Keep, a hanging was about to commence. The condemned man gained a brief reprieve as both he and his executioners paused to watch the armed horsemen race before them. They veered left into the Merchant Quarter, where the way grew narrower and more twisted, forcing the column was forced to stretch out, but the pace continued unabated.

They drew up before a nondescript warehouse, which like its neighbors bore a number of flats above the ground floor. The herald nudged his horse forward until it stood directly beneath an open window. He called out in a deep, loud, polished voice.

"Roscoe Appleman! You are summoned to the presence of Lord Drakar de la Pole! You will appear at once!"

Inside, Roscoe was already awake. No one could sleep through the thundering approach of the horsemen. But he had not, until he heard these words, had any inkling that their coming could be in any way connected with him. The realization filled him with dread. Drakar was known to be the most arrogant and ruthless noble in the kingdom. What would bring him in search of a lowly Adventurer?

The herald called again.

"Roscoe Appleman—present yourself at once, or I will dispatch men to drag you forth."

Roscoe looked out the window. Why had Drakar brought so many men? He waved an acknowledgment to the herald and then ran down the stairs to face whatever fate Lady Fortune was throwing his way. He felt awful. He and his comrades had sat up very late the night before celebrating their good fortune. All were boon companions once more.

Thurmond was entirely contrite and eager to redeem himself. Sarah was much more humble than before. Her encounter with Lady Renata had revealed the true nature of nobility. She had begged Roscoe's forgiveness, promising to never again let the accident of her birth guide her thoughts or actions.

Roscoe had long suspected that the jugged imp was having a poisonous influence on them all. It had been, he felt, the real cause of the darkness that had begun to grow over Sarah, playing on her insecurities and need for identity. Now that the demon was gone, she was, he prayed, free of its evil sway.

They had swilled a great quantity of ale. There was, after disposing of the witch's remains, much to rejoice in and much to put from their minds, and the ale helped with that. And after the ale, there had been uisge, so now Roscoe's head throbbed, and his stomach heaved. When he reached the bottom of the stairs, the herald looked down on him in haughty contempt.

"You may approach Lord Drakar, sirrah."

The old Adventurer gave a slight bow and spoke in a quiet, modest tone without raising his eyes.

"Your Lordship, I am Roscoe Appleman, Adventurer in good standin', at your service."

Drakar's reply was ice cold.

"I've received word that my sister, Lady Renata de la Pole, met her death in this abode. Is that true?"

This was no secret. Lady Renata's panicked grooms had blurted their tale to anyone who would listen. Various conflicting versions of it had quickly circulated throughout the city. Before answering, Roscoe lowered his voice as if in grief.

"Aye, Your Lordship, sadly it is. I wasn't personally present at the time, but that is what they tell me."

"The manner of her death?"

Roscoe though it best to lie a little about this.

"Carried off by a demon that got out of control is what I hear. There was a frightful splashin' of blood but no other mortal remains, sorry to say."

"Why would a great lady come to a place such as this? Tell me that."

"I am told that there was a great book of magical lore she desired. My men brought it from the hut of a dead shaman. Would you like it?"

"Nay! I have no use for it or any other book. And know this, sirrah, I am well aware that you do not tell the whole story, yet I care not one whit. Lady de la Pole died as she lived. My death will inevitably come on the battlefield, and I could wish for nothing better. Her life was devoted to the dark arts, and by them she perished. It was fitting, and I mourn for her not at all. But I did not come here to discuss her end. I have been tasked by Ralf Mortimer, Earl of Avincraik, to deliver this personally to your hands."

Drakar gave his warhorse a slight nudge with his heels. The spirited beast reared slightly, snorted, and took two prancing steps forward. The herald removed a rolled document from his wallet and placed it in his master's hand.

He handed it to Roscoe, who looked at it briefly, then looked up in confusion. The formal writing was beyond his ability to comprehend.

"Can Your Lordship kindly explain what this might be?"

"It is the deed to a freehold, a tract of land that until yesterday belonged to me. It includes the village of Grimsgard, where my sister made her residence. I am off to war and have ceded the holding to the earl in exchange for soldiers and weapons. Earl Ralf now presents it to you. You will hold it directly under him. I will be your neighbor."

Then Drakar and his men gone in a tumult of clattering armor and pounding hooves. Roscoe stood motionless in the street, deed in hand, while his friends peeked down from the window. He knew that Jarvis had found success in his dealings with the earl. Knew that, as of this moment, their lives were forever changed. He was mightily relieved, for he had expected Drakar to leave his bloody body in the street. And he could feel the first stirrings of an overwhelming, delirious happiness.

There was fear as well—fear that these changes would not bring out the best in himself and his companions. Their friendship had come nigh to being destroyed by ambition for titles and gold. Would they be able to withstand such temptations in the future?

Thurmond, Sarah, and Torgul now came bounding down the stairs. They would have many important things to discuss.

†

Later that afternoon, Thurmond was sprawled on his pallet, still suffering from ill effects of too much uisge. He looked up at the sound of booted feet approaching. Here came Roscoe and Torgul, standing very straight and marching in lockstep, with their broad-brimmed Adventurer's hats seated firmly on their heads. Roscoe spoke in a voice charged with deep solemnity.

"Thurmond the Lucky…"

Thurmond possessed no last name, forcing Roscoe to concoct the designation on the moment.

"…you are commanded to rise and stand before us."

Thurmond was puzzled, uncertain, a bit scared even, but he did as bidden without question.

Roscoe continued.

"You have sought membership in the exalted Brotherhood of Underworld Adventurers, Gorgonholm chapter, a most grave and demandin' aspiration. Havin' survived the perils and deprivations of the underground, is this still your desire?"

"Aye, it is. Above all else."

The dwarf took up the interrogation, his voice deep and gruff, his words slow and deliberate.

"As a hang-around, you are not even a candidate for membership in the Brotherhood, just an outsider we've allowed to tag along. Durin' our adventure, your every deed was closely scrutinized for signs of cowardice, weakness, and stupidity. We witnessed some tremendous bad judgment. What do you have to say for yourself? Why should we continue to consider your application?"

Thurmond became flustered, his tongue seemed to swell in his mouth.

"Well…I tried to do my best to take orders and do my share…"

Roscoe interrupted, his tone softening.

"Aye, we saw that. And your best was pretty good at times. You had the good sense to come to me with the map. And you slew an assassin before we even left the city."

Thurmond felt his confidence starting to return.

"Aye, and I thought to use uisge on the giant slug, and killed I don't know how many goblins and kobolds."

"So you did, so you did. And more importantly, you came to the rescue of your comrades at great risk to yourself—that's how a true Adventurer must act. You saved Sarah from the shadow thing by strikin' it with Torgul's axe."

"Aye, and I pulled the witch bat out of her hair with my bare hands."

"And I seem to remember you savin' my own sorry hide from that nobleman with the long bloody hair. The odds was all against you on that one."

"And I used the demon jug to save Sarah from the witch-woman."

Torgul stepped in again.

"All right, we can agree that you ran up a fine tally. You're not wantin' for courage or loyalty or strength of character. But what of your mistakes? We all know what they were. What have they taught you?"

Thurmond had a ready answer.

"I've learned that the real monster an Adventurer faces often lurks in his own heart. That greed and ambition are more dangerous than trolls and goblins. That an Adventurer must recognize and overcome his own inner weakness, or he will become just as bad as the fell creatures of the underworld."

Roscoe and Torgul looked at each other and nodded, apparently satisfied. Then the dwarf spoke again.

"We are minded, boy, to elevate you to the rank of Prospect, makin' you an official candidate for admission into the Brotherhood. Prospectin' is hard, and lots of strong men don't make it. You'll spend at least a year doin' every dirty and disagreeable task that Roscoe and I can think up. This is to challenge your determination. And you'll be at the mercy of any other Adventurers that come along. They'll all want to test your mettle. Do you think you're up to it?"

"Of course I am."

Roscoe smiled and drew a deep breath.

"Thurmond the Lucky, you have demonstrated a sustained loyalty to your comrades, unbendin' courage, and exceptional skill at arms, at least for a beginner. In spite of your blunders, you have answered our questions intelligently. You had the skill and darin' to steal the treasure map, and then you had wit enough to bring it to me. These all recommend you for membership. But mostly it was your bringin' away that packet of gems that made us all so rich.

"Therefore, we, Roscoe Appleman and Torgul Bonelip, twenty-third of that name, bein' members in good standing of the Brotherhood of Underworld Adventurers, Gorgonholm chapter, do elevate you to the coveted rank of Prospect, and duly convey unto you all privileges and responsibilities of said title. Congratulations, laddie. You made it."

The two Adventurers then removed their hats, kissed the bemused Thurmond on both cheeks, pounded his back, replaced their hats, about-faced, and marched away. It was short and to the point as an initiation ceremony could possibly be. Typically, the creation of a new Prospect was celebrated with a monumental drinking bout, but all were currently too hungover to even contemplate such an undertaking.

Thurmond was left in a state of complete befuddlement. Sarah looked up from where she sat with her book of magic open in her lap.

"What was all that about?"

Thurmond was not sure what to tell her. A lot of Adventurer lore was secret, secret, secret. Roscoe and Torgul had certainly made no effort to conceal the brief ceremony, but were the rules the same for mere Prospects? Was he allowed to explain things to Sarah? He certainly wanted to—he had just taken a giant step in the achievement of a lifelong goal. He was so giddy that he cast caution aside.

"By God's holy backside! I did it! I'm a Prospect! I've been accepted! I'm going to be an Adventurer! They still like me, even after all the times I failed them. This is what I always wanted! WHOOOOO!"

"Then it sounds like I should give the new almost-Adventurer a kiss. You know, to celebrate."

CHAPTER SIXTY

GRIMSGARD

Jarvis arrived in town the next day and sent his servant, Milburn, to summon the others to his shop. His leg still pained him, but he believed a substantial bleeding by a qualified surgeon ought to bring the swelling down. He was looking forward to it.

When Roscoe and the others appeared, he explained the particulars of his compact with Earl Ralf. He had convinced the earl that a grant of land would be an appropriate reward for the return of the gems, especially since it could be accomplished at no cost to himself.

When news of Lady Renata's demise arrived in Norwerk, Jarvis had been in the midst of his negotiations with Earl Ralf. Though he had had no inkling that her death was in any way linked to Roscoe's adventure, he immediately recognized that he could use it to his own ends. Ralf now had an untenanted estate at his disposal.

Jarvis's network of informants kept him well abreast of current news and gossip. He knew, for example, that Renata's brother Drakar was planning a military expedition but lacked the funds for the necessary men and supplies. Why not, he asked the earl, call upon his vassals to send soldiers to Drakar in fulfillment of their feudal obligation? Then the cost would fall on the various nobles instead of on himself. In return, Drakar would cede to him Renata's estate, a property for which he had no real use. This could then be given to the Adventurers upon completion of their mission. A neat little scheme, no?

Earl Ralf had loved the plan and adopted it at once. His vassals were always concocting schemes to cheat him. How wonderful, then, if he could turn the tables. He was so delighted with Jarvis that he remained entirely unsuspicious when the heavy cost of his adventure kept coming up. There could be delays, the merchant warned, while he sold off inventory to raise capital. Even then the party might be smaller and less well prepared than it should be. Concerned that a shortage of funds might lead to failure, the earl had insisted that he be allowed to contribute to the financing. He actually seemed to believe the idea was his own.

Jarvis's one grave worry was that Roscoe and the others might let the truth be known. That would spell disaster for them all. Roscoe was to be the only survivor of the fictional adventure. He must learn and remember the events Jarvis had devised as a cover story. Any of Roscoe's associates—the dwarf, the girl, and the young man—would have to portray newcomers who had joined him after the adventure.

He then turned over to them, most scrupulously, five-eighths of the gold the earl had given to him. This was enough to last them for a very long time.

†

The holding they received was a fine parcel of fertile bottomland, two leagues south of the city. It was bordered to the north by the boundary stones of the Gray Friars and to west by the Mad River. To the south, Snake Creek, also known as the Little Mad River, separated it from the holdings of Lord Drakar. The Royal Highway marked the eastern limit. Renata's tower and the village of Grimsgard were located near the center.

It had once been a prosperous and fruitful estate with well-tended fields, hives of bees, orchards, and workshops, but Lady Renata had cared for such things not at all, and the village had been allowed to fall into decay. The trees no longer yielded fruit, and the fields were choked by weeds.

In the village a small ale shop was the only surviving business. Most of the houses were uninhabited and falling to ruin—Renata had kept very few tenants. Her staff of personal servants was gone, taken by her brother, so only a few disheveled residents remained.

As part of his arrangement with Earl Ralf, Drakar had agreed to include forty serfs along with the land. These were not slaves, properly speaking, for they had certain guaranteed rights by law and custom, but serfs were legally bound to the land and could not leave without the lord's permission. Nor was there anyone to complain to when their rights were violated.

These men and women were scheduled to arrive the next day to begin clearing the fields and restoring the dilapidated dwellings. Drakar, of course, used the opportunity to rid himself of his weakest and least capable serfs. He also sent a crew of servants to remove any of his sister's belongings that had value. Wagonloads of goods were taken. Much shattered glass and smashed crockery was left behind.

†

The companions came early the next morning to take possession of their property. They paused on a small rise to take stock of their new home. A broadsword now hung from Thurmond's hip—nothing fancy, just a good, serviceable blade. He sat astride the back of a horse, not the fiery warhorse of his dreams, but a broad-chested cob that was black as the night. A hat of the same color perched on his head—not the broad-brimmed campaign hat of the tattooed Adventurer, but a smaller, more circumspect chapeau befitting his rank of Prospect.

Sarah too was mounted, sitting astride her horse in the fashion of a man. In sooth, both were novice riders and held the pommels of their saddles in a death grip. Lars and Bodo followed with the cart, the latter's family perched in the back.

Drakar's serfs—men, women, and children, spindly and hollow eyed— were just arriving as well, driven forward by the clubs and whips of the overseers. Though they knew it not, Fortune's Wheel was at that moment making a sweeping turn in their favor, for they now belonged to Roscoe. The abject misery these people had suffered as the chattel of Lord Drakar was coming to an end.

Roscoe was now what was often termed a franklin, a wealthy landowner of common birth. He was the de facto Lord of the Manor, with great power over his tenants, but being the man he was, Roscoe was loathe to use his authority.

Under his sway, the serfs would endure no more beatings and maimings. Food would be abundant. New brides would no longer be forced to submit to the desires of the lord. Indeed, he would give his serfs a reason to work hard by affording them the opportunity to better their own lives.

But most shocking of all was Roscoe's declaration that all important decisions would be made by consensus—never would his own opinion prevail over that of the others. This was a potentially dangerous step, for empowering a stable boy, a female, and a dwarf would certainly be viewed as a threat to the natural order of things.

Responsibilities were shared. Roscoe Franklin—he had eagerly foregone the surname Appleman—oversaw the buying of provisions and the selling of their crops. He adjudicated the squabbles of the serfs and did what he could to relieve their privation. His wit and charm proved most useful in establishing good relations with their neighbors, the church, and Earl Ralf.

To be honest, Roscoe was more given to a life of leisure than to hard work and was eager to indulge his love of good eating to a degree never before possible. His big, round belly, pitifully depleted by the deprivations of their strenuous adventure, swelled to its former girth. By winter, too much red meat gave him the gout, and he was forced to spend his days with his foot propped on a cushioned stool. A flagon of mead was always close at hand in case his foot should experience a sudden flare of pain.

Torgul, a master craftsman, at once set to work repairing the dilapidated village. The blacksmith shop was put in excellent order, and hammers began to fall like ringing bells. He used the mule and cart to fetch several hives of live bees, which he deposited in a field of clover. He would repair there at night and croon grim dwarven love songs to the sleeping insects, swearing that this would instill the honey with a lovely piquant quality. Soon the doughty dwarf was producing the best mead anyone had ever tasted.

Sarah kept the manor's records and wrote the necessary correspondence. She added the sums when their produce went to market and recorded the births, deaths, and marriages of the serfs. She was delighted to discover that most of Renata's magical workshop remained intact. The majority of the books and papers had been removed, but most of the herbs, potions, and strange pickled creatures had been left behind. Drakar's workmen had been loath to touch such things. The young sorceress immediately fell to experimenting with new spells, but being such a novice, it was inevitable that some of these would go awry. One botched operation called down a rain of fish that lasted for three days. Another raised deep peals of hysterical laughter from the village well.

Thurmond, born and raised in a farming village, was put in charge of the flocks and fields. In fact, he possessed only the most rudimentary knowledge of such things, but when compared to fighting goblins, the intricacies of sowing and shearing were hardly daunting. So he set out to learn the correct depth to plant turnips, the proper techniques for the castration of calves, and the most effective countermeasures against crop-destroying worms. Happily, there were serfs to shovel the dung.

But his bucolic pursuits were purely secondary. In fact, he sorely neglected them. The lad remained steadfast in his desire to earn his tattoo and big, black hat by preparing for the next adventure. He practiced tenaciously with sword, shield, spear, and bow. He learned to ride at a gallop, to jump low fences, and to guide his horse with his knees. His mentors taught him tracking, rock climbing, and navigating by the stars. With Sarah's help, he learned his letters and attained a competent literacy. Roscoe and Thurmond were good to their word and tested his resolve with every dirty or disagreeable task that came to mind. He fulfilled them all without complaint. None were as foul as scraping dung from the floor of a troll cage.

†

Thurmond and his companions had survived a long journey through a perilous wilderness and had outmaneuvered or outfought every foe that came against them. They had successfully frustrated the malevolent designs of Lady Renata and Bartholomew Staynes. Thurmond, an illiterate, nameless peasant, had slain Rupert de Pugh—a trained swordsman—in single combat. He had overcome monsters and escaped hordes of goblins, kobolds, and conniving villagers. Because of his good luck, they had recovered a fabulous treasure, and by deceiving the Earl of Avincraik, received a magnificent reward.

Given these achievements, the problems of running an estate did not inspire dread. Certainly there would be problems. Lord Drakar, in particular, might prove to be a difficult neighbor. But when rapacious nobles and covetous churchmen threatened their lives or prosperity, they would, as they always had, stand as one to defend what was theirs. Their strength came not from birth or rank or accumulated wealth but from the deep devotion they held for one another.

They would, before long, need all their courage, intelligence, wisdom, and loyalty, for the next adventure was soon to begin.

EPILOGUE

F or the rest of his days, Jarvis recalled his role in the recovery of the Mortimer gems as one of his greatest accomplishments in his many decades as a merchant. Despite his initial misgivings, his relationship with the earl remained sound throughout the duration of the latter's life. Jarvis had demonstrated his trustworthiness to Earl Ralf, and powerful people are always in need of people they can rely on for discretion and honesty.

Jarvis remained convinced that his concocted story had saved the earl from falling into the deadly sin of avarice. Had Ralf been told the simple truth, the temptation to simply seize the gems, Jarvis believed, would have been too great. The merchant was aware that his deception was also a sin— albeit a venal one committed in a righteous purpose—and made a generous love offering to Bishop Boniface to return him to a state of grace.

Jarvis also took great satisfaction in his meticulous observance of the stipulations in his agreement with the Adventurer and his minions. He had promised to negotiate a deal that would give them a life of ease, and he had made good on this. They had also received a lavish financial reward. His clients were completely satisfied with the transaction, and that was important because merchants, like nobles, are always in need of people who they can rely on for discretion and honesty.

Best of all, of course, he earned a tidy sum for himself.

†

Contrary to everyone's expectations, Lord Percy Staynes did not die. Though he was for practical purposes a living corpse, his foul and reeking body continued to cling to the single flickering spark of life that remained. There were whispers of certain dark rites and forbidden rituals, of hellish sacrifices to keep his heart beating and his blood flowing. Or perhaps it was the very corruption in his veins that kept death at bay. His household servants began to slip away, at least the younger ones did. The old ones and the devoted butler Giles remained as if they had become somehow enmeshed in their master's web of sin, unable to escape.

†

Whisper found a new home in a tiny woodland glen just a short walk from Grimsgard. Sarah planted him in the dark, rich loam next to where a small mineral spring forced its way through a fracture in a slab of rock and formed a clear, deep pool. Here the young sprout thrived and grew.

The site had been, of old, sacred to the Goddess, to She Who Abides, as evidenced by crude carvings on the rock face, but it had been neglected since the coming of Charonism to the area and most especially during the tenure of Lady Renata. Soon after the arrival of Whisper, however, footprints began to appear on the little path leading to the spring—always those of women. Small offerings of food were left on the stones at the pool's edge, and bits of cloth were tied to the branches of the overhanging bushes.

†

In the autumn word came from the docks that a large party of rivermen and their Keltin friends had raided and burned a remote riverside village to the south. Their tales, though vague, inconsistent, and often garbled by language difficulties, spoke of retribution against a blasphemous cult that had waylaid a party of honest boatmen.

The approach of the stealthy rivermen had gone unnoticed, and the villagers had been taken completely by surprise. Most had sought refuge in an immense structure of aberrant geometry that seemed to function as their unholy fane. This was set ablaze. Those attempting to escape the flames were cut to pieces by the blades of the rivermen. A few fled into the river, but these were believed to have drowned, as none were seen to come to the surface for air.

Of the enigmatic cleric James, nothing was known. The raiders were well apprised of his appearance, and certainly one so strikingly handsome should have been readily noticeable among the slack-jawed villagers. Yet no trace of him was found, either in the initial attack or during the subsequent burning of the village. It must, therefore, be assumed that he survived.

†

Scrymgeour retrieved his boat from the accursed village and resumed his freight-hauling business on. True to his word, he set about forging some new sons. He bartered for a new and younger Keltin wife and was soon thereafter boasting of her swollen belly. Apparently, he still had some fire in his forge.

†

Things went hard for the goblins following their defeat on the riverbank. Roscoe and company made a valiant effort to keep the particulars of their adventure secret, but word inevitably leaked out. Large adventuring parties soon began to invade their caverns in quest of the gold that had been left behind. With their fighting strength so reduced, the goblins were unable to mount an effective resistance. In the end, they abandoned their caves, taking the bulk of their treasure with them. The location of their new lair remained undiscovered. The kobolds likewise disappeared, but it was unknown whether they followed the goblins or simply burrowed more deeply into the hillside.

†

At Yuletide, a strange and disgusting creature emerged from the river and scuttled through the streets of Gorgonholm. Convinced that the Archfiend had sent it to defile their good cheer, the citizens scattered before it and locked themselves in their homes. It was like nothing they had seen before—somewhat resembling a flabby hand, swollen to grotesque proportions. A long, spongy tumor extended from the wrist, like the vestigial remains of a boneless forearm. The scaly skin was corpse gray and puckered from long immersion.

The hue and cry was raised—the ancient call of bills and bows—and a host of armed citizens came running with weapons of all configurations. The hand, obviously aware of their hostile intentions, attempted to hide itself in a cesspit. When driven out by plunging spears, it erupted in a spray of filth that sent its pursuers reeling back in disgust. It then attempted to wiggle beneath the foundation stones of a nearby house but was caught between the tines of a wooden pitchfork and dropped into a burlap sack.

Squirming and flopping, the loathly thing was carried to the cathedral, where a conclave of holy priests tried to ascertain its true nature. Unable to arrive at a satisfactory explanation, the learned fathers, in their wisdom, declared it to be an official Yuletide Miracle.

A special hand-shaped reliquary was commissioned to contain the still-writhing appendage, and it was placed beside the cathedral's other holy artifacts. But even encased in stout bronze, it continued to quiver and jerk. In time the hand became the cathedral's most popular relic and greatest moneymaker. Pilgrims from far and wide paid handsome sums to ask a personal question while clasping it palm to palm. The subsequent spasms were interpreted by a priest famous for his spiritual sensitivity.

✝

Winter yielded to spring, as it will, and spring to summer. As that warm and pleasant season waned, nearly a year had passed since our heroes embarked on their adventure. Early one morning, in the street before Staynes Hall, a loud clatter of hooves and shouting of men aroused the household of Lord Percy. Windows were thrown open, and heads popped out—all but that of Lord Percy. The curious eyes fell upon a troop of armored horseman, their steeds prancing and rearing in the street in a wanton demonstration of martial prowess. Their leader was none other than Bartholomew Staynes.

He was much transformed from the Bart who had gone sailing down the river in search of goblin gold. His naturally muscular physique was leaner, and his previously bland countenance was infused with a vindictive intensity. His cropped blond hair had grown long, and a fresh, bright scar, running diagonally along his left cheek, disappeared into his new beard. The elaborate custom-tailored armor was replaced by a simple soldierly harness of leather and mail. And he was now adorned with the white belt and golden chain of a knight.

At his side rode a short, stocky, squint-eyed soldier, whose left arm seemed stiff and encumbered—Drax. After a brief display, Bart gave a signal, and the troop sped away.

WHAT HAPPENS NEXT?

Turn the page to read the first chapter of

CASTLE OF THE RED CONTESSA

CHRONICLES OF THE MEDIEVAL UNDERWORLD
VOL. 2

Despite the success of their first adventure, Thurmond and his companions, Sarah, Roscoe, and Torgul, are out of money and about to be expelled from their new home at Grimsgard. The only solution—a raid on Castle Sathas, the home of an infamous witch-cult. To get there, they must undertake a long and perilous overland journey through a wilderness rife with ruthless bandits, voracious wolf packs, and greedy robber-knights. Along the way, their every step is shadowed by an unseen nemesis bent on their destruction. Beset by treacherous landscapes and deadly enemies, it seems their quest is doomed to fail. And even if they win through, will they survive the ancient evil waiting in Castle Sathas? *Castle of the Red Contessa* takes the reader on a heroic quest of throat-gripping medieval adventure.

CHAPTER ONE

WEIRD TIMES IN GORGONHOLM

Thurmond was worried. Sarah was up to something, something he probably would not like. For three days now she had been distant and preoccupied. When he asked her about it, her response had been vague and evasive. When she announced at breakfast that she intended to go on a stroll through the forest, he had offered to accompany her, but she declined. She needed, she said, a chance to be alone, to collect her thoughts, to find her feelings.

Thurmond did not believe any of this, not for a minute, and so had followed her at a discreet distance. As he suspected, her steps had taken her not to the forest but straight to the city of Gorgonholm and then up Castle Wynd toward Market Square.

This was the heart of the great city. The outer edges of the square were given to the respectable, semi-permanent booths from which reputable merchants sold their wares, but the center was a wild labyrinth of crude wooden stalls and shabby canvas rainscreens tied to farm carts. Here peasant families sold their radishes, cabbages, and leeks. Itinerate tinkers plied their trade, and fish-wives sang the praises of the day's catch. A group of screaming boys fought a merry battle with horse turds.

Citizens of all castes and professions picked their way through the maze of guy ropes and wagon tongues, browsing the myriad stalls in search of bargains. Pompous nobles and blustering guildsmen pushed through crowds of sullen apprentices and loud, drunken laborers. The prostitutes did a good bit of business, as they did on every Market Day. So did the deft and canny cutpurse.

Actually, it was rather quiet for Market Day. No caravans had arrived recently, so there were no swarthy foreign merchants with exotic spices and fine silk cloth from the lands to the east. There were neither dwarves nor elves, though members of those races were sometimes present as they passed through the city on some business or other.

The Blue Friar's cathedral rose on the left, monstrously huge, a great stone fist demonstrating the supreme authority of the church. Gargoyles gaped open-mouthed along the rooftop. Imposing stone statues flanked the massive, iron-bound doors and frowned with grim disapproval at the bustling Market Day scene before them.

Thurmond concealed himself in the structure's shadowy portico and watched as Sarah made her way to the far side of the square. She was typically quite forthcoming about her personal business, so her duplicity made him uncomfortable. What could be prompting her to deceive him in this way?

Sarah was, he knew, entitled to her privacy. He had no control over her comings and goings, no right to thrust himself into a matter from which he had been deliberately excluded. She was not his ladylove. She was just … well … he had no idea how to accurately define their relationship.

The previous summer they had joined forces with an old Adventurer named Roscoe to pillage a hoard of gold from a nest of goblin river-pirates. They had faced deadly peril side by side and saved each other's lives multiple times. They had suffered terrible hardships and defeated fearsome enemies. Such experiences had forged an indelible bond between them.

Trusted friend and ally? Boon companion? Partner in crime?

Certainly she was all these things, but his feelings for her went well beyond that. It was just that he could not explain, even to himself, exactly what those feelings were. They had been through so much together—why would she deceive him in this way?

Thurmond shrank back further into the dark recess of the portico. Sarah would be furious if she discovered he was following her, but he had to take that chance. Maybe she was in trouble—something she was afraid to speak of. If so, he would be on hand to come to her aid.

Sarah seemed distinctly nervous as she pushed through the throng of merchants and shoppers. She kept turning her head, scanning the crowd, obviously looking for someone, and growing increasingly agitated when that person failed to appear. Thurmond was more and more positive something was deeply amiss.

Sarah suddenly stopped pacing, stared intently on a small street that opened into the far end of the square, and strode briskly in that direction. Something in her gait seemed unnatural, as if she had to refrain from running toward her assignation.

Sarah was happy. Happy like hell, in fact. She had met someone—someone who could give her what she had been needing for so long. His name was Gavin, and despite his youth, he was a highly skilled magician. Actually, he was not all that young—she guessed his age to be perhaps five-and-twenty—eight or so years older than herself. More important, his soul seemed old and wise.

Gavin was tall and muscular, which pleased her well, for she too was tall and broad-shouldered. He had shaggy, dark brown hair that fell nearly to his shoulders and even darker eyes—eyes filled with mystery. Not that his appearance was of any import—*nay, nay, nay*. Sarah wanted him to be her mentor in the occult sciences. As a master magician, his thoughts would be far removed from anything like dalliance.

Sarah's most fervent desire was to become an expert practitioner of the magical arts—that and to have her skills recognized through admittance to the local sorcerers' guild, The Most Sacred Fellowship of Spell-casters, Alchemists, Diviners, Sorcerers, Philter-Mixers, and Thaumaturgists of Gorgonholm. Such distinction would enable her to live without having to ask aye or nay from a father or husband.

As the illegitimate daughter of Lord Percy Staynes, Sarah had enjoyed a comfortable, perhaps even pampered, childhood. Her keen intelligence was recognized at an early age, and she had been educated, even in the use of letters. This was indeed an unusual attainment for a girl, and it had been a significant turning point in her life. She became a voracious reader and advanced her learning far beyond the limited scope provided by her tutors.

Late in his life, her father had become an avid collector of ancient books and manuscripts. This was fortunate for her, as it allowed access to scores of moldering volumes stacked on the shelves of his library.

There were works of geography, history, philosophy, and even poetry. But mostly there were grimoires, treatises on a wide array of arcane subjects— sorcery, divination, even the dreaded and forbidden practice of necromancy. Yellowed papyrus scrolls explained the summoning and controlling of infernal entities. A massive tome with greasy leather bindings provided hundreds of detailed formulas for philters and potions. Another listed the secret names of imps, demons, cacodemons, and archfiends.

Sarah knew from the start she had found her true calling. She was to be a great enchantress, a witch, a *magicatrix*—or whatever a female magic user was called. She set out to read every book in her father's library and was making good headway when—just over a year ago—her studies were interrupted by the sudden need to flee her childhood home.

Her father, Lord Percy Staynes, had experienced a steep decline in health. He was an extremely aged man, and no one expected him to live long. It was no secret that Sarah's half-brother Bartholomew awaited his sire's demise with gleeful anticipation. He lusted for the prestige and wealth that would descend to him along with his father's title. And he had made it plain to Sarah that his lusts extended in her direction as well.

So she had fled into the night with a young housebreaker whom she had caught in the act of pillaging her father's home. This turned out to be Thurmond, who had been hired to steal a magical mirror from her brother. Ironically, they had become friends, and Sarah joined him on his quest for goblin gold.

She, like Thurmond, came away from that adventure with several hundred gold sovereigns, most of which she was currently carrying in a bag tied beneath her skirts. The rest she had invested toward the advancement of her occult skills and knowledge. This entailed the purchase of many odd and unpleasant materials magicians always deem indispensable. There were foul-smelling incenses and even worse essential oils. Then she had needed some liver of sulphur and milk of lead, some goat gall, and a pair of howlet's wings.

The problem remained that Sarah was only a self-taught novice. She was a quick learner, and her magical intuition was quite good, but her workings often went wrong. An ill-conceived spell involving the mummified thumb of a drowned ship-captain had resulted in a terrific blast of wind that nearly sucked her up the chimney. On another occasion she had summoned, entirely by accident, an infestation of small invisible creatures that scratched, bit, and pinched unmercifully, forcing her to flee her workshop for several days until the spell dissipated.

It was clear that if she wanted to advance to mastery level, she would need formal instruction. This typically involved serving as an apprentice and enduring years of abuse at the hands of a magus. Thurmond, who had once been apprenticed to a dyspeptic carpenter, was adamant in his condemnation of this option.

Sarah had been dejected, frustrated, and angry over her inability advance in her craft. She had spent a year dabbling on her own but made no real progress. Then she had, by great good fortune, met Gavin, who was to be it seemed the answer to her problem.

Continue the adventure...

Read

CASTLE OF THE RED CONTESSA

Available on all major online retailers and at
robertjohnmackenzie.com

ACKNOWLEDGMENTS

A thousand thanks to my friend and fellow educator Carol Wolf for her generosity and expertise in helping me shape the first draft. Carol, your advice and encouragement were invaluable. You are as mighty with the pen as with the sword. I would also like to thank my son Andrew and daughter Kate for reading, rereading, proofreading, and suggesting. And special thanks to my wife, Christine, for, well, everything. I couldn't have finished this without your support. Thanks so much for all your help!

www.ingramcontent.com/pod-product-compliance
Lightning Source LLC
Chambersburg PA
CBHW020231110726
47898CB00004B/1224